JAVA GIRL

"Javanese Dancer"
Woodcut by Johannes Frederik Engelbert ten Klooster (1873–1940).

JAVA GIRL

By

Baron Willem thoe Schwartzenberg

and

Mary Bennett Harrison

Edited, Illustrated and Expanded by
Kent Davis

Featuring

Javanese Women in Photos:
Emerging Technologies and World Views
by
Kent Davis

DatAsia Press
MMXX

About the cover:

Adinda, René's Javanese servant whose fate becomes intertwined with his own, sits gracefully in a jungle setting. Javanese photographer Kassian Céphas captured several elegant images of this young woman between 1867 and 1910 but her identity remains unknown. Your editor chose to cast her in the visual leading role of this novel for reasons that will become apparent.

Acknowledgements

The editor is sincerely grateful to Kassian Céphas, Isidore van Kingsbergen, Walter Bentley Woodbury and Ohannes Kurkdjian, whose early photographs of Java more than a century ago brought this story to life.

In addition, special thanks to modern digital archives that preserve and share images that make creative and educational projects like this book possible:

Rijksmuseum.nl

Leiden University Library/Wikimedia Commons

The Koninklijk Instituut voor Taal-, Land- en Volkenkunde (KITLV)

The Royal Netherlands Institute of Southeast Asian and Caribbean Studies

Production Credits

Editor: **Kent Davis**

Cover Design: **Becca Klein**

Text Design: **Daria Lacy**

Photo Restoration: **Artsiom Yatsevich**

Colonial Literature Consultant: **François Doré**

DatASIA Press — www.DatASIA.us

First Edition

ISBN 978-1-934431-33-7

Library of Congress Control Number: 2019952224

Printed simultaneously in the United States of America and Great Britain.

TABLE OF CONTENTS

JAVA GIRL

APPENDICES

To all women of the world
who have loved unselfishly.

And to all men of the world
who have proven themselves worthy of that love.

Foreword

Two housholds both alike in dignitie,
In faire Verona where we lay our Scene
From auncient grudge, breake to new mutinie,
Where ciuill bloud makes ciuill hands Vncleane:

From forth the fatall loynes of these two foes,
A paire of starre-crost louers, take their life:
Whose misaduentur'd pittious ouerthrowes,
Doth with their death burie their Parents strife.

> *Romeo and Juliet*
> **The Prologue, 1-8 – Original text – 1592**
> **William Shakespeare**

Love stories always have the potential to end tragically or happily ever after. In the tale of *Java Girl*, two "star-crossed" lovers face challenges far greater than those Shakespeare penned more than 400 years ago.

Romeo and Juliet were from the same nation, culture and religion, they spoke the same language and they lived in the same town. Their only challenge—which was not insignificant—was that their families were sworn enemies. This alone led to tragedy for all involved.

But what about the story told by *Java Girl*, set circa 1900 in the Dutch East Indies?

Here, driven by the finances and politics of Dutch colonial expansion, we have European culture coming face to face with the ancient cultural roots of Indonesia. As in myriad other lands during that era, colonial "masters" exploited native populations for labor and natural resources without any commonality of language, culture, history or religion. They achieved "cooperation" with local inhabitants using cannons, guns and whips, often with the help of local leaders who accepted offers of money, power or force that they could not resist.

Searching for a stable income to build his future, young Dutchman René van Landsberg travels more than 7,000 miles to join his older brother Alfred supervising a sugar plantation on the tropical island of Java. From the day of his arrival south of the equator, he struggles to adapt to mores that are alien, and even contradictory, to his previous life experiences and morality.

Despite having a "girl back home" it doesn't take long for René to encounter young ladies…several in fact…and there the complexities begin. As René ponders, "The web about the dwellers in Alfred's house was slowly weaving. In and out went the shuttle—in and out—a pattern begun, as yet no broken thread, no weak spot. But Life laughed."

The authors, Baron Schwartzenberg and Mary Bennett Harrison, spun a wonderful story based on the Baron's four years working on Java circa 1900. How many vignettes, characters or women in their tale he drew from actual experiences or acquaintances is unknown. But based on my extensive work in colonial literature they ring true.

I confess that I, like co-author Ms. Harrison, have never been to Java. My experience is focused on Southeast Asia, and the areas formerly known as Siam and French Indochina. But thanks to the author's vivid descriptions, and the miracle of modern online archives I have learned a lot, and I believe that readers will find the text, photos and supplements both entertaining and educational.

The antique photos that bring the story to life were a serendipitous addition to the text, particularly thanks to the extraordinary online archives of the Rijksmuseum in the Netherlands. Their enlightened policy of freely sharing their images for creative projects made it possible for me to accurately illustrate much of the story's action. I am grateful for their generosity. These photos show the actual locations, views, villages and cities you will visit in the story. The people, however, are only to suggest what René, Arthur, Missah, Adinda, the Van Heecks, the de Kochs, Daisy and the rest may have looked like in that time and place.

Finally, in the appendices, you'll find my Publisher's Notes, with details about how this book came to be after nearly a 90 year hiatus. Also, biographical profiles of the authors; my article "Javanese Women in Photos: Emerging Technologies and World Views" with more than a hundred early photos; excerpts from *Isles of the East*, a contemporary travel guide with advertisements and an amusing set of "useful phrases" for communicating with the "natives"; an excerpt from the 1929 book *Malay Poisons and Charm Cures* to try some recipes mentioned in *Java Girl*; a glossary of Indonesian terms appearing in the text; and detailed period maps of the region.

As René thinks upon his arrival, "This was Java—the end of his journey—and he was a little frightened at all that the suave, exotic name implied."

Welcome to Java, my friends. I sincerely hope you enjoy your stay.

Kent Davis

December, 2019 — Snead Island, Florida

JAVA GIRL

This was Java—the end of his journey—and he was a little frightened
at all that the suave, exotic name implied.

1

Cheribon reunion

RENÉ VAN LANDSBERG stood alone on the deck of the
steamer, which was slowly making its way and churning up
mud to stain the tropical blue waters of the channel. Instead
of a harbor, there was but an open roadstead here. It would
be necessary to anchor some two miles out from Cheribon,
the port of René's destination, on the North Coast of the
island of Java.[1]

He was ready to disembark. His trunks and bags were
piled about his feet. But his heart faltered as he realized that
there could be no turning back to Europe now. This was
Java—the end of his journey—and he was a little frightened at
all that the suave, exotic name implied.

Leaning with both elbows on the ship's railing, he was
sunk in so deep a reverie that he scarcely perceived what
was going on about him. Gradually, however, the sights and
sounds of a glamorous human activity impinged upon the
young Hollander's consciousness.

---

1 Now called Ciribon, this Indonesian port city is located on the north coast
of the province of West Java. Founded as a fishing village in the 15th century, it
blends influences of Sundanese, Javanese, Arab, Chinese and Dutch cultures.

The towering liner was passing through a fleet of small fishing craft. With bulging rattan sails, the native boats sped seaward for the day's catch.

Cheribon, the port of René's destination, on the North Coast of the island of Java.

The towering liner was passing through a fleet of small fishing craft. With bulging rattan sails, the native boats sped seaward for the day's catch. Men and women swarmed at their tasks, or lolled in the shadow of the sails, laughing and chattering and from time to time pointing toward the big vessel. René noticed that the men went naked to the waist. Many of them wore only a loin cloth. Here was a different civilization, indeed, a primitive simplicity that suddenly charmed the newcomer. He wondered whether all he had heard about the allure of the women of Java was true. As he looked down upon the colorful flotilla, the girls seemed attractive enough, with their light brown skin glistening in the early morning sunshine and white flowers artistically set in the thick coils of their jet black hair. The gossip of the smoke room on the voyage out had made much of their beauty. But they were savages, surely—no more than that!—and destined to remain somewhat vague and impersonal to him.

The deafening clatter of the anchor chain aroused René from his musing. The boat had stopped. Before him stretched an unknown land, hazy and green, with the roofs of houses showing here and there above the mass of verdure. Beyond, lifting their mighty heads, soared two peaks: the extinct volcano Tjirmai, and to the left Semeru, with its stately plume of smoke rising to the sky.[2]

---

2 Known today as Mount Ciremai/Cereme (or Ciremay), this 10,000 ft. tall symmetrical stratovolcano is prominently visible to the southwest of Cirebon. It is the highest mountain in West Java.

Mt. Semeru, with an elevation of 12,000 ft., is more than 300 miles to the ESE of Cirebon in East Java. René and Alfred could not have seen it, even as an active smoking volcano (which it still is today). By the way, an old formula for calculating line-of-sight is 1.23 times the square root of the height. This 12,000 ft. tall mountain has a square root of 109.54 X 1.23 so it is visible from roughly 134.73 miles away.

It seems that the authors confused Mt. Semeru with Mt. Slamet, an active, 11,220 ft. tall volcano in Central Java. Mt. Slamet is a little over 50 miles SSE from Cirebon and, using the formula above, is easily visible at more than twice that distance.

Beyond, lifting their mighty heads, soared two peaks: the extinct volcano Tjirmai, and to the left Semeru, with its stately plume of smoke rising to the sky.

"The East!" he said to himself. "Cheribon! The name is like a song. Java at last!"

When the launch that brought him ashore approached the dock, René picked out his brother Alfred waving his *topie* in the midst of a crowd of white men and native coolies. How sun-burnt Alfred was! And what a large mustache he had grown! René trembled with excitement as his brother hurried forward to lend a hand in tying the launch to the pier. Another moment and they had fallen into a continental embrace, and were pounding each other heartily on the back.

"So, here you are! Welcome—welcome to your new country," said Alfred brusquely to hide his emotion.

After the usual formalities were completed, the two passed through the custom house shed and out into the harsh sunlight.

"My word, is it always as hot as this, Alfred? The sun beats down as from an oven."

"Yes, my boy, this is Java. You are in the Tropics now. It's right about face from everything you have known."

The brothers walked along the streets of the little seaport Cheribon, towards the club, "for a drink and to meet a crowd of good fellows," as Alfred had explained.

René was grateful for the change when they stepped into the semi-darkness of the cool clubrooms. They joined a group of men seated about a large round table. Introductions followed, and at once whiskey splits—as the Dutchmen called whiskey and soda—were placed at every elbow. The Colonials were men from the sugar plantations, some Government officials and a few rich merchants. They all made much of René, and were eager to hear an account of his voyage. The young man quickly fell in with their mood. He drank glass for glass with them, and talked effervescently.

It fascinated him to meet types so different from any he had known at home. No doubt they were the true conquerors of the wilderness, he thought. The sugar planters especially were carelessly dressed and coarse of speech. They had an indolent manner, as though they vastly enjoyed relaxing in town. Most of their conversation was vulgar. The jokes that they bandied among themselves caused much merriment, but were as yet beyond René's comprehension. The lonely years these planters had passed in the interior of the island had left a mark upon them.

"Going to stay in Java, van Landsberg?" one man asked with a slight lifting of his eyebrows.

"Yes, indeed," replied René warmly, and earned a chuckle of approval around the table.

Alfred studied his young brother covertly. A nice-looking chap, he reflected, clean and fresh, tall and strongly built for his nineteen years. A chap who would be well liked.

"Then remember, my young friend…
that you have come to a land of much heat and—and women."

"Then remember, my young friend," the planter who had just spoken continued, "that you have come to a land of much heat and—and women."

Several of the others laughed scornfully. "I say, de Bruin, you old *roue*" one of them commented, "this is the first time I have ever heard you warn anyone against the women of Java. You certainly haven't been a saint during the fifteen years that you have lived here."

"Admitted," replied de Bruin amiably. "But just because of that I have the right to warn this jolly newcomer, this *totok*"—he pointed his thumb toward René —"against the pitfalls of the damned island. You, for one, would let him go to the dogs cheerfully. Let's have another drink on it."

Everybody laughed boisterously, and more whiskey splits were ordered.

René stared out through the slats of the French shutters. Far in the distance, a moving black spot under a feather of smoke reminded him that the last link he had had with his native country was broken. The steamer was on her way again, the steamer which had seemed such a safe, familiar place compared with his new surroundings. Playtime was over. Boyhood was over. He had come to Java to prove his mettle. A fleeting picture passed before his eyes: His home life in Holland, his mother and sisters, his sweetheart, and his anguish at parting from them all. This was quite a different life, but never mind. He wanted adventure, and from the appearance of things he was going to have plenty of it.

A sonorous beating on a brass gong announced that luncheon was served. After the many rounds of drinks, René was far from being clear in the head. He staggered slightly as he walked to the dining room. He had never been feted before by older men, and he felt inordinately happy. As the conversation at the luncheon table grew rougher, he noticed that he was less shocked than he had been at first. They were talking about women. Women seemed to play an important part in the lives of all these men. Those from the plantations had almost no other subject of conversation.

"But to the devil with the women!" René told himself.

"They can keep their native women. It's a sure thing that I'm not interested."

Alfred kept a close eye on his brother, and he acted as soon as he felt that René had taken more wine than was good for him.

"Come on, boy, it's time for us to be on our way," he said, pushing his chair back from the table.

Alfred's horses and buggy stood ready for the homeward trip.

René steadied himself and rose at once. *Au revoirs* were exchanged. The brothers stepped out into the sun-smitten street, where Alfred's horses and buggy stood ready for the homeward trip.

2

The girls back home

AUTOMOBILES were as yet unknown in Java.[3] The steam-trolley had left for its daily trip hours before, and so Alfred's buggy was their only means of transportation. René's glance took in the spirited span of horses from the Sandalwood Islands, the mango tree in the welcome shade of which they stood, and Brahim the native groom.[4] The latter was an interesting little fellow with his large brown hat, shaped like a shallow dishpan, loose trousers and a *sarong* of beautiful batik[5]—batik René's sisters would have given a pretty penny to own. If the boy found René of any interest, he gave no sign. But Alfred knew that not one of the newcomer's movements escaped the native's seemingly indifferent eyes.

---

3 Though the novel was not published until 1931, this key point reveals that the storyline is set close to the turn of the 20th century. Your editor chose to include some circa 1910–1920 photos showing cars to give readers visual references, but keep in mind that automotive technology was not part of colonial life as our story unfolds.

4 Sandalwood ponies were originally bred from Arabian horses on the Indonesian islands of Sumba and Sumbawa, named for sandalwood trees that are the island's major export. Sandalwoods are renowned as among the finest breeds in the country. Despite the authors' repeated romantic references to carriages with multiple horses, not a single contemporary photo found showed more than "one horsepower." See pages 10, 60, 62, 154, 161, 165, 191, 262 and 273.

5 Batik is a technique of wax-resist dyeing applied to whole cloth that originated in Indonesia.

"The tradition of batik making is found in various countries; the batik of Indonesia, however, may be the best-known. Indonesian batik made in the island of Java has a long history of acculturation, with diverse patterns influenced by a variety of cultures, and is the most developed in terms of pattern, technique, and the quality of workmanship. In October 2009, UNESCO designated Indonesian batik as a Masterpiece of Oral and Intangible Heritage of Humanity." [Wikipedia].

**Huge tjamara trees lined the road on either side, meeting overhead
to form a solid roof of green leaves.**

They were off with a dash, the small, lively horses taking
all of Alfred's attention. René was thrilled with the beauty
about him. Huge *tjamara*[6] trees lined the road on either side,
meeting overhead to form a solid roof of green leaves. Many
varieties of palms grew somewhat lower, and their lovely
drooping foliage made a curtain through which the lad caught
glimpses of white houses, salient in the vivid sunlight. He was
conscious of a feeling of unreality. The enchantment of a fairy-
tale world must surely lie just beyond the emerald vistas.

Scarcely a leaf stirred. The air hung hot over the drowsing
land. Only René appeared to care that this tropical paradise
was beautiful. He wondered what was going on in the cool
darkness of the quiet homes he saw, and in the hushed
depths of the motionless foliage. Even the military barracks

---

6   Australian pines (*Casuarina equisetifolia*) grow 20–115 ft. tall and are common
throughout Southeast Asia, Northern Australia and the Pacific Islands.

Once beyond the suburbs of Cheribon,
they passed an almost unbroken string of native villages.

he passed a little later showed no signs of life. Men, beasts and birds awaited the hour of sunset when, as though in response to a magic wand, they would revive joyously.

The heat did not trouble René. The swift motion of the buggy and his cool European blood protected him. Soon the horses had spent their first playfulness, and Alfred was able to take his mind off them and to ask questions. He wanted to know a hundred things about home, about his mother and sisters, the news of old friends; in fact, all that René could tell.

Once beyond the suburbs of Cheribon, they passed an almost unbroken string of native villages. René halted Alfred's flow of questions to ask some of his own. He was fascinated by the sights about him. At a certain point, long rows of bamboo buildings lined the road on either side; he pointed at them speechlessly.

The stoves hung at either end of a huge yoke, which made it easy for the owner to move his small restaurant at a moment's notice.

"Native stores," Alfred explained. "The roofs are mostly of palm leaves extending far out, as you see, to protect the wares and the customers from sun and rain."

"Are they cooking things to eat?" René demanded, staring at the queer stoves covered with steaming dishes which gave off savory odors.

Alfred laughed. "Oh, yes! You can have hot rice at once, if you are hungry."

"No, thank you, but I would like to get out and look at their arrangements more closely."

René walked down the length of the market alley. There was much to hold his attention. The stoves hung at either end of a huge yoke, which made it easy for the owner to move his small restaurant at a moment's notice. There were baskets of

The women strolled about, superbly erect, with great bamboo trays
loaded with fruit balanced gracefully on their heads.

all shapes, filled with a variety of fruits and vegetables. The men sat cross-legged on the ground beside their wares. The women strolled about, superbly erect, with great bamboo trays loaded with fruit balanced gracefully on their heads. Even the children carried trays in this fashion. It was not surprising, René mused, that they had such well-developed figures and walked with an exquisite rhythm which no white woman possesses. The loads on their heads accounted for it.

Some of the native men were naked to the waist, their brown skins smooth and glistening as satin. The women wore white and blue jackets, and always the *sarong* of batik. Beyond the shops one could see bamboo huts, rice *goedangs* surrounded by hedges, mango trees, feathery fern trees, and long shaded paths, cool and clean. It was a gorgeous panorama, Oriental and beguiling. René's breath came quicker, and his mood mellowed.

"There is just one detail that spoils this picture," he said at last to Alfred.

"And that is?"

"The modern lanterns and student lamps hanging from the ceilings of the little stores."

"They must have light, René, and are mighty glad to have found a safe device. It's a great improvement over their old-time coconut oil lamps, which were always setting fire to the thatch."

"Yes, that's right. One spark among these dry palm leaves, and everything would be gone."

The brothers climbed back into their buggy, and were soon speeding forward. The Sandalwood horses fell into a steady gait, and kept it up for mile after mile. Alfred nodded in the heat, but René was full of all he saw. He frequently touched the older man with his elbow, in order to arouse him and to

Javanese countryside painted by Franz Wilhelm Junghuhn, circa 1853.

pose some naive query. Finally, Alfred took a sidelong glance at the youngster, sighed and spoke awkwardly:

"René, I feel that I must tell you an important thing. Or rather, let me ask you a question first. Have—have you ever had anything to do with women—at home, in your life in Holland?"

"No, of course not," René answered, with a touch of indignation.

"That being so, I must explain a situation you are going to encounter in the Tropics." Alfred was losing no time about shouldering his responsibilities as an elder brother.

René, as though anxious to get the subject over with, interposed:

"I take it that what you have to tell me has to do with the native women. I heard about this from the old-timers on the

The lad stared at the open countryside—here and there a rice field, a few patches of corn and far in the distance the foothills, covered with a growth of tropical forest, and topped by the mighty peak of Tjirmai.

boat coming out. But I'm not much interested. I haven't the slightest idea of paying attention to the native women."

"Well, well, René, you certainly guessed exactly what I had in mind!"

The lad stared at the open countryside—here and there a rice field, a few patches of corn and far in the distance the foothills, covered with a growth of tropical forest, and topped by the mighty peak of Tjirmai. Across the beauty and wonder of all this, a tiny speck seemed to flit before his eyes; somehow, he must brush it away and regain the poignant joy that the new land had created within him. What had he to do with the question of women? But of course Alfred thought that he was being helpful. He resented this spoiling of the present happy moment, but he suppressed his impatience as he answered:

"I can save you a lot of trouble, just by telling you a piece of news about myself."

"Oh, I can guess what it is!" Alfred replied quickly. "You are in love with a girl at home."

"Precisely."

"That's one reason the more why you should listen to me," Alfred insisted. "Do you remember that I was engaged to marry Kittie Welter when I left home? Perhaps you don't, for you were too young then to understand that sort of thing. It was only six months after I came to Java that Kittie broke off our engagement, because we would have to wait too long. This island was too far away from Holland, the interior was too lonesome, and what not! All my illusions went up in the air. In a little while, I took a native girl; she has been a better companion for me than many a white girl might have been."

"I remember Kittie very well, Alfred. What happened to you does not prove that every white girl would behave as your Kittie did. My fiancée, for instance, would not be capable of it. You may remember her—Betty van Voort, daughter of Mr. van Voort the mayor of a neighboring town? She will wait for me, and come to me wherever I may go. I tell you right now that I intend to lead a clean life for her sake."

Alfred's laugh was without bitterness, as he replied: "That's the way they all talk. It's the way I talked at the beginning. But, my dear boy, I admire you for your convictions. Hold strongly to them. I'll be the last one to drive you into the arms of a native girl. I'm only trying to explain to you why others do so, why I did it."

The speck in front of René's eyes seemed to expand to a cloud, yet he answered sturdily:

"Whatever may happen, I swear to seek the company only of decent white women."

Alfred moved his shoulders impatiently. A sneer twisted the corners of his lips.

"What a child you are!" he said. "You know nothing about conditions here, and yet you rebel against listening to straight facts from me."

René shivered. He did not like the brutal note which had suddenly come into Alfred's voice. It shocked him that his brother should sneer at a white man's ideals about love.

"Well, all right, tell me the whole story," he muttered. "I'll listen."

3

The *totok* meets the *njai*

"**ALL THAT YOU SAY** sounds very respectable," Alfred began, "but don't forget that we are going into the interior of Java to work for a living, and not to some holiday resort where you can pick and choose your girls. There are no white girls at our sugar factory. Among the white employees, only one is married properly to a white woman, and that dear lady is fifty-four years of age. If you stay out here, you may not see a European girl for years to come. I feel I should save you the shock of finding it out for yourself; I know from experience that it *will* be a shock to a *totok,* as we call newcomers like you."

"It's certainly better that I should know about it," René interrupted vehemently, "but it won't affect my stand. I can't see myself playing around with natives. I came here to work, not to degrade myself."

"Very good, boy, very good," Alfred replied more amiably. "Don't forget, however, that life in the interior of the Dutch East Indies is frightfully lonely. There is no true companionship between the whites and the mixed-bloods— a veiled alertness or suspicion on the part of the mixed-blood, a touch of scorn from the white man—you can imagine how bad that is for fraternity. We meet in a social way at the club, play cards or billiards together, drink a bit—and there it ends. The gap is too wide to be bridged.

"Our evenings are deadly. We can't go to the club every night. It's too boring to meet the same men over and over again, and hear the same old gossip. So we stay at home. Oh yes, we can ride horseback after work is done, but even that becomes tiresome! There's not much sense in riding from one factory to another. No dances, and hardly a white girl in all the land. We're thrown back upon a domestic existence, so it has become the custom for the white man to take into his home a native girl, a *njai,* as they say here."

Alfred glanced sideways at René, expecting some comment, but his younger brother was huddled against the cushions, and staring moodily into the distance.

"Look here, René, before passing judgment on a situation about which you hardly have had time to think deeply, place yourself in the position of the Hollander in Java. No man can take care of a house and about fourteen servants, and expect to attend to business too. Again, the colonist cannot handle the native servants—it takes a Javanese to do that. The *njai* assumes full charge of your affairs, does the marketing for you, looks after your every comfort, and in fact takes the place of a wife.

"Some of these girls are very beautiful, and you can't help feeling drawn to them. That makes a difference, too. Bear in mind that a man is all man out here. The heat and the highly seasoned food have a lot to do with this. The isolation of his life completes the job. He is swept away from his moral moorings and does things which he might consider to be wrong in normal circumstances."

"That's all well and good, Alfred, as far as the white man is concerned, but how about the girl?"

The sugar factory, Kerang Sawah, where Alfred worked as an overseer, now came into view through an opening in the solid mass of palm and mango trees.

"Don't think for a moment that the *njai* is lowering herself in the eyes of anyone out here. She actually betters her position. She can dress well, and she is treated with respect in native circles because of her responsible standing in the white man's household. In most cases, she is very happy. Then, their religion teaches them that a virgin cannot enter Heaven. A Javanese girl can see no wrong in overcoming that obstacle to her future happiness. Her standards are quite different from ours. There are many sides to the question, René."

"Does a man *have* to do this?" the lad asked despondently.

"Well, you don't have to take a young *njai,* if you feel so deeply about it; but for your own well-being you are forced to have some sort of female native housekeeper. This brings me around to the main object of my chatter. I have confessed to having a *njai* in my home. She is beautiful, efficient and wholly satisfying. You are to live with us, and my Missah

**Traffic along the road increased as they neared the *kampongs*
surrounding the factory.**

will make you just as comfortable as you would be in your
own establishment. Unless and until you break loose from us,
you won't have to violate your moral principles. I hope that
that makes you feel better about it all."

René could not answer. He had always admired Alfred,
had looked upon him as only a younger brother can, had
respected him through the years he had been away from
home. Now he could see but one side of his *njai* question:
Alfred had become embittered, following his disappointment
over Kittie. René's thoughts turned to his own Betty; her
influence would protect him from imitating Alfred. The
native girls could not tempt him. Nevertheless, he should not
judge his brother too harshly for living the way other white
men lived out here. What a mess, anyway!

They drove on in silence. It was all so strange, and René
had absorbed about enough for the moment. His emotions

"There is my home—and yours, too, now!"

were still jumbled.... So Alfred had a native wife, save the mark! Not so good!

The horses shied sharply as a boy with a heavy load on his shoulders stepped suddenly into the roadway. The incident afforded a welcome break in the train of René's thoughts. His interest in the sights about him revived. The sugar factory, Kerang Sawah, where Alfred worked as an overseer, now came into view through an opening in the solid mass of palm and mango trees.[7] The buildings were of terra-cotta, and much more pleasing to the eye than the glaring white structures of the city. A tall smoke stack stood high above the roofs of the various warehouses and sheds.

Traffic along the road increased as they neared the *kampongs* surrounding the factory. It was almost six o'clock and deliciously cool as compared to the heat of the midday sun.

---

7 Kerang Sawah means shellfish in Malay. Your editor could find no location, past or present, with this name.

The *kampong* Kerang Sawah, set in the midst of mango trees, was teeming with life. Encouraged by the evening shade, the natives had flocked out to buy food for their supper.

As the buggy jolted along among the shoppers, hats were raised on all sides. Everyone seemed eager to pay his respects to the white *tuans*. It was a lively scene, but to the sweaty René it passed as a picture. Even the houses they drove by, where white men were sitting on the verandas, failed to make much of an impression on his worn emotions. Yet as Alfred announced, "There is my home—and yours, too, now!" René's heart missed a beat.

He observed white buildings, long low-roofed verandas, great mango trees and a driveway flanked by deep hedges. Details somehow escaped him until he got out of the buggy, entered the porch and saw Missah there.

She was a smiling, graceful little creature, not black or thick-lipped, not greasy or woolly-haired—none of the things René had imagined a native girl would be. She was actually beautiful; her skin the color of rich coffee with much cream, a dull, pale brown, just light enough to show a pretty flush on either cheek; her hair jet black and combed straight back into a knot low on the neck, held by glittering hairpins interwoven with white, sweet-smelling flowers. René's senses reeled at the heavy odor of the flowers. He noticed that her eyes were brownish-black, set deeper than the eyes of Japanese women, and yet with a slight upward slant. They twinkled now in a wholly intelligent welcome to the *totok*. Her small mouth, of a natural red such as any white woman might envy, was curved in a seductive smile. Missah wore a fine white linen jacket open at the throat. A lovely *sarong* of batik fell to her ankles, and her feet were bare. Her figure was girlish, soft and rounded.

…her hair jet black and combed straight back into a knot low on the neck, held by glittering hairpins interwoven with white, sweet-smelling flowers.

With a delicate movement of her hand she tried to express what she felt. René took the hand in greeting; it was cool and soft. He stared at her in wonder as they entered the house; her charm was a revelation.

She understood René's admiring glances quickly enough, and smiled back at him. With all his senses beguiled, he was now much better able to understand what Alfred had been driving at on their journey from the city.

"*Slamat datang, tuan* René," Missah said softly.

"She means, 'Be welcome, Mr. René,'" Alfred interpreted.

Both Alfred and Missah showed René to his room. The elder brother breathed a sigh of relief as he turned away to his own. He had been far from sure of René. The boy could have caused plenty of trouble in the household if he had persisted in his attitude of hostility toward the native girls—and especially toward Missah. There remained no doubt, however, of his admiration for her, nor of hers for him.

4

...Don't mix your values

ALFRED'S HOUSE was large and rambling. It was L-shaped, the main section containing a living room and bedrooms. A large veranda was used as the dining room. On the right of this were René's quarters, while on the left was Alfred's office and his sleeping chamber beyond. He had chosen the position of the latter, so as to be able to overlook the factory buildings. In the outer wing were the servants' quarters, the kitchen and the bathroom.

The rear of the house commanded a fine view of the garden. René glanced at the garden first, admiring its wealth of flamboyant blossoms, and then looked about his room with curiosity. There were no screens or glass panes in the windows, but merely French shutters to keep out the rays of the sun. Around his bed was a *klamboe*, or netting, to protect him from the mosquitoes and other small insects which invaded the place in great numbers as soon as the lights were lit.

Brahim brought in the trunk and bags; as René watched the native put down his baggage carefully, he experienced a swift wave of apprehension. This room was to be his, perhaps for many years. It was now a part of him. Here, between these

The rear of the house commanded a fine view of the garden.

four whitewashed walls, he might have to wage many an emotional and moral struggle. Nevertheless, no matter what the new land of Java had in store for him, he would see it through, head up. He had now plunged into the realities of life, and he was ready to do his share, for better or for worse.

A knock at the door aroused him. "Come on, René," Alfred called, "I'll show you the bathroom. You'll just have time for a bath and a change for dinner."

The bathroom was a different affair, indeed, from what he had been used to at home. In one corner was a large cement tank filled to the brim with crystal-clear water. He was making ready to plunge in when Alfred held him back,

"No, son, you don't get into the tub in this country. Just stand beside it and dash water over you with those long-handled pails. You see, we all have to use the same tub. There is no running water here. The water-boy fills the tank every day with water brought from the river down below."

Upon his return to the bedroom, René found laid out for him a white linen jacket and loose trousers of batik, with soft slippers for his feet. He was now full of fun and mischief as he donned this strange clothing and went to join his brother at dinner. The cold bath had entirely washed away his misgivings.

He supposed, of course, that Missah would be at the table with them; he anticipated much pleasure in hearing her musical voice, watching her at close range and getting acquainted. She had withdrawn to the servants' quarters, however. Hot rebellion again surged in the boy. He told himself that Alfred was not treating her as his wife. All Alfred's talk had been meaningless, just so much hypocrisy and evasion which left the problem as difficult as ever to understand. As though sensing his struggle, the elder brother was silent while dinner was served by Kasdjan, the man servant, and one young girl, Adinda. Missah had seen to it that many European dishes had been prepared in honor of René's arrival.

Outdoors the swift twilight had come and gone, and a steady rain had begun to fall. The tropical night was loud with the croaking of frogs and the patter of the rain; other bizarre sounds were heard from time to time, but these competed vainly with the vociferous frogs. Insects of every description swarmed in, until they fairly infested the table. On the walls René saw curious little reptiles crawling. The sight of the latter took away his appetite, until Alfred explained that they were harmless.

They are lizards, the *tokkes* and their smaller relatives the *titjaks*. We never disturb them, for they feed on insects and serve to make the house more habitable on that account, Alfred said.

René's
repulsion slowly grew.
His feeling of distaste
gradually took in the
whole island of Java. He was stunned and
sick at heart over the very thought of having to stay there
indefinitely. The day had been one of contradictory reactions.
Homesickness as well as disillusionment now tipped the
balance to the darker side.

Alfred made conversation: "I have turned over a large
room to the men around here as a club room. They gather in
the evenings to play cards and to gossip."

"Do you expect them tonight?" René asked listlessly. He
had decided that if they came, he would not join them.

"No, it's raining much too hard for anyone to venture out.
This is the season of our wet monsoon. The storms rage for
hours sometimes."

"I'm glad, Alfred. I'm too tired to talk tonight."

"Then we'll turn in early. You've had excitement enough."

They left the table and took easy cane-bottomed chairs
in the living room. Missah came at once with cigars and
cigarettes, seating herself on the floor at Alfred's side, as
though quite accustomed to it, her legs crossed under her.

"What do you want here?" Alfred demanded severely.

"*Tida apa apa,*" was the laconic reply.

"Well, you can stay a little while."

Missah smiled at René, apparently not in the least
offended by Alfred's curt remark. René was sorry for her,

and showed it. He was furious at his brother for speaking in such a rough way to a beautiful woman. If he had had any knowledge of the Malay language, he would have said something kind to Missah. Alfred watched this little byplay with an amused smile.

"I treat them in the only possible way. They are all right, but they are not our equals and have to be put in their places every once in a while," Alfred said. "This girl is really a good girl, and I am almost certain I own her exclusively. She is honest, but of course not a lady. She gets on my nerves at times."

"Own her—exclusively! Is it possible that she might deceive you?" came from René's indignant lips.

"Oh, one can't always be sure! I happen to believe that Missah is true to me. In fact, I know it, and to that extent I regard her as a lady."

Alfred spoke on a coarse, jesting note, while he glanced down at Missah's expressive face.

"I say, Alfred! Its bad business... I don't accept it one bit."

"Rot! Get it straight, boy, and don't mix your values. You're no longer in Europe. When Missah, or any of these native girls, marries later on nothing could tempt her to leave her husband or to deceive him with a lover. The Javanese women have a profound respect for marriage. You can't always say as much for your white women, who get a divorce one day and take a new husband the next. Many of them have one illicit love affair after another. If the world finds them out, they are banned from decent society—at least in Holland—but they figure on not being caught.

"In this island, on the other hand, the girls indulge their sex impulses before marriage, openly and unashamed, driven solely by a natural force which they do not try to suppress. No native, man or woman, will point a finger at them for following their instincts. The old Indian tribes considered it marriage when a brave took the maiden of his choice by the hand and led her to his tepee. Every race has its own notions of right and wrong."

"Well, maybe so," answered René slowly, at a loss to combat Alfred's powerful argument.

"You can't get this thing in a few short hours, René, and of course you're too young to be patient. Forget it for a while and go to bed."

Alfred arose as he spoke, said good-night, and went toward his room. Missah followed. At the threshold, she turned to give René a single eloquent glance.

The lad made his way to his own room and leaned on the window sill, looking out into the gloomy, rain-drenched night. Strange, inarticulate passions buffeted him; he seemed to be swimming in an unknown sea. Now that he had been left to himself, his homesickness increased. He knew that the only sensible thing to do was to fight it down. A good sound sleep would give him renewed strength to face another day. Turning away from the window, he prepared for bed. The instant his head touched the pillow, he was lost to the waking world.

5

A false Garden of Eden

JAVA, lying almost under the equator, knows no leisurely dawn or twilight. The sun rises about six o'clock all the year around, and half an hour later it has flooded the earth with light and heat. At six in the evening it dips behind the horizon, and darkness comes almost at once.

The inhabitants, therefore, take full advantage of the twelve hours of daylight. Alfred and René had breakfast at seven. This being the quiet season, they could afford to idle a bit. At crop time, they would be at work an hour earlier.

René was astonished at himself. He felt as fresh as the morning; the emotions of the night before seemed already dissipated. He concluded that it was none of his affair, anyhow. He knew what he would do about women; the compromises of other men, even of his brother, need not affect him. He had come to Java to work, so that he might marry Betty and be able to give her a home. The very thought of her cheered him. Decidedly, the day had started well.

He had but a fleeting glance at Missah, for the young Adinda waited on them at the table. To Adinda he gave scant attention, other than to notice that she, too, was pretty, dainty

He was given the task of weighing the sugar cane
as it was brought in by natives in oxcarts and trucks.

and graceful. Evidently Alfred liked good-looking women in
his household.

At the office, Alfred introduced him to the employees of
the sugar factory. René proved to be the youngest among
them. They treated him cordially, making him feel at home.
It was good to be with the men, to talk about business, to
plan for work.

Alfred posted him about the employees, as they walked
through the factory; told him, for instance, about Terloak,
one of the engineers whose grandmother was a native, and
several others of mixed blood who held responsible positions.
Alfred then left for the sugar cane fields, where ordinarily he
stayed until late in the day.

René tackled his new work with zest. He was given the task
of weighing the sugar cane as it was brought in by natives

in oxcarts and trucks. The job was simple enough, but paid better than anything he could have obtained at home. This made him feel at peace with the world.

Later, he was given a variety of chores to do, in the factory and outdoors. But he often had whole days to himself; these he used to advantage in learning the Malay language. All foreign tongues were easy to him, and Malay proved no exception. "Take a sleeping dictionary," the men aboard-ship had advised, but René was satisfied with Missah's friendly help. He soon realized that but for Missah he would have been many months learning Malay. So efficient a teacher did she prove that in eight weeks he was able to talk fluently with his men. This made his work much more pleasant. He learned, also, to understand Missah better, and to admire her. They got along famously, to Alfred's satisfaction.

About a week after René's arrival, the mail carrier brought the dreamed-of letter from Betty. He had little to do that day, so gave himself up to the luxury of reading and re-reading it a score of times. What a perfectly sweet letter she wrote! Her naive, girlish words made him feel as happy as a king.

"You just wait, darling, and be very careful of yourself. In

Nevertheless, Betty's letter was delicious,
and made him long for the next one.

the meantime, I will pray for you, and someday we'll be together in a cozy little home under a big palm tree." He stopped to think a minute about the lovely word-picture that Betty had painted.... "I want you to keep amused," she continued, "and I hope that you can find some nice European girls out where you are, to play tennis with and go on picnics."

René chuckled over her well-meant suggestion. There were no white girls for miles and miles around. He hadn't heard of any picnics since his arrival. But Betty's unselfishness surely proved her love; there seemed as yet no way for him to test his love for her.

The mention of tennis was the best joke of all. It reminded him of what an old friend of his mother's had said the night before he left for Java: "It will be one continuous holiday for you on the plantations. They usually go horseback riding after breakfast on horses provided by the company, and you'll play a lot of tennis." What a queer, mistaken idea the good Dutch home folk had of life in Java! Did anyone in Holland, he wondered, really know what it meant to work on a colonial sugar estate?

Nevertheless, Betty's letter was delicious, and made him long for the next one. He set about answering her at once, pouring out his heart, detailing for her all the small matters so dear to a sweetheart, and explaining that it was for her alone he was working.

It was a fact that he almost felt Betty's physical presence beside him as he went about his tasks, and the long, intimate bulletins he sent her every few days proved to be a safety valve for loneliness.

The *njai* question did not trouble him while his mind and heart were full of Betty.

He paused before her picture on the dresser.

This proved to be the period of his greatest contentment in Java. Then he began to fret over the long wait between letters from Holland; it was high time for the next one. But the next one never came. Instead, there was a letter from Betty's mother—a cruelly tactful epistle—explaining that the girl was much too young to choose a husband.

"At sixteen she cannot know her mind upon so serious a question," wrote Betty's mother, and went on to disprove her dictum by adding: "Betty loves you very dearly and is heartbroken, though she has promised me she will not communicate with you again. I forced her to agree to this. You will realize, I am sure, that I have Betty's future happiness at heart. If later you both still feel for each other in the same way, neither her father nor I will make further objections."

There was more, much more, of the same cold reasoning. It wounded René immeasurably. On the back of the letter, Betty had been permitted to write a little note, a farewell message: "Poor boy, when you receive this news you will be terribly hurt; but, darling, I am sure Mother is right. I can say so little to comfort you. But time will work this out for us."

He sat in his room, trying to choke down his hot tears. His love, the first he had ever experienced, was very real; it possessed his whole being, it was the pivot on which his life turned. For love's sake, he had gone abroad to make his fortune. Betty had been his safeguard from temptation at Kerang Sawah. His hours of solitude had been occupied with letter writing, the telling of little things he thought and felt, what he wanted to do for her in the future, all the chatty confessions he could make to a sweetheart and to no one else. There was no dream girl for whom he could live and work now. The prospect became drab and the struggle meaningless. Java was a false Garden of Eden where all men went to the devil.

He was partly right about this. The white man is apt to deteriorate anywhere in the tropics, but the way down is made easier for him in the interior of the Dutch East Indies than in other colonial lands. It takes a strong will and a fine character to hold firm to one's ideals.

René was in the making; it was almost brutal to put him in such a place. There were no gentle, cultivated white women within a day's journey of him. He was at swords' point with the accepted theory of morals between Dutchmen and Javanese. The whole population lived against every line and precept, as these are usually understood by the rest of the civilized world. René's own brother had slacked off into a low sensuality, which the boy had sworn he would never imitate.

René van Landsberg, in short, was like a smooth, clean slate without any indication of what Life intended so soon to write upon it.

Loneliness engulfed him as he sat for hours in his room. He was made sick by the very thought that he must mingle again with the men of the plantation, must join them over their everlasting whiskey splits. Why did they drink so continuously in this hot climate? It was the destruction of them. Why did they do any of the things they did? Oh, to have someone nearby in whom he could confide! Some of his relatives or old friends from home who were familiar with the cause of his unhappiness. Just anyone to whom he could talk about Betty!

René arose and walked back and forth, back and forth, in his room—too stunned, now, even to think. So short a time ago, Betty had pledged her love, her life, to him! And already...

He paused before her picture on the dresser. She was a pretty youngster, with sweet little dimples, her hair down her back, and big eyes that seemed to follow him. So she was not old enough to choose a husband! Merely old enough to love him, and then to throw him over in his hour of need! In a sudden rage, he ripped the picture into small fragments, which he scattered upon the tiled floor. Yet he did not hate her, nor felt any profound anger at her mother. He scarcely knew what he felt. But if the affair must be ended, he wished to wipe it out of his memory as completely as possible. That was René all over. He did not believe in moaning about the past. "Never say die!" was his motto. "A good loser," men remarked of him in later years.

By means of the trivial act of tearing up the photograph, he commenced to face the future. His courage was low, however, and he felt unequal to working at the office that day. His room seemed small and stifling. Stepping on to the broad veranda, he almost ran into Missah's arms. She had been listening at his door, worried at his remaining so long in the room, and at the sound of his restless, pacing feet. She now poured out a flood of Malay words. René could not make out what she said, but her sympathetic smile conveyed an eagerness to help him in his trouble, whatever that might be.

He felt a sudden, intense desire to take her in his arms, just to hold someone close, to know the soft touch of a woman's embrace, to be comforted in his first great sorrow. The two stood only a few inches from each other. A magnetic current ran between them. Both seemed to be expecting some extraordinary event. René's self-control weakened, though it was not quite clear to him what he ought to resist. Missah's beautiful dark eyes burned deep into his; her young bosom rose and fell in great agitation.

6

Missah's infidelity

THE LAD BRUSHED PAST HER and seated himself in an easy chair. Missah remained standing, her expressive face full of sympathy for the *tuan,* yet slightly puzzled. For the moment, he refused to meet her eyes. His mood had become indifferent; he wanted no contact with a native girl.

He clapped his hands, which is the only system used to call servants in the Dutch possessions. Missah was in front of his chair at once.

"A glass of cold lemonade," he ordered, and raised his head to watch her as she walked towards the kitchen. Her step was graceful, her head held high, her slender back as straight as an arrow.

But it was Adinda who brought the cooling drink. As she handed it to René, she said softly: "Missah cries in the kitchen."

"*Knapa?*" he asked curtly.

"*Maoe tuan,*" came the simple answer.

Now, what in the world did that mean? René's knowledge of Malay failed him. He thought over the words. Ah, he had it now: "Wants master!"

For the second time that day, he was stunned. What excuse had the girl to want him, the brother of her own master? He had never given her any cause to think he was even interested in her. She had been kind to him, true enough. Surely she had not interpreted his gratitude as sex attraction! Obviously, she had sent Adinda to tell him of her desire. He felt disgusted, furious.

Here he did Missah a wrong; she had had nothing to do with what Adinda told him. The young Adinda had perceived Missah's passion for this *tuan,* and had thought to help her. That René might have standards of his own had not occurred to her, for she had never seen or heard of a white man who refused a beautiful native girl.

With a great effort, he restrained himself from breaking out into curses at everything connected with Java, and these two girls in particular. Unable to trust his voice, he merely frowned and shook his head. He then wisely decided to say nothing to Alfred of Missah's infidelity; it would only cause trouble. While he was still brooding over his personal disillusionment, Alfred came in from the fields.

As was his custom, the older man called loudly, *"Bawa kabaya,* which notified Missah that her *tuan* was home and wanted his negligee brought to the bathroom at once. This call was repeated by a large *beo* perched on a bamboo near the kitchen. It was a beautiful bird, with dark blue feathers and a yellow beak. Its powers of mimicry were amazing, and it remembered what it had learned. Often it called to Missah before Alfred could.

This time, despite all the calling, Missah did not come. Adinda brought the master's jacket in her place. Alfred asked no questions. Missah often shopped at this hour, or visited her friends. He went on into the bathroom, refreshed himself and put on cool clothes. He was ready then for a chat with

René, but he found his young brother in so dejected a frame of mind that he became alarmed.

"What is it, René. Has something happened to Mother or the girls. Tell me, quick!"

"No, not that," was the brief answer, while René struggled with the desire to unburden his heart to Alfred, tell everything and clear it up.

"What is it, old man? Let's hear it."

"Bad news for me, Alfred. I had a letter from Betty's mother, breaking our engagement. She thinks Betty is too young, and so on—you know the kind of thing."

"I'm damned sorry, René." Alfred put his hand affectionately on his brother's shoulder. "That is certainly rotten news. Of course, I expected it would happen sooner or later. But so quickly after you got here, it beats anything I ever heard! Brace up, my boy!" Alfred blustered a bit, in an effort to hide his feelings. "You're still young. She may wait, anyway. However, having gone through the experience myself, I know what emptiness it leaves in your heart. Take it like a man, and don't let it change your ideals about life in general."

René, feeling very forlorn, choked back his tears while the other talked.

"Here's the letter, Alfred. Maybe you will see a ray of hope in it."

Alfred read it through, feeling more sorry than ever for René. "Can't get a thing but dismissal out of that, boy, though I wish to God I could."

René was surprised at the emotion Alfred showed. He felt drawn to him the more since he had never known this side of his brother's nature.

Luncheon promised to be a rather solemn affair, but when René saw the many appetizing dishes of rice, curried chicken and several kinds of vegetables, he felt hungry and ate heartily. He was surprised at himself. This was by no means his idea of the way a man with a broken heart should eat.

"Where is Missah?" Alfred asked of Kasdjan.

Kasdjan, stiff in his white jacket, replied laconically: *"Tida taoe"*—I do not know—the usual answer from a native, meaning without fail that he knew all about Missah, but did not choose to tell. It was a good way to keep out of trouble. There was not a thing going on in the household the servants did not know. The Javanese have a nose for news; they also have the appearance of innocence, but this does not fool their masters.

Alfred spoke impatiently to René: "That rascal knows very well where Missah is, and whatever it is that is keeping her away."

To the native he said: "So! You don't know anything about Missah?"

Under the *tuan's* fierce glance, Kasdjan relented a little:

"Missah *sakit.*"

"Where is she?"

"Di dapoer."

"Well, tell Missah for me that if she is sick, she shouldn't stay in the kitchen."

Saja, tuan," Kasdjan replied with an expressionless face. That ended the matter.

A few minutes later, Alfred came from his room, dressed for the fields. He wore high boots to protect him from snakes and mud, a white drill coat and trousers, and on his head a huge hat at least two feet in diameter. He seemed to René well

He concluded that he would put on walking clothes and go out.

insured against both insects and heat. With a cheery flourish of his whip, he was gone—with not a thought of Missah, not a glance into the kitchen to find out how she fared.

This was not kind, René thought. What was the state of affairs between Alfred and Missah anyway? Did she expect such treatment? Was it what she had always received, or was Alfred a bit vexed at her and taking this means of showing it? Not much companionship in such an attitude, as far as he could see. He felt more and more puzzled as he thought it over. He must ask his brother. He understood there was a real liking between the man and the girl, which made the affair more nearly right; but it was all distasteful to himself, and his old feeling of rebellion flared up.

He concluded that he would put on walking clothes and go out, get away from the house into the open where he would be able to think things over more clearly. When he had dressed, he left his room only to find Missah again waiting, as though for him. She stood in the doorway, an appealing little figure of wistfulness. René's heart thumped; for an instant he paused. Missah smiled one of her ravishing smiles, her dark eyes melting into his.

But René turned and entered the garden. He was disturbed beyond belief; hot waves of emotion swept over him. He was indignant at himself for responding in this way to his brother's *njai*. Poor young René. Life was writing fast on the slate of his sensibilities. He longed for something familiar, something that would help him to perceive his values clearly and snap them back into their proper places.

In Alfred's room Missah wept, her quivering girlish body stretched out on her master's bed. At the coming of the fresh-looking young *tuan,* she had experienced new and haunting desires. It amazed her that he did not respond to her in the least. No man had ever failed to be glad of her smile; but this one was different, and so she wanted him more than ever. He seemed to care for no woman, and for that reason, too, he was a wonder and a delight.

The web about the dwellers in Alfred's house was slowly weaving. In and out went the shuttle—in and out—a pattern begun, as yet no broken thread, no weak spot. But Life laughed.

7

Adinda vs. the "Dutch wife"

A PARTY HAD BEEN PLANNED for that evening, a sort of initiation for René as a member of the club. Upon his return from his walk, he wished he could run away from it all. He did not feel like seeing the men he knew would be there: a few white men, but more of the mixed bloods. The boy was in no mood to meet the latter kindly.

Alfred was late, so there was no opportunity for a talk before the guests began to arrive. Everyone wore white and was in high spirits. Young native boys served the drinks. As the glasses were emptied and filled again, the affair became extremely lively, with each man trying to outdo the others in cordiality to the *totok.*

Innumerable healths were drunk, all in René's honor. Tongues loosened. Jokes were cracked, some not at all to the lad's liking. He was young, however, and this was only the second time that older men of position had treated him as an adult. It went to his head. He drank with the rest, although he was still able to observe that Alfred kept sober and did not enter into the coarser jests.

The talk was at first about their work, the sugar factories, the fields, and how material things were progressing.

Everyone wore white and was in high spirits. Young native boys served the drinks.

But it drifted around to women, as René had known it would. Coming out on the steamer, every smoking room conversation had taken the same turn. The Colonials of the Dutch East Indies were simply obsessed by women; by native women, it went without saying. René despised them for it.

Midnight found him more intoxicated than was good for him; not being used to whiskey, it did not take much to go to his head. He felt unequal to playing cards when a table was dragged to the center of the room, and poker for small stakes was started. So he killed the time over additional drinks until the party broke up at two o'clock.

Most of the men returned to their homes. A few, however, felt keyed up to wilder dissipations and started for the native *kampong,* announcing without the least embarrassment that

The whole country was a panorama of rarest beauty…

they intended to amuse themselves with the public women. Alfred and René bade their guests good-night at the gate and went back to their house.

Halting on the veranda, they seated themselves in easy chairs, to enjoy a last cigarette and cool their heated blood in the delicious night air.

It had rained a little during the early evening; now the sky was clear and the stars shone in resplendent loveliness, closer to earth than René ever remembered seeing them. He had a keen sense of the beautiful. This, perhaps, was one of the main reasons why he felt he could stay in the enchanting land of Java. The whole country was a panorama of rarest beauty: the mountains, the trees with their foliage so dense and green, the scent-laden flowers—everywhere an abundant, exotic growth filled with fauna he knew nothing of. At night, when the symphony of life slowed down to a murmur, the sense of mystery in all things around him deepened. The call of the *tokkes* on the walls and the shrill chirping of the cicadas from the flower-beds in the garden were the most salient sounds to break the brooding stillness. Small bats, attracted by the lamplight, fluttered noiselessly about in their quest for insects.

Far in the distance, the watchmen had built their fire, a vertical spiral of ruddied smoke going up toward the dark dome of the sky.

René was moved to speak his feelings: "Did you ever see such a night, Alfred? I want to become part of it. I want it to last forever."

"Merely too much whiskey and soda, my boy. You'll get over it."

Feeling that Alfred knew better, René did not resent his flippancy, yet refrained from saying more.

The squeaking of a door was heard suddenly. A shadow could be seen moving towards the edge of the veranda.

"Who is that?" Alfred called.

"*Saja, tuan.* Adinda," came back the soft voice of Missah's helper.

"Rather late for that girl to be out, isn't it?" René remarked.

"Oh, no! The girls go to bed at nine, but often get up in the night to sit outdoors a while, then turn in again. You see, René, they don't read or sew and the housework is easy; they really can't sleep all the time. It's necessary for you and me to get a little rest, though, and if you're through crying at the moon we'll go to bed."

They said good-night and went to their rooms. René undressed quickly. He felt battered by all the emotions of that long, long day. It seemed ages since he had stood in his room reading Betty's letter. It recurred to him now with a new power to hurt him. He threw himself on his bed, a low affair without covers, the nights being too warm even for a sheet. But René longed to cuddle under blankets, to snuggle down, hidden from sights and sounds. The pillow was hard, and the *goeling,* a long, narrow bolster often called the "Dutch wife," to put between the knees for coolness, bothered him. As soon as he tried to sleep, he was covered with a dripping perspiration. He opened the French shutters to let in more air, but found that this would not do at all; too many mosquitoes and other insects came swarming in. With a sigh, he shut out the lovely night, sank upon his bed again and slept heavily, stupefied by the whiskey he had drunk.

He was aroused later by a tapping at his shutters and a whispered, *"Tuan, tuan, tuan!"* The words only entered his mind as part of a dream. But they were repeated, softly, urgently. René tossed from side to side, not fully awake yet. Soon, the tapping became a little louder, and René sat up.

"Tuan, tuan," came the whisper.

"Who's there? What do you want?" he called.

"Sh-ss-sh, not so loud, *tuan!* It is I, Adinda. I want to come in. Please open the door."

René, in full possession of his senses now, replied angrily: "I'll not open the door. You must be crazy. Go away." Arising, he walked to the window, where through the shutters he glimpsed the faint outline of a figure in a white jacket. To his nostrils floated the deadly sweetness of the melati[8] blossom, which the native girls twine in their hair.

---

8 *Melati putih,* one of the three national flowers of Indonesia, is a vine with fragrant flowers formally called *Jasminum sambac.* The other two flowers are the Moth Orchid (*Phalaenopsis amabilis*), and the Stinking Corpse Lily (*Rafflesia arnoldii* or *Padma Raksasa* in Indonesian language). These three are chosen because they are described in three words: Purity, Wisdom, and Elegance.

"It is I, Adinda. I want to come in."

"Hurry, *tuan,* open the door. I want to come in. I have waited a long time for you. Missah belongs to *tuan* Alfred; I want to belong to *tuan* René."

Adinda slipped away from the window. René heard the faint patter of her bare feet as she re-entered the house and came down the corridor to his door. His anger left him—here was an adventure! Adinda was a most attractive girl, slightly darker than Missah, but more fully developed, a bit taller and withal very beautiful. She had delicate features, a small well-shaped nose, dimples in her cheeks, and curved rosy lips. René formed a vivid picture of her in his mind, and his heart beat fast. Perhaps it was the whiskey, he argued to himself. He was unused to drinking, and it might be better for him to lay off the stuff. Things looked queer in the dim light. He was excited, a trifle giddy. Hurriedly he lit his candle.

Adinda tapped gently on the door. "I am here, *tuan.* Quick, so that I am not seen by the household!"

Yes, it was an adventure—a most usual one in Java, if he had only known it. He moved over to the door, and opened it a crack. There on the threshold stood Adinda, smiling up at him, while the perfume from the melatie blossoms made his senses reel. The hot blood mounted to his face; wave after wave swept him, as Adinda spoke:

"Let me come in, *tuan,* I will be yours only."

René still held the door on guard. What had Alfred said about these girls? Not all of them belonged to just one man—a fellow must be careful. As though reading his mind, Adinda spoke again:

"I am young, *tuan,* and I have never belonged to any man. I want only you, never any one but you."

She smiled again, sure of her welcome. Had she not done her part, proved her readiness to give all to this so nice *tuan*?

All he had to do was to open the door—that was his part of the ceremony—and then she would be established as his *njai*.

René stood tense while the melatie blossoms pleaded for Adinda, yet still he held the door. Finally, he slowly opened it a little wider. Turning his head away as he did so, his eyes fell on the letter from Betty's mother, just beside the candle. Shocked, he braced himself, and pushed Adinda away with one hand while he held the door firmly with the other.

"But *tuan*, open quickly!"

In broken Malay, he answered: "Go away, Adinda, I do not want you. Go to your room." Then, as she still pleaded: "No, no, girl, not tonight. I am tired. Go away."

Reluctantly she withdrew, not understanding in the least this novel order of things. René heard the patter of her feet as she hastened towards the servants' quarters.

"Poor girl," he thought. "She can't see why I am different."

René sighed fretfully, realizing it was only a truce when stillness settled once more over the house. There would be no peace for him now. He had conquered for the time being, but how about the future? Had it not been for the sight of the letter on his dresser, what might he not have done tonight?

He knew he had at last arrived at his full manhood, physical as well as spiritual. He wanted to be honorable and clean, to keep his high standards, to respect himself, to respect women of no matter what race—but God, it was hard! Here, in one brief day, two native girls had offered themselves to him. They had sensed his loneliness and sorrow—yes, that must have been it. They were not lowering any personal or racial standards of their own. They had been human—and tender!

On his bed again, he tossed from one side to the other, doubting himself, hating himself, and hating the country. But at last he fell asleep from sheer exhaustion.

In the servant's quarters, little Adinda lay awake, staring into the darkness. What manner of man was this young *tuan?* She had twined flowers in her hair for him, she had told him she would be his alone, she was ready to serve him in every way, to cook his food, mend his clothes, and keep his house cool and clean; but it had all been for naught. Wounded and with tears on her soft cheeks, she, too, eventually slept.

8

Codes of honor vs. dirty dogs

A KNOCK AT THE DOOR awakened René the next morning. Alfred called: "I say, boy, are you going to get up? Breakfast is ready."

René tossed and mumbled. He got out the word, "Coming!" and finally staggered to his feet, feeling very much exhausted. His head ached, and his limbs were heavy. A bath would put him right, he thought. On his way to the bathroom, he stopped for a moment to speak to Alfred.

"How are you?" he asked.

"Pretty rotten. Whiskey does not agree with me, and I drank less than you did. You had better keep away from it, René. I see you are none too fit this morning."

"How in the world do those men manage to do business, Alfred? At the rate they go, I should think they'd drink themselves to death."

"Many of them do," was the crisp answer.

René continued on his way to the bathroom. He noticed Adinda standing by the kitchen door, waiting to serve breakfast.

The Sandalwoods were fidgeting, eager to be off…

"Tabe, tuan," she greeted him.

"Tabe, Adinda," he answered.

He made much noise in his bathing. No more hanging about the house for him today, no more love scenes, either! Cold water was the thing! He dashed bucketsful of it over his shoulders, and when he joined Alfred at the breakfast table he felt like another man. He gave Adinda only an indifferent glance as she stood, fresh and sweet and very sedate, ready to serve them from the buffet.

"Would it be all right with you, Alfred, if I went to the fields with you today?" he asked. "I have nothing much to do here."

"Yes, surely; come along. Better stop at the office and tell them you'll be absent. I'll pick you up in about fifteen minutes."

They passed strings of natives on the road, going to the marketplace with their wares carried on their heads.

The Sandalwoods were fidgeting, eager to be off, when René came out of the office. Brahim was holding the heads of the spirited little horses, and Alfred already held the reins in his hands. René jumped into the seat beside his brother, Brahim to the perch behind them, and they started at a brisk trot. It was barely seven o'clock and enchantingly cool.

They passed strings of natives on the road, going to the marketplace with their wares carried on their heads, all in single file, a carry-over from the days when Java had been a vast jungle and the paths very narrow with thick tropical growth on either side. There was no necessity now for walking one behind the other, but the natives do not readily change their customs. They smiled pleasantly at the white men. René commented on this, and Alfred grunted:

"Oh, I suppose they're all right. They will serve you well so long as you treat them fairly."

Kampong **Koevang Tengah, an important trading place for the natives.**

René thought of Adinda's earnest face at his door, her smile, her freedom from pretense—the memory troubled him. No matter how hard he might try, he could not forget her now. Betty, also, was in his mind as they drove on through the sweet morning air; but Betty he must forget!

They arrived at the *kampong* Koevang Tengah, an important trading place for the natives. René observed many large *warongs* with a variety of merchandise displayed on low tables. The *warongs* were bazaars, mostly owned by Chinamen and Arabs, and quite attractive in appearance. An abundance of fruit was offered: succulent yellow mangoes, pineapples, rambutans, lemons, mangosteens[9] and bananas. Other merchants displayed rice, potatoes, sweet corn, dried

---

9 The original text used Dutch and local spelling for these three fruits: ramboetan, *djoeroeks*, mangistans.

The *warongs* were bazaars, mostly owned by Chinamen and Arabs,
and quite attractive in appearance.

fish, shrimp, ducks, chickens and buffalo meat. There was a
wide choice, to suit the taste of everyone.

Small restaurants offered cooked foods, and here many
of the natives were seen eating. Native policemen walked
about barefooted, but garbed in blue uniforms with brass
buttons. Each officer of the law had a large sword dangling
by his side, held in place by a yellow leather belt and buckled
with a shining brass plate on which the coat of arms of the
Netherlands was very conspicuous. René responded warmly
to this new phase of the colorful Javanese pageant. He liked
the way the natives raised their hats out of respect for the two
tuans, and the friendly attitude of the Arabs and Chinamen
who waved their hands at them as they passed. Impulsively
he spoke his mind to his brother:

Javanese fruits (from left): jackfruit (split), bananas, longan, mangosteen
(bottom center), durian (with the spikes), pineapple, corn
and jackfruit (with rough exterior) etc.

"They are a good sort, Alfred. I begin to see some of their fine points. Until now, it has all been so strange that I could not be sure I would like it. The country is lovely, and I guess the native has his code of honor."

To his surprise, Alfred answered fiercely: "Honor! That is too much. Really, I want to be just, but I think the natives are dirty dogs. And I don't like the country. I never wanted to live here. I was forced to come because nothing else was offered. At first, I felt that I could never stand it; but I had to learn how! I was older than you are, René, and I did not get romantic impressions the way you do." He spoke bitterly. His handsome face with its huge mustache looked vindictive as he spat out the venom he had been secreting for years. His

When they reached the sugar-cane fields, they left the horses in the care of Brahim and proceeded on foot.

blue eyes became somber as he raged helplessly against the loss of his youth, the permanence of his exile.

He gave the horses a sharp cut with the whip, and drove on madly. Alfred's loneliness was telling on his disposition. René could see that he handled his men in the wrong way, and naturally they showed him their worst side.

To his great astonishment, the young fellow discovered that he, and not Alfred, had come to Java because he had wanted to do so. He, René, had subconsciously welcomed the opportunity, and his sunny nature would be able to shrug aside all the disadvantages. It was not so with Alfred, who brooded over the loss of his Kittie and saw life through blue glasses.

…now engaged in laying the tracks for a narrow-gauge railroad which would be
used to transport the cane to the factory.

The brothers were silent as they drove along a road lined on
both sides with magnificent old tjamara trees, the branches
of which were interlocked to make a perfect tunnel of green.
Here and there beyond the trees, René could glimpse native
dwellings of bamboo, embowered in beautiful shrubbery and
blossoms of all colors. He felt that he could never tire of such
scenery. Grudgingly, after the tunnel had been left behind,
Alfred admitted that it was worth seeing once.

When they reached the sugar-cane fields, they left the
horses in the care of Brahim and proceeded on foot. The
cane grows in stools; it has long, narrow leaves, topped by a
waving plume. As the wind sways the thousands of plumes,
there is a musical clamor about the field. As the two men
walked between the rows of cane, with the plumes rustling
above their heads, René again had the feeling of being in an

**René saw men and women working in the irrigation ditches,
pulling out weeds and debris…**

enchanted land. Alfred, however, cared only about the work
there was to do.

And there was plenty of work. As overseer, Alfred received
the reports of the native *mandoers* concerning the day's
activities. Each *mandoer* had under him a score of coolies,
now engaged in laying tracks for a narrow-gauge railroad
which would be used to transport the cane to the factory.
Cutting time was about a month away. When the harvesting
started, the men would know little rest until all the cane was
in. Alfred showed executive ability and real knowledge of
the industry in dealing with his *mandoers*. He issued crisp
military orders, and swiftly passed on to the next field.

René saw men and women working in the irrigation
ditches, pulling out weeds and debris, and getting everything
shipshape for the water to be turned on. In every section the

**Farther yet, there was a purple, unbroken line of mountains
with the extinct volcano, Tjirmai, dominating all.**

natives were busy, but Alfred showed them no mercy. His
bullying manner galvanized them into greater activity. The
brothers followed a roundabout course that totaled several
miles. Alfred, who was used to the heat and the hard-baked
ground underfoot, seemed incapable of tiring. But René was
almost prostrated. His head burned and his feet ached. He
was just about to call quits when the signal for luncheon was
given by a native beating on the trunk of a hollow tree.

They had not far to go to reach the next rest hut, which was
merely a palm leaf-thatched roof supported by four posts. A
low couch made of split bamboo stood in its welcome shade,
and René stretched himself out with a sob of relief. Alfred sat
in an easy chair, smoking a cigarette.

The view in front of them was one of unsurpassing beauty:
a long stretch of sugar-cane and rice fields, beyond these a
jungle of incredibly green trees, and the tall smokestack of

Kerang Sawah rising straight to the sky. Farther yet, there was a purple, unbroken line of mountains with the extinct volcano, Tjirmai, dominating all.

Alfred was forced to confess that the landscape was both impressive and beautiful.

9

Status of the *njais*

RENÉ CONCLUDED that it was a good opportunity to ask certain questions that had been tormenting him. "Alfred, what is the exact status of the *njais* among their own people?" he began. "You've already told me something about it, but I want to know to what extent they really keep their standing with their own men after having lived with one of us."

Alfred smiled indulgently. "It still troubles you, boy, doesn't it? Well, let me explain. Their social dignity is not impaired in the least; it is enhanced. These girls hold a position of trust in the white man's household. The natives are smart enough to realize that. The *njais* learn many things from their daily contact with the white man, their manners improve, they dress better than the ordinary girl, their authority over the servants gives them much poise."

"I can't get used to it, Alfred. The girl is degraded morally, though she may gain in a material way. I don't think it is fair to her."

"Do you realize that a Javanese girl is given in marriage when she is a baby?" countered Alfred irritably. "She may never see the man she must marry until the very day of her wedding. Is that fair? Can she possibly feel anything for a fellow who was picked out for her by her parents. Then, when she becomes his wife, what is she? Just the bearer of his children. Is it any wonder that most native girls would jump at the chance to be a *njai* in the house of a white man—at least as a preliminary experience?"

"That's partly what I mean, Alfred; the poor girl gets the short end of it. It is unjust. Look at Missah, and"—He hated himself for hesitating, but if Alfred noticed he said nothing—"and Adinda. They are sweet and pretty, dainty, too, and they serve us faithfully. Shouldn't they be treated more like human beings, and not like chattels?"

"Oh, I don't know! I think Missah has a darned easy time of it."

"That's not the question. Suppose that a feeling of love for their masters should spring up in their hearts. What then?"

"They don't know what love is, René. That word is absolutely foreign to them."

"I don't believe that, and I never will. They have hearts, and I'll wager they can love deeply."

"I advise you not to experiment in that direction. You might land yourself in a pretty pot of trouble. I'll admit one thing about them: they have their own ideas about the particular white man they want. If they've made up their minds in a given direction, no one else can buy them with money or the promise of beautiful clothes. They have a primitive mating instinct, and they follow it. Now, what do you say to that? You won't find that all over the civilized world."

"I don't know, Alfred. I need more time before I can give you a rational answer."

The breeze died down, the heat increased, and both men rested gratefully in the shade. Alfred at last broke the silence that had fallen.

**But clouds were forming over the mountains,
and already the higher peaks were hidden from view.**

"Don't think for a moment, René, that I love Missah. She is as dumb as a donkey."

"Hold on a bit!" René laughed in spite of himself. "It isn't as bad as that. Why don't you teach her something? You have many spare hours. She isn't too stupid to learn, and she could become more useful to you. That's what I would do, if I had a *njai.*"

"I wouldn't think of it," Alfred scoffed. "No native girl is worth the trouble."

"What do the few white women who live in the interior think about all this—the married ones, I mean, the wife of our head manager, Mrs. de Kock, for instance?"

"Well, René, they don't seem to mind. I certainly am invited to their houses; they, in turn, come to mine—with their husbands, of course. They know perfectly well that behind the scenes some woman is directing my household. It has to be, so why fuss about it?" Alfred stood up as he uttered the last words, "Come on, boy, I've two fields yet to inspect. We must be getting along. We won't stop for lunch. It's too hot to eat, anyway."

What he said was true; the heat was almost unbearable as they walked out into the fields again. But clouds were forming over the mountains, and already the higher peaks were hidden from view.

"That promises relief for tonight, and rain will be a fine thing for the cane," Alfred commented. "It needs another soaking to help it along."

An hour later, they climbed into the buggy and started for home. Along the country roads they met many natives with their portable stoves. Little children were gathered around one of the stoves, eagerly awaiting a turn at the hot rice. René laughed heartily at them. They were clothed scantily, or not at all. One tiny tot, completely naked, stood like a statue, gazing with round, wide eyes at the *tuans.* His little body was as perfect as a cherub's, his skin like soft glistening satin.

"Look, Alfred, did you ever see anything more ideal than that youngster? I wish I could paint."

"Ideal little pig," was the gruff response.

The streets in the *kampong* were all but deserted as the two men drove through; no one ventured out in the heat, except on the most important business. At home, René rested in an armchair on the wide, cool veranda, while Alfred took his bath first. Adinda brought him lemonade, and lingered behind his chair for a moment. He caught the heavy fragrance of the melatie blossoms in her hair and smiled to himself. Her wiles were lost on him. He even shrugged his shoulders scornfully.

The streets in the *kampong* were all but deserted as the two men drove through…

Both men, refreshed and in comfortable white, finally sat enjoying the spectacle of the gathering thunder clouds.

By five o'clock, the sun was overcast and towards the mountains it was as dark as night. Thunder could be heard now, faint but almost continuous. Nature seemed to stand in tense expectancy. Birds had disappeared, the chickens went to roost or hid themselves under the hay bins; only the horses were restless, stamping nervously on the hard boards of their stalls. The very insects were looking for shelter, and noxious flies entered the house and stables, stinging viciously: one of the surest signs, this last, of an impending storm.

It was dark in a few moments, and the tropical gale broke in all its fury. René had never seen anything like it. Lightning played across the sky without intermission, peal

He also supervised many odd jobs connected with cutting
and pressing the sugarcane.

after peal of thunder followed, and then the rain came down
in great sheets. The garden was soon a lake, and the men
were forced to leave the veranda to escape being drenched.
In half an hour it was all over, the sky clear as a bell. But
much damage had been done in that brief time; many
buffaloes had been killed, chickens drowned by the score,
and whole rice fields ruined.

Adinda served them at dinner, taking great care that René
had the best of everything. Alfred observed it, and being
in a good humor he chuckled frankly, to René's annoyance.
Afterwards, Missah brought the smokes, but did not smile
or stay long by Alfred's side. The men retired early; the night
was cool and promised a refreshing sleep. Just before oblivion
claimed him, René fancied he heard the patter of bare feet on
the veranda.

The following three weeks were filled with work. René was told off to oversee the coolies who were laying a solid roadbed to the weighing house. He also supervised many odd jobs connected with cutting and pressing the sugarcane. He had mastered the Malay language sufficiently to be able to direct his men with ease, and he was, all in all, very happy rushing preparations for the coming busy season.

One morning, unable to sleep longer, he arose early, dressed and was out on the veranda in time to see the sun burst in splendor over the land. The gorgeous conflagration in the East thrilled him; he longed for someone with whom to share his delight.

As though in answer to his thoughts, the door of Alfred's room opened softly, and Missah stood on the threshold. Her hair hung loosely down her back. Her *sarong*, which fell to her knees, was fastened tightly under her arms, leaving her shoulders and rounded neck bare. She was a picture of youth and beauty, and René caught in a melting mood, gave her an unexpected smile.

She moved slowly towards him, encouraged by the admiration that she read in his eyes. Kneeling by his side, she lifted his hand in hers, stroked it affectionately and held it against her cheek. She touched with her soft fingers first his hand and then her cheek, saying without words that she wished her face were as white as his hand. Then she arose, gave him a sad little smile, and left him.

René was moved to pity, stirred by her futile longings.

Somehow, the bloom had been taken off the morning for him. Alfred was all wrong—Missah had a heart, and she suffered. He wondered again at the strange way of living in Java, so different from the old country. In Holland, if a woman lived in a man's house without being married to him, she would be an outcast from decent society; but not so the man. There was a double standard at home. The young René struggled with his problem, while the sun mounted its golden chariot and rode in glory.

10

"...Love must not enter into it."

A FEW DAYS before the busy season started, René and Alfred were invited to take dinner with Mr. and Mrs. van Heeck. The latter lived at Tjilarang[10], a sugar factory about two hours' ride from Kerang Sawah. Both Mr. and Mrs. van Heeck came from old Dutch stock, but had lived for twenty years in the interior of Java. Mrs. van Heeck was a charming matron, and a great champion of all the young men who came to the island. She knew so well the difficulties that beset them; in her candid, sympathetic way, she put them right about many matters. On this occasion, she had also invited another couple, Mr. and Mrs. Inger, and the evening promised to be a gay one as such things went on the plantations.

Missah, of course, had Alfred's clothes ready for him when he came home, and René found that his best suit had also been carefully laid out on his bed. Had Missah or Adinda seen to this?

Alfred and René dressed in eager anticipation of the break in the monotonous routine of their evenings.

---

10   Your editor could not locate any references to this town or factory.

René and Alfred were invited to take dinner with Mr. and Mrs. van Heeck.

Missah stood in the doorway as they drove off, a smile on her lips, but sadness in her eyes. Alfred did not even glance at her; René, however, smiled and waved a friendly goodbye.

They enjoyed the ride through the beauty of the cool evening. When they reached the van Heeck home, the brothers mounted the steps quickly, to where Mrs. van Heeck awaited them on the porch. As René bowed low over her hand, he was too delighted to say much. It seemed like heaven to the lad to be in the presence of charming white women again. He had almost forgotten how attractive they were, and it was an especial pleasure to hear them speak his own language. Mrs. van Heeck had a sympathetic manner with men, and notably with young bachelors. She put René at his ease at once.

**When they reached the van Heeck home, the brothers mounted the steps quickly,
to where Mrs. van Heeck awaited them on the porch.**

He decided during dinner that it would not be difficult to
ask her all the questions that were in his mind. Accordingly,
when coffee was served on the veranda, he contrived to get a
seat next to the matron.

"May I—may I consult you on a few points," he began
hesitantly.

She smiled into his earnest face. "Of course you may, René.
I hope you will let me call you by your first name, because
I'm old enough to be your mother."

"Oh no, you're not! But you may call me anything you like.
I'm all excited about being in the presence of white women."

"I see you can turn a pretty phrase, young man. Perhaps you do not need my advice so badly after all."

"On the contrary," René assured her, "I need it very badly."

Mrs. van Heeck laughed softly, pleased at being taken into his confidence. Then, seeing that he was really serious, she, too, became grave at once.

"What is it, René? I do hope I can help you. Let me try;"

"You can set me straight on a certain matter, I am sure. I want your opinion about the way our men live out here. How can they feel justified when they go home in a few years' time and abandon the girl who has made life bearable for them in this country? It seems like taking a mean advantage; I think the native girls are capable of a lot of sentiment, don't you?"

Mrs. van Heeck waited a full minute before answering, while from the other end of the long veranda came scraps of a heated argument.

"René, it is hard to explain to a newcomer," she said at last. "The *njais* accept the arrangement for precisely what it is. If you did not live with your brother, you would be very uncomfortable unless you were to take a *njai* of your own. A white man must have someone to attend to his household, and no laws—no local precepts—are broken when a native girl lives with a Hollander. It is not that which ruins our men in Java; it is whiskey and gambling." She spoke with considerable warmth. "Believe me, René, I know what I am talking about. Many who began as fine fellows drink themselves to death, and on their way down to destruction they indulge in excesses of every kind. They run after other women, though they may have perfectly beautiful *njais* at home."

"It is clear that you feel deeply about this question," René interrupted.

"I do, because it is so misunderstood. It is not the faithful young *njai* who hurts our men. It is their own loss of dignity and manhood, their own debauchery."

"But I still feel for the *njai*, Mrs. van Heeck. I'm thinking more about her than the white man, who ought to know how to take care of himself. She has a heart—she should be treated as an equal."

"Wait a minute, René. How would your brother's *njai* behave if he brought her here as a guest. Do you think she would be happy with us? Would she be at her ease?"

"I'm afraid not," he was forced to admit.

"To be sure, I know some men who seem to be really devoted to their *njais*," Mrs. van Heeck went on. "They have raised a family and apparently are well content; but the children are sure to be miserable when they are old enough to understand their social position. Such children are neither white nor native—you must have observed that. They are nobodies."

René mulled over her statement for a while, and then remarked stubbornly: "As long as a native girl lives as a white man's wife, she should be treated at least with consideration and loved for her beauty and the service she gives."

"No, no, René, it cannot be. Love must not enter into it. Respect, yes; but if you were to love a native girl you would have done a real injury to her. No white men or at least very few—ever spend their lives here, and you can't imagine a Javanese girl entering society in Europe, can you?"

"If she were educated, she might well prove to be good enough for Dutch society. How can you tell what talents a girl may have, if she is not given a chance to develop them?"

"You are an idealist, dear boy, and I admire you for it."

"They have raised a family and apparently are well content;
but the children are sure to be miserable…"

"I'm no saint, but I like to see justice done," he said with a touch of embarrassment. "Maybe I'll learn to see all this differently after I've lived in Java long enough."

Mrs. van Heeck leaned towards him, her eyes tender. "I want to say one thing to you, René: Be strong, be your own master! Write that on your heart, keep it before your eyes wherever you go. I somehow know that you will; I have no fear for you."

Before he could answer, Mr. van Heeck called merrily: "I say, Annie, is the session of the secret society about over?"

"Just about, Jack. Get us all some cool drinks, and then we'll have a game of cards."

As she and René moved in the direction of the others, the boy said under his breath: "I can't thank you enough. You have made me feel much better about things. Please let me come to see you as often as I can get away."

She smiled at him graciously, and nodded. They seated themselves around a large table on the veranda for the promised game. Lemonade was brought for the ladies, and whiskey splits for the men.

"Hey now, René, how do you like this country?" van Heeck boomed.

"Splendidly. I'm mighty glad I came. I'd not have missed it for anything. I could't find work at home, but here there is plenty to do. I believe I'm going to get along in great shape."

"That's the way to talk! That's what I like to hear," the neighbor Mr. Inger cried, slapping René on the shoulder. I have no use for men who come out here to make their fortune, and then say not one good word about Java. I feel like packing them right back where they came from. He

"The cool air will do you good," van Heeck yawned.

turned around and looked Alfred squarely in the face. "Yes, I mean you," he added.

Alfred grinned, not at all disconcerted. "Give me time, Inger. I may come around."

"I hope that you will. We all raved against Java when we first came, though in our day we had some excuse for doing it. We old-timers really suffered—this was a wild country then, and the white man was hated by the natives. But under present conditions, you fellows have no kick coming."

"I agree," smiled René. "Just let me see some women from home occasionally, and it won't be so hard." His glance went to Mrs. Inger, a young and pretty matron.

Inger made a wry face at Alfred and then chuckled. "That young brother of yours is a fast worker. He seems to be making progress with my wife."

"That's all right with me," Mrs. Inger defended herself. We don't see half enough young men from Europe, do we, Annie?"

"No, we don't. I wish Alfred and René didn't live so far-away. We could have many jolly times together."

"Well, there isn't much time left for social doings," van Heeck remarked. "The busy season starts in a couple of days."

"What a cheerful outlook for us, Annie! Three whole months of cane cutting, and the men coming home at night too tired to talk."

"You women had better take a vacation. Go up to Soemedang[11] in the mountains. The cool air will do you good," van Heeck yawned. "We may join you later."

The wives hailed the suggestion, and when the party broke up the usual promises to visit each other soon and often were heartily exchanged. They all knew that there would be little leisure for vacations or visits.

---

11 Called by its former name in the text, Sumedang is about 50 miles west of Cirabon, a little more than halfway to Bandung.

11

"The Eye of the Day"

IT WAS A BEAUTIFUL MOONLIT NIGHT, one of the few that had occurred of late. Quite noticeably, the seasons were changing, the wet monsoon being about over and the dry monsoon coming on. The latter would last for three months; it was the ideal time for cutting and pressing sugar-cane.

As Alfred and René drove along, they could see the whole countryside, near and far, flooded with a silvery haze which made drab objects lovely. The palm leaves glistened as though dipped in mercury. The distant mountains, as well as the dwellings and factory buildings, were transfigured by the moonlight. From time to time, as they passed the police stations along the road, someone would challenge them; but when the officers saw that the travelers were white *tuans* the call was not repeated.

The hideous squeals of the *kalongs, or* flying foxes[12], was the commonest sound on all sides. From tree to tree the *kalongs* sailed with a slow, indolent motion, their foxlike heads showing plainly in the strong light, their white teeth

---

12 These Asian mammals of the genus *Pteropus* are the largest bats in the world with wingspans up to 5 feet. They're also known as fruit bats because (fortunately) they only feed on fruit, flowers, nectar and pollen that grow in their habitat of tropical and sub-tropical Asia.

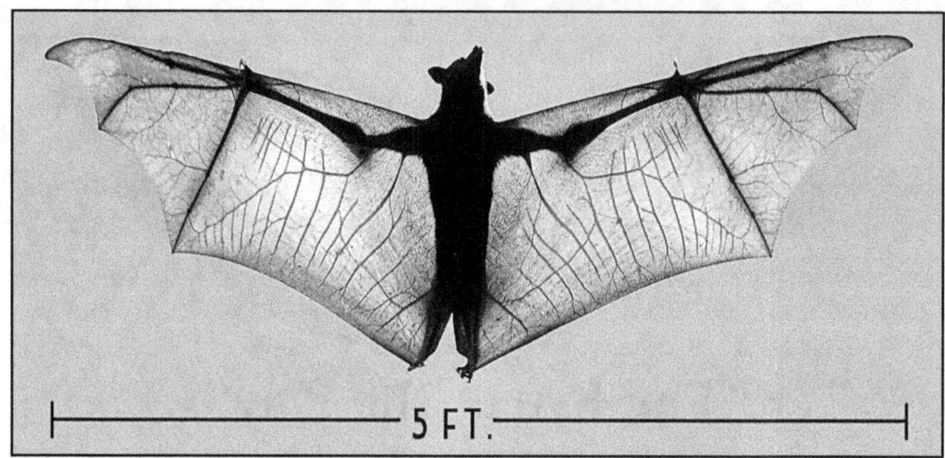

The hideous squeals of the *kalongs*, or flying foxes , was the commonest sound on all sides.

gleaming as they fought over a mango or some other fruit. In the daytime, these ugly creatures find a shady nook and sleep, hanging on by their sharp claws, and at night they come out to seek food.

Later the brothers passed a graveyard, where four-footed beasts were seen slinking around, fearful of detection.

René shuddered. "What are they? They behave as if they were robbing the graves."

So they are, but not in the way you fear," Alfred answered. "Those are half-starved dogs. The native never feeds them, because his religion teaches him that they are unclean. The graveyard is the best place for the dogs to find food. It is left there beside the tombs in small dishes, on the theory that the departed spirits crave it. The dogs devour the food, and the native thinks that ghosts have made away with it, so everyone is satisfied."

Alfred's laugh was scornful, but René found the Javanese superstitions fascinating. The whole land was steeped in tradition, in quaint and fearful beliefs. He had just begun to realize it.

The evening following René's visit to the van Heecks,
he attended the opening of the native festival.

They reached home at two o'clock. René found his
nightclothes carefully laid out on his bed. "Comforts!" Mrs.
van Heeck had said. Well, he surely had them.

Every year before the cutting began it was the custom
to hold a festival, a sort of street fair at which the natives
made merry. This lasted two or three days and put everyone
in good spirits for the hard work to come. The religious
ceremony conducted at the factory was one of the principal
features. There, under Dutch auspices, the Javanese besought
their god to bless the harvest and keep evil spirits away.

The evening following René's visit to the van Heecks, he
attended the opening of the native festival. He was attracted
by the dancing girls, who whirled to the music of a queerly
assorted orchestra consisting of drums, gongs, flutes and one-
stringed violins. All these girls were professionals. They were
not of good repute, and were never received in the homes of

He was attracted by the dancing girls, who whirled to the music of a queerly
assorted orchestra consisting of drums, gongs, flutes and one-stringed violins.

the natives. The men might dance with them to their hearts'
content in public, but nowhere else.

Their manner of dancing was different from anything
René had ever seen. The girl postured in a given spot, while
the men circled about her with slow, graceful movements. A
girl was never taken into a man's arms. Round and round
went the female dancers, their bare arms waving, their bare
feet keeping time, their *sarongs* of batik fastened at the waist
with a beautiful buckle and falling in decorative folds, their
hair surmounted by elaborate headdresses which they held
high or dipped skillfully as the dance required; and the men
dignified, aloof, absorbed in the ancient ritual.

It was at street festivals of this type that the fabulous Mata
Hari learned by observation how to perform the dances
of Java. She spent six years in the island as the wife of a

Dutch army officer. Then she returned to Europe, where she deluded the critics into believing that she was a dancing priestess who had fled from an Oriental temple.

The name she assumed—Mata Hari—means in Malay "The Eye of the Day," a synonym for the sun. The success she made on the stage has almost been forgotten, but the world still talks about her work for Germany as a super-spy and her sensational death before a French firing squad in the woods of Vincennes, near Paris.[13]

No respectable Javanese girl ever dances, but René saw the maidens watching the dancers with something of yearning in their big eyes. They are very musical, and the throbbing of the drums stirs their blood.

"How strange!" the lad mused. "It is a disgrace in their opinion to dance, but not to be a white man's *njai*." Then and there, René began to see all the women of Java in a new light. The struggle he had been waging with his European scruples began to die down, and he felt freer. Realizing this, he enjoyed his immediate surroundings the more. Unconsciously, he was ready to become a part of the life of Java, which is the only way to get the best that a foreign country has to offer.

Alfred had not come with him to the fair. Alfred hated the turmoil and din, and was thankful when the whole affair was well over. René longed for his brother's company and advice; he did not feel sure how deeply he was expected to enter into the festivities, but since the white men seemed more or less on the outside of everything he, too, kept aloof. Nothing would have pleased him better than to join in the

---

13 The authors included a prochronism here, and not just because your editor was itching to use that word in a sentence! The Baron set his story at the time of his stay—circa 1898-1900—which is also when "Mata Hari" began her residence on Java. The First World War and her unfortunate demise, however, were still more than 15 years into the future. See page 92 for more details.

This 1897 photo shows the 21-year-old Margaretha Geertruida MacLeod-Zelle (Aug. 7, 1876–Oct. 15, 1917) seated left front, with her new husband Captain Rudolph John MacLeod behind her. The group appears on the deck of the *SS Prinses Amalia* departing from the Nederlands for Java. [Wikmedia.org]

At the age of eighteen, Zelle answered a newspaper ad placed by MacLeod (Mar. 1, 1856 – Jan. 9, 1928), a Dutch Colonial Army Captain living in the Dutch East Indies (now Indonesia) and seeking a wife.

MacLeod returned to Amsterdam to marry Zelle in 1895, with the couple returning to Malang in East Java in 1897. There, the marriage quickly deteriorated as the alcoholic MacLeod regularly beat his young wife while keeping a *njai*, or local mistress. Due to his abuse Zelle separated from MacLeod, during which time she studied Indonesian dance traditions. She later returned to Europe to become an well-known exotic dancer and entertainer, adopting the stage name Mata Hari.

During the First World War, Zelle gained the confidences of French and German officers, and was ultimately accused of becoming a double-agent who epitomized female espionage as a game of sexual strategies. Biographer Pat Shipman best captures her life's considerable dramas in her 2008 book, *Femme Fatale: Love, Lies and the Unknown Life of Mata Hari*. As noted in the text, a French court ultimately sentenced Zelle to death by firing squad for spying, but she declared her innocence to the end saying: "A harlot? Yes, but a traitoress? Never!"

dancing. His impulse was to slip an arm about a native beauty's waist and whirl her away in a fast and furious polka. Were Missah and Adinda somewhere in that crowd? How the deuce would they respond to a polka, and could the musicians be taught to furnish the right music? He chuckled.

The white men stayed only for a little while, because the natives did not fully enjoy themselves until they were free of supervision. René started for home reluctantly; he was having a great time. He concluded that he might with safety take a look at the Javanese theater, and was very glad that he had not omitted it. The actors were all wearing headdresses even more magnificent and fantastic than those of the dancers. Each one displayed the gauds[14] of his own ancestors. Pride and supremacy were depicted in the brown faces sweating under the weight of their symbols of vanished glory.

René finally departed in earnest. As he took a last glance about him, he saw Missah and Adinda. He walked towards them, because that seemed the natural thing for him to do. They were very pretty in their best clothes. He knew of no reason why he should not talk to them. Then they caught sight of him, and except for a flash of their brown eyes they gave him no greeting. The lad was astonished, but he understood that there was a life here which he was not permitted to enter; there were customs which he was expected to respect.

"Well, did you manage to live through it?" Alfred asked lightly, as René sank into a chair on the veranda.

"Live through it? Man alive, I had a jolly time! It was the most interesting spectacle I have seen since I arrived. I wanted to dance and have a bit of the fun myself, not just look on."

---

14 A gaudy or showy ornament or trinket.

The actors were all wearing headdresses…

"Good Lord, you didn't attempt that, did you?" Alfred was scandalized.

"Don't get excited, most august brother! I haven't brought shame on you yet. Everybody was well behaved, including myself. I didn't see an intoxicated person, or a single glass of whiskey served to anyone."

"Of course not, René. They never drink. They leave that to the fool white man. As much as I hate Java and as much as I dislike the natives, I am forced to give them credit for

even more magnificent and fantastic than those of the dancers.

their temperate way of living. They are a simple people, who observe a rational code of existence."

"I am glad to hear you praise them."

"You think me indecent because I have Missah here," said Alfred, pursuing his own train of thought. "Well, the natives would have considered you the lowest of the low if you had taken a girl in your arms and danced with her. All our white women are disgraced in the eyes of the natives because they dance."

"They are steadfast and true, these Javanese. I see that, Alfred."

"Steadfast? I should say so. Think of the example we are for them. Think of the men at the club who drink so much they cannot walk straight. Does such idiocy make the native follow suit? Not a bit of it. He goes along the way he always has. He still thinks his own thoughts and acts for himself, and he always will."

"I saw Missah and Adinda," René broke in. "There I was held back again. I wanted to talk to them. I'd have been glad to have someone with whom to share the fun. But they didn't even nod to me."

"Certainly not." Alfred stiffened. "They are not your social equals. Don't make any mistake about that."

"Gad, Alfred, I'm sick of such bunk. Social equals! I hear nothing else. Who cares, anyway?"

As usual, when René became heated, Alfred ended the argument with a superior smile. Then he remarked tersely: "The fair will be over in a couple of days, and we'll get down to business."

12

"You will soon get used to earthquakes."

AT DAWN on Monday morning the factory was humming with activity. The smokestack belched forth great clouds of smoke, the huge wheels of the presses were set in motion, the hiss of escaping steam filled the air and the men bustled about, intent upon their labors. By noon the first truckload of cane came rolling in on the narrow-gauge road. Thereafter René was a busy lad. Each load was run onto the scales, weighed and sent forward to be stacked beside the presses. He saw to it that the weights were correctly registered. There was no relaxation of the work until seven o'clock at night.

And this kept up for three long months.

René was happy on his job. The bustle and steady grind of the daily tasks kept his mind occupied and sent him home at night too tired to be troubled over little problems. Missah and Adinda kept the brothers well fed and clothed, looking after their comfort with more than a servant's interest. If Adinda harbored any further longing for *tuan* René, she wisely hid it until a more propitious moment.

By noon the first truckload of cane came rolling in on the narrow-gauge road.

A letter came in the mail one day from Charlie Melton, one of René's oldest friends. They had come to Java on the same boat, had shared the same stateroom, and each had been seeking his fortune. They had promised each other to maintain high standards of morality in the new land. Now Charlie wrote to say that he had broken his promise. He had taken a *njai,* but he begged René not to blame him. As the latter sat for a moment thinking things over, he found himself making excuses for Charlie, who doubtless had been lonely and tempted. René felt grateful for his work and his home with Alfred.

The days slipped by quickly. The white men were up at sunrise and through at sundown. René had to be on hand as early as the coolies—otherwise they would loaf—and the great presses were never stopped. So the season drew to a close, and the boy began to wonder what he would do with his time when the let-up came. He had not been there long

...the great presses were never stopped.

enough to rate a vacation, but as soon as the factory closed down Alfred would be off for a month.

The wheels turned for the last time, the fires went out and quiet settled once more over the drowsy land. That first night René could not sleep, accustomed as he had grown to the rumbling of the presses and the whirring of the dynamos. The stillness was oppressive. There was no clanging of iron trucks in the morning. The hollow sound of the gong meant nothing but six o'clock.

At noon as they sat at the luncheon table, Alfred said: "The men are coming over to the club room for a little celebration tonight. They're all eager for a good time. Mr. de Kock will be there too."

They sipped their coffee in silence while Adinda stood quietly at the buffet. Feeling her glance, René turned to look squarely into her eyes. They flashed him a message, and he was covered with confusion. Alfred seemed to take no notice.

In the lazy afternoon, Missah sat for a brief hour at Alfred's feet. Her demure smile twinkled out at René and was as quickly suppressed. Funny, he thought, how girls played a large part in one's life as soon as one was idle. He had not been disturbed by the memory of them during the busy season. There now swept over him a sudden, wild desire to override all his prejudices and ignore the consequences. It was a very natural, boyish impulse. The doings of the men at the club did not particularly interest him. He was full of life, and eager to express himself.

After dinner, the two men strolled into the club room, where already a few had gathered. Whiskey splits were brought at once, and as they drank and talked others joined them and things became more lively. Mr. de Kock and

**After dinner, the two men strolled into the club room,
where already a few had gathered.**

Alfred planned the latter's vacation. He was to leave soon
for the capital city of Batavia.[15]

"Lord, won't it feel good to stretch one's legs under a real
dinner table again and see some white women!" Alfred
spoke to no one directly, but de Kock answered him:
"You've had a busy time, van Landsberg. You deserve a
vacation. But don't let the city wean you away from the
interior. Your best opportunities lie here."

"Oh, he'll come back, all right!" one man interposed, with
a slight lifting of his shoulders.

____

15   The colonial capital of the Dutch East Indies from its founding in 1619 until
1942 when it was occupied by the Japanese. On August 17, 1945 Indonesian
nationalists declared independence, renaming the city Jakarta in deference to
its pre-colonial name Jayakarta. The city is on the northern coast of West Java,
about 110 miles west of Cirebon.

René sensed that the man meant that Alfred's *njai* would bring him back. He had scarcely given the matter a thought until now—what would Missah do while Alfred was away? More to the point, would Adinda stay on? He became serious, thinking this over.

"Hey there, René ! What's the trouble? Has the girl at home stopped writing? You're as glum as a disappointed monkey."

"As terrible as that?" he laughed back.

"Cheer up. You have nothing to do for a long time now. Alfred will be away, and you're a free lance."

René started to speak, but was interrupted by de Kock, who asked anxiously: "What is that noise?"

"Thunder in the mountains," a club member answered.

"There it is again. It's coming nearer. It isn't like a storm."

Everyone was silent as the frightful rumbling noise approached nearer and swelled in volume. It was like the growling of some huge beast in anger. Louder and louder it grew. Suddenly, it reminded René of a train thundering in a tunnel. He glanced out at the sky, and was absurdly surprised to find that the stars were shining. The next moment, the house and everything in it was jerked back and forth with great violence. The roof of the veranda creaked and groaned. In the billiard room, the balls clicked together as though driven by some unseen player. The floor heaved, the walls swayed, and there did not remain a single steady object to fix one's eyes upon. René was almost overcome by nausea, and the other men were no better off. Fear kept them silent. A mighty force was at work, laughing at puny man.

Then the tremor eased down. The grumbling traveled on. Another slight jerk or two, and the earthquake had rolled

An original "free-lancer" from *Ivanhoe*; 1905 MacMillan, London edition.

Now used as a compound word, the original text with the words separated inspired an inquiry into the origins of this expression for independent workers. Merriam-Webster. com quotes Sir Walter Scott's 1819 historical novel, *Ivanhoe*, as the earliest known recorded usage when a feudal lord gathers a mercenary army:

> "I offered Richard the service of my Free Lances, and he refused them—I will lead them to Hull, seize on shipping, and embark for Flanders; thanks to the bustling times, a man of action will always find employment."

The site goes on to say "Interestingly enough, the phenomenon of freelances was well-documented throughout medieval warfare (and earlier), even if the word freelance was a 19th-century creation. Hired soldiers were common after about 1000 A.D. and were important pieces of major military campaigns between the 12th and 14th centuries. But most of the fancy words English has for these hired soldiers in the Middle Ages came about well after the Middle Ages: *condottiere*, which refers to a leader of a band of mercenary soldiers, and *lansquenet*, which refers specifically to German hired soldier during the 15th through 17th centuries, showed up only a hundred or so years before freelance did. So what were freelances called before we had freelance? Latin records from the Middle Ages show that, most often, hired soldiers were called *stipendiarii* (or stipendiaries, meaning they were given a stipend for fighting), *soliderii* ('soldiers'), or simply *mercennarius* ('mercenaries')."

upon its way. But from the *kampong,* a fearful yelling burst forth, accompanied by a deafening beating on gongs and drums, a sound more frightful than the groaning earth. One of the men servants dashed out of the club, crying at the top of his voice: "Lindau, Lindau, *aya, aya!*" meaning, "We are here, we are here!" Other natives took up the cry until the night was made hideous with the racket.

"What in the world—?" René managed to gasp.

"An earthquake," Alfred told him, "but not so bad as I feared. The smokestack still stands."

"But the screeching of the natives?" René faltered.

"Don't worry about that. They're only telling the evil spirit, Lindau, that they are still on earth."[16]

"What do you mean?"

"They believe that an earthquake is the passing of Lindau to find out whether any living creatures are still on earth. If he hears shouting, as he makes his way under the ground, he knows they are still here and he will not destroy the world. So you can see it is most important in their minds that they let him have no doubts about their being alive." René blinked and called for more whiskey. He felt he would need a good deal of it to straighten out his nerves.

De Kock arose, excusing himself to hurry home because his wife would be anxious, and to see what damage had been done to his house. He spoke to René in parting:

"You will soon get used to earthquakes. We have many here, but not always as severe as this one."

After he had gone, the men started a lively game of poker, apparently no worse for their fright. René, however, could

16 There are countless tales of Indonesian folklore associated with volcanoes, earthquakes and the creation of the islands. Your editor could find no references to Lindau in modern sources available.

not pass it off so lightly, and he drank more than was good for him. Alfred helped him to his room and to bed.

13

Three servants for René

THE HEAT WAS INTENSE when René awoke the next morning, and he felt unusually depressed. He decided the earthquake must have alarmed him greatly to cause him to drink so much whiskey, and again he made a resolution to keep away from liquor.

After breakfast, as he and Alfred sat in cool white linen on the veranda, Adinda brought the smokes. This was Missah's own pet service, and Alfred could not help commenting on her absence. Alfred puffed away in silence for a moment, while his brother, smelling trouble, took a side glance at Adinda. Her downcast eyes told him nothing.

"I don't know where Missah is," Alfred declared abruptly. "She told me last night she was unhappy and did not want to stay with me any longer." René did not dare to look at him; he felt he knew the cause of Missah's defection. "She has been with me three years, and she has been very good to me, though I haven't always been easy. I pressed her for her reason and told her I would send her to visit her parents, thinking she might be homesick. She cried more than ever and begged me not to send her away from Kerang Sawah."

Adinda rose from her seat on the floor and slipped quietly towards the kitchen. René's eyes followed her, then fastened themselves on the mountains. Alfred also stared at the mountains, as though they might tell him the secret of Missah's worries.

"She said she was in love," he finally admitted. "Whatever she thinks that is, I don't know. These women are incapable of love—"

"I wish you would get over that notion," René interrupted sharply. "You place the Javanese women lower than the beasts of the jungle, for even the beasts have affections. How can you say that of Missah, who has shown you such devotion? If she had not cared for you, she wouldn't have come at all, and now if she finds she loves someone else she is not unique in that."

René paused, his face flushed, his eyes flashing. Alfred did not laugh. Missah had disturbed the even tenor of his life, and although he did not for a moment agree with René he felt the boy's earnestness and respected it for once.

"I am certain of one thing," Alfred replied. "There is some other reason why she wants to leave me. She cried for a long time, and at last got up and went out; but before she did, I told her in no uncertain terms that she must move away from this house before I go on my vacation. It would cause a great scandal if she stayed on here with you while I am absent."

"Oh, of course, a terrible scandal!" René took his turn at sneering. "Upon my word, Alfred, it would be a comedy if it were not already a tragedy."

"You needn't feel that sorry for her. She will get over it quickly enough." Alfred gave his brother a keen glance.

"The funniest part of Missah's confession was, that she could not rest until I agreed to send Adinda away also. I intended to in any case, since you don't want her. Kasdjan and cook will look after you."

"I'm sure they will, and I'm very glad that you have disposed of both girls," René said hastily. "I was worried about it. I didn't quite see what I should do with them."

"No?" Alfred queried, so meaningly that René blushed.

"No, no—I didn't! You needn't suppose that I have changed my way of thinking."

"Certainly not. That would be weakness, indeed," Alfred bantered. "I'll also leave Brahim with you. That gives you three servants. You should be very well protected."

"Three servants is more than I ever had before," René laughed. "We'll get along all right; don't worry about us. And here comes Missah now."

Missah tripped up the driveway, a smile on her pretty face. She carried a brightly-colored Japanese parasol. Her *sarong* was drawn tightly about her, permitting her to take only short steps and making her light body sway gracefully. She mounted to the veranda, the eyes of both men following her with admiration. Perceiving this, she dimpled the more. She spoke to Alfred, but her eyes were on René.

"I am going to stay, *tuan*, with Tan Loh, the Chinese merchant. I shall be quite safe with him and his wife."

"Very good, Missah. They are friends of yours, I know."

Smiling frankly at René, she turned and went to the servants' quarters.

"Hey-ho! I hope she marries before I get back," Alfred remarked.

"Marries?" René exploded. "Won't you want her back?"

"Not I. We might make the mistake of becoming fond of each other," Alfred said ironically.

René was both angry and suspicious. Missah had involved him in a well-laid plan of hers, he decided. While Alfred was away, she would attach herself to him. That was why she had made Alfred understand she was no longer his *njai*. Because Adinda knew of Missah's feeling for *tuan* René, the former had been disposed of as suited Missah. She was a clever schemer.

The youngster felt that Alfred had been more dependent on his *njai* than he had been willing to admit. He became sure of it when his brother left on his vacation, a week later. Never had Missah been sweeter than during that last week, and so devoted to Alfred's comfort that he called for her whenever he sat on the veranda. When she was on the floor by his side, his hand wandered often to her glossy hair; hers crept up to meet it, and a smile would pass between them. To René's mind, that was all as it should be. He was sure Missah would not abandon Alfred, despite what she said.

Sunday afternoon found the brothers ready for the trip to Cheribon, where Alfred would take the steamer early Monday morning. The whole world seemed to sleep in the heat of the tropical sun. Flowers closed their petals, and the leaves hung limply in the still air. There was silence everywhere, and seeming peace. Above the deep blue of the mountains stretched a pale sky; below them the waves of heat shimmered like silvery gauze. The beauty of this slumbering land profoundly affected René. His soul sprang to meet it half way; all the good in him leaped toward the Creator of such loveliness.

Alfred saw none of it. His imagination launched itself ahead to Batavia, to the white women who waited there and the sights worth seeing. He paid scant attention to his adieus

His imagination launched itself ahead to Batavia…

The comforts of Batavia: Above, the barbershop in the Grand Hotel.
Below, the dining room in the Hotel des Indes.

He stood perfectly still until he could no longer see his brother…

with Missah, barely speaking and climbing into the buggy without a backward glance. Strange, after three years with her, thought René. They were a queer couple, but perhaps they had said a more affectionate farewell in the privacy of Alfred's room. He hoped so, for Missah's sake.

As they drove away, René took in the house at a glance: Missah on the wide veranda, the cook in the kitchen doorway with Kasdjan, and Adinda's pretty face peering out of his bedroom window. He hated to think that when he returned only men would serve him. But maybe it was better so; he would be free.

At seven o'clock the following morning, the brothers again stood on the dock where René had landed; but this time it was Alfred who had to do with ships and traveling.

He was a changed man, friendly even to the coolies who carried his baggage. So happy was he at the thought of regaining civilization! He waved his *topie* to René from the launch, calling jovially: "So long, old man, take care of yourself."

René waved back. He stood perfectly still until he could no longer see his brother, then he turned and looked towards the city. A queer feeling came over him. For the first time in his whole life, he was unattached, unwatched. There was no member of his family within reach, to tell him what he should or should not do. He felt like shouting and throwing his hat into the air, but he did neither. Instead, he went to the club, where he was greeted cordially.

After luncheon, he climbed to the driver's seat of the buggy, Brahim hopped up behind him, and they were off. Laughing in boyish delight, René sent the Sandalwoods speeding homeward.

14

The "comforts" of home

RENÉ REACHED KERANG SAWAH in the cool of the evening. No one greeted him, no voice broke the stillness until the big *beo* on its perch near the door called, *"Tabe, tabe."* It made the absence of human beings more noticeable. "This is not so good," thought René. "I'll be feeling sorry for myself if I don't look out."

He mounted to the silent veranda, stretched himself in an easy chair and marveled that the absence of two native girls could make so much difference. He clapped his hands. No one came. He clapped again and again. Finally, Kasdjan appeared, a very sleepy, disheveled servant, stifling a yawn with the back of a lazy hand. René ordered lemonade, which was served after a long wait, and was very badly made at that.

"What do you mean by this? Can't you prepare me a decent drink?"

"Tida taoe," came the usual answer.

"Well, put out my clothes. I'll bathe, and as soon as I've finished you can serve dinner."

"Saja, saja, tuan," was the indifferent reply.

René bathed, went to his room to dress and found all the wrong clothes on his bed. There was not a thing he generally wore. "Damn the man, is he trying to show he is Alfred's servant and not mine!" he swore. Searching his closet for the right coat and trousers, René managed to knock down everything from the hooks, and then he stepped on his white jacket, leaving dirty footprints.

He was in no mild temper when he went out to dinner. Kasdjan, with his insolent, slack air, served him badly. There was no dainty Adinda at the buffet to watch his every need. The meal was like the service. René made no attempt to eat it. He wanted to wring Kasdjan's neck, but he merely vented his spleen in black looks which Kasdjan met with a grin.

The big house was dreadfully lonely. René strolled into the club room where he wiled away a few hours, and then sought his bedroom. There were no nightclothes on the bed. The things he had taken off in the afternoon were still in a heap on the floor, and his closet was a mess. He had been in the tropics long enough to have lost the habit of waiting on himself; he knew the servants would think less of him if he did. Servants! He laughed. Three servants, and he had thought he would be well cared for! He dropped off to sleep fitfully.

He had recovered his sunny temper in the morning. He whistled a merry tune as he splashed the cold water over himself. Breakfast was somewhat better than the dinner had been, although still far from being a good meal. He gave Kasdjan a severe lecture, winding up with a great show of authority.

"See that I have a luncheon fit for a white man, or I'll kill you."

"*Saja, saja,*" was the serene answer.

Three servants, and he had thought he would be well cared for!

René flung himself out of the dining room. There, squatted on the veranda floor by his chair, was Missah. A natural position for a native woman in the presence of a white man, a sign of respect and not at all of slavery, rather the old custom retained of showing deference to the ruler of the land. For the same reason, she would not speak first.

René was shocked out of his anger for an instant, only to have it return twofold. Damn these natives! and again, Damn them! They seemed determined to ride right over him.

"What do you want here?" he asked bluntly.

Missah replied in her sweetest voice: "I come to see that *tuan* René is served well, and his clothes in order."

"Well, it's not necessary for you to trouble about me. You'd better get out."

His voice thundered through the quiet house. He turned his back on the girl. She rose slowly, looked for a moment at his forbidding back, then slipped quietly away. René breathed more freely.

He went about his work. It seemed a loafer's job, after the strenuous days just past. He simply supervised the cleaning of the factory in an unhurried way. The natives worked in the same lazy fashion. His meals were awful. When he tried to see the cook, she was always absent or asleep. She was an old woman, long in Alfred's service, and evidently felt she could manage as she pleased. René hurled his complaints at Kasdjan.

"Tell cook I must have something decent to eat, do you hear, damn you!"

"Saja, tuan."

"*Saja, saja!*" sang out the clear call of the *beo;* it sounded very much like mockery.

René ordered the Sandalwoods to be hitched up, and went for a leisurely drive through the countryside. He tried to plan a course of action if Kasdjan and the cook should continue their show of disrespect. Perhaps he had better give Kasdjan a beating. He wondered whether it was an organized rebellion, or merely a let-down following Alfred's stern rule. Or had it been Missah's rule? He would have to be more severe—well, he could be!

Two weeks went by, and René was sick of his tussle with the house servants. Try as he would, nothing went right. The dwelling had an air of neglect that drove him from it in despair. His clothes were in wretched shape, his socks full of holes, and his meals were almost too bad to eat.

Smoking on the veranda after dinner one evening, he was in no amiable frame of mind when Kasdjan came to ask some question. René roared at him: "Get out of here! For God's sake, don't ask me anything. Get out, and stay out!"

He wanted to be left alone, and he proposed to be even if he had to thrash someone. After he had chased Kasdjan, there was silence. René smoked on, moodily satisfied. But suddenly he heard the faint pitter-patter of bare feet. He turned, to find himself face to face with Adinda.

Instantly, she sank to the floor, her head bent, her whole attitude one of submission. Neither of them spoke. René's blue eyes had become slumbering fires, his breath panted in his chest, and his hands were clenched.

Adinda slowly raised her head. Her eyes were melting loveliness, her soft bosom rose and fell in rhythm with the beating of the man's heart. Time stood still—old customs battled with new—race struggled against race— woman for man, and man in a fierce effort to suppress his physical nature.

15

Primitive man and primitive woman

ADINDA WAS THE FIRST TO MOVE. Lifting her head a bit higher, she gave René a ravishing smile. He relaxed, trying to speak easily, naturally.

"What do you want here?"

"I am sent by Missah, *tuan.* She has forgotten some of her clothes."

"Well, you may get them. I suppose they are in *tuan* Alfred's room. Why didn't Missah come herself?"

"Oh, *tuan,* she is leaving for the mountains with an old sweetheart!"

"What!" exclaimed René, in great surprise. "Is Missah getting married?"

"Saja, tuan."

"Well, that beats the Dutch! Only two weeks ago, she was living here with Alfred—now she is getting married!"

"Saja, tuan."

Adinda's eyes sparkled. René laughed. The minx! She was glad to have Missah married off.

"I suppose it's better so—one worry the less."

"*Saja, tuan.*"

"Hey, what's that? What do you know about it?"

"*Tida apa apa.*"

René sought his easy chair, the eternal easy chair of the tropics. Quickly, Adinda brought the smokes. He accepted them from habit, and then started up.

"I say—I say, go get Missah's things and hurry along!"

"*Saja, tuan.*"

Adinda moved towards Alfred's room. René watched her go. What grace, what beauty! Of course, Alfred would take her to fill Missah's place, and not a bad exchange at that.

His cigarette went out, it dropped from his lax fingers. Later, much later, he arose and went to his bedroom. It was clean and orderly; his clothes were hung neatly in his closet, or folded in the drawers of his dresser; the pajamas of beautiful batik laid out on his bed. He went slowly to the window, opened the shutters and lifted his eyes to the stars. They hung like sparkling jewels in the dark dome of the sky; they twinkled and scintillated a message of power and beauty. From the garden came the over-burdened sweetness of the melatie blossoms; it touched the man but faintly. The stars won.

At breakfast the next morning, which by the way was very good, thanks to Adinda's parting suggestions, René questioned Kasdjan about Missah's marriage.

"Did you know of this? How is it possible Missah could find a sweetheart so quickly and arrange for marriage?

"Tida taoe."

The same old answer. René was sure the wily servant knew everything, and that a bit of coaxing was all he needed.

"Does Missah's sweetheart live in Kerang Sawah?" he asked, putting a friendly, human note into his voice.

"Tida, tuan, in Kerang Tengah. He had a house all ready for Missah when she should leave *tuan* Alfred. She was given to Artam when she was only a baby—she must marry him sometime."

"But why didn't she do it sooner?"

"Oh, *tuan,* she loved *tuan* Alfred and never would have left him! But since he sent her away, she knew the time had come to marry Artam."

René had his own opinion about this, but as Kasdjan had been drawn into a talkative mood he asked more questions.

"Do all your girls live like this and then marry?"

"Oh, no, *tuan!* Very few of them are fortunate enough to find a white master. But most of our girls are given in marriage by their parents."

"Poor girls! Aren't they often unhappy—and the men, also—in marriages of that sort?"

"Why should they be, *tuan?"* Kasdjan stifled a sigh over such ignorance, such queer ideas of marriage. "They are true to each other, have a home and children; the children are always good to their parents. What more is there?"

"True, Kasdjan, I overlooked the children. But about Adinda? Has she a lover, also, one she was promised to?"

"No, *tuan,* Adinda has never been promised to anyone. Her mother died when she was born, and her father shortly after. Adinda has always been free. Many men have wanted to marry her—men who are rich, with land and buffaloes. One man—Oh very, very rich!—thought much of Adinda. He could have given her beautiful clothes and silver ornaments. Him she was going to marry—when you came, *tuan.* Then she wanted only you."

"That will do, Kasdjan."

René arose from the table with dignity, failing to observe the servant's twitching lips and heaving shoulders. Going into his room, he tried to write letters home. His mother, greatly interested in all he did, would have been shocked had he written the full truth about life in Java—yet this life was absorbing him at present. He gave up the letter as a bad job.

Several days went by, and again René's room was disordered, his meals unfit to eat. The heat seemed much worse with the house uncared for.

He had been out all day looking over the machinery, and had come home to bathe and dine. No use to ask Kasdjan for a clean suit. Rummaging in his closet for one, he found nothing but crumpled linen. He ate little.

Later, from his lounging chair he watched the stars come out, and looked with lazy interest at the smoke from the watchman's fire, kept burning to chase the mosquitoes away. Thoughts of home drifted through his mind, of his mother, his sisters, the well-ordered life there. But he was unable wholly to dismiss the lure of the tropics. Kasdjan came, begging for a night off.

"Yes, go on, go on!" René ordered testily. "Be back in time for breakfast. Where is cook?"

"In bed, *tuan.*"

René doubted it, but never mind. He was glad the loafing servants were gone, out of his sight. He rather enjoyed the big house to himself. He turned the lights low, in order to discourage the mosquitoes.

From his chair could be seen the Southern Cross, shining clear and beautiful in the sky. All was still, save for the faint call now and then of some wild animal in the jungle. Resting his head on the back of the chair, he half dozed; his surroundings seemed to drift away—only the sky, the stars and himself remained. He did not hear footsteps on the gravel walk or in the house; the first he knew of another's presence was a low whisper that came as from far away. He could not understand what it said.

Again he heard the soft, pleading murmur: *"Tuan!"*

"Yes, who is there?"

"Oh, *tuan,* it is I—Adinda! Do not send me away. Let me come near to you and explain."

Then and there, the stars lost out. In the dim light of the veranda, René could see only the faint outline of a figure. He hesitated—his traditions, his precepts, capitulated before the wild beating of his heart.

"Yes!" He hardly recognized his own voice. "Come, sit on the floor beside me. What is it you want to tell me, Adinda?"

She slipped toward him like a shadow, sank down on to the floor and took his hand in both of hers. He drew it away. He could not distinguish her features, could barely see the white blossoms in her hair, although their fragrance made his head swim.

Neither of them spoke. The quiet moments were precious to Adinda. She did not know the ways of this *tuan* whom she loved, so she held her peace. At last, René broke the throbbing silence:

"What is it you want to tell me, girl?"

Instead of answering, Adinda took his hand again in hers, holding it tight so that he could not draw it away. She pressed it caressingly against her cheek, then laid it over her beating heart, while hot tears fell upon it.

There was no longer any conflict of races, or of color—but only primitive man and primitive woman.

Stooping quickly, René gathered her close into his arms.

All was tranquil now on the deserted veranda. The calling of the *tokke* to its mate could be heard at brief intervals. The stars shone calmly on, resplendent, glittering symbols of power and beauty.

16

"C'etait plus fort que moi!"

RENÉ'S HOUSE now took on a new aspect. Kasdjan in immaculate dress served deliciously cooked meals with the air of a well-trained servant. Adinda in the costume of her rank—a white linen jacket with lace at the neck and sleeves, a rich *sarong* about her slender body—gave orders in a soft but authoritative voice. The long living room and veranda were clean and inviting. René's bedroom, now Adinda's also, was a marvel of order and freshness. His clothes hung in fine array in their closet, his linen was crisp and white. Adinda was beautiful in her happiness and desire to please her *tuan*.

René had been fearful of awakening from the fascination of his first surrender, but found to his surprise that he was more contented than ever before. The great loneliness was gone, for Adinda always waited at the steps to greet him when he came home. Adinda with fresh blossoms in her hair, and soft lace at her rounded throat.

As he sat in his armchair one evening and watched the girl roll cigarettes for him, he reached out and tenderly touched her glossy hair.

"Adinda with fresh blossoms in her hair, and soft lace at her rounded throat."
Above, a Javanese seamstress making lace.

"Tell me, Adinda girl, what did you want to explain to me the other night when—when I interrupted you?" Sure of her *tuan*, she glanced up, smiling very sweetly and shyly.

"I wanted to tell you why I had come, *tuan*. I had to come, I could not stay away. I was free to give myself to you, and I knew *tuan* wanted me as much as I wanted *tuan*." René's eyes were tender as he looked at her.

"How did you know all that, girl?"

She shook her head. "I do not know, *tuan*. I felt it here." She put her hand over her heart. "It was a longing inside of me. It kept me from eating. It was so big it hurt me. There was no use trying to get away from it. I said: 'When I feel this so strong in me, *tuan* must feel it, too. It must go on and on; we two must come together and go on and on.' It was so clear, *tuan*, it just had to be."

She raised earnest eyes to his, full of unshed tears and burning with anxiety to explain herself to him. René caressed her warm, satiny shoulder.

"And do you call that love, Adinda?"

"Oh, no, *tuan!* Love is only between parents and children, with no passion."

René was shocked for an instant, endeavoring to see into the mind of this child of nature.

"Where did you get your wisdom, girl? You talk like a grown-up woman, yet you are only sixteen. White girls don't talk that way at your age."

Adinda smiled knowingly, and answered demurely enough: "But I have been told, *tuan,* that white girls feel and talk just as I do. Do we not all seek a mate? I cannot tell how you would say it, but do not the birds of the air mate? Do not the animals that live in the water, and all those in the forests and fields? You would not blame them, *tuan.* I felt as they feel—it was here, in my heart. I had to come to you because you were my mate. Now I am happy and at peace; I am *tuan's njai"*

She burned with conviction. René could not doubt her. He wanted to hear more about her life from her own lips.

"Why have you never married, Adinda? Most Javanese girls do at your age."

"Oh, *tuan,* I could not! I am different from the girls at the *kampong,* though a few I know are like me. We would rather risk dying virgins and so miss heaven than marry men who are not our mates. If my parents had lived and had given me in marriage when I was a baby, I would keep the pledge they had made for me; but I am glad now that they did not."

René was taken aback. Did she think he would marry her? Her soft voice went on:

"My father was of high caste, and my mother of an old and honorable family."

René could well believe this, for Adinda had all the marks of high birth, including tiny hands, with long tapering fingers, and small feet. Her very walk denoted rank. The proud lift of her head when she gave orders to the servants was not assumed for the occasion.

She went on with her story, as if glad to tell it. A sadness crept into her voice when she spoke of her years of struggle for a living. "There was no money for me, *tuan*, so I worked for some white ladies." René felt sorry for her; she looked so young, so desirable, seated there on the floor, her slender hands folded in her lap, her head bent. Sensing his sympathy, she raised big brown eyes to his face, a wistful little smile on her lips.

"Are you satisfied now, Adinda?" He touched her cheek lightly.

"Yes, *tuan*, I am very happy. *Tuan* has always treated me like a white lady, never like a servant. I have only one fear."

"And what is that?"

She took his hand, bending her smooth brow over it, holding on to it as though she would never let him go.

"What are you afraid of, Adinda, girl?"

In a whisper, she answered without looking up: "That you will send me away some day. Oh, *tuan*, never send me away. I want to be with you always, day and night. I will serve you as no white woman could."

"Silly girl," René assured her, "I have just found you and taken you as my *njai,* and you already fear I will send you away! Do not think about it."

He felt that his speech did not convince Adinda. She still clung to his hand, while her tears fell. A short silence prevailed between them. Then Adinda arose, looked long into René's eyes and turned away. What was she thinking? Did the memory of the sufferings endured by other girls rob her of her present happiness? René could offer her nothing lasting, and as he watched her go to their bedroom he had long thoughts. Of course, she would serve him submissively. That was expected of the native women; they were well aware of it. Adinda's standing in the community had been raised by her position in his household—but what about his own honor, the purity of his motives? To his credit, it must be said that René was not satisfied with himself.

He followed her to the bedroom a few minutes later. Adinda was already asleep, lying on her side like a nice little girl, her knees drawn up and hands outstretched. She made a picture of youth and beauty, and—yes, René had to admit it—of innocence. Her cheeks were still wet with tears, but her pretty mouth was curved in a smile, as though happy dreams had stopped her weeping.

What a wonderful creature a woman was, he mused, and this one was his alone—her body, her service, her every thought! Was he being quite fair to her? She opened her eyes slowly, her slim hand reached up to him and he sank down beside her, contented for the time being because she was happy.

The next morning a long letter from Alfred arrived, the first René had had since his brother's departure.

"I am writing you from the Concordia Club."

"I am writing you from the Concordia Club[17]," Alfred began. This is the real life. I have met more decent white men and women in this short time than I did in a whole year in the infernal interior. I had no idea that I had deteriorated to such an extent. Why, I even avoided meeting white women when I first came! I was afraid of them! Can you believe that, René? I did not know what to say to strangers. I longed for Missah, who never expected me to say anything. But it is different now. I have gotten over my silly fear, and I am enjoying the company of the charming women I meet. And I like the way people dress here. No white suits or cartwheel

---

17 The two largest private clubs for Europeans in colonial Java were the Concordia Society (Sociëteit Concordia) and the Harmony Society (Sociëteit Harmonie). Each built luxurious clubhouses in major cities like Batavia, Bandung, Surabaya and Malang. Most facilities included a large ballroom, restaurant, billiard tables, theater and library to serve as gathering places where elite locals and visitors could meet, relax and conduct business.

hats. At night, the men wear tuxedos, and the women are in fashionable evening gowns. Lord, it is living again! I hated to get into a boiled shirt[18] at first, but now I enjoy it. The conversation is about big affairs, the doings of the world instead of the petty subjects we discuss in the interior."

At the end of the letter, he added: "Tell Missah that I don't want her anymore. And you, old man, don't get tangled up with any native girl. You were right about that. Stick to your resolution."

When he replied to Alfred, René stated: "You need not worry about Missah. She is happily married to Artam and has gone to her mountain home. As for me, alas, *c'etait plus fort que moi!*[19] I consider a pale brown complexion charming now. When you return, you will find Adinda doing the honors in our house. Did you not tell me that these girls are better at making a man comfortable than any white woman? I agree with you."

René glanced up at Adinda as he sealed the letter, and met her affectionate, trusting smile. So far, so good. He had chosen his woman of Java, and was well pleased with her.

18   In the 1800s into the early 1900s white dress shirts consisted of separate components: collar, cuffs, studs (only a commoner would use buttons!), a bib to hide the studs, and the shirt itself. When cleaned, the shirts (collars and cuffs) were boiled in highly starched water and ironed to so stiff that wrinkles would not appear, so a gentleman always maintained his impeccable appearance. Think James Bond.

19   French expression, literally "It was stronger than me."

17

The boar hunt

"I SAY, RENÉ, you are a fortunate lad. Bring her in, won't you?"

The speaker, a tall mixed blood, one of the employees of the factory, sipped his whiskey and soda, lounging comfortably on René's veranda. He had come to ask René to join a group of seven or eight men in a wild boar hunt, leaving the next morning at daybreak. Adinda, on her way from the kitchen to the bedroom, had stood for barely an instant in the doorway, making a pretty picture. René's fair face flushed at the light allusion to his *njai*.

The speaker laughed loudly. "I take it she's not on inspection then?"

"Certainly not," was René's dignified answer.

"Don't take them too seriously, boy. It doesn't pay."

René hated the man. Ignoring the offered advice he took up the subject of the hunt. "I'll be very glad to join you—you'll find me ready at daybreak." The matter closed, the man left, a slight sneer on his lips. René could have killed him cheerfully. At daybreak he was up and ready.

Here and there natives had started to plow their fields for the rice crops.

"Oh, *tuan*, you will be very careful?" Adinda's face was anxious.

"Don't worry about me, girl. I'll come back safe and sound."

He waved a happy goodbye and joined the men in the yard. There were four buggy-loads, some of them whites and some of them mixed bloods. They were all experienced hunters, while René had only bagged a few of the *kalongs*, or huge bats. He was thrilled at the thought of bringing in a wild boar.

At the head of the procession rode the inspector, Feldman, a mixed blood of enormous size. They started out at high speed, passing many natives huddled together on the ground of the stores and eating houses, their *sarongs* pulled up about their shoulders, as the morning was still chilly. The sugar cane fields, stripped of their green foliage and graceful, flowery plumes, appeared deserted and desolate. Here and there natives had started to plow their fields for the rice crops. The lands in Java remain for all time the property of the natives and can only be leased by the white men.

After an hour's swift riding the hunters came to the foothills, where the jungle begins. Here the native overseers and their coolies awaited them. They carried great clubs to start the drive with and to kill smaller game aroused by the tramping of the men. Feldman again headed the little procession as the men left the buggies and took to the mountain trail, a path made by the wild animals of the jungle on their way to the stream to drink. Overhead was heavy timber, dense foliage on either side. From time to time came the plaintive call of the gibbons, or long-armed apes. These went from tree to tree, showing curiosity rather than fear, swinging low to see what all the commotion was about.

The drive was to begin when Feldman fired a signal of two shots. The hunters were stationed along the trail some few rods[20] apart, a native accompanying each white man. The whites were armed with guns, the natives with their *klewangs*, or short daggers.

René found himself the third from the front. With him was his own native overseer, Kass, of the scalehouse. Everything about them was indolent and tranquil; sitting on the ground, they lit their cigarettes and talked in a whisper. René, ever quick to see beauty, was charmed by the jungle. He felt as though he had entered some mighty cathedral, a solemn abode of loveliness where God walked and where one should speak but little. It was cool and very still, a wonderful resting place in the daytime, but a turmoil of rampant life after nightfall. The eternal battle for existence is fought ruthlessly in the jungle, with every animal, however small or great, a prey to one mightier than he. Man is too puny to cope with the beasts at night. Though René would have preferred not

---

20 A rod is an English unit of measurement equal to 5 ½ yards, 16 ½ feet, or ¼ of a surveyor's chain.

Feldman again headed the little procession as the men left the buggies and took to the mountain trail…

to torment them now, he stifled the feeling in order not to appear faint-hearted.

Two shots brusquely shattered the stillness, and echoed back and forth. René sprang to his feet, his gun in position, while overhead the gibbons chattered furiously at the unexpected disturbance.

"No hurry, *tuan*," Kass murmured. "It will be another hour before any game will break through."

René stood a moment, listening intently. "I think you are right, Kass. I cannot even hear the drivers shout or beat the brush."

"Besides, *tuan*, the wild boar will not keep running. He runs a short distance, then stops, running again when the men get near him. He may not come our way at all, but switch off the trail into the brush, trying to get down the side of the mountain."

René settled down, a bit nervous withal, but game for whatever was coming. The men were seated at the foot of a large hardwood tree. Its limbs were covered with a wild growth of orchids so lovely in coloring René could not keep his eyes from them. Great vines trailed from the trees about them, some in flower, some like ropes of silvery threads, others rich green or of pale glossy sheen—too gloriously beautiful for anything but matins, this jungle where man had come to kill.

René and Kass sat perfectly still, not even whispering. Above them a flock of many-colored parrots took to roost, screaming and chattering over the strangers at the foot of their tree.

"Look, look, *tuan!*"

René looked where Kass pointed. There stood a beautiful mother deer with two young ones. Her soft eyes wide with fright she glanced this way and that, then dashed off down the other side of the ridge.

"The boar must be nearer. She senses him, I am sure," René whispered.

Kass raised a warning hand, while René stood ready to shoot, tense with excitement. The shouts of the drivers came nearer and nearer, closing in from all sides.

"Now we have him pretty soon, *tuan,*" Kass muttered, preparing to use his dagger.

René grew more nervous. A shout of: "On guard! The boar!" caused him to dash behind a tree followed by Kass. They waited on the *qui vive*[21], but nothing materialized.

"Must have turned off in another direction," Kass spoke, close to René's ear.

---

21 Latin meaning alert, or lookout.

There were several minutes more of anxious waiting. They were just about to lower their weapons when Kass cried hoarsely: "Look! They are coming. The gibbons are on the run!"

Seventy or eighty of the little apes could be seen, swinging rapidly from tree to tree, yelling in a frenzy as they tried to outdistance the menace on the ground below them.

The shouts of the drivers converged from right and left. René raised his rifle to his shoulder—but still there was no tusker. Then suddenly the undergrowth rustled and broke just in front of him. The huge, dark head of a wild boar emerged from the tangle of twigs.

René fired twice, and both shots missed their mark. The boar charged by, making a side lunge at him which barely missed the calf of his leg. Kass stabbed fiercely with his dagger, but the boar was too quick for him. Grunting furiously, the ponderous beast rushed off unhurt.

Shots were heard in all directions, then three blasts from Feldman's horn, announcing to the drivers that it was safe for them to draw in. The round-up of the hunt showed a good killing—eight boars and one deer. These the men hung on poles and carried to the buggies.

René took his teasing in good humor, realizing he had failed badly. "Better luck next time!" he laughed.

"Well, you cut your eye-teeth, boy. You've been face to face with the biggest game in the jungle," one of the planters assured him.

The men rested and smoked, talking over the fine points of the hunt. René listened respectfully, acquiring much lore from the seasoned oldtimers.

At home, Adinda greeted him joyously.

"I made a sad mess of it, girl," he said. "I missed a fine boar that was right in front of me."

"Never mind, *tuan,* you are safe. The great boar might so easily have wounded you. I rejoice to see you back uninjured."

18

Bound by silken cords

ALFRED RETURNED a few days later, a changed Alfred, who said: "Batavia is a wonderful city, René. That's the place for me. I dread to face things here—and I'll never take another native girl."

René answered with some heat, unconsciously defending himself: "Why can't you accept things as they are? You always see the present in the wrong light, always comparing your own life with the lives of others, and forever dissatisfied. Why, you're getting to be a regular crank."

"Yes, I know, René, I'm thinking in the wrong direction. But are you happy the way you are living?"

"Of course, I'm happy. Who wouldn't be with a beautiful girl like Adinda? She's far too good for me."

"Don't begin to talk or think that way. You're forgetting your birth and race." Alfred was out of patience.

"I know that according to civilized Dutch notions she is not my equal, but she gives me everything I want from a woman. Why shouldn't I be content—for the present, anyway?"

"Oh, well, let's forget it!" Alfred parried. "Let's walk over to see Mr. and Mrs. de Kock. We haven't paid our respects to her since their return from Europe."

Accordingly, they went to the home of the de Kocks, had a pleasant visit and returned about midnight. Mrs. de Kock insisted that she would send her man over each morning with fresh milk for René, saying she could not use it all since her daughters had left for school. Adinda very happily poured the rich creamy milk for her *tuan* the next morning, René remarking upon its fine color.

About a week later as he lifted his glass to his lips he paused. "See here, Adinda, I don't like the looks of this milk. It's bluish, as though it had been watered. Someone has stolen part of it and filled the bottle with water. What do you know about it?"

"*Tida taoe, tuan!*' was the laconic reply.

René flared in quick anger. "No, of course you don't! You people never do—you never know anything. I'll soon find out! Bring that man to me when he comes in the morning."

Adinda did not answer. She was hurt when René put her on a level with the other natives. She had seen him lose his temper at some blunder of the coolies, but never before at her. She slipped away without a word.

The next morning, according to her *tuan's* orders, the man was brought in, carrying his bottle of milk. He squatted on the tile before René, submissively handing him the bottle, not speaking or looking at him.

"Well, Sintang, what have you got to say for yourself? What did you do to that milk yesterday?"

"*Tida taoe,*" Sintang murmured.

"Let's walk over to see Mr. and Mrs. de Kock. We haven't paid our respects to her since their return from Europe."

"So! You don't know, you dog! You stole it and filled the bottle with water. For that you can take the milk. I'll teach you to fool a white man." And René, angry beyond control, dashed the milk in the man's face.

"Oh, *tuan*, please don't!" Adinda interfered, grasping his arm as she pleaded.

René looked at Sintang, sitting humbly on the floor, milk dripping from his face; at Adinda, pleading for him.

"You shut up!" he shouted. "Go to the kitchen where you belong. And you, dog, get up and get out."

Sintang rose and left the room. Adinda stood as though stunned, then turned and fled to the kitchen. René sank in his chair, exhausted by this outbreak of temper. A few minutes later he left for the factory without saying goodbye to Adinda. Remorse overtook him before he reached there; turning back he hurried home to find Adinda weeping on the bed.

"Come, come, Adinda girl, I was not fair. Do not cry. See here, I am going to stay home today with you. Get your books and we will study."

He picked her up gently, and peace was made. All day Adinda sat at his feet, crooning patiently the letters of her *tuan's* language. She was an apt pupil.

Soon, he promised her, "you will be reading my books and speaking my language."

At this she smiled happily, bending her dark head over the difficult tasks—nothing too hard for her if it pleased her *tuan*.

The next day was Sunday; the household usually slept late, but René awakened early, and missing Adinda, got up to seek her. Voices from the kitchen sent him that way— what did she mean by disturbing him with her talk? Rather impatiently he started to open the door. Her voice came to him clearly, although she spoke low. Something in the command of that quiet voice made him pause.

"Bring me that bottle of milk, Sintang."

René pushed the door open just far enough for him to see what was going on in the kitchen. Adinda stood with her back to him. Sintang was too agitated to see anyone but Adinda. Slowly he came to her, put the bottle of milk in her outstretched hand. She took two glasses from the table at her side, poured the milk in them.

"Drink this with me, Sintang," she ordered.

"I never drink milk," was his agitated answer.

"You don't?" Adinda looked into his strained face. "Then I will."

She raised the glass to her lips. Instantly Sintang dashed it from her hand, the glass breaking into tiny bits at her feet.

"I thought so, Sintang! You would poison my *tuan* because he was unjust to you yesterday. I love him and I would gladly die to save him. I could have you killed for this—you know it. I won't if you will promise me to go home and never do such a thing again. Cook took the milk, and you were not to blame. How was *tuan* René to know that? You have tried to do a terrible thing—remember, I will not spare you another time."

Sintang slunk away, glad to have saved his head.

René went slowly back to his bedroom. He was overcome with what Adinda had done for him—how could he repay her?

A curious feeling of being bound by silken cords, many of them, around and around him, swept over him; made him hide his face in his pillow. He said nothing to Adinda about what he had heard—later, perhaps, he told himself.

19

Sakit

ALFRED SAID but little to René about Adinda. How she came to be established in the house and why René changed his views was as yet a sealed matter to Alfred. He was troubled over René's assertion that Adinda was too good for him; some day they must talk it out. Adinda served Alfred because he was René's brother, but she never gave him the best of things. She feared him, thought he was too stern with the servants. Alfred took her services without a single acknowledgment. He was still dissatisfied with life in the interior as compared with Batavia and did not prove too amiable about the house.

Coming home from the factory one day René found Adinda beside the bed where Alfred lay with closed eyes. She cautioned, pointing to Alfred's head.

"*Sakit*" she whispered.

As René seated himself, Alfred slowly opened his eyes and smiled at Adinda.

"She is wonderful, René. I came home very sick, fainted on the veranda. When I regained consciousness this sweet girl had somehow gotten me to bed. She has been putting cold towels on my head all day, taking care of me for seven long hours. You are a fortunate boy, René, and Adinda is a dear girl."

Alfred stroked her glossy hair as he spoke. Adinda beamed over such praise from the stern Alfred.

"Will *tuan* take care of *tuan* Alfred while I go and fix some nice food for him to eat?"

"Yes, go, Adinda," René told her, "and get some rest if you can. We don't need to eat for a while."

Adinda was too happy for words. Both *tuans* were being so kind! She went to René's side for an instant, stroked his hand lovingly, looked deep into his eyes, her own full of real love, then went out quietly.

Alfred was astonished. He had never seen that look in a native girl's eyes, nor such gentle ways.

"How did this little lady happen to become your *njai?*" René told him how it had come about, repeating some of the things Adinda had said to him. Alfred was a bit scornful.

"Well, she must have been pretty badly off to come to you like that!"

"Oh, don't say that, Alfred! She is not like the other girls. She could have married many times, but she would not until she had found her true mate."

"That's rich," sneered Alfred. "I never heard of a native girl refusing anyone who could give her plenty of nice clothes and ornaments. I can see Adinda is above most of the girls, and I don't doubt but that she will be very true to you. That's as far as it goes. Do you really think she loves you?"

René thought of the poisoned milk, wondered if he ought to tell of this to his brother, and finally decided not to.

"Yes, I think she loves me, Alfred. She is even studying hard to master our language, and does everything possible for my comfort and happiness. Adinda may not quite yet understand the word 'love,' as we mean it; it was never spoken to her until I explained it in relation to the feeling between man and woman, but there is no mistaking her devotion to me. Most of these girls have never had a chance to know what love can be. The majority of them are promised in marriage before they are a week old, and go to their husbands at fourteen or fifteen; they bear children and labor on until all feeling is killed. Adinda being of high caste is different in this respect; she proved it by refusing to marry a rich native."

"Who told you all this?" Alfred asked in surprise.

"Adinda, of course. She has a fine mind. She sees that the women of this island have never been treated right, hardly as human beings at all. I am sure that these women can love as truly as white girls, and more unselfishly. Time was when the widows were burned on the funeral pyre of their husbands. That, thank God, is all changed. Other changes are coming. You have not found that out, Alfred. You still treat them as slaves."

"I have never thought of things in this fashion, René. And to think I should learn it from my young brother! I meant to teach you. But beware, boy, you know you can't think of real marriage. You must not bring children into the world by Adinda—they would only be miserable. East is East, you know. You can't make a race over. But here comes the little girl with something good to eat."

Alfred was in a most lenient mood, now that the pain was better. Adinda fed him patiently, even smiled at him.

He tried after this to follow some of René's suggestions, with the most happy result. He was more kind to the house servants and relaxed a bit in his stern rule in the fields. He watched Adinda very closely and came to the conclusion that she really did love René. She managed their household infinitely better than Missah; there were as many servants about and as much food served, yet the expenses were not nearly so great. She was gentle and kind where Missah had been imperious. She never failed in her devotion to René, and Alfred was quick to see that his brother was being drawn closer and closer to this beautiful native girl.

The weeks slipped by uneventfully. The very ease of it all, even Adinda's sweetness and continual service, began to make René a bit restless. He could not tell why. After all his vaunted praise of her to Alfred, after all she had done for him, what was it that fretted him? It came to a head a few weeks later when he was taken ill with the fever so many white men have in the Tropics, but which is not serious if broken up at once.

"Better stay in bed and take no risks," Alfred cautioned him.

This pleased Adinda greatly; she had her dear *tuan* all to herself, and he needed her. His fever would come up at night, making him restless. But it would die down by morning, leaving him weak and fretful. Adinda scarcely left his side. For fear of disturbing him she slept on a mat on the tile floor close to the bed, where at a touch of his hand she could spring up to bring a cool drink.

"You must not do this, Adinda girl, it is too hard down there. You will wear yourself out."

"Oh, no, *tuan,* I do not feel it hard. I might trouble you if I slept in the bed."

René tossed in despair; it hurt his feelings of chivalry to take all from her and give so little in return. He did not want a slave—perhaps he had judged her too highly. She should demand some service from him, or at least expect it.

He learned that night what she did wish of him, and found it more than he could give. It was towards morning, and, his fever gone, he was weak and very dependent upon his little nurse. He drank the broth she had made for him, holding on to her hand when she started to lie down again. So she sat on his low bed, caressing his hand, soothing him as she would a restless child. He was tender with her, and found her a great comfort in his weakness.

A hot tear fell on the hand she held.

"What troubles you, girl? Tell me."

"Oh, *tuan,* I fear to tell you."

"You should not, Adinda. I want to help in whatever is troubling you. Just tell me."

She caught her breath in a little gasp.

"*Tuan—tuan—*could we not have a—a little baby in our home?"

She waited breathlessly, in her anxiety clinging hard to his hand. She waited long. René was too stunned to answer at once. A baby—his baby, dark-skinned! God, what was he doing? He had not dreamed Adinda would ever want this. He could not think of her as the mother of his children, while she had been dreaming that if it happened she would have her *tuan* forever. He would not leave her in that case; she felt sure of it.

The moments slipped by, and Adinda still clung to his limp hand. Sick at heart, René understood clearly that he could never grant her wish. He was not proud of himself.

In and out went the shuttle. Life had the ghost of a smile on its mocking lips.

When the dawn came in a burst of splendor, René slept at last. Adinda, on her mat by the bed, stifled her sobs, her slender body shaking from head to foot, her heart sick over her *tuan's* silent refusal.

20

A telegram from Bandoeng

ABOUT A MONTH before the cutting season would begin, Mr. de Kock dropped in on Alfred. The brothers were at breakfast, and not a little surprised to see the manager at such an early hour.

"I am sorry to disturb you so early," he explained, "but I have just received a telegram from Bandoeng[22] asking me to come and take possession of some very valuable papers in connection with a big deal I concluded for the factory last week. It is impossible for me to leave the plant just now. I came to ask you to go in my place, Alfred. I know it will be a hurried trip, but I thought it would be nice for René to go with you. Can you boys get ready to leave tonight? It may do you lots of good, René, you haven't been any too strong since the fever."

---

22 Now spelled Bandung, the city is about 90 miles southeast of Batavia (Jakarta) and 90 miles west-southwest of Cirebon. Surrounded by fertile land in the Parahyangan mountains it is ideal for growing tea. In the early 19th century, it developed into an exclusive European resort known for its cafes and shops that attracted rich plantation owners and businessmen from all over West Java.

Like Batavia, Bandung also had a Concordia Society clubhouse, built in 1895 with a large ballroom and theater. In 1926, the original structure was replaced with an art deco style building that is known today as the Merdeka Building (Gedung Merdeka) and serves as a museum.

René jumped up. "That's fine, Mr. de Kock, I'd love to go."

"I appreciate your confidence in me, Mr. de Kock. We'll be ready to start tonight," Alfred replied composedly.

"That's a load off my mind, van Landsberg. You know the carriages on the inland route leave Cheribon at one o'clock in the morning.[23] By steamer would be much more pleasant, but there won't be one leaving for three days and this business can't wait. You might return that way,

"We don't mind," René shouted. "It will be a great adventure to travel all night."

"All right, boys. I'll have the bookkeeper make the reservations, and here is the paper giving you, Alfred, the authority to act for me. Good luck and goodbye."

René jumped about the veranda like an excited little boy. He had not been on a real outing since his arrival in Java, and the thought of seeing Bandoeng was thrilling. While he was going over the trip with Alfred, Adinda came in. She had never seen René so happy. He sprang to her side in his joy, taking her in his arms, holding her close for an instant. For a brief moment her head rested on his breast, making her almost swoon from happiness. Alfred laughed at his brother's prank, knowing the embrace meant little, yet seeing how deeply it affected Adinda—time, he thought, that the boy should go away for a bit.

"Adinda girl," René cried, "I'm going on a trip with *tuan* Alfred for a few days. Pack my bag, will you?"

The girl's vivid color left her cheeks; she put one hand on a chair as though to steady herself.

---

23 Bandung is a bit more than an overnight carriage trip from Alfred's home on the outskirts of Cirebon. The following comment about the steamer, however, does not make sense. Bandung is more than 50 miles from both the north and south coasts of Java and is inaccessible by boat. We explore additional problems about the way the authors described their trip in footnote 26.

"Going away?" she whispered.

"Oh, don't worry, I'm only going to Bandoeng for several days. You be a good girl now, and take a rest while I am away."

"I don't want a rest," was her spirited reply. "I'm going too. I must go with *tuan*."

"No, girl, that is impossible, and you know it is." René tried to soothe her. "You just be good now. I'll bring you a nice present from the city."

"*Tuan* is too good to me—but the only thing that will make me happy is for *tuan* to come back very, very soon. I cannot live without *tuan*."

"Don't be silly, Adinda. I can't sit at home all the time. Run along now and get my things for the trip. Tell cook we won't be here for dinner—we will get that in Cheribon. Oh, but I'm glad to go!"

Tears blurred the girl's eyes while she packed her *tuan's* clothes; as she kneeled down by his leather grip they fell on his things unheeded. Going to the city! Ah, how many had she seen do this—they never came back the same. How she hated the white girls! How she hated her dark skin! Would all she had done for him be forgotten when he saw those girls of his own race? What had she left undone to bind him to her? How could she bear the days of waiting? She had studied so hard to learn his language; she could say many things as he said them. She could say, "My darling," and that meant much, very much.

Just then René stepped into the room. Adinda rose, put her arms tight about him, held him close, looked deep into his eyes.

"Will you see white girls, *tuan*?"

Brahim took his little seat and the brothers were off.

"Oh, I don't know about that," he evaded.

"But I know, *tuan.* You will see them and talk with them—will you forget me?"

"You dear, sweet girl, of course I won't forget you. How could I ever forget you after all the wonderful times we have had together. Besides I am not going there to see girls. We are away on business."

"You must think of me, *tuan,* when you do see them. You are mine, all that is me is yours—can any white say that? Nature made you mine—*no one else shall ever have you.*"

René's heart sank, but only for an instant. He was too excited to realize the meaning of Adinda's words.

"You are the best girl ever, little Adinda, and when I come back I will tell you about the sights, the wonderful sights I am sure to see."

He unclasped her arms. Still Adinda worried. Centuries of other religions, other blood, other ideals stood between them forever, and she knew it. He could never feel it as she did.

"Well, hurry," he interrupted her, giving her shoulders a little shake. "There is plenty to do. My clothes must be right for the city."

Then, seeing he had hurt her, he hastened to tell her some jokes, calling her all the pet names she loved and again promising to bring her a very nice gift from the city. While she was busy packing René moved about restlessly. He had never known hours to have so many minutes, nor one day to be so long.

Alfred entered into his spirit and laughed and joked while getting ready. Eventually, Adinda, too, tried to show a happier face. She was aided in this by many ages of training. The women of the Orient know the men come first, and the women are only there to serve. Tears and sobs had never changed things for women; they would not help her now.

She said goodbye quietly enough, standing by the side of the buggy where René sat waiting for Alfred. When he came, jumped in quickly and took the reins from Brahim, Adinda pressed her lips suddenly to René's hand, and could not still their trembling. René did not notice. Brahim took his little seat and the brothers were off, both waving joyously as the Sandalwoods dashed out of the driveway.

21

"He is dead, *tuan*."

BANDOENG, capital of the Preanger Regencies, is located on a high plateau in the southwestern part of Java. This is one of the most beautiful parts of the island, and may be reached by coach or train.[24]

The brothers arrived at Cheribon in time for dinner at the club and a visit with some of their old friends. At one o'clock they climbed into the coach for Bandoeng. The coach, a rather clumsy affair, had two large wheels and was drawn by a span of Javanese horses, tandem fashion. The seat in front held the driver. Just back of him was the seat for the travelers, and attached to the rear of the coach a running board on which a native stood, whip in hand, for the entire trip. His duty was to lash the horses when they slowed down. To do this he would jump off, run up to the horses, cut them across their backs two or three times, then at the risk of his life make a spring for the running board. He was called the runner and never allowed to relax in his effort to keep the horses up to top speed. The rear seat could be moved backwards or forwards as might be necessary to keep the

---

24 As mentioned in footnote 23, Bandung's inland location allows access by coach and train, but *not* by steamer.

The brothers arrived at Cheribon in time for dinner at the club
and a visit with some of their old friends.

balance perfect, making it as easy as possible for the pull on the horses.

Alfred and René boarded this old fashioned affair in high spirits. The bags were settled comfortably, and they were off. They were driven slowly through the city, although at this hour all was quiet. Once out in the country the runner sprang down and applied his whip vigorously. A slight rain now began to fall. The night was very dark, but the driver assured the boys the horses knew the way quite well without any guiding. René trusted he knew what he was talking about. Watching his bobbing head gave one a most uncomfortable feeling; he was doing more than his share of sleeping, René felt sure. Alfred, not so trusting, gave the fellow a prod in the ribs.

"I say, there! Wake up! Do you want to land us in the ditch?"

The driver responded with a sort of whistle, a sign for the runner to use his whip, but since the horses knew this sign they started running before they felt the lash. This kept René in constant anxiety over the runner; how he managed to return to the coach remained a mystery. As the night wore on he was smart enough to neglect his duty, trusting to the effect of the whistle on the horses. The driver, quickly seeing this, or perhaps already well accustomed to the runner's tricks, called louder than ever. The two kept the boys laughing over their pranks.

The changing posts are about five *paals* apart, and soon the lights of the first post could be seen shining through the rain.[25] The horses, too, knew that a meal and a good bed were near; they sprang forward and drew up to the post with too quick a stop for the brothers' comfort. Two sleepy natives

---

25 A *paal* is about 1,500 meters, or a little less than one mile. According to the description above, they changed horses about every five miles.

unhitched the horses and brought fresh ones, and again they sped into the dark night.

René was thrilled with the speed and the element of danger, which he felt was large, judging from the driver's nodding head. On they went, and soon the lights of another post were shining in the distance. The horses leaped forward—the driver slept. Crash! At full speed they ran against the station. Groans were heard, and curses from Alfred. The carriage was on its side and René was on top of his brother.

He extricated himself with considerable difficulty and turned to pull Alfred out. Alfred's face was covered with blood and he seemed badly hurt, but not too much to keep him from swearing vigorously, and for once René was glad to hear the curses. René escaped any injury, but his brother's face, hands and arms were cut and bruised. Limping into the station Alfred demanded the driver.

"He is dead, *tuan*," said a frightened native. "His head was crushed when he hit the post."

"Well, curses on him, anyway," was Alfred's ungracious reply.

René felt differently, and was shaken and nervous over the accident. He bound Alfred's cuts with a handkerchief, torn into bandages.

Another carriage was procured and they set out again. This time Alfred instructed the driver in no uncertain terms. It worked perfectly, although neither of the boys dared close his eyes for fear of another accident.

At six o'clock the sun came up brilliantly. At seven they had breakfast with the manager of a sugar factory, at New

At seven they had breakfast with the manager of a sugar factory, at New Tersana.

Tersana.[26] He was a friend of Alfred's, and at his home they changed their muddy clothing and Alfred's wounds were washed and dressed. Later they took the train to Bandoeng, a ride of about two hours from the factory.

In Bandoeng they stayed at a very fine hotel, a long white building with rooms opening on a wide, cool veranda. Its grounds were beautiful with rare palms and ferns, and shady walks bordered by exotic flowers. René felt like a stranger in so much luxury—the well-trained waiters, the different quality of food, the polished manners and elegant clothes of the women, the dainty little children with their native *baboes* watching over them, the whole atmosphere of a civilization finer than he had known for many a month. He was dismayed at his feeling of being out of this atmosphere.

How could so short a time make so great a difference? He had kept up his reading, he had not dissipated, yet he was not at home among his own kind. He felt everyone must notice his awkwardness. How could life in the interior change him so quickly? Sitting just outside their room,

---

26 Here the travel account's accuracy breaks down as we learn that the coach was not on the 90 mile trip to Bandung by road from Cirebon (which would have taken longer than 6 hours). Instead it traveled 36 miles *east* of Cirebon (moving *away* from Bandung) to Alfred's friend's plantation in New Tersana. With two changes of horses, as per footnote 25, that's a total of 15 miles. Leaving at 1AM from Cirebon and arriving at 7AM, with two sets of horses, means they averaged 6 miles per hour. This seems slow for a small carriage with fresh horses (moving so fast at one point that a fatal accident took place) but horses can either walk slowly for a long time, or can run quite fast for a short time.

Another problem is that the train station that circuitously connects with Bandung was just *north* of Cirebon so, once again, their itinerary does not make sense. From their home they arrive in Cirebon in time for dinner at the club, take a dangerous 6 hour carriage ride (at 6 mph) to New Tersana to meet Alfred's plantation owner friend. Then they somehow travel more than 40 miles to the train station for the "two hour" trip to Bandung. Today, in 2019, that train trip takes more than 4 hours (see www.rome2rio.com/map/Bandung/Cirebon).

Your editor notes that the main author, Baron Schwartzenberg, only spent four years on Java as a young man (circa 1900), and there is no indication that Ms. Harrison ever visited. Somehow, these logistical errors appeared in the text of this section.

Later they took the train to Bandoeng…

smoking on the wide veranda, he became terribly lonesome. His thoughts went to Adinda. He wished he were back with her—here he was nobody. He was glad with a new gladness that Adinda was there at home, waiting for him. What would she be doing at this hour?

At home Adinda was being very unhappy indeed. She had not slept, imagining all sorts of evils that might befall her *tuan*. She did not get up for breakfast, preferring to lie in bed and think of René. How jolly he had been, how funny—she smiled a bit, remembering his pranks, throbbing with joy over that quick, loving embrace. Soer, one of the new maids, knocked at the door, but Adinda did not even answer.

Life itself seemed to have left with René's going. She had never realized he was so much to her—she worshiped him, she could kiss his feet, her wonderful, wonderful *tuan!* She would fill his life with joy, she would be more to him than

In Bandoeng they stayed at a very fine hotel, a long white building with rooms opening on a wide, cool veranda. (Seen here, the Grand Hotel Preanger. The cars indicate this is about a decade after our story takes place.)

any woman ever had been to a man, she would learn his language, his ways, be his equal mentally, serve him, love him! She liked that word—"love."

Thinking all this restored her happiness. With a smile she arose, donned her *sarong* and with free, easy stride went down to the river to bathe.

22

Poison *again*

WHILE RENÉ WAS BROODING on the veranda, Alfred had gone to fulfill his mission for Mr. de Kock, returning in about an hour. They decided they would go out and see the city. It was a pretty place, situated high in the mountains; the air was cool and stimulating, very different from the interior. They walked through the business part and out to the mansion of the Resident, a large beautiful house befitting the representative of Holland's Queen. René, enjoying the sights, still felt out of place, although he did not speak of this to Alfred, who was very much at home.

Returning to the hotel René was on the point of going to their room when he caught sight of a familiar face. He was sure it was his old friend, Adolf van de Wal, although now so worn and haggard he was only the ghost of the young fellow René had gone to school with.

"Well, well, Adolf!" he said in greeting, holding out both hands. "What in the world are you doing here? And whatever ails you?"

Adolf smiled wanly. "It's good to see you, René. Sit down and tell me about yourself."

Above, Winkelstraat in Bandoeng (note the car, dating this photo to about ten years after René and Alfred visited). Below, the Concordia Society clubhouse.

"Don't ask how I am," René interrupted. "I want to know what ails you. Come, old pal, let's hear it."

He was trying vainly to see the rosy cheeks and merry smile of the Adolf of former days in this wasted man before him.

"It's a sad story, René. I hardly know where to begin." Adolf paused as though collecting his thoughts. "I studied in Germany for the sugar business, then came out here. I've been here two years, but I'm going back home soon, now."

"Are you in trouble?" René asked anxiously.

"Trouble a-plenty, René. I'm done to the death."

Was the fellow crazy? "Not that bad, Adolf. Maybe I can help you."

Adolf's lip curled in mockery. "No, René, I'm beyond help, though what I have to say may help you." For the fraction of a second he paused, then looked up at René with miserable, haunted eyes. "I just want to say this first of all: if you have a *njai*—you don't need to tell me whether you have or not—keep her, and for the love of heaven be true to her!"

"I don't mind telling you, Adolf, that I do have a *njai*. I am very much attached to the little girl; she is good to me."

"Now, listen," Adolf broke in. "I know all that stuff myself. All *njais* are good, and mine was *very* good. She finished up by poisoning me, and that's why I'm off for Europe."

"Poisoned you?" René broke in, astonished. "But why? Didn't she have any reason at all?"

"Oh, yes, son, reason a-plenty. It's my own fault, but I didn't know these women and their weaknesses, and by the time I did it was too late. I was already done for."

René was horrified. "Tell me about it, Adolf."

"Well, I had a very pretty *njai*. We lived together most happily until about five months ago. Then one night I went out with the boys, drank too much of their damned whiskey, hardly knew what I was doing—I spent the night in the *kampong*. Of course my *njai* knew all about it the next day—damned gossips saw to that. A week later I was taken very ill and have not been able to eat much since, just a little liquid food. I'm not in much pain now, but I'm weak as a rag."

"Surely you've seen a doctor—can't he help you?"

"Oh, yes, I saw a doctor! He signed my death warrant at once. No hope for me, René. These natives when they use poison do it thoroughly."

"But who did this to you?" René asked, frightened.

"Well, who do you think? Just as I said before, my *njai*, of course."

Adolf looked off with staring eyes. René was silent, horrified over what he had heard. Then, with a ray of hope: "But, Adolf, if you have lived this long, surely you are getting over it."

"No, no chance, son. The natives get this poison from the old grandmothers, who take it from the bamboo, just where the leaf joins the stalk, and grind it up fine to be put in the food. The fine powder clings to the lining of the stomach and nothing can remove it. It finally eats through—and that's all. The natives know to a nicety how to time your death—at once, a week later, a month or ten years, according to the depth of their revenge." [27]

---

27 Your editor was intrigued to hear of this bamboo poison that slowly eats through your guts when added to food. Why, my wife has been feeding me bamboo soup for years! I quickly grabbed my handy 1929 edition of John D. Gimlette's *Malay Poisons and Charm Cures* and, right there in the first chapter, he mentions both bamboo *and* "time-poisons"! Gimlette's classic scientific inquiry also describes Kelantan poisons from plants and animals with details of charm cures, witchcraft, spells and lifting of spells. You'll find the first chapter in the appendices for your own cooking needs. Sadly, my guess is that Adolf drank himself to death, as many expatriates did, and still do.

"But, Adolf, if your *njai* cared for you, this act of hers would not bring you back."

"She didn't want me back after what I had done. Say, René, you can just tell some of those old timers for me that if they think the native girls don't love, they don't know Java or her people.

"There is no court of justice to help a *njai* when her *tuan* is untrue to her, so she goes back to the old, old method of taking the punishment in her own hands. The old women herb doctors who secure the poison for the girls are glad to see the white man suffer for his sins. I'm paying all right."

Adolf seemed to sink into his chair; he looked white and drawn. "It was the whiskey, René. Keep away from it."

Very tenderly René helped his friend to his room, leaving him on his bed with closed eyes and pallid lips.

The remainder of the day was spoiled for René, nor could he sleep that night. He did not connect this ghastly story with Adinda—she could never do such a thing nor, for that matter, could he be untrue to her. Lying awake, staring into the darkness, her words came back to him, "Nature made you mine and no one else can ever have you." He shuddered a bit, and was glad that Alfred was near him.

23

Batavia

THE NEXT MORNING Alfred and René left for Batavia, deciding to go home by boat. This would give them a day and a half in the city, and René hoped to get a little pleasure there. He had tried to see Adolf and say goodbye. "Too weak to see any one," the nurse said. René was ashamed of his relief.

Batavia, capital of the Dutch East Indies, pleased him from the first. They put up at the Hotel Netherlands, a large hostelry in the fashionable section of Weltevreden. That evening they went over to the Concordia Club for dinner; this was Alfred's favorite rendezvous. René, remembering his brother's letter written from there, was prepared to meet ladies beautifully gowned and men in evening clothes, nor was he disappointed.

Almost at once they were invited to join Alfred's friend, Mr. de Jong, and his wife and two daughters at their table. As de Jong was interested in sugar he and Alfred were soon absorbed in the topic. The older girl, Wilhelmina, who was, René judged, about nineteen, took immediate charge of him. She was a perfect blonde of the Dutch type, big blue eyes, full lips parting over white teeth, rounded and rather

Ingang Paviljoenlaan Koningsplein.
Avenue entrance.
HOTEL DER NEDERLANDEN
BATAVIA.

The rich history of the Hotel der Nederlanden began when Pieter Tenzy built it as his private residence in 1794. In 1811 Thomas Stamford Raffles purchased it as his private home for 27,000 rupees while he was working as the lieutenant-governor of Java. When Raffles concluded his post and sailed to England in 1816 he sold the home to the government of the Dutch Indies (it's worth mentioning that Raffles published *The History of Java* in England the next year).

Two decades later, in 1837, the expansive residence was converted to the Hotel Palais Royale. With further construction it became one of the most luxurious accommodations in Batavia, finally acquiring the name Hotel der Nederlanden in 1846. By the early 20th century the hotel had grown to become a complex of private bungalows, coach-houses and stables, with a grand dining hall in the main building serving both European cuisine and local Indies Rijsttafel for up to two hundred guests. By the 1920s, rooms featured running water, electric lighting, call bells and private bathrooms.

Like many grand hotels around the world it gradually lost its elegance, with its final role as a headquarters for the Tjakrabirawa Regiment, the presidential bodyguard unit for former Indonesian President Sukarno.

They were invited to join Alfred's friend, Mr. de Jong,
and his wife and two daughters at their table.

stocky throat. Too stout altogether, René thought, comparing her with Adinda's slender grace. Her sister Johanna, much younger, watched him with shy eyes.

"Do you play tennis?" Wilhelmina asked after they had exhausted the topic of the weather.

René chuckled. "Oh, yes, Miss de Jong, I play tennis in the jungle with the gibbons."

A good laugh at this set René at ease.

"Well, I play every day," Wilhelmina informed him, "otherwise I would get too stout. I don't do a bit of work—I hate it. Besides, we have a bevy of servants, so why should I?"

"You'll save your working days for your married life," René ventured.

"Not I, Mr. van Landsberg. I don't ever intend to work."

"Oh, yes, Miss de Jong, I play tennis in the jungle with the gibbons."

"You'll change your mind, young lady, if you marry and live in the interior."

She shrugged her plump shoulders. "I won't live in the interior. The man who marries me must live in the city.

"You are not a believer then," René asked, "in the old idea of a wife following her husband wherever he goes?

"Oh, yes, that's all right, but I'm nobody's wife as yet, and you may be sure I shall pick my husband very carefully. I'm not a native woman. Poor things, they are not given a chance to marry for love—though they don't know the meaning of the word, now do they, Mr. van Landsberg?" She leaned towards him eagerly.

"Don't you believe it!"

His over earnest answer brought a long "Oh!" from the girl. René flushed and changed the subject. Had she heard

Daisy sank into her chair, dazed, withholding from René
her beautiful, dreamy brown eyes.

of his *njai?* He felt exceedingly uncomfortable, and hated the thought of having anything in his life that called for diplomatic evasions.

The orchestra struck up a lively tune. Miss de Jong hesitated for a moment, and then said: "Shall we dance—or don't you care for it?"

"There's nothing I enjoy more," he answered heartily.

They moved to the rhythm of the music, and René grew more and more delighted with the evening. He had Johanna for his next partner. When they returned to the table, he was presented to a young girl who had just arrived.

"Daisy," said the elder Miss de Jong, "meet Baron René van Landsberg and make him dance with you."

It was true that René was entitled to the courtesy title of Baron, but he had never intended to use it in Java. Wondering where Miss de Jong had obtained her information about him, he bowed to Daisy Vermeer and politely offered his arm for the next dance. The orchestra played a dreamy waltz which made René's pulses tingle—or was it the girl he held in his arms that thrilled him? The soft hand he held seemed to cuddle into his. They went round and round the floor, swaying in perfect harmony, forgetting the people about them, feeling only each other and the quivering sweetness of the music. Daisy's head was almost on his breast, and his lips were close to her fragrant hair.

Their breath came faster as they went on and on, lost in the poetry of motion and music. Once, Daisy looked up and smiled into René's eyes. He smiled back, but neither of them spoke. There was no need for words; they had communicated with one another in the language that all the world knows.

The music stopped. Daisy sank into her chair, dazed, withholding from René her beautiful, dreamy brown eyes, and René, throbbing with the magic of her presence, forgot other brown eyes, saw only white shoulders, felt the tug of his heart towards this lovely girl of his own race, white as a snowdrift, whiter than he remembered a woman could be, slim in her white dress, slender white hands, rounded white arms, a white satin ribbon binding her fair hair and ending in a bow at her throat—gentle, yet aflame. But the music was playing again; he must do his duty. Her eyes were still shielded when he led Miss de Jong on to the floor.

"Wake up," she twitted him. "Daisy won't melt away."

René was sure he didn't like Miss de Jong.

Obediently then he danced with Mrs. de Jong, and again with little Johanna. Free at last, he asked Daisy for the next, a lively polka.

"Oh, no, Mr. van Landsberg, that wouldn't do at all after our lovely waltz. Shall we go out on the terrace?"

She raised her eyes and smiled. Little electric sparks seemed to fly from her to him. Outside, Daisy seated herself on a marble railing, swinging her feet. René dared lift his admiring eyes to her.

"We don't have nights like this at home, do we?" she asked. "All silvery with moonlight and fragrant with the sweetness of many flowers—almost too sweet. It makes me feel unreal."

"It is more wonderful in the interior where I live," he told her. "The nights are beyond description. What I like best, though, are the mysterious sounds one hears. Every cluster of trees, every sugar cane field, every hanging vine seems to give forth its own particular rhythm. There is where one feels creation."

René spoke eloquently. Daisy caught his spirit.

"I see you love the interior. I have never been there, but have felt almost afraid of the jungle with its dense growth and wild life."

René, leaning close to her, answered, "Maybe someday I can show it to you." Then he told her a bit timidly of his boar hunt and of his feeling as he waited in the cathedral-like jungle.

"I may have to live where I will see plenty of that," Daisy answered. "Papa is a captain in the cavalry and likely to be sent to Makassar[28] at his next promotion. But it doesn't matter. I'll like it anyway, since there is always something nice about any place."

"I'm glad to hear you say that," René replied impulsively. Why he was glad would not have been apparent to a listener.

"We must go in now," Daisy told him, slipping from the railing. "This is a terribly gossipy place."

"Give me one more dance," René pleaded.

"Not tonight—but you may call me Daisy—René."

His answer was a whisper of her name.

All eyes turned towards them as they joined the others at the de Jong table. Wilhelmina mischievously pulled Daisy into a chair near her.

"How do you like the good-looking baron? I've a notion to fall in love with him myself, but perhaps I'd better leave him to you. He seems to have fallen too far your way to recover himself."

"Oh, that's charming of you," Daisy laughed.

---

28   The capital of what is now the Indonesian province of South Sulawesi. Historically, it has always been an important trading port, being the center of the Gowa Suttanate and a Portuguese naval base before being taken in the 17th century as a possession of the Dutch East India Company. Makassar is nearly 900 miles due east of Batavia (now called Jakarta).

"Baroness van Landsberg, née Vermeer," Wilhelmina teased. "It sounds really good."

"I can't marry on a sound," was the saucy reply.

Mrs. de Jong rose. Good-nights were said, a bit slowly.

"You must both come to luncheon with us tomorrow," Mrs. de Jong invited the boys.

Daisy gave her cool slim hand to René.

"I'll never forget that waltz," he told her. *"Bonne nuit"*

"Goodbye and good luck," was her answer.

Outside Alfred asked René mockingly, "Jolly life, isn't it? Now dare tell me you don't like it."

"I don't though. It's too far from nature. This is artificial."

Alfred's laugh was hearty. "Methinks the gentleman protests too much. Nice girl, that Vermeer girl."

"Very nice," came the crisp reply.

"You're a funny bird, René. Give me this any time and you can keep the jungle."

24

"You are just used to brown ones..."

RENÉ'S SLEEP was troubled. In the dark hour before dawn, he was aroused by a vigorous shaking.

"Hey, there! Hey, boy, wake up!" Alfred's voice was kind, but anxious. "Come out of that nightmare. You'll bring the whole management up here with your yelling. What's bothering you, anyway? Are you sick, or is it a bad dream?"

"God! It was a dream—a horrible dream about Adolf van de Wal." René struggled to compose his voice, while Alfred climbed back into his own bed. "I saw Adolf as I used to know him, full of fun, jolly, a round-faced chap who wouldn't hurt a fly. Then I caught sight of him in a great river, floating with his mouth open and his eyes staring upward. I tried to save him, I strove madly to get to him, but he was always just out of reach. Then, somehow, it was Adinda floating there. I couldn't save her either."

René groaned. Alfred, who knew exactly what had inspired the nightmare, said morosely:

"It's terrible, and I'm sorry for the boy. The native girls will do it, though, if given sufficient reason. Missah had the heroic stuff in her, but I was pretty careful not to arouse her jealousy."

René did not answer.

"You see now why I cautioned you not to be too serious. It's best to keep them in their place. Your teaching Adinda to read and speak your language may encourage her to expect more from you."

Out of the darkness came René's answer at last, "If she must be kept in ignorance just to serve me, then I'm the worst cad on earth."

"Oh, no, I wouldn't say that." Alfred smiled a little in the darkness at his brother's self-condemnation. "You'll save her suffering later. All your teaching but binds her the more to you—and when you leave, as you must, think how lost she'll feel. You're storing up suffering for yourself, too."

"That's all right," came from the other bed. "It doesn't matter what I suffer—the thing is to keep her from anguish."

"You're a fine lad, René. You're right, in the main, but think of Mother. You can't live here always."

"It's because of Mother I'm thinking of Adinda— womankind, the man's duty to protect them."

Alfred, wide awake now, was silent, fearing that after all René might marry Adinda. He had done wrong to bring the boy into such temptation. Betty, curse her! This wouldn't have happened if she had been faithful.

Then, later, when he had hoped René was asleep, there came out of the silence, "How white Daisy Vermeer is, Alfred, like snow."

"No," came the relieved, laughing reply, "she's no whiter than any of our girls. You are just used to brown ones, that's all."

A little before daylight, René spoke again: "I wish I had met her in the interior with all the trimmings of city life left out. I'd know better how real she is."

But Alfred was asleep.

Luncheon at the de Jongs' proved to be a royal affair. René was astonished at the warmth of their greeting and the elaborate meal served. Although Alfred had told him the Colonials were always most cordial, he was unprepared for such splendid entertainment. The de Jongs said by their manner, much as the Spaniard puts it in words: "Our house is yours."

Alfred thoroughly enjoyed himself, but René was a bit ill at ease. He did not like the way Wilhelmina teased him with her air of repressed laughter. He had half hoped Daisy Vermeer would be there, and would have inquired about her had he not known that this would simply add to Wilhelmina's amusement. Not daring even to mention Daisy's name, he decided again more definitely that he did not like the elder Miss de Jong. He said as much to Alfred, as they walked back to their hotel.

"She's too self-satisfied and rather tactless," he added. "But you can't criticize the magnificent way we were treated—a true Holland welcome," Alfred countered.

During the remainder of the warm afternoon they sat on the veranda of the hotel, smoking and chatting. At six o'clock they boarded the steamer for home. René was not sorry. Work was the best thing for him, he concluded, though social life was beguiling and Daisy Vermeer decidedly seductive. On the way to the boat, he purchased a beautiful gold bracelet for Adinda—and fell to wondering how it would look on a snow-white arm.

During the remainder of the warm afternoon they sat on the veranda of the hotel, smoking and chatting.

The steamer dropped anchor in Cheribon roadstead early the next morning.[29] Brahim was at the dock with the Sandalwoods, and the brothers were soon on their way to Kerang Sawah. As they sped over the familiar road, René's thoughts flew ahead. He felt again the joy of the open, the freedom of his life here, the lure of the interior where conventions were sloughed off, with the real and the unreal made equally clear; here he could develop unhampered, could call his soul his own—and here, too, was Adinda.

As they entered the driveway to the house, René was out of the buggy and dashing up the veranda steps before the surprised Brahim could jump from his little seat. Meeting one of the maids, he demanded eagerly:

---

29   The distance from Batavia to Cheribon by ship is roughly 135 miles.

"Where is Adinda?"

"In her room, *tuan*" the girl answered, bowing.

25

Sonario

THROWING HIS *TOPE* ON THE TABLE René strode across to their room, opened the door with a rush, banged it shut and stood still, taking in his little *njai* with a smile of joy. She in turn stood perfectly quiet, one hand grasping the bedpost as though for support, the other over her throbbing heart.

One long look into his face and she knew he was her own *tuan*. Her emotion almost overcame her. Tears filled her eyes. Still she did not move. In two long strides René reached her side, took her tenderly in his arms, holding her close while moments ticked by. Her head was on his breast. The fragrance of the melatie blossoms swept him. "Oh, Adinda, little girl, you at least are real."

She could not answer, happily resting in the shelter of his arms. He did not kiss her, although now she raised her face to his, lips trembling.

"You are mine. I feel it, *tuan*, I know it."

"Of course I am yours. I could hardly wait to reach you. My longing for you grew stronger at every turn of the propeller, and when we reached the grounds I had a hard time sticking to my seat." René laughed happily. "I thought something had happened to you when you were not at the steps to greet me."

"I could not greet you there, *tuan*. I did not want the servants to see our meeting. They have seen enough of my longing for you—too much already."

"Well, I'm glad to be back, Adinda, you beautiful little thing!" and René swung her off her feet for an instant, making her eyes sparkle, her dimples come and go.

"What kind of a time did you have, *tuan*, in the city?" Adinda asked, demurely settling her *sarong*, straightening the lace at her sleeves.

"Oh, all right," was the somewhat evasive answer. "Rather hurried. I heard some very unpleasant things while in Bandoeng."

"Tell me, *tuan*." Adinda was full of anxiety. "Anything serious about *tuan's* relations in Holland?"

"No, no, it's not that, girl. Don't let's talk about it. I will tell you sometime—not now."

"Did you see some white girls, *tuan*?"

Adinda was not fearful, yet she would like to know about those girls. René laughed heartily, taking her by the shoulders playfully.

"I not only saw them, girl, I met them, danced with them, talked with them. Artificial—that's what they are! Oh, but nice, if one likes them that way."

Adinda's arms went about him. "I do not care, *tuan*, how many you saw, now that you are back and still mine."

"Come, child, we must unpack. Don't you want to know what I have for you?"

René opened the door, calling loudly, "Bring my bags, Brahim." Brahim brought them, and Adinda began to unpack, finding the little box with the bracelet carefully wrapped in tissue paper.

"For me, *tuan?*"

"But yes, who else?"

"Put it on, *tuan!*"

She held up her slender arm to him. Playfully René took the bracelet. As he clasped it about her wrist he glanced at her wide eyes. Suddenly he became serious—this was more than a gift to Adinda, it was a ceremony, a sacred rite, drawing her still closer to her *tuan,* binding her to him, him to her, in a circle of gold, symbol of unbroken faith. This she knew from the books he had taught her to read.

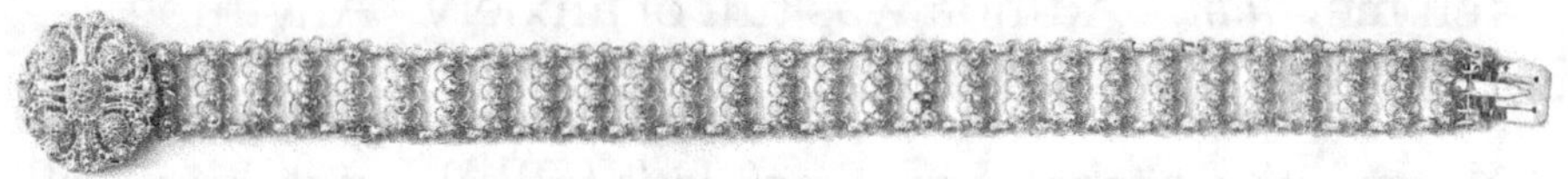

He purchased a beautiful gold bracelet for Adinda—and fell to wondering how it would look on a snow-white arm..

She bent her head to kiss his clasping fingers, a new caress for her, learned also from her *tuan's* books.

Suddenly René dropped her arm, turned to rummage in his bags, saying nonchalantly, "And what have you been doing—resting while I was away?"

"*Saja, tuan,* I am all rested and ready to serve you better than ever before. I slept and slept—I simply could not get up in the morning. Oh, how I loved to lie in bed with my eyes closed and picture you before me! It was the only way to bring you really close to me. It was beautiful to dream that way. Now I will go after the household again—you will want for nothing, *tuan!'*

"Did you see any one while you were here alone?" René asked, trying to appear indifferent.

"No,—" Adinda hesitated, "no, I didn't really see any one—but yes, I met one person, *tuan,* outside of the servants."

"Yes?" René did not meet the quick glance of the girl.

"Sonario came to see me the second day after you left. Please do not be angry with me, *tuan.* I did not want him to come."

"Well, go on," said René seriously. "What did Sonario want from you?"

"You remember, *tuan,* I told you there were two men in the *kampong* who wanted to marry me? I refused both. Sonario was one of them. He came back to see whether I had changed my mind—he asked me to be his wife. I told him no, I wanted only *tuan.* He pleaded with me, he promised beautiful batik *sarongs,* gold and silver ornaments and a servant all to myself—and children." She paused, a bit breathless.

"Yes, yes, what more?"

"That's all, *tuan.* There could be nothing else. I explained to him that gifts did not matter—you only were the one I want. He said I was cruel, that I could not marry *tuan* René anyway. You are—are not angry—*tuan?*

"You know I am true to you. In your heart you know that. Speak to me, *tuan.*"

She came closer to him, one hand on his arm, pleading with her brown eyes searching his. His hands hung limp by his sides.

He answered, looking unseeingly into the distance, "No, Adinda, I am not angry at his coming. I know you are true to me, never expected anything else,—but, girl—"

"Oh, what is it, *tuan?*"

"Would it not be better for you to marry Sonario?"

And while René said this Daisy Vermeer's picture passed ever so quickly before his eyes. Adinda saw his faraway look, knew his thoughts were elsewhere.

In a frightened voice she cried out, "*Tuan,* you don't want to get rid of me, do you? Tell me, *tuan,* are you tired of me? Oh, is it that you have seen the white girls? It is the cruel, cruel city!"

Her bitter crying hurt him.

"Listen, little one, I did not say I wanted you to leave me. Whoever said I did?"

"No, no, *tuan!*" Adinda spoke between sobs. "You did not say it, but Sonario did. He said you would be through with me before long—you would take a white woman to live with always. Then I was angry with him and told him to go away. Why did you want me to marry Sonario, *tuan?*"

"Wait, Adinda! I didn't say I wanted you to marry Sonano. I thought only of your good. If Sonario is well-to-do and can give you a good home, make you his wife, wouldn't it be better for you?"

"No, no, *tuan!* Don't say it!"

"I must, Adinda. You know I can't marry you—our laws do not forbid it, but our blood does. There could be no lasting happiness for me, away from my own people forever, nor for you among my people. Our children would be of mixed blood, and miserable."

"But I would be happy, *tuan,*" came the anguished cry. "Our children need not be unhappy. I could be a good mother."

"Yes, little Adinda, you would be the sweetest mother on earth."

Adinda squatted on the floor, head bent. René turned away—never had he felt himself such a rotter. He hated his sunny nature, living just for the day. How could he have done this thing, taken all from the slender girl at his feet, believing what Alfred had said? He cursed that fateful night when she had come to him. He was a weakling without backbone. He deserved to go the way of Adolf. He had not thought a native girl could love so, yet he had taught her the meaning of that word and she was heartbroken now. "Cad, cad, thief!" he called himself. Let her take revenge—justice was on her side.

But Adinda, feeling his self-accusation ran quickly, put her arms about him once more, held him closely, brave, strong, for her *tuan*. "I did not expect you to marry me. I refused Sonario because I want to be with you, just to be near you and serve you for the rest of my days.

"It is not asking too much, *tuan*. If *tuan* should not want me then I'd rather be dead. No other man shall ever have me. I am yours forever. What I did, I did of my own free will; always I shall be glad. I know at last what is love—your word, *tuan!* And I can be truer than a white girl. Do not be sorry. I will serve you always, *tuan*."

She loosened her clasp and rushed from the room. She had overwhelmed him with her eloquence, her faith, her love.

He spoke, half aloud, "Adinda, you wonderful girl!"

26

The next steamer for Batavia

NOT ANOTHER WORD was said by René or Adinda regarding the subject of marriage. He bent to his work with renewed energy and to the delicate task of making Adinda forget the hurt he had unwittingly given her. She deserved the best in him. Regardless of what Alfred might say or think, he continued to teach her his language. Evening after evening found her dark head bent over the book on her knee. She displayed the native characteristic, patience; this, coupled with her great ambition to be to her *tuan* all a white woman would, made her difficult task much easier. In the daytime every spare minute found her jotting down on paper what she had learned. This René corrected, and he was not astonished when she read to him from some of his own books.

Thus the weeks passed. The sugar cane season started up with all the festivities and all the hubbub connected with the putting in motion of this great industry. René was at his post at the scales. When the work was done he would sit, thoroughly tired, on the cool veranda, Adinda by his side. Often she refrained from asking him about her day's studying, seeing how worn he was from twelve long hours

One evening Alfred and René were invited to the home of Mr. and Mrs. Inger.

at the factory. It agreed with him, however, for each morning found him fresh and ready for the day's work.

One evening Alfred and René were invited to the home of Mr. and Mrs. Inger, and, as always, they accepted gladly. After dinner, as the men sat smoking, Inger asked René, "And what will your future work be? Are you going to follow in Alfred's footsteps and wind up eventually in the fields?"

"I would like to," René told him, "but you see, Mr. Inger, I am not a chemist, as Alfred is. I would have to stop as an overseer—that would be my limit."

"Too bad, René. So many men in the Colonies do not fit themselves for advancement."

"Mr. de Kock has promised me my present position," René informed him, "until I become thoroughly familiar with the work, the people and the language."

Inger laughed as he jokingly replied, "Well, so far as I can see, you are getting along with the people very well, and your language has been especially looked after." René flushed. He didn't quite like this reference to his *njai;* it was the first time anyone had referred to Adinda in this covert way.

"Say, boy!" Inger spoke abruptly, banging his fist on the table. "I have a great idea. You know, Alfred, I am still interested in the tea estate, Tjidani.[30] My brothers, George and Henri, are the managers. What do you say to my trying to get René in there?"

"Bully!" was Alfred's response. "That would be wonderful!"

"That would be great, Mr. Inger," René interrupted. "I certainly appreciate your offer to help me."

"You'd better, René," Alfred said. "That is one of the largest tea estates on the island. You are to be congratulated if you find a position under the Inger brothers."

"It may not pay so much at first," Inger informed him, "but there is hope for advancement. Your foot will be in the stirrup anyway."

At home René felt impelled to tell Adinda of his hopes for the future. She was sound asleep, but awakened at the sound of his voice, dreamily opening her eyes; one arm went around his neck.

"Listen, child, I'm telling you I'm going away from Kerang Sawah, far away to a tea plantation."

---

30 The authors apparently named the plantation after the Tjidani River (now called the Cisadane River), that has its source at Mt. Mandalawangi in central West Java and flows north into the Java Sea west of Batavia (Jakarta). Though the river was not truly useable for transport and communication—being too rapid at its source, and too sandy and shallow in the lowlands—it provided irrigation to the region and served as a tangible boundary line between the Dutch region of Batavia and the rival territories of the Banten Sultanate to the west.

"Sama djoega," came sleepily from Adinda's lips. "I am going with *tuan* wherever he goes."

"Would you leave your birthplace to follow me?"

The question was fraught with meaning, but Adinda had dozed off. René speculated long on this problem, sleeping at last, leaving it in the lap of the gods.

Time went on, with no word of the new position. Then, one evening Inger telephoned, asking René to come over at once.

"Good news, my boy! Come and hear about it."

René lost no time in ordering the Sandalwoods and in changing into a fresh white suit. Mr. and Mrs. Inger greeted him cordially.

"You're a lucky boy," Inger told him. "Here read this."

"Van Landsberg must be here not later than ten days from the date of this writing," René read. "We are very busy just now with the tea picking and shipping of a large order, and we must have help at once. Please wire immediately."

With a beaming face René tried to thank Inger.

"No thanks are necessary, my boy. I'm glad to assist you. Get permission from Mr. de Kock to leave and don't delay your going."

"It's all settled," was René's joyous greeting to Alfred and Adinda, who had waited patiently his return.

"You have the job?" Alfred asked.

"Yes, it's mine if Mr. de Kock will let me go."

"Oh, he will, René, and I'll say your future is assured. But I'll miss you, boy! It will be damned lonesome here without you."

His eyes went from René to Adinda.

"Yes," René said with no sign of hesitation, "Adinda goes with me."

She rose quickly; going to his side took his hand in hers. "I knew you would take me, *tuan!* When do we go?" They laughed at her eagerness.

"I'll tell you tomorrow," was René's answer.

The next morning René had his talk with de Kook, and although the manager was somewhat embarrassed about filling the place on such short notice he knew it was too good an opening to be refused. Without hesitation he consented to René's departure on the next steamer for Batavia, just three days later.

Those three days were difficult ones. René had found many friends during his three years at Kerang Sawah; he had attached himself strongly to this, his first home in the tropics. He was going to a place where a different dialect was spoken, where no one knew him. He realized with a throb of gratitude that Alfred had smoothed many rough places for him—now he would be alone. It was like starting all over again.

But his pangs at leaving were as nothing compared to Adinda's. René knew that no native ever leaves the district where he or she was born unless forced to. They belong to that particular piece of soil, grow up, work and die in the same place where they blinked at the sun for the first time. Adinda, too, was leaving a position of envy among her people, for she had become a personage. Her acquired knowledge and the weight it gave her among her people reflected very favorably, too, on René. Everyone knew he had taught her to read, write and speak his language. They respected him for that.

René felt deeply the sacrifice she was making for him, although no words of grief, no signs of trouble ever came from the girl. She went about the task of packing up for René as she did everything for him, quietly, efficiently. All the little knickknacks he had brought from Europe were handled with reverent tenderness. She saw that not one detail of the move was left to him. When he came home at night she was fresh and sweet as always, ready to sit quietly by his side, rolling his cigarettes or chatting.

Then all was ready, and René found to his disgust that he would not be permitted to travel with Adinda. The laws of the country were against it. It seemed unfair—she who had managed the whole move so efficiently must now go all that distance alone. He knew that secretly she feared this. It was her first real trip; she was absolutely ignorant of travel, of meeting strange people, the changing from carriage to boat, and from boat to train; but it would have embarrassed her greatly to be put into the first class compartment, so she took calmly what had to be.

René hired a carriage for her, a two-seated affair, packing her bags and his into it, and leaving barely enough room for her. This would take her to Cheribon, where she would board the steamer. When all was ready, Adinda came out of her room to find the servants gathered with Alfred and René on the veranda to say goodbye. Everyone was sorry to see her go—not a few shed tears. Adinda, however, was the poised lady throughout. With a sweet grace she gave each servant her hand in farewell. Coming to Alfred she took his hand in both of hers.

"You had better get a *njai* to look after you, *tuan* Alfred. You can't live here alone." Then she added in Dutch, so the servants might not understand, "I love you because you are *tuan* René's brother."

Alfred was moved by this. "You are a wonderful girl, Adinda, and I am glad you are going with *tuan* René." She did not bid René goodbye, but smiled, saying, "I may see you on the boat."

She was gone, and René set about making his adieux. The brothers had a few moments to themselves before it was time for René to start, but neither spoke much. René could not reconcile himself to the idea that Adinda must travel alone, but he knew that railroad and steamship companies do not permit natives to travel first class. He had a constant feeling that he wanted to do more for his *njai*. She was a woman, and his; he was not ashamed to say this to the world. The Oriental idea of woman's inferiority had never been accepted by him.

"You have done all you can, René," Alfred comforted him. "Don't let it spoil your trip. You'd better be going now, old chap."

A hearty handshake was the brothers' goodbye.

27

A new life

RENÉ ASSURED HIMSELF that Adinda and the bags were safely on board, then went on the upper deck. Again he stood at the ship's railing, looking thoughtfully towards Cheribon. This time he had no fear in his heart. A new life opened for him. Adinda was a grave responsibility, but he had learned much in this strange, fascinating country, having crowded into a few years experiences that would ordinarily fill a lifetime.

The trip passed uneventfully. Adinda proved a fine traveler, many times showing her knowledge of white women's ways as learned from reading René's books. Always she was quiet and dignified, quite sufficient unto herself. Often, watching her at a distance René was surprised and pleased at her ladylike manner. She commanded service from those beneath her, gave it freely to those above her. He fell to wondering what European travel would do for her, and if it were possible successfully to transplant an Oriental woman.

The house they were to occupy at Tjidani stood on a high cliff above the tea gardens. It was made entirely of bamboo, and consisted of living room, dining room and bedrooms, with a wide veranda across the front. The kitchen, bathroom,

Again he stood at the ship's railing, looking thoughtfully towards Cheribon

and servants' quarters were in another building, entirely detached from René's house.

From the veranda one had a magnificent view of the entire valley. The tea gardens stretched in front, fresh and green. To the left, towering high above the gardens, was the cloud-encircled cone of the one-time mighty volcano, Salak.[31] Its sides were covered with dense tropical growth. In the distance could be heard the faint rumbling sound of waterfalls, while the playful shrieks of monkeys came from the back of the house.

Often René and Adinda went to the edge of the cliff to watch the lovely scene that was spread below them. There would come, morning and evening, the wild animals of the

---

31   Mt. Salak, an eroded volcano that last erupted in 1938 (just seven years after *Java Girl* was first published), rises to a height of 7,200 feet. It is located about 12 miles south of Bogor.

The house they were to occupy at Tjidani stood on a high cliff above the tea gardens.

From the veranda one had a magnificent view of the entire valley.

To the left, towering high above the gardens, was the cloud-encircled cone of the one-time mighty volcano, Salak.

jungle, great tigers and gentle-faced deer, stealthy wildcats, clumsy, leaping jackrabbits. At the rushing, foaming stream of cold water they drank their fill, showing not one fierce desire to kill the little creatures that gradually gathered to slake their thirst.

Adinda was as happy as a child, hanging over this great wall. For fear they might fall René fastened a rope about them, the other end tied securely to a tree. Then freely they hung far over, never tiring of watching for the first animal that would come down the well-worn path to the water's edge.

"They do not kill each other, *tuan!*" Adinda whispered in astonishment.

"No, Adinda, they never kill unless hungry or attacked. It is left for man to take his sport that way."

"Our men in Java do not do that."

…later mounting his beautiful white Australian horse to ride over the tea gardens.

"I know, girl. The white men in Java have forced that pastime on the natives."

René liked his new work, although it was much harder than the sugar business. There were no days off, no festivals of any kind. The tea leaves must be kept picked closely; when one field was worked another stood ready, day in and day out, never slacking. The first little tender leaves must not be allowed to unfold completely; they make the finest tea and bring the best price. René had to watch the women who did the picking very closely. He had to learn, too, their dialect. In this Adinda was a great help. She mastered the language at once. When the native overseers came in the evening to report she was by René's side to interpret for him.

At seven every morning the *mandoers* came to René for instruction. When they were sent about their tasks he went in for breakfast, later mounting his beautiful white Australian

She managed his household beautifully. Ten servants were hers to command.

horse to ride over the tea gardens. This was his rule day by day, and Adinda saw but little of him.

She managed his household beautifully. Ten servants were hers to command. Each one must do her work well, that *tuan* René be served properly. He felt he could never have taken this position but for Adinda. Tighter and tighter the tiny threads of service and love bound him. He ceased to struggle.

Sitting one evening on the veranda, tired after his day's work, René was enjoying the view before him. The faint sound of the falls was like distant music, the peace and quiet rested his spirit. Adinda sat on the floor by his side, reading. She could never be persuaded to sit on a chair in her *tuan's* presence, nor had she ever called him "René"—always it was "*tuan*" or "*tuan* René" when she spoke of him to anyone.

The sun set and it became too cool to remain outside. Going into the living room Adinda lighted the lamp swinging from the ceiling.

"Better put something warm on, Adinda. We're not in the lowlands now."

"*Saja, tuan,* but I like it cool. It makes me feel full of life, better than in Kerang Sawah."

"You like it here, then?"

"*Saja, tuan,* I would like it anywhere if you were there."

"You are a very dear girl, Adinda, you have never said one word of regret about leaving your home, though I knew it was hard."

"Harder, *tuan,* to stay without you."

René thought the "Song of Ruth" must have been written for Adinda.

"Whither thou goest, I will go;

Where thou diest, I will die,

And there will be buried."[32]

"Someday, Adinda, I will teach you to read a great book. There is a song in there about you."

"About me?" she laughed. "How funny! Have you the book here? Let me get it now, *tuan.*"

---

32 Condensed from the Holy Bible, Ruth 1:15-17, King James Version:

[5] And she said, Behold, thy sister in law is gone back unto her people, and unto her gods: return thou after thy sister in law.

[16] And Ruth said, Intreat me not to leave thee, or to return from following after thee: for whither thou goest, I will go; and where thou lodgest, I will lodge: thy people shall be my people, and thy God my God:

[17] Where thou diest, will I die, and there will I be buried: the Lord do so to me, and more also, if ought but death part thee and me.

"I keep it always in my trunk," René answered. "I'm afraid I don't read it often enough. Someday I will bring it out and read you the 'Song of Ruth,' but tell me what you have been doing today."

She told him the day's doings, though he slept in his chair and did not hear.

"Come, *tuan*," she roused him, "you must go to bed."

When ready for bed, asleep almost as soon as his head touched the pillow, René was conscious of gentle, loving hands tucking the blanket about him. This was what kept Adinda happy, the quiet evenings with her *tuan*, the night, her hours of delight.

As the work grew heavier René had to stay away from home several evenings at a time, often having to take the night shift himself. Another employee, Rudolf Homan, who lived with his sister Anna at the other end of the great estate, about sixteen miles from René's home, shared the night shift with him. Rudolf was his own age, of European stock, although born in Buitenzorg, where his mother and other sisters lived.

At midnight one night René gave the work over to Rudolf and set out on his horse for home. It was a beautiful night; no moon, but the high deep dome above him was studded with myriads of stars, stars only the tropics can boast of, very bright and seemingly very near. The Southern Cross glowed high in the heavens, keeping watch with twinkling eyes over the sleeping, mysterious land.

René rode with slackened rein. His horse would keep the road better than his master, knowing well every turn of the way. René loved to ride this way—alone with creation. To the left, far down the mountain slope, the hazy valley was shrouded in a white veil of mist, but with miles and miles

Straight ahead of him soared the mighty peak of the still active volcano Gedeh, sending out occasional puffs of smoke and red-hot stones.

of palms making a veritable sea of green, with here and there a twinkling light suggesting life. Straight ahead of him soared the mighty peak of the still active volcano Gedeh, sending out occasional puffs of smoke and red-hot stones.[33] A flare against the dark velvet of the sky, a rumbling from the bowels of the earth, a whorl of ruddy smoke—over and over again, until one ceased to fear any greater disturbances from the giant.

To the right, the jungle, dark and threatening, reached almost to the mouth of the burned-out crater Salak. Strange noises came from the woods, the wild shriek of a monkey frightened in its sleep, the startling call of the *toetoel*, and

---

33 Mount Gede, or Gunung Gede, forms one peak of a twin volcano rising to 9,700 ft southwest of Bogor. Though observers have recorded volcanic activity there since the 16th century, the volcano is not seen at risk of producing a large eruption. That said, the major cities of Cianjur, Sukabumi and Bogor are quite close, with a total local population of roughly three million people.

René began to whistle, softly but clearly, an air from the opera *Faust*.

other weird cries which could not be identified. As an overtone, there was the rhythmical splashing of many waterfalls—a music that seemed to soothe the rumbling within the earth.

Then a lisping wind blew down from the harsh forest, singing a new song for René's attuned ears. This, surely, was the harmony of the whirling sphere, and he was at one with it. Life was almost too good.

He threw his head back to watch the blinking stars. His horse, slowed to a walk, seemed to catch his master's mood. René began to whistle, softly but clearly, an air from the opera *Faust*.[34] It helped him to express the inward exultation that possessed him; he made of it a hymn of praise. Never had he felt nearer to his Creator. Under the star-studded dome, his spirit took wings. This, he felt, was the moment and the place in which to give thanks, to be filled with beauty and love.

The reins slipped from his hands as, still with his gaze upward, he mused about the many happenings of his life in Java—Betty, Alfred, Kerang Sawah, Adolf, Daisy and Adinda—yes, Adinda, ever Adinda! His horse went slower and slower while René's thoughts dwelt on his little *njai*. She would be sleeping by this time, worn out with waiting for her *tuan*, curled up on the bed like a weary child, a beautiful picture. At his coming she would rouse just enough to make him feel he was not alone in this lovely world.

---

34 The German legend of Faust has inspired numerous books, plays, poems, songs, artworks and operas since the late 16th century. The tale is based on the historical figure, Johann Georg Faust (c. 1480–1540), an alchemist, astrologer and magician well-known in his time.

In the story, Faust is a highly successful man, but remains dissatisfied with his life. Upon meeting the Devil (called Mephistopheles) he makes a pact exchanging his soul for access to unlimited knowledge and worldly pleasures. The adjective "Faustian" is therefore used to describe situations where an ambitious person surrenders their integrity to gain some measure of power, fame, wealth or success.

The horse took the steep hill with steady step. Now on either side, close to the road, stretched the tea gardens, the short bushes touching each other. Horse and rider seemed alone, shut in by fields of green with only the road winding like a narrow ribbon up hill and down dale.

With a sudden short jerk, the great white horse came to a stop, rearing in terror and whinnying pitifully and trembling. René tried to grasp the reins too late. He slipped from the saddle and went sliding off the horse's back, catching sight as he fell of two brilliant green spots staring at him from under the tea bushes. He landed in the road with a bounce, raised himself quickly on one arm only to see those steely eyes shining at him sharply.

It seemed an eternity that he looked into the menacing points of light. Then he sprang to his feet, the eyes withdrew, and the rustling of the leaves told that the prowler had fled. Unsteadily René walked to his horse's head. The sleek animal stood as though rooted in the soil, his nostrils quivering, his eyes protruding, too frightened to run.

"Well, my boy!" René spoke soothingly. "We had a narrow escape that time. Come on, old fellow, the danger's past for the present anyway."

With much petting and talking he persuaded the terrified horse to take a few steps. René jumped into the saddle and, still unsteadily, they traveled on, master and horse with eyes and ears alert. Then, gaining courage, the horse gained speed. Faster and faster it went, as though to put as many miles as possible between itself and the place where it had seen those burning eyes.

René did not object. Now, however, he kept the reins well in hand. At home he found Adinda fast asleep. He wanted to talk to her, sure of her sympathy over his fright, but she appeared too peaceful to awaken.

Adinda was more attractive now than when she had first come to him; she was about nineteen and at the peak of her beauty and youth. In a very few years she would age, as did the women of her race, although René did not think of this as he watched her soft bosom rise and fall while she slept.

A smile of happiness curved his lips as he made ready for bed, quietly for fear of waking the sleeping girl. How safe this home was, how sheltered and protected he felt after his dangerous ride.

28

Rudolf, Anna, Oerip and...

WORK IN THE TEA GARDEN, while exacting and more or less of a routine, was nevertheless absorbing. René found the responsibility satisfying. As he rode on his tall white horse through the gardens the women, bending over the picking, kept one eye open for their young *tuan,* admiring him while they served him. He was always kind to them, and jolly, depending upon them to make his efforts a success.

There was peace seemingly in his bamboo house, set on its high cliff on the edge of the jungle. René told himself over and over that this was living, putting from his mind the picture of Daisy Vermeer in her flopping hat covered with roses.

Outside of business he had little to do with his manager, Mr. Inger. He lived with his *njai* in a very nice place some miles from René, but he never entertained the young Hollander. The only time René went there was after work to report on the progress of the business. Inger had one hobby, photography, and to this he devoted all his spare hours.

René was not sorry; he had much more in common with Rudolf Homan. They were both great lovers of nature, and René went often to the delightful Homan place to visit. Anna

As he rode on his tall white horse through the gardens the women, bending over the picking, kept one eye open for their young tuan, admiring him while they served him.

Inger had one hobby, photography, and to this he devoted all his spare hours.

Homan was a jolly, hospitable sort of a girl, so homely she made a joke of it; but compensating for this was her beautiful spirit of understanding, of cheer, quick wit and service. Her home was a bit of Holland itself and a revelation to the men who were entertained there; her homekeeping an art, her meals delicious and daintily served, her many servants handled with consummate skill.

Rudolf, because he lived with his sister, kept no *njai* in his home, but he did keep a small house in the village, where his *njai* lived. René expressed himself to Rudolf one day while talking this over.

"It does not seem fair to Anna—does she know about Oerip?"

"Yes," Rudolf answered, "Anna knows all about her. It doesn't seem just fair, does it? But if I had my way I would

René went often to the delightful Homan place to visit. Anna Homan was a jolly, hospitable sort of a girl, so homely she made a joke of it.

have Oerip at the head of my household. Mother insists that Anna keep house for me, so there I am. What can I do?"

"You don't need a *njai* with such a sister to look after you."

Rudolf shrugged his shoulders. "Well, I have her,—a baby girl, also. What do you say to that?"

"Does Anna know that, too?"

"Yes. She's a brick—she has never told Mother. She sews for the baby,—what is more, loves her."

René was astonished. "Does Oerip care for you, Rudolf?"

"Care for me?" Rudolf repeated. "She's crazy about me. She loves me so much she would never hear of my marrying a white girl; she'd poison me first. You must meet her, René, she is a fine girl. Come home with me to dinner tonight. Later I'll take you over to see 'Mrs. Homan' and the baby."

René was troubled all day over what Rudolf had told him. How unfair the whole thing was to Oerip and the baby! The problem that had slumbered for months again reared an ugly head. His own net seemed to draw closer about him; it hurt him ever so little.

At dinner time Anna greeted him with warmth. She soothed by her very presence, she made life real again, she fed his mind as well as his body.

"You spoil us fellows," René told her.

"I must do something to make life worthwhile," she said laughingly. "I'm a blot on the landscape at home."

"You are an angel of mercy, Anna. When I am here, it is like being in Holland. I rather imagine you hold us back from many evil things." René's voice took on seriousness. "Somehow our values get jumbled. Tropical life is so difficult for a white man."

"I know," Anna comforted, taking in Rudolf with her kind glance. "I have often doubted the wisdom of sending very young men out here. For me, it is the only thing."

"No, no, Anna," Rudolf interrupted. "You shan't be permitted to stay here all your life—too many limitations."

"Well, anyway," his sister responded as she rose from the table, "I'm here until you find a blind man to marry me."

And though she laughed merrily, René noticed she sought a shaded corner in the living room. Thus shielded she dominated the lively chat, her rich, mellow voice coming pleasantly from out the semi-darkness. Later she bade the men *bonne nuit* and went to her room.

"She's a dear girl, Rudolf."

"Yes, René, she is. She'd make a glorious wife for some man, but come on, let's go to the village before Oerip gets to bed."

They found Oerip still up, playing with the baby.

They found Oerip still up, playing with the baby, while the grandmother, a woman of fifty—old for a Javanese,—watched their frolic with evident pleasure. Oerip's eyes sparkled at Rudolf. She acknowledged René with a pretty gesture of welcome. He compared her with Adinda much to Oerip's disadvantage; though petite and dainty she was not intelligent and charming, as Adinda was. There could be no ties of the mind between her and Rudolf; she had, however, bound him by the strongest of all ties. There was no denying the parenthood of the baby girl, she was so like Rudolf in every feature. Oerip had an air of assurance because of this.

Rudolf was booked for life in the interior, René reflected, but he was not as sorry for him as for the baby, whose life was doomed to be unhappy. Why, he wondered, did the white man look down upon a race he himself had produced? The natives, too, did the same, leaving the mixed bloods to stand alone. They were between the devil and the deep blue sea. René did not enjoy the visit.

Much serious thinking and hard work tended to sober René's buoyancy. As the months went by Adinda noticed this. She searched her brain for some fresh service for her *tuan*, something to bring back his merry laugh and happy, carefree air. She studied the harder, reading prettily to him in the evenings. Her mind unfolded like a flower. René was delighted and surprised at the beautiful thoughts her reading brought out.

"And the big book in your trunk, *tuan*, when do we read that?"

"It is about my God, Adinda; would you care to read it?"

It was then she amazed him by her reply. "Your God, *tuan*, and mine. But one Allah made the world, the stars, you, and me. What difference does a name make? You love God, I love Allah—all the same. Is it not true, *tuan?*"

René put one hand tenderly on her glossy hair.

"You are wise, Adinda."

"Love has made me so, *tuan*"

With almost a sob he lifted her in his arms, not speaking—but thinking, thinking!

29

An apt little pupil

ADINDA, sitting on her mat on the wide veranda, was busily mending her *tuan's* clothes. Her house was clean and orderly, herself a picture in her white linen jacket, with lace at her throat, and the gay batik *sarong* drawn close about her rounded figure.

Rudolf Homan drove into the yard. Adinda slipped quickly into the house. She must not be seen by a stranger, although she knew Oerip very well and went often to visit her, playing with the baby or caring for her while Oerip went to market. René seldom called Adinda in when there were visitors, and of course she could not come unless he did.

Rudolf called loudly for René again and again. When he received no answer Adinda came out on the veranda, much against conventions.

"*Tuan* René is at the stables," she told him.

Rudolf did not move. The sight of Adinda's beauty astonished him. He had never seen her before and could only stare in admiration.

"Where is your master?"

"At the stables," she told him again, then squatted quickly on the floor. Even in her position as René's *njai* she did not forget the respect due the white man bred in her through ages of submission, first to the native rulers, then to the Hollanders.

"Shall I call *tuan* René?" she asked, "or will you go to the stables?"

"Go call him!" Rudolf spoke in quick and short tones, regarding Adinda as a servant merely. He prided himself on keeping these people in their places.

"Yes, *tuan*," Adinda smiled.

Rudolf dismounted, tied his horse to a post and came up to the veranda and seated himself in an easy chair. Here René greeted him with outstretched hand.

"This is quite an honor, Rudolf. In all the time I've lived here you have never visited me."

"No, I'm a lazy chap, René. Being born here makes us as easy going as the natives. I sometimes envy you the way you go about your work, full of life and ambition. By the way, I compliment you on your little 'wife.' She is cute as can be, and pretty. Better watch out, René—if the boss sees her you'll lose her."

René resented this. "Please, Rudolf, do not speak so loud. Adinda understands Dutch very well."

"What!" exclaimed Rudolf. "She understands Dutch!"

"Yes, she does; speaks and reads it also."

"Well, that beats everything I ever heard. Did you teach her?"

"Why, of course I did. During the long evenings to gether I not only taught her that, but many other things. It makes life much pleasanter for both of us. She is very bright and learns quickly."

"Say, old chap, if all the white men did that with their *njais* what would become of this island? The more they know, the more independent they are. I'll never teach my *njai*, I assure you."

"She couldn't learn, she's too dumb," was René's thought, disliking Rudolf's manner.

"Call her out and let me hear a little of this grand work of yours," Rudolf suggested.

René called in Dutch, "Adinda, please bring the cigars."

In her own language she responded, "Forgive me, *tuan*, I am not dressed. I cannot come."

Rudolf smiled, as though to say. "Independent—you can't fool me."

René called again, a friendly call without any touch of command, "Well, dress quickly and come out."

"Just a few moments, *tuan*, then I will come."

The men sat in silence while Adinda dressed. When she came she was in her best, the finest white linen jacket, exquisite lace about her neck and sleeves, a rich *sarong* of batik falling about her slender ankles. She paused an instant in the doorway, a picture of loveliness framed in bamboo. Two pairs of eyes told her she was beautiful; no woman ever received this homage more gracefully than did little Adinda. A swift glance from her brown eyes, then her long lashes swept her cheeks as she waited for René to bid her come nearer. Rudolf could only stare, forgetting his manners.

"Have you the cigars?" René asked her in Dutch. Quickly she took the cue and responded in the same language, "Yes, *tuan*, I have them."

"Very well, bring them here and sit next to my chair while you tell *tuan* Homan what you know of his language."

She was quite willing to show off, not only because of her own pride but to let Rudolf see how much René had done for her. She did it in a sweet and simple, though dignified, manner, never once forgetting herself.

Rudolf listened, dumfounded. Adinda led the conversation, talking about the work and the narrow escape René had had with the tiger. Her winning dimples came and went, her musical voice flowed on, while René enjoyed Rudolf's amazement.

"Isn't she an apt little pupil?" he asked.

"Say, old man," Rudolf replied, "that is the sweetest thing I have heard in a long time. I admire you for what you have done for your little beauty."

Adinda bowed her head in great confusion.

"I believe I'll try it with my Oerip—only she's so dumb I can't imagine her learning a language."

Adinda caught René's look of approval. They smiled at each other, well pleased over her performance. Shy, now that she had done her part, she asked permission to go to her room.

René gave it, then turned to Rudolf. "Anything particular about your visit?"

"Yes, indeed, old man. I just came from the boss—what do you think he said?"

René laughed. "Oh, he wants to raise our salaries! Is that it?"

"No, not that, but almost as good. He wants us to go to Buitenzorg for the week end, thinks a little holiday would please us. The rain made the gardens too wet to work in just now, anyway."

"That's bully, Rudolf! When do we go?"

"Right away. If you dress quickly we can be in town by dinner time. We have to be back for roll call Monday morning."

"Just order my horse saddled while I dress, will you?" And René hurried inside.

To Adinda he said: "I'm riding into Buitenzorg for a weekend visit. Do you mind, girl?"

"Surely not, *tuan*. You have worked hard and need a change. But do be careful. You know I am still here."

He smiled into her eyes. "I shan't forget, Adinda."

When ready to go, he did not kiss her—he never had. The caress was unknown to the Javanese. She took his hand, held it to her cheek affectionately; this was quite enough for her. Suddenly René thought of Daisy—would this have been her farewell to him? He knew it would not—there would have been long, lingering kisses; Daisy in his arms. A gulf seemed to widen between his *njai* and himself.

"And now what will you do while I am gone? I don't want you to stay here alone."

"I will visit Saina, *tuan*. She will be happy to have me." Saina was the wife of one of René's *mandoers* and a good friend to Adinda.

"Fine! I say, girl, I was proud of you today! Now, goodbye, don't worry about me."

He was gone in a whirl. Both young men dashed out of the yard on their spirited horses, René waving his *topie*. A turn in the road hid them from Adinda's eyes. Perhaps, she mused, he will laugh when he comes back.

30

Those three ladies with the fire-eaters...

RUDOLF AND RENÉ kept up their mad pace for miles. Like two boys just released from school, they reveled in their freedom. They laughed and sang, sending their horses recklessly down steep hills, planning what they would do in the city, enough joys for a week instead of two days. When the white foam flew from their horses' flanks they drew rein—slowly now, stirrup to stirrup, talking in quiet tones.

The road led through a dense forest, so thick at times as to obscure the sun. It was deliciously cool in these natural avenues of tropical verdure. Here and there were open patches where the sun's rays poured through the thinner layers of green as in a Spanish cathedral. Tempered mysterious lights played on the leaves, while gorgeously colored parrots flitted from branch to branch, uttering guttural sounds, as though talking to each other. Little gray monkeys peeped out at the travelers; huge, brilliant butterflies fluttered from the great streams of orchids; a tall stately deer crossed their path, eyeing them quietly without fear. Crystal-clear mountain streams made music near-by.

The men became silent, thrilled by the beauty and stillness about them and the
peace in this great place as yet untouched by man.

Out of the heavy timber at last, they came into a small clearing
where some enterprising natives had built their homes.

The men became silent, thrilled by the beauty and stillness about them and the peace in this great place as yet untouched by man.

Out of the heavy timber at last, they came into a small clearing where some enterprising natives had built their homes. These were charcoal burners, usually the first men to penetrate into the jungle. They carried huge loads of charcoal in baskets hung from either end of a yoke fastened to their backs. This was taken into the city to be sold for use in the kitchens.

Again the riders entered forests where every shrub fought for sunlight. René broke the long silence.

"Why didn't you bring Anna along? This would be a fine trip for her."

"Oh, no, she doesn't care for horseback riding. The road's too rough for a carriage. She won't mind being alone, she likes to read. Then she loves my baby girl too much to leave her."

"Do you, Rudolf?"

It was an unexpected question. Rudolf pondered before answering.

"It may sound strange, René—it's an awful thing to say—but I don't care for that youngster. I don't care for Oerip, either."

"Whether you do or not," René's voice was stern, "you must look after them. It's a rotten way to live. I don't feel right about this thing—those poor native girls and that helpless child. You must take good care of them, no matter how you feel."

"You can say that, because you love Adinda. She is very beautiful and very intelligent."

"Look here, Rudolf, I can't say I love Adinda. I have a great affection for her. I loved—really loved—once. I know what it is. But East is East and West is West—I can't forget it. I hate myself. I am often cool to Adinda, and yet never a girl served a man more wonderfully."

"Oh, come, René, let's forget our *njais* and enjoy ourselves. This is a pleasure trip."

They sped along and soon entered the city. Rudolf went to his home, while René went to the Bellevue, the finest hotel in Buitenzorg.[35] The majordomo gave him a room, the windows of which had a splendid view of mountains and winding river so close he could hear the laughter of the bathers.

---

35   Built by the Dutch government in 1856 to house official visitors, it was originally named the Dibbets Hotel after its founder, J. Dibbets. Later it became known as the Binnenhof (which means courtyard, in Dutch) or the Bellevue.

René went to the Bellevue, the finest hotel in Buitenzorg.
The majordomo gave him a room, the windows of which had a splendid view of
mountains and winding river…

...so close he could hear the laughter of the bathers.

A cool bath and fresh white linen clothes made a different man of him. With the donning of city dress his manners took on the polish he was accustomed to. As he stepped into the reception hall and looked about for a possible chance acquaintance he was as remote from Adinda as the skies. Subconsciously this troubled him always. He lived a double life, and this was against his nature.

Two men strolled in from the garden, one much the worse for liquor.

"I declare," the latter exclaimed loudly, "can this be my old friend René? Is it really you?"

"You're too drunk to recognize me, Louis," taunted René.

"Oh, no, never too drunk for that. Hit me with a brick, I do believe it is René van Landsberg!" He took René's hand, shaking it vigorously. "And how is Betty?" he sang out.

"She threw me over years ago," was the laughing answer. "Can't you think of something cheerful to say?"

"Meet my friend, George van Horn, René. He's working on the same plantation I am."

René acknowledged the introduction and the three men moved towards the great table in the center of the hall where, as was the custom, stood a large decanter full of Dutch gin and a smaller bottle of bitters. They mixed their drinks and sat down to enjoy a bit of gossip. Louis Bartels, with whom René had spent his boyhood, told of his life in Java, and listened to René's story in return.

"Tell me, Louis, what did become of Betty? I've never heard."

"She went to school, made her debut about a year ago. Haven't you gotten over that yet, René?"

"Oh, yes, long ago. I just wanted to know what she was doing."

Rudolf Homan stepped into the hall and René hailed him, introducing his two companions and saying, "Four is a fine number. Let's go in to dinner."

One long table was spread in the dining room, individual tables being as yet unknown there. The four men were seated at one end and made things lively at once. They had all drunk too much, nevertheless René ordered champagne. That gone, Rudolf ordered another bottle, Louis followed suit and, not to be outdone, George van Horn demanded the fourth. With much hilarious talk by the four hotheads dinner was consumed, to the amusement of the other guests.

"Now, boys," spoke up George, "there's a circus in town. Let's go."

**One long table was spread in the dining room,
individual tables being as yet unknown there.**

His proposal was hailed with delight. They sought the big tent and secured seats in the first row, making so much noise the native policeman came three times to quiet them. The last time René sobered up; he was too much a gentleman to relish being made an object of comment. His eyes roamed over the audience—a shock ran through him. Just across from him in one of the boxes sat Daisy Vermeer. She was with two men in uniforms of officers of the Colonial Army, a man in a tuxedo, and two ladies. René became quite himself immediately.

At last he asked, "Say, boys, do you know that party over there, third box from the entrance?"

"You mean those three ladies with the fire-eaters? Well, I don't know them, they're too highbrow for me. I'm only a poor planter," Louis replied.

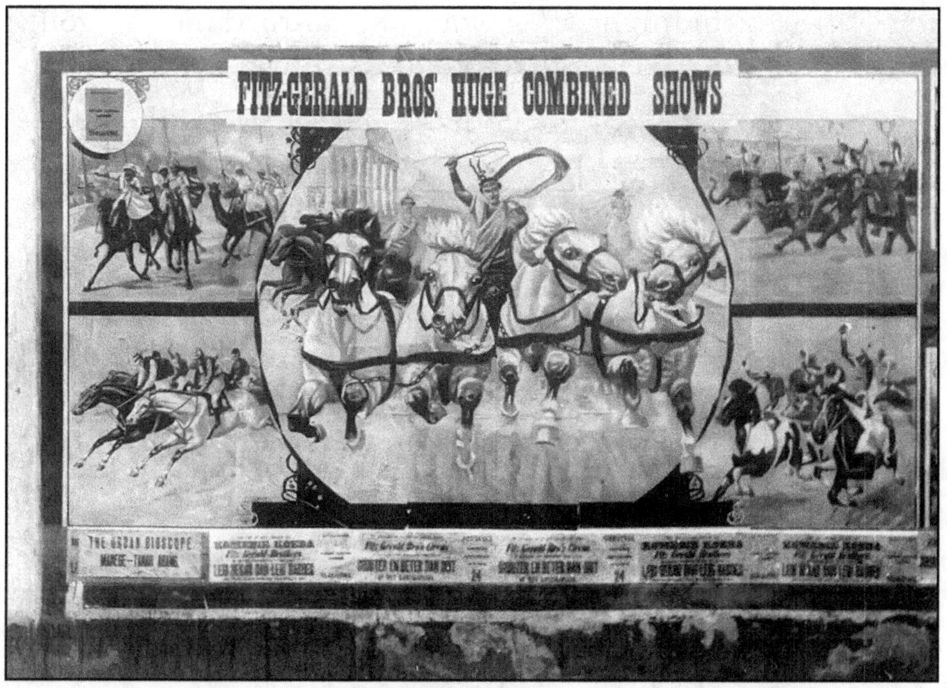

"Now, boys," spoke up George, "there's a circus in town. Let's go."

"Let's go," René suggested. "I've had enough of this." On the way out, he tried to catch Daisy's eye. She was, however, too absorbed in the handsome officer by her side to notice anyone else.

"And now where?" asked Louis.

"If it's the same to you boys," Rudolf stifled a yawn, "I'm going home to bed. I'm dead tired after that long ride. Isn't anything else to do anyway."

George van Horn laughed scornfully.

"Nothing else to do! Of course there is—come with me to the *kampong.*"

"Not on your life," the other three men objected vigorously.

"You poor dumbheads! Your *njais* won't let you, is that it? Imagine coming in from the bush for a good time, and going to bed before midnight. Well, you can't railroad me. I'm going down there alone," George roared boastfully.

"No, you're not, George." Louis seized his friend by the arm. "You're coming to my room. We'll have a game of poker, if you like. But to hell with disgracing yourself with the women of the *kampong*."

George raved on, until his companions finally dragged him to Louis's room. It was three o'clock before the party broke up. René lost more than he could afford, but decided not to worry. He did not allow himself to worry very often, and least of all about money.

31

The Homan house

RENÉ SLEPT LITTLE AND LIGHTLY. At seven o'clock
the next morning, he was up and on the veranda. In answer
to his call, a native servant brought him coffee. In front of
him stretched a majestic panorama. The sun stood high, but
the mountains were only faintly visible, being obscured by
the vapors rising from the moist forests. The volcano Gedeh
emitted a flattened cloud of white smoke. The palm trees
close by shone like silver.

The lad sipped his coffee. He felt very fit; a little short of
sleep, it was true, but with a clear head and a contented heart.
Champagne, after all, was a good drink. He did not care for
breakfast, preferring to stay outside and enjoy the glorious
view, a spectacle thousands of tourists would have been
willing to travel from the four corners of the earth to see.

He leaned back in his rocker, and suddenly he recalled that
Daisy Vermeer had been at the circus the night before. So she
hadn't gone to Makassar, as she had thought she would.

"I wonder if she is engaged to that fire-eater?" he mused.
"The fellow certainly looked at her as if he wanted to carry
her off. Funny how girls fall for shining buttons! She looked
quite happy, too. Well—I don't care a damn!" Having settled

233

The sun stood high, but the mountains were only faintly visible, being obscured by the vapors rising from the moist forests.

the point, he arose and went out to the swimming pool. A plunge into the chilly water restored his vigor, and drove away the last trace of drowsiness.

Rudolf was waiting for him when he returned to the hotel. "Hello, old man, how are you feeling? But I don't have to ask; you look handsomer than ever. Had a fine time, didn't we? I'm only sorry you lost so much," Rudolf remarked.

"Oh, forget it! I'll make that up in a jiffy—it was worth the fun," René answered. "If we had a crowd of the boys on our plantation, we'd enjoy a good game oftener. But what are we doing today? I must see the botanical gardens."[36]

---

36 Founded by the government of the Dutch East Indies in 1817, the 210 acre garden now contains roughly 14,000 different kinds of plants and trees. It remains a top attraction today, attracting tourists as well as botanists and biologists from around the world.

"I must see the botanical gardens."

"That's one of the things I have in mind. Mother wants you over for dinner at one, and then we'll all go in the carriage to the gardens."

"Bully! Do I have to meet your sisters? I may not know how to behave in a flock of educated young white girls."

"Surely, you must meet them. Anna has told them so much about you, they are all eager to see you. I'll throw you out if you don't do the right thing."

**"Talk about everything and anything at home, but for the love of heaven
keep off the *njai* question."**

On the way to the Homan house, Rudolf added: "Talk about everything and anything at home, but for the love of heaven keep off the *njai* question. Mother has a fierce hate of it. You can't explain it to her, nor to most white women for that matter.

Mother loves to get hold of an unspoiled youngster like you. She'll tell you how wrong it is."

"Never mind, Rudolf. It *is* wrong, and I know it, but there seems to be no other way of living in the interior. It's a pretty serious problem, however you look at it."

René stayed with the Homans the rest of the day. They made much of it, and he enjoyed himself to the full. After dinner, the whole family took him out in an open carriage drawn by two tall, black Australian horses. The party spent several hours in the famous botanical gardens, driving through avenue after avenue bordered with rarest tropical trees and shrubs, and finishing up with a visit to the palace

…finishing up with a visit to the palace of the Governor General
of the Dutch East Indies.

of the Governor General of the Dutch East Indies. They then returned to the Homan residence for supper.

As Mrs. Homan said goodbye to René, she took his hand. "I am so glad Anna is with Rudolf. He will not be tempted by native women so long as she keeps such a good home for him. I am happy, too, to know that you do not live like some of the men out here. Rudolf has told me how fine you are. Please come to see us again."

It was a dark, lonely ride back, but the boys preferred it to getting up at four in the morning and riding fast and furiously, in order to report for their jobs on time. As they left the city, René turned his head for a final glance at the twinkling lights. Somewhere down there, Daisy was smiling at her handsome officer. For an instant, he had a mind to go back, hunt her up and look once more into her eyes. But he shrugged the impulse aside.

"You won the family," Rudolf told him, as after a stiff gallop they slowed their horses to a walk. "It's hard to say who liked you best, Mother or the girls."

René chuckled. "It was a new lease of life to be with white folks again."

"Yes, wasn't it? I wonder why we bury ourselves in the interior. But, my God, René, I'm in deeper than you are."

"There's no denying that," René answered soberly.

It was pitch dark when they entered the jungle. René thought of his last midnight ride and kept a sharp lookout, with his reins well in hand. The horses were nervous. In the open again, they began to climb the foothills, the lights of Buitenzorg far below them, and to the left Gedeh tossing red-hot stones into the sky. They stopped talking by mutual consent, and mused about those dear to them until they came to the parting of the roads. Rudolf turned to the right, with eleven miles to go, while René kept straight ahead for the half-hour's ride to his home.

"*Tabe, tabe*," Rudolf called.

"So long, old chap, I had a fine time."

René handed a very tired horse over to his stable boy and went into the house. No one greeted him, and everything was dark. Lighting a candle, he sought Adinda. She was not there, her bed had not been slept in. She must have stayed with Saina, he thought; but how unlike her that was, since she was expecting him home. He found the house dismal and quiet after his comfortable room at the hotel and the Homan's beautiful place.

A door creaked on its hinges. He heard the pattering of feet, and Adinda was in his arms.

René handed a very tired horse over to his stable boy and went into the house.

"*Tuan, tuan,* you are safe! I was afraid!" She clung to him, panting.

"But why? Why, dear girl?"

"The tiger! *Tuan,* he is here, somewhere close, just outside. He prowled about the house last night. I saw him through the shutters an hour ago. I have been watching, watching, and waiting to call to you not to come nearer. Oh, *tuan,* he might have killed you!"

Then, for the first time in her life, Adinda fainted.

René put her tenderly upon his bed, opened the shutters for more air, knelt by her side and chafed her cold hands. Slowly, her eyelids parted. When she saw the open shutters, she cried in alarm:

"Close them! Quickly, *tuan!* Quickly, quickly!"

At her wild warning, he turned just in time to see the great tiger slinking away toward the jungle. He fastened the shutters, and knelt beside the frightened girl.

"You are always watching over me, Adinda."

He pressed his face against her soft shoulder. Her trembling hands stroked his hair. She smiled now, almost too happy to break the sweet silence.

"I always will, *tuan,* always, always! Even in the life hereafter, I shall be thinking of you—maybe!" She laughed a little at her fancy. "Perhaps I could fly down to be near you, as a butterfly on your shoulder with golden wings and tiny eyes."

"Hush, child, hush! I don't deserve you, my little guardian angel."

She slept at last, while he kept vigil, moved beyond words by her love and devotion.

32

"A dead tiger is of little importance..."

AT EIGHT THE NEXT MORNING, the tea gardens were teeming with workers. René with one of his *mandoers* went first to a newly cleared patch of jungle where some young tea plants were to be set out. It was a delicate job, for the plants wilt and die unless carefully shielded and watered. He rode his horse over the new road, the *mandoer* keeping to the path on the edge of the jungle.

Nearly one hundred women were busy at the field, setting out the tender plants in the freshly-dug holes. The men carried the plants from the nursery beds, using large flat baskets which were swung on yokes across their shoulders.

It was a busy scene. René, remaining on horseback stationed himself on a little knoll where he could easily overlook the work. The *mandoer*, rifle in hand, was sitting on a tree stump, talking with one of his helpers.

Suddenly, there was a crashing of bushes, a roar from an animal's throat, a piercing yell from a man in agony, and only then a shot. René pressed the spurs into his horse and dashed over to the place where the *mandoer* had been sitting. The

Nearly one hundred women were busy at the field, setting out the tender plants in the freshly-dug holes.

poor fellow lay unconscious, face downward. His jacket was torn to shreds, his back was ploughed deeply by the sharp claws of a tiger. Yet he had fired in time to get the huge beast, which lay dead at his side.

The women were fleeing in all directions, and the men had thrown down their baskets in confusion. Gradually, the latter gathered about the wounded *mandoer*. The women, assured of the tiger's death, drew nearer.

René ordered a stretcher made of young saplings from the jungle. Fresh leaves were spread over this, and the *mandoer* was lifted carefully upon it. Four of the sturdiest men acted as bearers, and he was carried to René's house, where Adinda attended to his wounds. The fellow was in great pain, but his hurts were not mortal. The tiger, also, was triumphantly brought in. Everyone was rejoicing, for all felt sure this was

Yet he had fired in time to get the huge beast, which lay dead at his side.

the same tiger which had stalked René on his midnight ride and frightened Adinda the past two nights.

Sitting on the veranda with her that evening, René said: "I'm glad the tiger is disposed of. He scared you so!"

"But a dead tiger is of little importance," Adinda answered. "Did you enjoy the city, *tuan,* and—and your friends?"

René smiled in the dusk. "I passed some gay hours in Buitenzorg, but this is better. You don't know how lucky you are, girl, to live always in this beautiful country. You never think of getting away, and where ignorance is bliss—"

He interrupted himself, and Adinda looked up quickly, not comprehending. "*Saja, tuan*",' she murmured.

"Now, just think," René continued, not really speaking to Adinda. "What did I do that was worthwhile with all the hours I spent in town? I drank a lot, played cards and lost money, saw a circus that didn't mean a thing to me, gossiped with some white girls—and that's all. When you come right down to it, what did I accomplish?"

"*Saja, tuan.*"

René was fairly launched on a diatribe. Some of his inner struggle had boiled over; it was good to relieve himself, even if the girl at his side knew little of what he was saying:

"Civilization is so bred into our race, there is no forgetting it. It keeps drawing us and drawing us until we join the city mob, become one of many doing whatever everyone else does, not daring to be an individual, stifling one's inmost desires and making money—only to spend it. As far as I'm concerned, I don't want to be a money-getter if I must give up such beauty as Java holds."

At the word "money," Adinda was on her feet, quick as a deer. She had but half understood her *tuans* discourse, but she did know the meaning of that weighty word, "money."

"I hope you will never make much money, *tuan*. If you do, you will go away, as the others do. No white man with money stays in our country. They come here to use Java, and then leave it."

How clearly she had thought it out! René was astonished at her intelligence.

"You are right, girl. That is the trouble here. No one takes a real interest in the country. Everyone thinks only of himself, grabs all he can and leaves—and let the newcomers do the worrying!" He leaned towards her, speaking with conviction: "Never fear, Adinda, I am far from leaving. You have been a wonderful *njai*. If there were many more like you, our men would stay here and this would become one of the greatest countries in the world. I know that my success is due to you."

"Oh, *tuan,* you make me so happy!"

"You deserve it, child."

René stared towards the mountains, his pose an oddly prophetic one as his hand rested on the glossy hair of the girl at his feet.

33

Saina and the *mandoer*

WORK ON THE TJIDANI ESTATE WENT ON, one day very much like another. Orders for tea had come in and there was no time for holidays. Inger and his employees had hunted a few times, just a few hours snatched from the regular schedule. Overseeing the night shift was divided among the three men; even so, René had to be at work every morning. Not accustomed to night duty he was soon fagged out. It happened many a time that he was too tired to eat after hearing the day's report. Instead he went to bed as soon as the *mandoers* had lifted their heels. Adinda, fearful of disturbing him, slept on her little mat on the floor.

"You must not do this, girl, it is too uncomfortable there," René would remonstrate.

"*Saja, tuan,*" she smilingly replied, glad he noticed her sacrifice.

She missed the long leisure hours they had had together at the sugar factory. To fill in the day she visited in the *kampong*, sometimes with Saina, but more often with Oerip. Neither of these women understood Adinda. Saina born and bred in this mountain region, married early to a native, thought only as a native, felt as a native. She sought Adinda's friendship for

Since her husband was René's *mandoer* **Saina felt she might further his promotion by keeping close to Adinda.**

several reasons, one being the *njai's* nearness to René. Since her husband was René's *mandoer* Saina felt she might further his promotion by keeping close to Adinda. She was eight or nine years older than Adinda. Because of this she felt free to advise the younger girl.

Sitting in Saina's house one afternoon, Adinda happily playing with Saina's youngest, the conversation easily drifted to children. Both women spoke in the mountain dialect, although Adinda threw in a Dutch word occasionally, artfully sure of the supremacy this gave her.

Saina said, working carefully on a fine piece of batik, "You love children, Adinda; you should get yourself one or two."

Adinda smiled, catching the laughing baby to her. "So easy as that, Saina?"

"Yes, why not? You should see to it that your nice *tuan* does not leave you. You are too sweet a girl to be left alone when he is through with you."

"You must not talk that way to me, Saina. My *tuan* has no thought of leaving me."

"You cannot tell," was the wise answer, "what those white ones are thinking. But I can get you some magic medicine from old Grandmother Dassam. It will bind him to you forever."

"No, no, Saina!" Adinda looked up quickly. "I do not need anything to bind my *tuan* to me. You do not know how kind he is, how good."

"I do know, child, how quickly they change—like lightning. The white man who was here before your *tuan* came was good, too. When his *njai* felt he was growing tired of her she got strong medicine from Grandmother Dassam—now they have two children and are very happy. By that medicine she bound him to stay with her always."

"Oh, Saina, don't you know a medicine cannot make love?"

"Love? What do you mean? I don't ever hear that word. It may be there is no medicine to make that. I mean 'stay'; Grandmother Dassam has a special one for that."

Saina worked away, trying vainly to see Adinda's mind.

"How," she continued, "would you like a white woman to come now and marry *tuan* René?"

"If he does not care for me—love me," Adinda spoke with a catch in her voice, "then I do not want him."

"Silly girl, of course you do! Don't you wear the finest ornaments of any one around here? Aren't your *sarongs* the very best? And look at your house, your servants,—"

"Stop, stop!" Adinda put up a protesting hand.

"I must tell you, Adinda, before you get too foolish. If *tuan* René does take another girl you know there is the poison."

Adinda was on her feet, a young fury.

"Saina, you are a bad woman! I love my *tuan*—how could I poison him?"

"Silly, silly little girl," was the placid answer, "you may yet be glad Grandmother Dassam knows how to mix the poison."

But Adinda was gone. All the way home her breath came in little quick sobs. How terrible Saina was! She had no heart— no wonder the white men left such women!

She knew white men had left their *njais*. None of them had been like her *tuan,* nor for that matter had any of the *njais* been like herself.

She fingered the gold bracelet on her arm lovingly. Was she the only girl in all this mountain region to believe in a white man? Ah, hadn't he said to her when he came back from Batavia, "You, at least, are real?" He needed her, he had said so a thousand times, he had taken her in his arms, held her close—though he had never kissed her, and a kiss was the token of a white man's love. He must kiss her some day; then she would know.

She could hardly wait for his homecoming that night. He had been so tired lately and curt to her; tonight she would make him smile. He must have the best food she could order. Going into the kitchen she tasted the food.

"This is not good enough, cook, for *tuan* René. Give it to the stable boys; prepare more quickly."

Cook smiled at Adinda's retreating figure. To her helper she whispered, "A sign. I know it."

"Keep it in your head or you'll be looking for another home," was the warning answer.

René was late and very tired. Saina's husband gave his report. Adinda, squatting by her *tuans* chair, listened intently, eyeing the *mandoer* keenly.

"A pig of a man," was her inward comment. "I'd take poison myself had I to live with him."

When he was gone René leaned back with closed eyes. Adinda slipped away to return quickly with a savory dish. "Taste this, *tuan*. You are too tired to sit at the table."

He tasted and smiled. "Delicious! Let's have some more."

Daintily she fed him, bringing dish after dish of rarest vegetables, fish, curried chicken.

He drew her to his knees. "Taste this yourself, Adinda. Isn't that good?"

It was an hour of the closest, dearest intimacy she had ever known. It made her heart throb with joy.

At its close René reflected on the sweetness of the service he had received. Hang it anyway, why shouldn't he marry Adinda and make her happy for the rest of her life? It was only fair to her; she deserved all he could give her. She seemed more like an equal with him since she had learned to speak and read his language. Thoughts of Holland, his mother and sisters, Betty, flitted through his mind. Well, damn it, whose life was it he had to live? His own, he had to live it, not they. They would condemn him—that didn't matter. He would condemn himself if he didn't marry her. He was married to her already—he always felt so. Of course, in that case he must live here forever, but Buitenzorg had not been so diverting. Buitenzorg—Daisy Vermeer!

He sprang up. "Come, child, it's late. Let's go to bed."

With his arm about Adinda they walked to their room.

"You must not sleep on the floor tonight, girl, do you hear?"

"And you must not talk, *tuan.* You must go to sleep quickly."

She turned her back on him, and no amount of coaxing brought a word from her.

He smiled at her determined little figure lying there beside him, while Adinda smiled as she thought how wrong Saina had been.

34

Broken machinery...

ONE HOT, SULTRY AFTERNOON Oerip came to see Adinda. The baby was fretful, Oerip tired holding the half-sick child.

"She won't eat, she won't sleep," the mother complained. "What is the trouble? It may be she has the sickness."

Adinda took the crying baby in her arms while she led the way to a cool, shaded side of the veranda. She put the child on a soft mat, squatted down beside her. At the clap of her hands a little maid appeared.

"Bring some cool lemonade, Roae, not very sweet."

When it came she bade Oerip drink some. Giving the baby a few sips she was delighted to see it smack its lips.

"Go into my bedroom and lie down, Oerip. Take a good sleep. I'll care for the baby."

Oerip went gratefully. Left alone with the baby Adinda turned it over on its stomach while she rubbed its tiny back with her soft, slender fingers, slowly, soothingly until the child's fitful wail ceased and it slept deeply.

She was very quiet, watching over the sleeping child with a mother's solicitude. Her great brown eyes were pools of tenderness, her quivering lips beautiful in their soft curves. She looked shyly about—no one in sight, she bent quickly to kiss the dimpled feet, the little hands, lastly the soft cheeks turned towards her. She could give the caress her *tuan* knew, she liked it. The baby's skin was like satin, it thrilled her. If only it were her baby, hers and *tuan* René's! Yet then she would be much whiter, and every time she looked at her she would think of the hard, bitter life before her. *Tuan* had said so, it must be. Now she could pretend the sleeping child was hers. In a crooning voice she sang a low lullaby, sad and sweet, as though the baby had died. Time slipped away, and still Adinda kept her loving watch. Oerip slept on.

René's tall white horse thundered into the driveway. Adinda sprang up, ran to the steps to meet him.

"Hush, *tuan!'* she whispered. "Oerip's baby is asleep on the veranda."

"What's that?" was his astonished question.

"Oerip's baby. Come see her, she is so cunning."

She took his hand, led him to where the baby lay. The noise had awakened the child. She rolled over on her back, and, comfortable now, cool and rested, she kicked her chubby legs and cooed up at them.

"Isn't she—a darling?" Adinda stumbled a bit over the new word.

"She's a little brown imp." René looked into Adinda's eyes, where the tears were slowly gathering. His arm went swiftly about her. "Do you care so much, Adinda?"

Oerip came, fearful of being in the way. Adinda did not answer her *tuan's* question. As mother and baby ran hurriedly away she went inside to attend to her *tuan's* wants.

René was leaving for the gardens the next morning when a servant of Mr. Inger's rode up, jumped off his horse and squatted down before him.

"What is it, Sakit?" René asked.

"*Tuan* Inger say come to the factory."

"What is wrong?"

"*Tida taoe, tuan.*"

"Oh, well," was René's impatient reply, "it doesn't matter. Go tell *tuan* Inger I'll come at once."

Sakit dashed away.

"I hope nothing is wrong, *tuan*", Adinda said anxiously.

"Can't tell. The stupid fellow wouldn't say. I'd like to break his neck."

"*Tuan* Inger might break his neck if he did tell. The poor fellow, his life has been saved twice in one day."

René had to laugh heartily. Adinda joined him, one eye twinkling as she closed it slightly, a funny little trick that never failed to amuse her *tuan*.

"Don't worry, anyhow," was his parting admonition. "It's probably nothing that matters."

He hurried away. Upon his arrival at the factory he found things very much upset. Inger awaited him on the veranda of his home.

"Good morning, sir, what's up?"

"Sorry to take you from your work, René, but a small, very important piece of machinery broke this morning. I must send it to Buitenzorg to be mended. You know how the natives bungle a thing—can you go for me? You haven't had a day off for six months. I thought you might relish a change.

You can stay at the Mansion with my brother. It will probably take a day or two to mend the machinery."

"Very well, Mr. Inger, I'll go. I don't care about seeing the city, though."

"I appreciate your going, it's a long hard ride. Homan could not get off on account of the planting in the new gardens in his district. You may get a little pleasure out of it all."

"Yes, I'm sure I will. I'll go home, pack up and be off."

Adinda was on the watch for him. He was scarcely off his horse before she asked, "What is it, *tuan?*"

René went inside before answering. "I hate to tell you, girl. Mr. Inger is sending me to Buitenzorg again. A piece of machinery broke, and everything is stopped until it is fixed."

"Couldn't someone else go, *tuan?* Why didn't he send one of the servants?"

"It is too important to trust to a native, Adinda, but I don't see why he didn't go himself. Pack for me, that's a good girl."

"I can't let you go, *tuan.*" Adinda put her arms about him. "I'm afraid to let you go, I don't know why—there is some trouble ahead of us. The broken machinery, it is a bad sign. Before, you wanted to go and you came back still mine. This time, you don't want to leave, but some hidden force separates us. You must not let me out of your mind one minute, *tuan.* As soon as you forget me for even one minute life will change for both of us."

"Child, what are you trying to say? Why should the breaking of a bit of machinery have any influence on our lives? That is a good old superstition of your race—it has hold of you now. Don't be silly, Adinda, you needn't fear I'll forget you. Why, child, I'm only going for two days."

"I know, *tuan*." Adinda still held him—how to make a white *tuan*, even her own, see things as she saw them?

"I may be back tomorrow night," René told her. "You had better sleep in cook's room tonight. You are all upset, girl."

"I don't care what becomes of me tonight, *tuan!*"

"Now, aren't you ashamed of yourself? Can't you trust me out of your sight?" He tilted her face up, one finger under her chin. "Look at me, little girl. Aren't you going to smile at me before I go? Don't take this so seriously."

Adinda looked deep into his eyes, but her smile was sadder than tears. She seemed to be saying goodbye for the last time. She opened her lips as though to speak; instead, she drew his head down and kissed his cheek—a long, sweet kiss.

René was astonished. She had never shown her love in this way before. Of course she had learned it from his books. He was of two minds about liking it. She turned away to pack his things.

When René had almost disappeared around a bend in the road he turned in his saddle to wave to Adinda, but she was not there to answer his greeting. He went away in a different mood from the time he had dashed off so gaily with Rudolf.

He thought of all she had said, superstition merely, yet how sad she had looked—and her kiss! She knew how to kiss at any rate, put her very heart in it, too. He smiled happily, sent his horse along at some speed; the quicker there, the quicker back.

35

Face to face with the fire-eater

HE HAD ENTIRELY FORGOTTEN Adinda's words when he entered the gates to the grounds of the Mansion. Although practically the entire mountain slope of the Buitenzorg side of the Salak belonged to the tea estate Tjidani, the grounds surrounding this old palatial home were enclosed with a brick wall.

The Mansion, as it was generally called, dated from the time the coffee barons had made their fortunes on the island. It had more than forty rooms on the ground floor, and the walls of the corridors were of white marble. The outer buildings, with kitchen, bathrooms and servants' quarters, stretched out for half a mile. Beyond these were the stables, an almost endless line. The Inger brothers were famous for their pure-blooded horses, and more than eighty could be stabled there.

René entered the grounds from the mountain side. On his way to the house he passed extensive hothouses where rarest trees, shrubs and flowers were cultivated for the pleasure of the owners of Tjidani. A lawn like velvet sloped down to an enclosed swimming pool, built entirely of marble. On the other side of the house was another massive entrance, leading

**He had entirely forgotten Adinda's words when he entered the gates
to the grounds of the Mansion.**

from the road to Buitenzorg, two miles away. On the front
lawn graceful blue and white peacocks strutted, while among
the trees soft-eyed deer grazed.

It was a scene not to be forgotten, and René thrilled to
the beauty of it. A groom took charge of his horse as he
dismounted while George Inger, the oldest of the three
brothers and general manager of this great estate, came down
the marble steps to greet him.

"Come in," he welcomed, "my brother telephoned me of
your coming. How are you?"

"Fine, thank you," René answered.

Inger led him up the steps to a wide veranda of marble, and
down this to enter a huge room, the windows of which gave a
sweeping view of lawn, swimming pool and gate beyond. He
showed René to his room, saying hospitably, "I hope you will
find everything you want. If you need anything, just ring for

**The Mansion, as it was generally called, dated from the time the coffee barons
had made their fortunes on the island.**

your servant. I have a special one for you, and he will be at
your command day and night."

"Thank you, sir, you are very good. If I may I'll take a dip
in the swimming pool before lunch."

"Yes, do, René. Meanwhile I'll send one of my employees to
the foundry with this piece of machinery. We can no doubt
fix it quickly."

After his swim, René called Mrs. Homan on the telephone.
The old lady was astonished to hear his voice.

"You must have dinner with us tonight. It will be most
informal. We have a couple of guests coming in, but they are
old acquaintances, so it is merely a family dinner."

"I'll come with pleasure," he told her.

At luncheon Inger said, "I'm sorry, but that machinery
won't be fixed until tomorrow evening."

At luncheon Inger said, "I'm sorry, but that machinery
won't be fixed until tomorrow evening."

"I'd better go back, hadn't I? We're very busy at the gardens just now, and a servant can bring it in." René's thoughts flew to Adinda.

"No, indeed," Inger answered him. "I telephoned Henri, and he says you are to stay. You've been working pretty hard lately, a day's rest won't come amiss."

"It's a rare treat in a home like this. I'm happy to stay. I'm all fagged out, too, though I didn't realize it until I began to relax."

"Take it easy, amuse yourself in any way you wish. I have given the head coachman orders to have a carriage ready for you at any time. By the way, I'm out for dinner tonight. Can you get along?"

"Thank you, I'm out for dinner also. Mrs. Homan invited me."

Mr. Inger laughed. "Be careful of your heart, young man! There are five pretty daughters over there—no telling what they'll do."

"Never fear, sir. I'm immune."

"Immune," the older man teased. "There isn't any such state where women are concerned. Those girls will help you cut your eye-teeth, I'll wager my hat."

"Maybe," was the laughing answer.

How good it was to be free to wander through the spacious grounds. René went first to the stables; from there he strolled through the greenhouses, and back of these found a delightful spot, a rockery with tree ferns and all sorts of exquisite tropical flowers. A little brook of crystal-clear water ran through this miniature jungle, leaping over a small waterfall into a dark, cool pool alive with goldfish. Here he sat down.

It was so cool one could hardly realize this was in the Tropics. The sun scarcely penetrated the dense foliage, a soft breeze stirred the air and birds sang joyously.

Marvelous, to have such a pile of money, pondered René, a very paradise on earth. This was the place to live with a charming wife and raise one's children. He thought of Adinda, but could not see her at the head of such a household; she would not fit in this regal splendor. Still, he had heard that George Inger, who was a bachelor, kept a *njai*. Did she, he wondered, manage all these servants? And why need Mr. Inger live this way? Surely it was better for him to marry a white girl and have her openly at the head of his household.

**Even white men who did not know René saluted him,
recognizing the Inger carriage.**

"The Tropics seem to do things to us all," was his inward
comment. "But hang it all—it isn't my affair." He went in to
dress for dinner in a fresh white drill suit, which Adinda had
rolled carefully in a little bundle and tied to the pummel of
his saddle. Since the dinner party was informal, he felt quite
content in this simple attire.

The carriage, an open victoria, with two fine Australian
horses was waiting for him under the porte-cochere. The
coachman and footman on the box wore the Inger uniform.

"Very stunning and elegant," René chuckled to himself,
"more like the equipage of some visiting ambassador than the
humble employee of a tea garden."

They dashed out of the gateway and down the road in fine
style. Hats were lifted out of respect to this great *tuan*. When
some native carriage did not make room quickly enough the

He was at once introduced to Colonel and Mrs. Vermeer.

footman would call from his high perch, "Get aside for the white *tuan!*" strengthening his warning with curses. Even white men who did not know René saluted him, recognizing the Inger carriage.

To satisfy his pride the coachman swung up the driveway of the Homan estate with a smart dash of his horses, and while the spirited team stood prancing in front of the portico René descended, assisted by the footman who had jumped from his box while the carriage was still moving. Mrs. Homan, her daughters and guests were on the wide veranda, not a little impressed by René's royal entry into the grounds.

His hostess rose to greet him, saying laughingly, "Very pretty and dashing, much like the arrival of the Governor General, René."

"Thank you, Mrs. Homan, it was rather well done, wasn't it? I'm quite proud of that outfit. Much too stylish for me. I'm half spoiled now with this life."

He was at once introduced to Colonel and Mrs. Vermeer. Mrs. Homan was saying, "This is Captain Cramers, Mr. van Landsberg," and René was face to face with the fire-eater who had been with Daisy at the circus.

36

The scent-laden garden

THE SWINGING DOORS leading into the dining room were suddenly pushed open. Marie Homan came forward to greet René, while Daisy Vermeer stood speechless in the doorway. One hand went quickly to her heart as though to still its beating. Mrs. Homan began an introduction, but René interrupted.

"I have the great pleasure of knowing Miss Vermeer. We met at the Concordia Club several months ago."

"How do you do, René?" Daisy gave him her white hand, strangely cold now.

"So, so," teased Colonel Vermeer. "Calling each other by the first name? This will bear looking into."

Mrs. Vermeer, also, took in with a glance the way matters stood. She spoke to her daughter:

"Did you know that Mr. van Landsberg was coming here tonight?"

"No, Mother, I did not."

To René Daisy said, "I had no idea you were in this neighborhood."

Captain Cramers turned to René. "Imagine what we would have missed if Miss Vermeer had gone to that jungle land."

"And I believed you to be in Makassar. That is where you expected to go, wasn't it?"

Such commonplace words, fraught with so much meaning.

Colonel Vermeer answered for his daughter, "Yes, I did expect to be stationed there. I thank my stars I was placed with the general staff in Buitenzorg."

Captain Cramers turned to René. "Imagine what we would have missed if Miss Vermeer had gone to that jungle land."

His eyes sought Daisy's tenderly. Nothing of this escaped René, who took up his side of the banter readily enough.

"The Government should never send officers with beautiful daughters to an outpost. It isn't fair to the good bachelors on this island. We poor planters, however, have no chance, so what's the difference?"

Daisy looked at him with a naughty twinkle. "If the poor planters you speak of didn't hide themselves in their caves they might have a chance."

"I know one," René whispered, "who has come out, ready to do his cave act."

Mrs. Vermeer interposed: "Life on the plantations is too lonely for a white woman." Then, with a scornful shrug of her shoulders, "Conditions in general are too horrible."

A direct hit, René thought, at the lives of the white men with their *njais*. Mrs. Vermeer was bent apparently on making him uncomfortable. Of course Captain Cramers supported her.

"You are right, Mrs. Vermeer." He was very ingratiating. "It is too lonely altogether for a young white girl. Why, even Makassar would be better."

"Oh, I don't know," Daisy broke in, ever so slight a challenge in her manner. "So far as lonesomeness is concerned both places are about alike, but the plantations are far ahead in beauty. I might try visiting one; I could then tell you more about it, Captain Cramers."

"You should, Daisy," Mrs. Homan seconded, feeling that for some reason the air was becoming charged. "My Anna loves the life on the *Salak.*"

Before Mrs. Vermeer could respond a majordomo announced dinner. Mrs. Homan, on the arm of Colonel Vermeer, led her guests to the dining room.

René found himself between Mrs. Vermeer and the oldest Homan girl. Daisy, on the same side of the table, was between Captain Cramers and Marie Homan. He cursed fate, he couldn't even see her, much less speak to her; the dinner lost interest for him. His thoughts flew to Adinda, only to fly back quickly—he folded their wings and forgot everything but the lovely girl whose gay laugh reached his ears from time to time.

Mrs. Vermeer had set her mind upon belittling plantation life. She boasted of the wonderful doings in the city.

"Especially when one's husband is an officer in the army the wife has great standing in the community, an enviable position," she finished up, leaning over to smile at Captain Cramers.

Then Colonel Vermeer made a gross mistake in the eyes of his enviable wife: "That's all very beautiful, my dear, and quite romantic, but the salary of the officer does not permit the wife to play the leading lady long."

Again Mrs. Homan sensed that trouble loomed. Turning quickly to René she asked about her "mountain children," as she called Rudolf and Anna.

"Fine," he answered. "Rudolf is very busy just now. I don't believe he'll be in town for some time. Anna is a wonderful sister. She takes good care of him."

Mrs. Homan beamed. "I am so glad she is there. I feel perfectly safe about them both."

Poor old lady, René thought, the grandmother of a mixed blood. It would almost kill her if she knew.

Mrs. Vermeer's taunting voice penetrated his disturbed thoughts.

"A very unselfish daughter, Mrs. Homan. I would never permit a daughter of mine to do such a thing. I pray every night she will marry a city man."

Detestable old cat, was René's inward comment. She had succeeded in spoiling his evening. He decided with a setting of his teeth that nothing should send him into the city again. Why subject himself to the covert insults of a society woman or tear his heart with longing for her beautiful child? He had cast the dice for life in the interior. Daisy leaned over, giving him a quick glance from sparkling eyes—or had he cast it irrevocably?

At the fashionable hour of ten the party broke up.

René had no opportunity of speaking to Daisy alone, so, rather formally, he asked permission of Mrs. Vermeer to call at their home the next day.

As formally, she answered that both herself and her husband would be attending a garden party at the Governor General's in the afternoon.

"Perhaps you could come at eleven in the morning for a cup of coffee?" she suggested.

"Yes, yes," blurted out Colonel Vermeer. "Come at eleven and stay for lunch."

Again his worthy commanding officer withered him with a look, but the mischief was done. René accepted at once.

"Come early," Daisy added.

The evening was not quite lost.

Back at the Inger mansion, René, finding his host still away, went into the scent-laden garden. Alone, he might think his problem over. In the quiet beauty God seemed very near. It was not hard to tell himself he was Adinda's, hers by the great giver of laws. Daisy's face swam before his eyes, the tender little backward glance as she said good-night—and nothing was easy.

37

The song of the Lorelei

RENÉ SLEPT LATE. On coming out to the dining room he found Inger had finished breakfast and gone. Two young natives served him, shuffling noiselessly over the marble floor. Sipping his coffee lazily a feeling of well-being enveloped him, the luxury about him satisfying his beauty-loving side.

A native woman crossed the reception hall directly within his lazy glance. She was very beautiful; her lace-lined white jacket and batik *sarong* of rich design told him the story. Here was Inger's *njai*. Even the general manager of all this rich estate kept a *njai* at the head of his royal household.

But Inger himself was coming up the marble steps. René rose quickly to wish him good morning.

"Sorry, sir, to be so scandalously late. I had no duties on my mind and didn't waken. I surely slept my fill."

"Quite right, René. You've no reason to hurry. I just had word from the foundry. We'll have to wait another day for the missing link. Sometimes the slowness of those fellows makes me lose my hair, but I suppose nothing can be done about it."

"It is too bad," René seconded. "We're so busy at the gardens I feel I should be there."

"Well, be patient. Keep yourself amused a bit longer. I'm sorry I can't entertain you, but I'm off to Batavia on urgent business."

"Don't give it a thought, sir. I have an invitation for luncheon at the Vermeers'. I'll make out in great shape."

"Bully, René! I'll say *au revoir* now. I have many things to attend to before leaving. By the way," he called over his shoulder, "the carriage is yours at any time."

"Thanks, awfully."

René began to have a little insight into the great responsibilities the Ingers had shouldered. Not all play by any means—was it worth it? His old sense of freedom leaped— his was the better part after all!

He ordered the carriage and drove in state to the Vermeers', thinking on the way of the many snubs Mrs. Vermeer had given him the evening before,

She was very beautiful; her lace-lined white jacket and batik sarong of rich design told him the story.

He ordered the carriage and drove in state to the Vermeers'…

hoping she had not spirited Daisy away, although she was quite equal even to that. Upon entering the Vermeer veranda, however, he was greeted most cordially by his hostess.

"So glad," she gushed, "you could come for luncheon." She led him to the huge sofa and bade him sit beside her. "Oh, you naughty boy, why did you not tell me you are a baron? I just learned it from my husband at the breakfast table. My grandmother was a Baroness van Aldersheim. I always feel that as a class we should hold together. You must come to see us often."

"Snob!" thought René, glad, however, that Baroness van Aldersheim had lived, since she aided him in being near Daisy.

Aloud, he said, "That's very kind of you, Mrs. Vermeer. I shall be glad to come whenever I am in town."

"So glad," she gushed, "you could come for luncheon."

"Yes. My grandmother, the Baroness—"

But his talkative hostess was interrupted by the arrival of Daisy. She had just come in from the garden; in her arms she held great trailing streamers of pure white orchids, decorating her simple dress of white; on her head, a flopping hat covered with red poppies and blue bachelor buttons, a sparkling bit of color fitting in with Nature's exotic blooms of the tropics. Remembering the pink roses on her hat when first he saw her, he felt now they had been too pale—the flaming poppies matched the fire in his heart.

"Hello, René," was her simple greeting. "I didn't know you had come. How are you this morning?"

He was visibly disturbed by her beauty, much to the delight of her mother. Daisy gave him her hand, laughing softly. René held it long.

"If only I could paint you now just as you are—that dress, the orchids!"

"The Baron is quite a flatterer, is he not, Daisy? I do love the polite sayings of the true nobleman. It reminds me of the time when knighthood was in flower. My grandmother, the Baroness, used to tell us many tales of knightly valor."

"Oh, I thought Great-Grandmother died when you were a baby, Mother."

Mrs. Vermeer did not relish this checking up from her daughter. She was too pleased, though, at having a baron in her house to be disturbed for more than a passing instant—she had been willing to say anything. Having succeeded now in letting him know blue blood ran in her veins she overlooked Daisy's unfilial remark.

Colonel Vermeer came in from military headquarters, jovial, loud-spoken, and drawing the fire of his wife's displeasure.

"What do you say to a little drink before luncheon, van Landsberg?" he cried, slapping René heartily on the back.

"Excuse me, Colonel, I don't indulge. I've given it up since taking over the tea gardens. For some reason there is little drinking up in the mountains, perhaps because the men are so much alone; there's no fun in drinking by one's self. At the sugar factory there were always some fellows near—drinking was a daily pastime."

"Oh, this younger generation is hopeless!" said the colonel in disgust. "When I was young we drank alone and in company."

"But, papa," Daisy broke in, "I think René is perfectly right."

"Yes, so do I," joined in Mrs. Vermeer. "It shows weakness when a man drinks alone, and you, Colonel, should not do it at all at your age."

The colonel looked dejectedly at René.

"Well, my boy, you have two great allies. I might as well order retreat sounded."

Daisy smiled affectionately at her father, a real camaraderie in her glance.

"Shall we go in to luncheon?" Mrs. Vermeer rose with dignity. René, vastly pleased over the running of the tide his way, offered his arm.

Here again was encountered the charming hospitality of true Hollanders. Behind each chair stood a native servant, ready to anticipate every need. The food was a joy. The innumerable tropical fruits were too delicious to refuse. The colonel warned him:

"Careful, young man, about the fruits! They bring on rather quickly a serious illness hard to combat, much like typhoid fever in Europe."

"Others have told me that also. I'm afraid I have not been overcautious. Mr. Inger had fruit for breakfast. I helped myself generously, but I'm very strong."

"How do you like the food in the interior, anyhow?"

"Very well indeed, Colonel. I have a splendid cook—"

René stopped short. Evidently the colonel was keener than his wife knew, for he covered quickly René's embarrassment, knowing perfectly the cause of it.

"You must be pretty lonely out there, boy," he said brusquely.

"Yes," René admitted, "I am at times. The natives have different standards. It makes one feel alone morally."

"Why don't you marry, young fellow?" The colonel stroked his thick gray mustache, a sarcastic smile partly hidden.

"Any mother would be glad to have a baron for a son-in-law."

"Harry! How impossible!" came from Mrs. Vermeer indignantly, another of her withering looks accompanying the words.

Daisy blushed prettily, not daring to raise her eyes to René's. Above her head, he gave the old colonel an amused glance.

"I'm too busy to think of looking after a wife. Up at sunrise, working until sundown, I've no time for the making of a real home."

Oh, René, René, what about that home in the interior, made and kept solely for you? The song of the Lorelei[37] was in his ears, the inner voice hushed.

"You can't tell me, boy—"

37   The Lorelei is a 433 foot tall rock along the Rhine River at Sankt Goarshausen in Germany. Its name comes from old German words meaning "murmuring rock", due to a combination of heavy currents and a small waterfall echoing off the formation. Folklore associates cave-living dwarves with the rock, as well as a bewitchingly beautiful woman who was a siren who lured men to their deaths. Drawing by Howard Pyle, circa 1880-1910.

But Mrs. Vermeer had stood enough from the doughty colonel; she interrupted quickly:

"The Hollanders are hard workers. They have made this island what it is today."

"The only thing I regret," René interposed, "is they leave when they have made a fortune, not caring what becomes of the big industries that still need their care and wise management."

"Yes," the colonel broke in, "it's true, but some of my friends are buying here to stay. I'm thinking of it myself; it's an enchanted land and I am much attached to it."

He threw a quick glance at his wife.

"No, indeed, I won't stand for it, Harry. When you get your pension I want to live in the Hague and be somebody."

With a broad wink at René the colonel threw back, "That's all right, Julia, you are somebody wherever you are."

They moved to the veranda, where smokes and coffee were served. A few moments later Mrs. Vermeer rose.

"Come, my dear," she said to her husband. "We must take a little rest before the party. Excuse me, Mr. van Landsberg. I am sure Daisy will look after you for a while, won't you, dear?"

"Oh, yes, I'll guard this mountaineer! He won't escape, I can assure you."

"Just like your father," was the irate lady's muttered comment.

38

Steeped in love's potion

RENE'S HEART LEAPED WITH JOY. He showed it all too plainly in his eyes and voice. Before such ardor, Daisy was very quiet.

"Will you drive with me to the gardens, Daisy? The Tjidani carriage is waiting. You can show me all the beauty spots."

"I'd love to go, René. Just give me time to change my gown."

"Please don't—you are charming in that, sweeter than when I saw you last."

He was standing near her now, not daring to touch her, holding himself in hand. His eyes spoke his admiration. Daisy laughed, a bit confused.

"At your command, sir," she joked.

She put on her hat, which she had removed for luncheon, and they went out. They seated themselves in the carriage; the horses threw up their heads proudly, with nostrils quivering, a true sign of the pure-blood. Many turned to watch this royal equipage, which held a fairy prince and princess. Under the brim of her flopping hat, Daisy sent René a merry glance, thrilled, she knew not why, by his nearness.

Soon the prancing horses entered the gates of the botanical gardens.

"Happy, my lord?" she teased.

"In heaven, my queen," he whispered. "Shall I command that we go on forever?"

"As you will," was the breathless answer.

They were not joking now, some emotion throbbed too quickly in their throats. René could not carry on his part of the conversation. They drove in silence, while there quivered between them volumes of unspoken words.

They passed through beautiful avenues of stately *tjamara* trees, dazzling white houses on the wealthy, spacious lawns, rare fan palms and tree ferns intermingled with the scarlet *kambang sapatoe*[38] and dainty orchids—a fairy land, an

---

38   *Hibiscus rosa sinensis* is a species of tropical hibiscus known for its large, brilliantly colored flowers.

enchanted isle, they knew not what! It all passed like a flame of many colors before the happy eyes of Daisy and René.

Soon the prancing horses entered the gates of the botanical gardens. They drove down the hushed beauty of the canary tree avenue, aptly named Cathedral Aisle. Huge trees a hundred feet high grew on either side, touching overhead—a vaulted dome of green, save at the peak, where sunlight turned the leaves to dashes of silver. Streamers of orchids hung from the very tops of the trees, sprinkling their glorious blooms of every color, dripping red, rose, royal purple and palest lavender. Ropes of lianas[39] with round, glossy leaves twined about the trunks of the already burdened trees. And beyond, silvery ponds of water covered with huge lilies, their blooms resting on great leaves, some of them three and four feet in diameter.

Speech was impossible. Daisy seemed to see Cathedral Aisle for the first time, to catch the heavy sweetness of the tropical flowers; while René felt Paradise could not be more lovely. There were no words to express it. The horses walked slowly, as though they, too, were in the presence of some great divinity. Out of it at last, René found his voice.

"Will you walk with me, Daisy?"

She nodded, and together they left the carriage. Side by side they strolled down a footpath bordered with fragrant blossoms. René's senses were bewildered by Daisy's nearness. He found himself trying to carry on a conversation that would express something of what he felt—instead he was merely conventional with a stilted, formal, polite tone of voice, while his heart beat furiously.

---

39 The name applies to a variety of long, woody vines rooted in the ground that use trees for vertical support to climb higher in wooded canopies to get more light. The term is not a taxonomic grouping but a general description of the plant type, similar to "tree" or "bush."

Side by side they strolled down a footpath bordered with fragrant blossoms.

She was a stranger—she was nearer to him than any human being had ever been; she was a glorified spirit, endowed with warm flesh and warm, living blood! He was afraid even to reach out to touch her hand. When the path became narrow their shoulders touched accidentally, then he dared raise his eyes to her bent head. Before he knew it he had taken her hand in his. She did not withdraw it, but clasped her slender fingers closely about his tingling ones.

In a low voice she said, "I feel as though I had known you for years, René. We have scarcely spoken to each other alone, yet I know what you are thinking. Words are not necessary between us."

He could not speak, only press closer her clinging fingers. He saw none of the beauty about them; he saw, felt and had his being in the girl at his side. Bending near, gently removing her picture hat, he caught the fragrance of her abundant brown hair, the shine of her eyes.

From a great distance his voice came at last: "What a beautiful thing you are, a perfect creation! Nature is at her best in you!"

They turned into a cool, densely shaded avenue of bamboo with the leaves stirring lazily back and forth making a swishing sound as of gently lapping waves. Daisy sat down on the mossy, velvet earth, René beside her. She touched his hair with tender fingers.

"René," she began, but got no further.

With a whisper of her name he crushed her in his arms, kissed passionately her closed eyelids, her cheeks, her quivering mouth. In utter abandon she flung her white arms about his neck, giving back his kisses.

Like a flash from the sky René remembered. Quickly he released her, staring with unseeing eyes down the long, shady path. As suddenly he turned and took his fill of her kisses, touched the velvet of her white, rounded arms with his lips—closed his eyes in swift agony. Brown eyes, brown arms!

Daisy took his head between her cool fingers.

"You wonderful boy!"

"Daisy, Daisy, darling! I have been starved for this! I've tried to forget you, to kill my love for you—but I cannot! It is too deep."

He broke from her and flung himself face downward on the green earth. His muffled voice came to her.

"I'm not worthy of your love. It can never be. I must not see you—I must try *not* to love you—it is all impossible! Forgive me!"

"Hush, hush, my own!" Her voice was low and tender. "Don't go on—I understand. It does not matter. Nothing matters but our love. We are young, we can wait."

René sat up quickly.

"You say you understand, Daisy? You cannot! You are too good, too pure. I have lowered myself too far ever to ask a white woman to marry me!" His fierce tone died to a breath. "Lowered myself, even saying that! How can I tell you of—"

"Don't, René ! I do know. Don't we all know? Out in this country even the married men—my own father! But you have been truer than you guess—you had no wife, and your— your—" She could not say that word, *"njai"*; she paused an instant. "My love is big enough to understand that. Our love will work it out."

Impulsively she threw her arms about him, kissing his brooding eyes and then his lips.

How could she know the agony he was in? He dared not think the name of Adinda, that faithful little native girl! "If you forget me for one minute!" she had said.

He was not forgetting her, he was remembering only too poignantly.

"Please, dear, don't condemn yourself so seriously. Why, René, think of the men we know in Europe who live a dual life—we receive them in our homes, do we not? Out here it is done openly, frankly, because a man needs a native woman at the head of his household."

She smiled bravely into his face. He had to smile back. Leaning over her he gave her a long, sincere kiss, honest as herself now. He was trying with all his might to match her spirit. He was the offender, his the responsibility. This great love had come to him too late—he could see it in no other way. He became cool and silent. Daisy paid no attention to his mood.

"Would you feel better about it," she asked, "if I admitted your weakness, but forgave it?"

"I never expected it to be forgiven by the woman I might love—that you do so is a marvel! Your willingness to help me, your setting aside of all obstacles, has overwhelmed me. I must think it out. Oh, Daisy, my dear, why did I do it?"

"You have been fair with me, René. You might so easily have hidden it, even married me and said nothing about it. I trust you and will leave it all for you to work out. Now," she added, rising, "I will never mention this to you again—it is in your hands."

He stood still while Daisy looked into his clear eyes, blue as the sky, his fresh, boyish face, fair as a woman's.

"Oh, my dearest dear! You have done nothing base. I can't bear it to be this way, René." She leaned against him for an instant—hard to give him up when she had just found him! "Please say nothing to papa or mamma until we have settled things."

At four o'clock he was up and started on the journey home, ill at ease, feverish and almost too tired to ride.

He promised secrecy.

Hand in hand they started back towards the carriage. Shadows were growing long. They had been hours in the shady nook and the time had passed like minutes. Just before they left the dense shade René drew her again into his arms, and kissed her quietly, tenderly.

As they walked they planned, Daisy happily sure of his working it out, René with a very heavy shadow over his spirit. He had much to do before they could marry, but Daisy had persuaded him to do it. She had pleaded for their love until he promised to find some way to accomplish its fulfillment. And he was too young not to feel a deep exultation as they drove home. At her door he said goodbye.

"Darling, you are too good to me," he murmured.

"I love you," was the whispered reply.

He was not to write or see her until he had arranged his affairs. This was best—though it was hard.

At the Inger mansion he found the mended machinery. He made arrangements to start home early the next morning. He dined alone in state, his thoughts full of Daisy and the glorious hours they had spent together. He would not think of home now; he wanted these few happy hours just for Daisy. He did not see the way out—how could he plan when his senses were steeped in love's potion?

"Apres moi le deluge," he said to himself.[40] It must be. Poor Adinda, what would happen to her?

For a fleeting moment he thought of Adolf. He did not fear—if Adinda wished to follow that course he must take his punishment. An easy enough resolution since he was drunk just now with joy.

At four o'clock he was up and started on the journey home, ill at ease, feverish and almost too tired to ride.

------

40 French phrase meaning "After me the flood," attributed to Madame de Pompadour (1721–1764), lover of King Louis XV of France. Before the French Revolution of 1789–1799, the French royalty lived extraordinarily lavish lifestyles, with little regard for the common man. This phrase characterizes her total indifference to the lives of people outside the royal palace. To put it another way, she's expressing her self-indulgence saying, "who cares what happens after we are gone?" Likewise, the lovestruck René, overwhelmed by his passion for Daisy, knows that his relationship with Adinda must be sacrificed for this alternate future.

39

Straight as an arrow

IT WAS THE COLDEST TIME OF THE NIGHT. He had scarcely ridden half an hour before he was thoroughly chilled. He broke out in a dripping perspiration, his head burned like fire, while he shook with the chill. He sent his horse along faster, he must hurry or he would soon be too ill to go all the way.

He paid no attention to his surroundings, even when the sun rose in gorgeous pageantry. He thought at first that the excitement of the day before had wearied him; he knew as he went on that this was nothing so simple as weariness.

When he came to the road leading home it took all his will power to turn towards the factory instead. His horse, too, had strong yearnings for home. But the factory was reached at last. He found Inger testing tea.

"Hello there, stranger."

Without a word René handed him the mended machinery.

"Had a good time, René?"

"I should say I did!" He uttered the words with so much conviction Inger glanced at him keenly.

"What's the matter, old man? You look as if you had stared all the jungle ghosts in the face! Perhaps you didn't eat before you left. Better have breakfast with me."

But even as he spoke René fell in a heap on the floor. When he came to, Inger's *njai* was tending him.

"Feeling better, *tuan* René? What is wrong with you? You are as cold as ice."

"I don't know, Anima—yes, maybe I do. I ate a great deal of fresh fruit. Colonel Vermeer advised me not to. Silly of me. The best thing for me is to get home and to bed under warm blankets."

"Adinda will look after you well, *tuan.*"

With the assistance of Inger, René mounted his horse again and rode slowly home. He dismounted at the steps leaving the horse to go to the stables alone. Sinking into a chair on the veranda he fainted again.

Adinda, busy in the kitchen, saw the riderless horse. She rushed to the front of the house.

"*Tuan! Tuan!*" she called in great fear.

Running to him, she saw he was unconscious. Quickly she brought water, dashed it in his face until his eyes slowly opened.

"What is it, *tuan?* Tell me!"

"I feel rotten, girl. Help me to bed."

Leaning on her shoulder he reached his bedroom, where Adinda put him to bed. He was asleep at once. Pulling the blankets close about him and carefully closing the shutters she went just outside his door. She felt very forlorn and anxious, but it did not enter her head to leave her post. At eleven o'clock René awoke and called for her.

…entirely against Adinda's advice he mounted his horse and rode to the tea gardens

"Now, tell me, *tuan*, what made you sick? Did you drink too much in Buitenzorg and were you up very late?"

"No, girl, it isn't that. I ate too much fruit, foolishly thinking I was strong enough not to have it hurt me."

"It isn't a matter of strength, *tuan*. White men can't do it in our country, though I don't know why. Maybe you did not know this."

"Well, I know it now," René told her weakly. "I feel better after my sleep. Don't worry, I'll be all right tomorrow."

"Stay quiet, *tuan*, and I'll bring you some hot broth."

Although she was sorry her *tuan* was so ill, Adinda rejoiced over his return and the prospect of having him at home for a few days. She was a fine little nurse, anticipating his wants, never troubling him for news of his trip, but sitting quietly by his side on a small stool. When night came she unrolled her little mat and slept on the floor.

He slept most of the night; when he did waken, her hand was on his to soothe him and assure him of her nearness. He felt so much better the next morning that, entirely against Adinda's advice he mounted his horse and rode to the tea gardens. By noon he was too ill to keep up. Shivering with cold while burning with fever, he had barely strength to ride home.

He made light of it to Adinda, saying jokingly: "Here I am, doctor. I'm sick enough this time to mind your orders— no fooling."

That night Adinda did not close her eyes. Her *tuan* was very sick indeed. Hour after hour his fever rose. He tossed from side to side on his bed, trying to get up, muttering words she could not understand. It took all her strength at times to keep him in bed. At last he quieted down, worn out with his ceaseless efforts. Though his eyes were wide open he did not see. To the faithful girl, watching this was terrible; it filled her with an uncanny fear.

He talked unceasingly, first in a whisper, then louder and louder, and fully understandable broken sentences, all too plain to the girl at his side.

"Daisy," he called. Adinda sat up with a shock. "Daisy, oh, girl!" A pause. "Alfred, you said—" Another pause. "My love—your kisses—Daisy—I shouldn't—*njai*— the poison—" Then words she could not make out.

"Mother!" came from his parched lips, "Mother, please understand."

A long pause while tears fell from his eyes—gently Adinda wiped them away. Then suddenly he sat up in bed, taking Adinda's hand in a firm clasp.

"Daisy, you wonderful girl! I love you. Mr. Inger, I can't idle here. Forgive me, Daisy, I love you."

At last he fell back on his pillow. There was the stillness of death in the room. The man on the bed slept.

The girl on her little stool was like stone, cold, without motion. Even her breath seemed bated.

Feeling came to her slowly, torturously. Had she dreamed? Was it her *tuan* who had spoken? Had she been sitting there long—was he real—was she alive? He moved, tossing aside the blankets; she covered him gently, tenderly. The little service brought the hot tears. Unheeded they fell on his limp hand. Adinda looked at them as they glistened there in the faint light from the candle—then she leaned over and pressed her lips on her own bright tears. The touch broke her heart—she must never kiss his hand again nor serve him. He belonged to a white girl. All that she had feared and dreaded had come to her. In a broken whisper she poured out her grief in the language he had taught her:

"*Tuan*, my darling, have I deserved this? What have I left undone? Haven't I given all a woman can, forsaken my birthplace, learned your language, studied so hard, *tuan*, to speak to you in your own tongue, to keep you from being lonely. Did I not save your life? And yet it isn't enough!

"Nothing is enough! Even though I love you—you taught me to love! You wanted everything, and I gave it! I believed in you—they said you would do this and I did not believe them.

"You were so kind, so good to me! Oh, you love me and do not know it! *Tuan, tuan!* I cannot live. I am so cold—I will never be warm again."

Adinda rocked back and forth in her anguish. Suffering was coming to her now where before she had been stunned,

She was all Javanese—straight as an arrow, proud, jealous,
and revengeful in her primitive thoughts.

only half feeling her pain. Still she rocked back and forth. Her tears dried quickly in the fire of her sorrow.

She rose, stood still as a subtle change swept her face. She seemed to lay aside, as she would a cloak, the woman he had taught her to be, his language, the ways of the white woman, the culture of his race, the open frankness of an awakened mind, the tender beauty love had added to her face.

She was all Javanese—straight as an arrow, proud, jealous, and revengeful in her primitive thoughts. A fierce beauty glowed in her somber eyes.

Silently she moved towards the door. Seeing that René still slept, she went out and across the open passageway to the kitchen, where she prepared herself a cup of strong coffee. She muttered in her own language.

So this white man thought he could do with her as the others did, pack her up and send her off like a piece of old furniture! She had trusted him, the treacherous white man! Time some native put a stop to it—she was the one to set an example—it would not bring her *tuan* back to her, but other women could be saved.

She drank her coffee—she must have strength. Daylight was coming when she went out. At the edge of the canyon she watched the deep shadows grow lighter. Here he had taught her to see beauty in every tree and shrub, flower and bird, even in the fierce animals that dwelt in the jungle. Here her mind had quickened to truths hidden to her people. Here she had learned love! She could not hate that word though she wanted to.

The woman he had breathed life into struggled with the half-dead creature she had been.

A sob came from Adinda's lips. She turned and ran down the road towards the *kampong* and Saina's house. What she had to do she must do quickly before her courage failed, before she lost her high resolve to save the women of Java. She stumbled. The tears would fill her eyes. Her tired body was so hard to drag along.

The sun came up in swift splendor. It hurt her. She bent her head, not seeing the coolies who passed her on their way to the garden. They looked at her curiously, respecting her as the white man's *njai*—but what brought her out at this hour? The women too, going to work, looked at her in surprise; she did not know them except as those who would be saved by her.

How far it was to Saina's! Her feet ached, her head swam. At last she was there. Saina was alone, her husband off to hire his coolies for the day.

"Well, well, Adinda! What brings you here? You're crying— what troubles you?"

Then, seeing that Adinda could scarcely stand, she put her arm about her and led her to her *baleh-baleh.*

Sitting down beside her she asked, "But what ails you, Adinda? You look sick—and the tears?"

Adinda strove to answer. Why had she come? She was not brave—she was only one lone woman and very tired.

"Ah," said Saina, "your *tuan* has come back! You need my help."

A flood of tears from Adinda, and then she poured out her story. "I told you, Saina, about the broken machinery. I knew it meant dark, bad trouble."

"What do you want me to do, my little friend?" Saina knew in her heart what Adinda wanted.

"I don't know, Saina, what I want. I should be home now— *tuan* may need me any minute."

"Oh, hush! You are too soft-hearted. Your *tuan* need you! What if he does? Did he ever ask himself whether you needed him or not? Did he ever worry about you? You should hate him!"

"I know, Saina,—how can I force myself to hate? I can't—I love him!" Sobs shook her.

"Bah! 'Love!' Adinda, you always say that word he taught you—he doesn't know it himself. He'll soon get well, go off and marry the white woman. Then where will you be?" Saina laughed scornfully.

"Yes, yes!" came from the tortured girl. "I want the poison! Go to Grandmother Dassam for me. Now I must leave."

"Be strong," warned Saina with a satisfied smile as she watched Adinda hurry down the road, her little head no longer erect, but bent, weighed down by grief and dismay over what she had done.

40

She has the poison...

NOISELESSLY Adinda opened the door of René's bedroom.

"Who is there?" came faintly from the bed.

"It is I, *tuan*, Adinda."

"Come here, girl, where have you been? I am so thirsty. I tried to get some water, but I fell. The fever is burning me up."

She brought the water, holding his head while he drank.

"Are you better, *tuan*?" The words came with a sob.

"Why do you cry, Adinda? I am only sick for a few days. A Dutchman doesn't give up that quickly. Cheer up." He fell back on his pillow, a faint smile on his lips.

"I am glad you are here, girl. Don't leave me again."

"I won't leave again, *tuan*."

An hour of utter silence, then, "Was I very sick last night, Adinda?"

"Yes, *tuan*, very sick."

"Was I—delirious?" Anxiously.

"Yes, *tuan*, all night."

A pause. "Did I—did I talk in my sleep?"

"No, *tuan*, not a word," Adinda lied.

"That's fine!" came in relieved tones from René. "When I am better I have much to tell you, girl, yes, very much. Better to tell it than hide it." He grew excited, the fever still high.

"There, there, *tuan*! Don't talk now, it will make you worse. If you are not better soon I must call the doctor."

"I can't tell it now, girl. I'm too sick to talk." Another long silence.

"You know what my sickness is, don't you?"

"Just a fever, *tuan*. You will be well in a few days. Keep under the cover and don't worry."

"You're all wrong, girl. I have the terrible sickness the white men fear out here. I ate too much raw fruit. I am full of pain. The fever will burn me up before we can break it."

"Don't, don't say that, *tuan*! That sickness is dreadful. It is so hard to cure." She bathed his hot face, head and hands, bending over him anxiously. "I must get the medicine, *tuan*, from Grandmother Dassam. She can heal all the trouble very quickly."

Her eyes were on the floor as she spoke.

"You're a sweet girl, Adinda, but I will have none of your native medicine. I will call a doctor from the city if I don't feel better soon."

"Those doctors, *tuan*, cannot cure this sickness. It is only the native medicine can do that. No white doctor understands the fever."

"You're a fine booster for your own medicine. I don't want it, girl, I won't take it."

Night came, and again René's fever rose to an alarming height. He called Daisy's name many times, while Adinda kept her silent watch. Towards morning the fever went down, and René, rational now, sent her to the cook's room to get a few hours' sleep.

Free of the worst effects of the fever, he thought over the hours spent with Daisy. The very memory of them made him happy. How could he have dreamed of marrying Adinda—yet now leave her? The cruel duty that lay before him brought torture to his mind. How would it all end?

Meanwhile Adinda slept, too exhausted from her grief and long hours of watching to do otherwise. Stretched out on cook's *baleh-baleh* every line of her lithe figure was grace and youth—too young to meet such grave problems. A rap on the door awakened her; one of the maids came to announce Grandmother Dassam.

"Let her come in," Adinda ordered.

The withered, weather-beaten old herb doctor shuffled into the room.

"Don't talk too loud," the girl cautioned.

Grandmother Dassam obeyed by speaking in a weak squeaky voice.

"What do you want, my child?"

"Didn't Saina tell you what I wanted?" Already Adinda despised the old hag.

"Yes, yes, Saina said you were in trouble and wanted some of my medicine."

"Have you brought it? Tell me quickly." Adinda sat up, eyes wide.

"I have three packages," the whining voice went on. "Which one does Adinda want?"

"What do you mean? I don't understand."

"No? Well, this one," holding up a small package, "will kill a healthy person in one hour." Adinda gave a little moan. "This second one will kill more slowly—about a month—and this one will take several years, but he'll suffer much and die in the end."

Adinda's eyes were full of horror.

"The first one quickly. Here's your money." She flung the guilders on the floor. "Now, get out, get away from me!"

Grandmother Dassam bowed in submission, a leer on her wrinkled face.

"Wait," called Adinda. "Is there enough here—for two?"

"*Saja*, Adinda, for three."

When the door closed on Grandmother Dassam, Adinda lay back, panting. She kept her eyes turned from the small package of poison at her feet. Gradually she brought herself to look at it, sat up, one hand outstretched to take it—drew quickly back, then, as though fearful of her own weakness, she seized it and hid it in the tight folds of the *sarong* about her breast.

When she returned to René's room Mr. Inger was there.

She would have withdrawn, but René called her back.

"Water, please, Adinda."

As she handed him the glass Inger took her in from head to foot, his eyes all too admiring. She saw without caring—they were all alike, those white men. What did they know of love? Whether she could feel as deeply as the white *tuan* did not concern them in the least. She hated them all; she would not exert herself for them any longer. With head held high she left the room.

"Say, boy, that's a good-looking *njai* you have! Has she been with you long?"

"Three years," René sighed. "Too long, Mr. Inger. She's getting too fond of me. She's the best *njai* a man ever had, though."

"Come, come, René, don't worry about her. Someone else will take her when you are gone."

"That is true enough," was the dignified reply. "The trouble is she won't take any one else."

"Pooh, pooh, boy! She would be the first one then."

"Oh, let's talk of something else, Mr. Inger, if you don't mind. I'm too sick to argue just now. Perhaps I'd better have a doctor. I can't lie here forever."

"Very well, René, I'll call our doctor in the morning."

"Thanks, if you will."

Adinda found a very tired patient after Inger left. Wearily he watched her at little tasks about the room.

"Sit here beside me, girl."

"You must not talk, *tuan!*'

"I wish I could stop thinking as easily."

Adinda wished she too might still her thoughts. Sitting on the low stool by his side her hand went fearfully to the package hidden in the folds of her *sarong*. "Be strong," Saina had said—strong when her *tuan* lay so ill and weak a child could torture him! If he were up and about her courage might be sufficient. She sat with brooding eyes. The white girl was beautiful, so he said. Adinda's heart hardened—she should not have him! René stirred.

"Tired, girl?"

He smiled at her, the same dear smile he always had for her. She caught her breath, slid on her knees by the bedside and laid her cheek against his hand, sobbing heart-brokenly.

"Oh, but girl, brace up! This will never do! Why, you are not nearly so hopeful as I am. Don't see it all so black. Mr. Inger has sent for the doctor—he'll fix me up in great shape."

"But, *tuan*," Adinda sobbed, "it isn't—"

A sharp knock interrupted her. Wiping her eyes she hurried to the door.

"May I come in, Adinda?" Rudolf Homan was much more respectful than he had ever been before.

"*Saja, tuan!*" was the quiet answer, "if you stay only a little while and do not make *tuan* René talk. He is very tired."

Rudolf told of the work, spoke of Oerip and the baby, of little everyday doings to distract René's mind from his illness. René paid scant attention. The sun was setting, his fever rose, and he sank into a fitful sleep.

Rudolf rose, called Adinda out to the veranda and questioned her sharply while his eyes searched her face. "When was your *tuan* taken sick?"

"In Buitenzorg, *tuan!*"

"Are you sure?"

"*Saja, tuan.*"

"Did *tuan* René talk in his delirium last night?"

"*Tida*, tuan," Adinda lied again, asserting he did not, but she shrank back when he asked this question.

She knew why he asked it. He had heard from his people that her *tuan* was in love with a white girl and thought he had disclosed this in his delirium. Now he was trying to trick her into admitting she knew *tuan* René's secret—and the rest was plain. He suspected her of poisoning him!

Did her face betray her, could he have heard of Grandmother Dassam's coming? Had Saina told Oerip and Oerip told her *tuan?* In fear and shame Adinda hung her head, while Rudolf's glance seemed to penetrate the folds of her *sarong* where the poison was hidden.

"Well, you take good care of him, and no monkey business, do you hear?" was Rudolf's parting shot.

She watched him ride away with mixed emotions. It was getting harder and harder to do this thing she had set for herself.

Saina came up the walk. Instead of going around to the kitchen as usual she came swiftly up the steps.

"Listen, Adinda, I have some bad news to tell you! Come down the road where no one can hear."

Adinda hesitated.

"Come, hurry," Saina coaxed. "It will surprise you." Down the road, well out of hearing, the two girls squatted.

"What have you heard, Saina?"

Adinda's voice was none too friendly, her glance forbidding. Saina was too full of her story to notice.

"This morning, when the mail carrier from the Mansion passed the *kampong* he stopped to chat with my husband for a few moments. He told him that the assistant coachman and one of the footmen had driven *tuan* René and a beautiful white girl into the botanical gardens. They left the carriage and walked down one of the shady paths. They stayed for hours! When they came back they held each other's hands, and when they said goodbye they looked into each other's eyes—long, Adinda—long! That calls for revenge!"

Saina smacked her lips over this juicy gossip.

To her astonishment Adinda answered, "Please, Saina, will you mind your own business from now on?"

She got up and returned to the house without a further glance at Saina.

"And that's what I get!" was Saina's bewildered comment. "And yet she has the poison. She feels she's better than the rest of us. We can't read Dutch. We're strong, though,—we're not afraid to use the poison."

And she shuffled off down the road.

41

"Cure him?"

IT WAS DARK in the sickroom. René slept deeply. Adinda on her low stool by the bed kept her silent watch. Saina had only told her what she already knew. There was but one way open to her—others had taken it, why not she? Saina thought she was afraid, poor ignorant girl! It was not fear that held her hand, it was love. She would prove her love to all the world by dying with her *tuan*. She put her hand tenderly on his arm and whispered brokenly to herself.

"No one else shall ever have you! We will die together, close in each other's arms, my lips on yours, *tuan!* Did the white girl kiss them? It is not revenge, *tuan.* I know better than that. You have told me so many things—better ways than ours. No, it is not revenge. It is love!"

René stirred restlessly. Adinda sprang up guiltily. The package of poison dropped to the floor.

"Are you there, Adinda? Why is it so dark?" Desperately she searched for the little package on the floor, found it, restored it quickly to its hiding place.

"Yes, I am here, *tuan.* Do you want something?"

"Why don't you light the candle? I don't like it so dark."

"*Saja, tuan,*" Adinda lit the candle, shrinking from the light.

"Would you like a glass of milk, *tuan?*"

"No, no, not now."

"I will drink one, too, *tuan.* It will keep up your strength."

"No, I tell you," came fretfully from the sick man. "Sit down, Adinda, take my hand. The shadows seem big and fearful."

"The fever, *tuan.* It is nothing."

"Little Adinda, you are so good. Did something move? Over there in the corner?"

"No, *tuan,* nothing."

"Do you remember the little poem I taught you, girl? The one about God and cool, running waters?"

"*Saja, tuan.*"

"Say it now. I'm tired and cannot sleep."

Adinda repeated in her soft voice and attractive accent the poem he loved.

"You must learn many poems, child. You say them beautifully." A pause. "Your hand trembles, Adinda. Are you afraid?"

"No, no, *tuan,*"she said brokenly.

"You must be brave, Adinda girl. I will get well—it may take some time. I know your nursing will make me well." A little later: "If you need another maid, get her. I want you with me; you must not try to do any work. Don't get too tired, girl." A long silence, then: "I'm sleepy now. Go to cook's room and rest. Daylight is coming. Adinda!"

"*Saja, tuan?*"

"Lean down, girl. Kiss me before you go."

The bubbling of the rushing mountain stream on the canyon floor was all that broke the stillness.

A gasp, a pause—the heavens seemed to open. Golden light flooded the soul of the girl as she slipped to her knees, bent tenderly over her *tuan* and laid her soft lips on his brow.

He smiled, comforted, and slept.

A hint of light was in the sky as Adinda left her *tuan's* room. Over by the jungle the shadows were dark and deep. The bubbling of the rushing mountain stream on the canyon floor was all that broke the stillness. She walked to the very edge of the cliff, stood for an instant with her face upturned to the sky.

"God forgive," she breathed. Then she knelt with forehead touching the earth. "Allah! Allah, hear me, forgive me!"

"Well, old man, there's only one way open to you. You must be taken
into Buitenzorg for treatment."

She rose swiftly, straight and proud, sought the package
hidden at her breast, found it and flung it from her, far, far
out over the deep, dark jungle, watched it fall, a white speck.

As she turned the sun leaped into the sky. With a little
cry of joy she greeted it. No need now to hide her face! She
walked back to the house, her step sure. She was Adinda, the
woman, conquering and unafraid!

Dr. Jansen came from Buitenzorg towards evening.

After due consideration and asking many questions while
Adinda watched anxiously, he said cheerfully: "Well, old
man, there's only one way open to you. You must be taken
into Buitenzorg for treatment. I can't look after you at this
distance. It takes a long time to break the fever. Anticipating

this I have made arrangements with George Inger to keep you at the Mansion; there could be no better place."

René consented and talked it over with the doctor, unmindful of the girl, who had risen, trembling. Had she heard rightly? Take her *tuan* away? He might die. And she who had planned his death the night before now pleaded for his life.

"No! Oh, no!" she cried.

"What is it, Adinda girl?" René asked in a troubled voice.

"*Tuan,* you can't go away! No one knows how to nurse you. Only a native understands the tropical sickness."

Dr. Jansen looked on in surprise.

"What's all this?" he asked.

"She wants to go with me to nurse me."

"Why, yes, of course, she is just the one. You will need plenty of care, young man. You're mighty lucky to have her."

Adinda was full of joy. She heard the doctor's orders, planned the trip with him, became a tower of strength to René in his weakness.

Just before he slept she said: "You don't want my medicine, and I won't say anything more, *tuan,* only this—if the doctor fails, will you then take the medicine Grandmother Dassam makes?"

René assented quickly enough, feeling sure of the doctor, and saying, "I don't want your medicine, Adinda, but I do want you."

After he was settled for the night and sleeping deeply, Adinda flew down the road to Saina's house. She was happier than she had been for a long time. What a terrible, terrible thing she had planned to do! To lower herself as many *njais* had done when her *tuan* had set her so far above them—she was a wicked girl! She did not deserve to be taught the right way, she who had thought to kill the man she loved.

All the way to the *kampong* she flayed herself, forgetting the dark night and the possibility of jungle creatures prowling about.

At the entrance to the *kampong* the guard gave his challenge, "Who is there?"

"It is I, Adinda, *tuan* René's *njai*." And she sped on to Saina's house.

All was dark. It took much knocking to arouse anyone in the cottage.

"Who is there?" came a man's voice at last.

"It is I, Adinda. I want to speak to Saina."

Saina opened the door, glad to have Adinda seek her. She was afraid she had offended her and Adinda might cause the discharge of her husband. Saina knew only one law— revenge.

"What can I do for you, Adinda? Come inside. You are trembling!"

"I want to go to Grandmother Dassam's house. Will you show me the way?"

"Yes, I will go with you, Adinda."

They hurried along the deserted paths. Saina was burning with curiosity over this midnight visit. Whatever did Adinda want? She dared not ask for fear of offending her. "Over there, Adinda, is Grandmother Dassam's house." Saina pointed to a low bamboo hut.

"Wait here for me," was Adinda's order.

Grandmother Dassam was a sound sleeper. Adinda called and pounded many times before receiving an answer.

"Who comes at this hour of the night?" the old woman called crossly.

"Open the door. It is I, Adinda."

"Come in, come in. What do you want? Did I not serve Adinda well? Was the medicine not strong enough?" Adinda ignored the question.

"I want five guilders' worth of your famous medicine against the white man's terrible sickness, the bad fever. Don't ask me any questions." Her manner carried authority.

"*Saja, saja*, Adinda. I will give you good measure. I picked the herbs myself in the forest. It is a sure cure if you but follow my directions."

Grandmother Dassam opened a large bamboo chest, filling the small room with the refreshing odor of dried herbs. It was like walking in the forest after the sun had baked the grass and weeds. Adinda smiled; this would cure her *tuan*, as it had many a white man.

She paid the old hag and took her package of herbs. Not one word of explanation, although Grandmother Dassam was as curious as Saina. She stood in the doorway watching Adinda's hurrying figure. The girl's education made her as secretive as the white people, the crone mused. If all the native girls were like that what would there be to gossip about? She fingered the money lovingly.

The women sped away into the night. When near her home, Saina could bear the suspense no longer.

"Did you need more poison?" she asked solicitously.

"Poison!" came in severe tones from Adinda. "I had no need for poison. I came for medicine to cure *tuan* René."

"Cure him?" Saina exclaimed. "I thought you wanted to kill him."

"You know nothing, Saina. It is wrong to kill. Some day you must learn a better way. My *tuan* is going to Buitenzorg to get well, and I, Adinda—" her tones were proud— "am going with him. I ride in the same carriage with my *tuan!* Tell that in the *kampang* if you will."

She was gone down the road in the dark, leaving a sorely puzzled Saina. There would be no touching Adinda now; she was far above them all. She was a learned and much traveled lady. "Allah save us!"

42

"You naughty girl!"

AT EIGHT O'CLOCK the next morning, the Tjidani carriage drove up to René's humble house. It was the same royal equipage in which he and Daisy had been driven to the botanical gardens. There were the prancing horses, the uniformed coachman and the footman, too! Dr. Jansen accompanied it on horseback. Henri Inger and Rudolf Homan were there, to help transfer René to the carriage.

Adinda's heart swelled with pride, although she showed nothing but concern for her *tuan*. She eyed the footman keenly. So this was the fellow, she thought, who had spread the gossip about her *tuan* and the white girl! Let him see who now rode beside the *tuan*, and who attended to his wants!

Very carefully, they placed René in the carriage, making him as comfortable as possible with blankets and pillows. Adinda rode in the seat by his side. Just before they started, René looked backwards at his home on the jungle's edge, and wondered whether he would ever see it again. After all, he had spent many happy hours there; freedom and work had been his. His eyes sought the girl who sat so close to him; she smiled, giving him courage.

"Tell them to start." His voice was full of weariness.

Just before they started, René looked backwards at his home on the jungle's edge, and wondered whether he would ever see it again.

Slowly, so as not to jolt René's sick body, they began the long journey to Buitenzorg, and neck and neck beside them went the grim, unseen rider Death. For René grew weaker, hour by hour. He saw none of the beauty of the jungle, and paid no attention to the song of the birds. From time to time, Dr. Jansen stopped the carriage to administer a stimulant.

Adinda watched her *tuan* with a dreadful fear in her heart. Would he die before they got there? Would she be denied a chance even to use the healing medicine she was guarding so carefully? She prayed silently to Allah.

After four wearisome hours, they entered the grounds of the Mansion, where everything was in readiness for René. He was put in the same room he had occupied when a guest there before, a room of such beauty that Adinda could only stare in amazement. Flowers were everywhere, and she had never seen so wonderful a bed. A maid was hers to command; she was being treated with all respect.

René was unconscious, and had been so for the last hour of the wearing journey. Adinda had seen him in this condition before, and she used her own capable methods of reviving him. Dr. Jansen quickly recognized her value.

"No mean little lady," he said to Inger, "and a mighty fine nurse."

That night she kept her watch as faithfully as had been the case in her own little home. The native servants were impressed by her position of trust, and hastened to obey her every order.

René talked all night in his delirium. This time he called for Adinda, imploring her not to leave him, and vowing that she alone could help him. Was it time, she wondered, to administer her herb medicine. She had promised, though, not to use it until the doctor failed, and Jansen had not admitted failure yet.

Once during the night, Inger came in.

"Can I do anything for your *tuan,* or for you?" he asked.

"Thank you, *tuan,*" she replied, "you have done so much already that I know of nothing else."

Then Inger's *njai* had come. She brought with her a light meal she herself had prepared for Adinda.

"You must not use up all your strength. Your *tuan* may need you for weeks," the girl said.

Tears welled up in Adinda's eyes. "You are so good, and all is so lovely here! My *tuan* must get well."

"Of course, he will. Now, eat this and have your maid call me if you should need me."

She smiled into Adinda's eyes. They had liked each other at once. She gave Adinda a warm feeling of comfort.

Just as morning broke, Adinda slipped into the garden. The fresh air revived her sagging energy, and the young beauty of the world was good for her nerves. She was worn with thinking. Her mental struggle over the poison had been a bitter ordeal—a struggle for possession of her *tuan* in death as well as in life. Now, she had fully decided upon her course. She would do everything in her power for him, and if he died she would be there to close his eyes. If he should live and choose the white girl, then Allah would help her to bear it.

She had only been absent from the sick room for an hour, yet René had changed pitiably in that time. His cheeks were scarlet, and his breath came in little panting gasps. Terribly worried, Adinda sent a hurry call for Dr. Jansen, who gave the patient a brief examination.

"Better notify his brother to come quickly," the doctor said. "I do not believe your *tuan* will pull through. He is too weak to combat so high a fever. Have you given him the medicine as I directed?"

"*Saja, tuan.*"

"Well, keep it up, once every half hour. I'll be back later."

"*Saja, tuan.*"

As soon as she was left to herself, Adinda reverted to the immemorial medical wisdom of Java. The time had come for that. She got out her preparation of herbs, flew to the kitchen and used them to prepare a weak tea. Back in the sickroom, she poured out a spoonful and forced it between René's lips. Then she hid her brew on a far corner of the closet shelf, measured off a spoonful of Dr. Jansen's medicine and threw it away. She kept this up throughout the long day,

Now, she had fully decided upon her course.

never flinching, although at each stroke of the clock her *tuan* seemed nearer to losing his fight for life.

In the afternoon, his appearance had not changed greatly; he was perhaps more quiet. She often laid her ear against his mouth to learn whether he still breathed.

Dr. Jansen came with another doctor. They shook their heads at her. The battle, in their opinion, was about over.

Alone again, she administered her medicine, making it much stronger now. She forced a spoonful between his lips every ten minutes. If Inger's *njai* had not brought her a supper with her own hands, Adinda would not have eaten that day. A glance of swift comprehension passed between the two girls, as Adinda pointed first to the herb tea and then to the white man's medicine.

Another morning arrived—and Adinda had won, so far! The doctors paid their usual visit, and seemed greatly surprised that René was still alive. They praised each other, and ordered another bottle of the wonderful physic their skill had concocted. Adinda's face was inscrutable, though her heart beat fast with joy. Her manner was humble enough as the great doctors gave her explicit orders.

For another day and night, she continued her treatment, while René came slowly back from the dark valley. Alfred arrived, but finding René on the way to recovery he returned home, bluntly affirming his faith in Adinda's capable nursing. She prepared special food every few hours for her *tuan,* nurturing his strength and coaxing his will to live.

"I am not worth such devotion," he muttered weakly one day, as she fed him. "You are saving me singlehanded."

"Oh, I have plenty of help, *tuan!* You should see how great a lady I am here." Her eyes twinkled. "I say come, and they come; I say go, and they go."

Javanese herbal remedies vs. Dutch apothecary. .

René smiled in spite of himself.

"Shall I tell you a secret, *tuan?*"

"Yes."

"It was Grandmother Dassam's medicine that saved you."

"What, Adinda?"

"Yes, *tuan.* The great doctors said you were dying. They told me to give you their medicine often, though they felt sure you would not live. So I quickly made the herb tea and fed it to you—they never knew. I poured away their medicine each time. When they came and saw how much better you were, they said to each other, 'You are a wonderful doctor!' Oh, *tuan,* I laughed—inside of me!"

"You naughty girl!" René began, only to stop with a catch in his voice. "Adinda, Adinda! So many times, you have saved my life! I can never repay you."

"Yes, you can, *tuan*"

"How"

"Let me learn many things more. I would read your books aloud."

So, in the weeks that followed, Adinda read to René. The books were often too difficult for her to understand, yet she struggled through them with infinite patience. She wanted to know of other lands and other peoples.

"How strange it is, *tuan!*" she said. "You are born in one little spot on this great earth, I in another. It is all the same earth, all made by your God, or by Allah. Yet you are very white, and I must be like this."

Sadly, she held up her slim brown hand. He took it gently in his and carried it to his lips.

"The hand I love! Beautiful little hand of service!" he whispered.

And Adinda forgot her color, and mourned no longer that she belonged to another race.

43

"I am free."

EVERY DAY, Adinda had been expecting to receive some word from the white girl. She imagined she would write, or perhaps would pay a sudden visit. As time went on and neither of these things happened, Adinda ceased to think about her.

Light was steadily breaking in upon her mind. Racial differences, inherited traits and old superstitions were giving way to the big new truths her *tuan's* books taught her. She was fortifying her spirit for the final sacrifice she might be called upon to make.

Weeks slipped by, but René, although slowly gaining, was still too weak to sit up. Peace reigned in the Mansion until one bright morning a runner brought a letter for René.

"Open it, Adinda, and read it to me," he said.

Standing by the window, Adinda broke the seal and read it first to herself.

"What is it, girl?"

She could not answer. It had come—the thing she had dreaded! The courage she thought she possessed was not nearly enough.

"Tell me, Adinda, who writes to me?"

In a faint voice, she answered: "It is from *nona* Daisy, *tuan.* She wants to come."

René could not speak. He felt too weak to meet such a cruel situation, but Adinda met it for him.

Going to the door, she said to the maid: "Tell the runner *tuan* René will see *nona* Daisy."

With no further word to René, Adinda left the room. She went out of the house and down to the shady rockery. She did not sink onto the ground. She stood proudly erect, her arms folded across her breast, close to the dark pool where the goldfish darted swiftly back and forth.

The water seemed comforting—one little slip into its cool depths, no struggle, then quiet and rest! A few happy years had been hers—enough for one life. She had saved her *tuan's* life many times; would that win forgiveness for ending her own?

The white girl could take him. Let Adinda step bravely into the pool, and the way would be clear for her *tuan.* But would it be? And her own act might not be so brave. What was it *tuan* René had taught her: that life came from Allah, and was not ours to destroy. Weak, foolish beings destroyed themselves, those who lacked the courage to face the struggle. She had conquered once, and could conquer again!

At the sound of the little bell tinkling by René's bedside, Adinda turned and went to him. There was no trace on her impassive features of the conflict through which she had just passed, but in some strange, subtle way her beauty seemed greater than ever. Spiritual loveliness was shining in her big, brown eyes.

"Adinda," René began. "Oh, Adinda—"

He interrupted himself, stammering, unable to say more. But she sensed all that he wanted to tell her, and she smiled back at him. She prepared his luncheon, bathed his face and hands, clothed him in pajamas of beautiful batik, made his bed fresh and spotless, brought flowers from the garden, and then left him.

"Come," he called, in answer to a knock on his door. Daisy Vermeer entered. She was wearing the dress and hat in which he had last seen her. For a second, she hesitated on the threshhold, then flew to René's bed, dropped on her knees beside him and placed her warm lips against his trembling ones.

"You, Daisy—you—at last!" he whispered.

"Yes, my darling boy. I would have come sooner, but Papa and Mamma would not let me—let me encounter your nurse here—you know why."

René dosed his eyes. His problem was upon him with a vengeance!

"Daisy," he said slowly, "if it were not for that girl I would have died."

"I know, René," she answered. "I am grateful to her. But don't try to talk. Let me do that. I trust you, dear; you will work it out when you are well."

"Work it out!" he repeated. "There is only one way, Daisy. When we first discussed it, you seemed able to understand—"

He paused, too tired to go into the question now. He could not argue it out until he was on his feet again. He closed his eyes wearily.

Daisy became alarmed at his ill appearance. In a panic, she rang the little bell on the table by his bed.

Adinda came promptly. She knelt and bathed René's face and hands once more, whispering as she did so all the endearing names she knew. Daisy looked on, but Adinda had forgotten her. When his eyes slowly opened, Adinda arose and would have left the room.

"No, Adinda, not yet," said Daisy, and threw her arm about the native girl's shoulders. "You must stay. You know best how to care for him."

Side by side, they smiled down at the man they both loved. René was profoundly moved by the picture they made—Daisy, tall and fair as a lily, his by every law of love and race; Adinda, smaller, graceful as a wood nymph, devotion shining in her eyes, his by God's law and the bonds of her beautiful service. They were both ready to give all to him, both were generous and fine. In choosing between them, he faced the hardest decision of his life. No man had ever been given a sterner problem.

Daisy came frequently after that, much against the wishes of her parents. She read to René, while Adinda sat in the garden with her hands folded in her lap. When Daisy talked of their future life together, René listened with a faraway look in his eyes. It escaped the white girl that he never gave her an affirmative answer. She was so sure of him, she did not even resent the fact that Adinda was still his nurse. Only a short while more belonged to the *njai;* to herself a lifetime, she thought.

Little by little, René regained his strength. He was able to leave the bed at last, to sit up, to walk about the room. The long dreamed of day arrived when Dr. Jansen discharged him, and told him he could return to the tea plantation.

It became impossible for René to postpone the making of his choice any longer. The climax was reached swiftly.

Daisy ran over in the morning to bid him *au revoir*. She was gay for his sake.

"Sit beside me, Daisy," he muttered, "I have something to say."

Puzzled, a bit fearful, she sank into the nearest chair.

"You understood once why—why we men in the interior take native wives. Will you understand again? My dear, my dear!"

"What do you mean, René?"

"I am thinking of Adinda."

Daisy's head went up. "Adinda is surely no problem between us!"

"Don't speak that way, dear! I must play a man's part. You know I love you, Daisy. But love is not enough. I could not take you unless I came to you with a clean conscience. Honor—"

"I thought all that was settled."

"It is, now. I can never marry while Adinda remains single. She cannot be set aside like any common *njai*. She is a rare, beautiful character. I feel I belong to her."

"No law binds you to her," the girl said, her white lips scarcely moving.

"No law that is written in the books," answered René. "But she has saved me from death, and at any time she would give her life for me. I cannot betray devotion of that kind. I do not even want to betray it. I feel married to her by all laws. It's not easy to tell you this—but there, it has been told!"

"You intend really to make that Javanese woman your wife?" Daisy demanded fiercely.

Adinda came in a few minutes later.

"Not in a legal sense. It's not necessary. Legally and according to the custom of the country, I am free. Yet I am bound by my own conscience. That is the way I see it now."

Daisy Vermeer arose and left him without one word of farewell.

Adinda came in a few minutes later. She started to pack his bag. Suddenly, she turned to him, sank on to her knees and placed her arms around his waist.

He drew her to his breast, wordlessly.

Java had won.

APPENDICES

Publisher's Notes
by Kent Davis

Author Bios — 1931

**Javanese Women in Photos:
Emerging Technologies and World Views**
by Kent Davis

Isles of the East
1912 Travel Guide – Extract

Malay Poisons and Charm Cures
1929 – Chapter 1 – Extract
by Dr. John D. Gimlette

Illustration Credits

Glossary of Malay Terms in the Text

Map of Greater Indonesia – 1920

Map of the Dutch East-Indies – 1920

"Nederland's kostbaarst sieraad" — "Netherlands most precious jewel"
Dutch imperial art representing the Netherlands Empire holding its crown jewel: the
colonial Dutch East Indies (Now: Indonesia). Drawing by Joh. Braakensiek, published
1916-10-14 in "De (Groene) Amsterdammer" newspaper.

Publisher's Notes

The cure for boredom is curiosity.
There is no cure for curiosity.

Dorothy Parker (attributed)

I hope you enjoyed reading *Java Girl* as much as I enjoyed researching and reviving it. Here are some details about how the new edition and the original came to be.

Literary Archaeology

I've loved reading books my entire life, but the idea to publish them began in the 1990s when my wife Sophaphan and I returned to the United States after my five years working in Thailand. 1995 was the dawn of the Internet and soon bookstore inventories from all over the world began appearing online. I missed Southeast Asia, so I began collecting antique titles on the topic. We returned to Thailand annually but, despite my growing familiarity, every Asian visit unveiled new wonders. I knew then, as I know now, that a lifetime of secrets and surprises awaits there.

Meanwhile, my growing library confirmed that Westerners who preceded me by 50 or even 100 years experienced wonders and epiphanies similar to my own. Then a few of these men and women shared their adventures—real and imagined—in print as fiction and non-fiction books (for some, the two genres were hard to tell apart!).

The biggest frustration working with forgotten books is that their authors have usually been equally forgotten. What motivated them to share their stories? How many "fictional" events and people described were based on actual experiences? What really drove these authors to invest the time and effort needed to publish their stories? Answers to these questions were almost never revealed as the authors and their lives had vanished with the long out-of-print books they created.

So, in a nutshell, curiosity inspired my career as a literary archaeologist. My mission became finding worthwhile books about life in Southeast Asia that had vanished long ago, and bringing them back to life for new generations of readers. There were already services scanning antique originals for reprinting, but I had no interest in that. A "new old book" is still an old book. Since the original publication the entire world had changed. World events, trends, conflicts, tastes, technologies, language and everything familiar to the author and readers at the time were long gone, long transformed, or were never known to readers far removed from the Asian settings in the first place.

To make these lost histories and novels again relevant and accessible we build entirely new editions while remaining faithful to the author's original content. First, we reset the text as older books are often poorly typeset with small fonts on cheap paper. Many were self-published or produced on a shoestring budget, often by printers far from the authors. Time, costs, technology, poor communications, distance and almost always the printer's lack of familiarity with the subject matter limited the quality of many works right from the start. We fix these shortcomings while expanding relevant content.

The next task is making the long-gone author's immutable text intelligible for modern readers. We do this by adding maps, author backgrounds, supplemental articles and detailed footnotes that explain obscure terms and places on the spot, rather than forcing readers to hunt for answers. Appendix articles from sources contemporary with the original and from modern scholars add context and new perspectives.

Finally, "a picture is worth a thousand words" so we add images so modern readers can actually *see* the people, places and events the original authors experienced and described. We draw from our own catalog of antique photos, as well as from estates, collectors, private sellers and online archives around the world.

Though we began publishing in English, we quickly added French, and French translations to English. While we're proud to publish rare American contributions to Southeast Asian history by authors like Helen Churchill Candee and Harry Hervey, the breadth and depth of French experiences in Southeast Asia go far beyond what most Anglophones can imagine. Over the course of a century, French colonial writers created a vibrant library filled with adventures, hardships and bravery. And, of course, many romances.

A Shrine to Colonial Literature in Bangkok

Though most of these titles are long forgotten—even in France—a shrine to this genre exists in Bangkok, Thailand. There, curator François Doré presides over the Librairie du Siam et des Colonies, preserving one of the world's most complete collections of colonial literature. Over the years, François has been a wonderful mentor whose guidance has

A panorama showing part of the Librairie du Siam et des Colonies
in Bangkok, Thailand and its knowledgeable founder and curator, François Doré.

brought me to appreciate that the stories of French Indochina are every bit as thrilling as American tales of the "Wild West" (that are read in every language).

On every visit to Bangkok I make a pilgrimage to see François to ask for his recommendations of obscure books worthy of revival. In October 2016, he surprised me with a beautiful book bound in batik fabric. It was a colonial romance but, rather than being by a French

author, this one was written in English by a Dutchman who worked in the Dutch East Indies as a young man, circa 1900. I was intrigued but kept my literary focus on French Indochina and Thailand.

On Christmas that year, François emailed to tell me he saw a 1931 copy of *Java Girl* for sale in the US for only $2.69. How could I resist? I ordered the book. Apparently our conversations put the book back in François' mind as well because on January 7, he sent me Issue #117 of *Les Ecrivains de l'Indochine* (*The Writers of Indochina*) featuring his new review of *Java Girl*.

Just as very few French colonial works had been translated into English, he noted that though a vast body of Dutch colonial literature exists, almost none has been translated into French… *or* English. The rarity of this Dutch tale of romance in Java made it more appealing. I immediately read the book, was delighted by the adventure and planned to one day bring the book back to life. Suddenly 2 ½ years went by!

The Rijksmuseum in Amsterdam at night. 2014 photo by John Lewis Marshall.

Suffice it to say I encountered a few distractions, but in mid-August 2019 the wild idea popped in my head that this would be a fun book to quickly reprint before my next visit to Thailand. I'd just flow the text, make a nice cover, add a map, write the footnotes and finish up in a week or two. And that *would* have happened if not for me discovering the online image archive at the Rijksmuseum in Amsterdam. As I immersed myself in the text adding footnotes I began browsing through the thousands of images that the museum offers. Not only do they share their history at no cost to researchers, they actually encourage the free use of the images for creative projects. The Rijksmuseum photos brought the *Java Girl* story to life before my eyes, so creating an illustrated version became irresistible.

I completed the reading proof in eight weeks. By then my research folders had 1,829 jpegs, 828 tifs, and 100 pdfs. This abundance of images even inspired an additional appendix article about Javanese women in photos. Meanwhile, expert photo restoration artist Artsiom Yatsevich spent eight weeks working in Belarus to finish the project. If you're reading this I guess we finished!

East-West Romance in Colonial Asia

"If you come to Indochina to know it, then become intoxicated with it—and the surest draught is a woman.... The *congai*, she is our symbol—the symbol of the ability of the Frenchman to mingle with the natives, whereas the Englishman only conquers them."

M. Malardier's welcoming advice to Justin Batteur
Congai – Mistress of Indochine **by Harry Hervey**

Inspired by my 30 year love affair with my wife Sophaphan, East-West romance in literature has always been near and dear to my heart. My introduction to the genre was in the early 90s when I read Jack Reynolds' brilliant *Woman of Bangkok*. Despite being written in 1956, Reynolds described social interactions and romantic entanglements in the Kingdom that, in essence, hadn't changed a bit! A little more than 20 years later I'd be making my own contributions by reviving classic romantic works that had vanished.

I suppose it's human nature to think that what we are experiencing, learning and feeling now is unique in the history of the world. But while emotions and ideas may be unique to us in our lifetimes, a bit of historical reading may surprise you when you learn that people have walked your path before. Your loves, your fears, your ambitions, your obsessions, your heartbreaks, your passions, your fascinations...someone out there in time shared many of these with you, wrote them down and, if you're lucky, you'll find what they wrote. Their experiences may enhance your own, as a road map guiding you, as a cautionary tale warning you, or as vicarious confirmation that others have lived as you. Equally thrilling is the ability to walk paths that you have never, or could never walk...because the world has changed.

If this topic intrigues you then you can do no better than to read our modern edition of Harry Hervey's 1926 novel, *Congai – Mistress of Indochine*. In addition to being one of the

most exceptional and earliest English language novels in
the East-West romance genre, its supplements offer excellent
modern perspectives. They include a foreword by renowned
travel writer Pico Iyer, "The Book That Launched a Thousand
Ships," and two key appendix articles: "Through a Woman's
Eyes: *Congaies*, Heroines & Harry Hervey" by Hervey
biographer Harlan Greene; and "*Congaies* or Concubines?
Literary Views of Asian Women" by historian Walter Jones.

In addition to *Congai*, another relevant read is DatAsia's first
English translation of George Groslier's 1928 novel, *Return to
Clay – A Romance of Colonial Cambodia*. In a conversation with
the protagonist's wife, a French bachelor comments

> "The *congaïe*," he said, "is a little animal that must be
> changed every month, for by then, as I've had occasion to
> notice, she will either start to rob you or start sleeping with
> the cook."

> "How dreadful!" cried Raymonde. "What pleasure could
> one get from such women, I wonder?"

All is well until one day a local girl named Kamlang
catches her husband's eye...

> Claude recalled ancient statues he had seen...these fruits
> of human art, all measure and rhythm, were here coming
> to life, their marble turning flesh. A child and a goddess:
> so seemed one of these girls to Claude.

> She passed with lowered eyes...in her company was an
> old woman. Claude had his interpreter find out who these
> Cambodian women were...then he turned to Claude and,
> with an imperceptible turn at the corner of his lips, said
> simply: "Maybe possible."

Ah, these romances have been writing themselves for a
long time. But now let's get back to the book in hand!

Unraveling Mysteries of the Original Edition

While researching *Java Girl* in late 2019, I saw just one copy of the original edition for sale for $37. Only thirteen original copies are located in US libraries, with one copy in Leiden University Library in the Netherlands. There is also a copy of the dust jacket (but no book) in the Margaret Ayer Papers at the University of Southern Mississippi in the de Grummond Children's Literature Collection. This is a rare book.

Throughout the 1920s, there was a growing interest in Asian exoticism in the United States so it seems that the 1931 release of *Java Girl* was well timed. Given the colorful nature of the story, its New York publisher, and that the creators lived in California a mere 90 years ago I expected to discover much more about the book and the co-authors than I did. Not only could I find no articles or reviews about the book, I could not find a single photo or obituary for either author. Still, I found a few items that will let us make educated guesses about how the original came to be.

Genealogical records show that Baron Willem Herman thoe Schwartzenberg en Hohenlansberg was born February 27, 1879 in Bitgum, a small village in the Friesland province of the Netherlands. The original dust jacket bio (p. 346) says that he went to Java as a young man to work for four years before leaving for health reasons. His book notes that "automobiles were as yet unknown in Java" so it seems that Willem's four year stay in Java was around 1898–1902, from roughly age 19–23 (possibly slightly earlier).

In March 1910, three identical newspaper articles ran in Spokane, Washington and Montana announcing that the baron had begun "keeping books" for an unnamed "stock broker". Here, he claims he was born in "Wittengan Castle in southern Bohemia". This is more than 500 miles southeast of Bitgum, conflicts with genealogical records, and I found no records of such a castle. They go on to say he engaged in the "nitrate business" in South America before traveling all over Europe, visiting 40 American states and four Canadian provinces, and that "he speaks nine languages, writing six of them."

Oddly, the article adds that he "frankly confesses he did not locate to Spokane to marry an heiress", while a census record that same year notes two people living in his new home at 620 W. Sound Ave. in Spokane WA. Records later confirm that he married Sara Croockewit on March 22, 1913. He had just turned 34 and his bride, born June 6, 1892, was 31. Their honeymoon was evidently successful: on December 18, 1913 Sara gave birth to their only child, Katherina Mea Charlotte barones thoe Schwartzenberg en Hohenlansberg.

The baron again drops out of sight for 15 years, reappearing with Sara in Santa Barbara, California working as a banker at 1014 State Street. Their 3 bedroom, 2 bath home built in 1924 was a little more than a mile away from the bank, and it's still there at 32 East Isley St. If the phone numbers I found in this 1933 directory still worked I'm sure the baron and I would have had a lively chat about Java…and the rise in California property values!

> Schwartz S C Dr r 1518 Laguna....................22048
> **SCHWARTZENBERG W THOE BARON** 1014 State....6131
> Schwartzenberg W thoe r 32 E Islay................6553
> Schwarzberg Elmer A 1122 State...................27574

Sadly, from this point the only records I found of Willem and Sara are their dates of death, with no obituaries. The baron died March 23, 1972 at age 93, with his wife living 10 more years to pass on September 8, 1982 at age 90. I imagine that their daughter Katherina has long since followed her parents by now as she would have just turned 106.

The baron's co-author, Mary Harrison, is equally obscure. Despite the "journalistic experience" mentioned in her bio (p. 346) I found no bylines or articles under her name, or records of the publication "A Child's Garden". Worldcat.org came up with the following titles that seem to be her works, totaling just a little over 300 pages during her 13 year career. All appear to be religious plays:

1924: *By a way they knew not; an idyll of the first century.* New York, Chicago: Fleming H. Revell Co.–91 pgs, classed as "devotional literature."

1925: *Shining Windows.* Los Angeles: Harrison & Hathaway–26 pgs.

1926: *The Christmas bells of Kerin Town.* Los Angeles: Clyde Browne–34 pgs.

1927: *At Last Christmas.* Los Angeles: C. Browne–23 pgs.

1931: *The Singing Trees.* Los Angeles: Browne–28 pgs.

1934: *When Christmas comes. A Christmas play for Church school or club.* Los Angeles: Pageant Publishers–10 pgs.

1935: *The Golden Flame.* Boston, Mass: Baker's Plays–18 pgs.

1936: *As Easter dawns: a religious play in two episodes.* Los Angeles: Walter H. Baker Co.–30 pgs.

1937: *Thine shall be the glory, a dramatic adaptation from the story "He is here".* Los Angeles: Walter H. Baker Co.–25 pgs.

1937: *He is here; an episode from the story of the same name.* Los Angeles: Walter H. Baker Co.–22 pgs.

So how did Mrs. Harrison get involved in writing a romance novel about Java? She was a Christian playwright living in Los Angeles and the baron was a banker working about 100 miles north. Perhaps they met socially, perhaps through a church, or perhaps he found her through "her late husband's newspaper." My theory is that the baron needed to hire a wordsmith to help him complete a project he had been contemplating for nearly 30 years: to write a book related to his youthful adventures in Java.

The baron's personal connection to the story is there from the start. The young Dutch protagonist—who *also* holds the hereditary title of baron—arrives in Java to work on sugar and tea plantations. From this we can infer that some vignettes in the story describe real people, places and events that Willem encountered. More importantly, it's clear that emotional memories of his time in Java stayed with the baron and, even three decades later, were strong enough to inspire his collaboration with a professional writer to share them. Above, I mentioned that sometimes in colonial novels it's hard to tell fact from fiction. This is one such case.

He being a banker, and she a widowed playwright with two children, suggests that she may have welcomed the work, and that he could afford to hire her. This was the baron's only book, so we have no idea how much of this story he had

Java Girl
Original dust jacket art by Margaret Ayer – 1931.

previously written down. Mrs. Harrison may have helped him organize his notes, or even taken dictation. In any case, it was a laborious task to assemble the text, make grammatical corrections, and to manually type the 63,000 word manuscript to submit to the publisher. The fact that Willem retained exclusive copyright also indicates that his co-author may have been engaged on a "work for hire" basis, with the bonus of adding a book to her own credentials.

In 1931, Brentano's published the elegant original edition in New York. Batik fabric covers, copper stamped spine titles, artistic interior culs-de-lampes and a lack of modern copies suggest that this was a costly limited edition. The dust jacket even featured an illustration by Margaret Ayer before she became well known. Ayer spent her childhood traveling with her parents in Mexico and the Philippines, and lived in Thailand (then called Siam) from 1918-19. During her long career that followed, she authored and illustrated six children's books, and illustrated 52 other books, many of which were on Asian themes including *Anna and the King of Siam* by Margaret Landon in 1944.

Despite its provocative cover by a talented artist, quality writing, expensive binding, reputable publisher, and fitting the trendy Asian exoticism theme I could not find a single article or review about the book's publication. To me this implies a labor of love. I believe the baron subsidized the creation of this book for himself, primarily to share within his circle of friends. Still, we're left to wonder why a 52 year old banker would be driven to write a fictional love story about a place that he hadn't seen for three decades? Perhaps he was exploring a path that he chose not to take under the guise of fiction? We'll probably never know, but we can still enjoy the fruits of his obsession to tell this tale.

KENT DAVIS BIO

Having worked and traveled extensively in Southeast Asia since 1990, Davis is an editor, author, translator (English, Thai, French), independent researcher and literary archaeologist.

Since founding DatAsia Press with his wife Sophaphan in 2005, they have published a series of exceptional books about the history, art and culture of Southeast Asia and French Indochina. Covering topics from ancient times to the mid-20th century, DatAsia editions include contemporary academic analysis, expanded restorations of rare, long out-of-print books, and English translations of French colonial literature.

Davis and his wife also conduct extensive research documenting the *devata* (goddess) images carved in stone in Cambodia, Thailand and Laos (see www.Devata.org).

In 2007, DatAsia funded construction of Srei Devata Middle School in Baray, Kompong Thom through World Assistance for Cambodia (www.CambodiaSchools.org).

Author Bios

From the 1931 edition

Baron Willem Herman thoe Schwartzenberg en Hohenlansberg is of the 22nd generation of a noble Dutch family. Born in Holland in 1879, he went to Java as a young man to learn the management of sugar, tea, coffee, rubber and rice plantations, but owing to ill health returned to Holland after a four years' stay on the island. Subsequently, he adventured in the Argentine and Chile, but it was in Portland, Oregon in 1913 that he met the lady who became his wife. He is now an official of a Santa Barbara, California, bank.

Mrs. Mary Bennett Harrison, born in Chicago and brought up in Topeka, Kansas, is the mother of two stalwart sons and a young daughter. She has had a good deal of journalistic experience on her late husband's newspaper, and for two years was on the editorial staff of "A Child's Garden." Mrs. Harrison is also the author of "By a Way They Know Not," (Revell.) She is a resident of Los Angeles.

JAVANESE WOMEN IN PHOTOS:
EMERGING TECHNOLOGIES AND WORLD VIEWS

by

Kent Davis

"She was all Javanese—straight as an arrow, proud, jealous,
and revengeful in her primitive thoughts."

Arrayed in the brilliant colors of exoticism and exuding a full-blown yet uncertain sensuality, the Orient, where unfathomable mysteries dwell and cruel and barbaric scenes are staged, has fascinated and disturbed Europe for a long time.[1]

Malek Alloula

BY THE DAWN of the 20th century, photography had become a crown jewel in a constellation of communication and transportation technologies that not only changed our world, but forever changed the way people saw, understood and interacted with our world and each other. In searching various archives for this book I found so many obscure colonial photos of Javanese women that I decided to share the best images to both honor their memory, and to reconsider the contrived context of many. All of these women, except for a few royals, have slipped into total anonymity. Their hopes, dreams, accomplishments, loves, losses, hardships and identities have all disappeared into the sea of time. Yet today, more than a century later, we can still look into their eyes while wondering who they really were, and how they lived out their lives.

First we'll have a brief look at the history of photo technology, and learn how it became part of everyday life by the late 19th century. Next we'll meet some of the

---

1 Alloula, Malek. 1997. *The colonial harem*. Minneapolis, MN: University of Minnesota Press. Pg. 3.

photographers who pioneered the art in Java. Foremost among them, from my personal perspective in creating this book, was Kassian Céphas, the first Indonesian photographer. In his lifetime, Céphas created a wealth of important photographic records of his land, including those of the young lady to whom I assigned the visual role of "Adinda" in our novel.

In total the article features 103 vintage images featuring Javanese women in various genres of photography, from royal portraits to advertising images. Please refer to the Illustration Credits on page 513 in the appendices for all photo sources. My goal for this short essay is to give readers a basic background for understanding the images, and to introduce expert sources that will provide a deeper knowledge of the topic for those interested.

A Short (But Long) History of Photographic Technology

The working principles of photography have been known to humanity for well over two thousand years. That's not a typo, but it certainly surprised me. The Chinese philosopher Mozi wrote about projecting images from a bright place to a dark place through a narrow opening using the "camera obscura" effect as early as 400 BCE. Other records suggest even earlier knowledge. The Greek mathematicians Aristotle and Euclid were also describing the effect in the 3rd and 4th centuries BCE.

Eighteen hundred years later(!), Leonardo da Vinci (1452–1519) was actively studying optics and human vision, and he drew 270 diagrams of the camera obscura in the course of his work. By the end of the 16th century, the introduction of lenses improved the device to the point that it became a popular

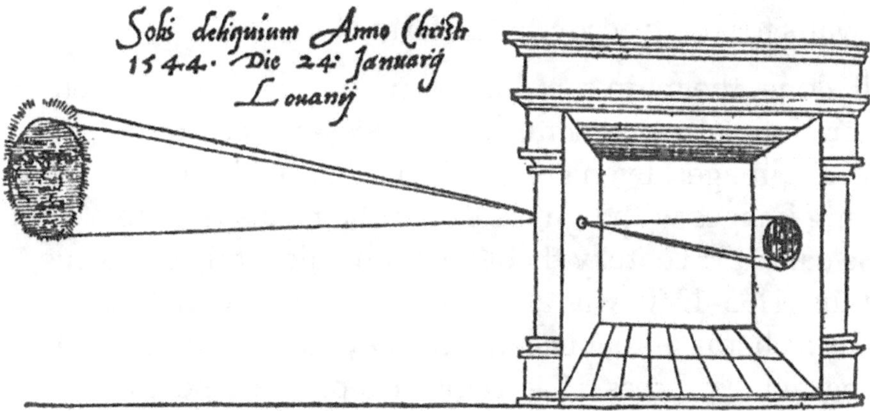

The first published picture of camera obscura in Gemma Frisius' 1545 book
De Radio Astronomica et Geometrica [Wikimedia].

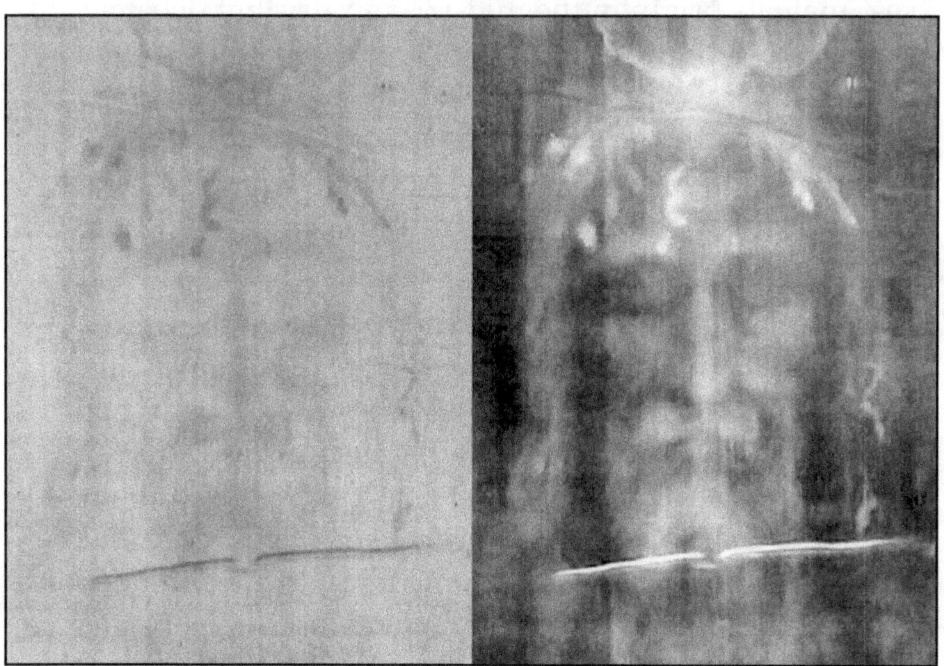

The Shroud of Turin

Technologist and Wikipedia contributor Dianelos Georgoudis processed this
image in color using digital filters. These are mathematical functions that
make existing image information more visible to the naked eye without adding
information. Readers should consult his color original as this image was converted
to black and white and adjusted for publication. All that said… sure looks like a
photographic chemical process to me!

tool that artists used to project their subjects onto canvases and walls for more accurate renderings.

All along, the main component missing to turn a camera obscura into a true camera was a process to record the projected images. Even here, we find that the idea of creating images with light sensitive chemicals is quite old. In the early 13th century theologian and alchemist Albertus Magnus (1193–1280) was already experimenting with silver nitrate, a chemical that became the key element in the early photographic process. Historians also point to the image of Jesus Christ on the 14ft long linen cloth known as the Shroud of Turin as a possible example of photography. In 1988, Oxford University scientists used radiocarbon dating to estimate its origin in the mid-13th century, but debates about the technique used, the age and origin of this relic continue. In any case, from the 16th through the 18th centuries experiments with aspects of the photographic process continued, but it wasn't until the first half of the 19th century that we begin to see true photographs.

That started around 1800 when Englishman Thomas Wedgewood (1771–1805) successfully recorded the first images on a composition of silver nitrate…the same stuff Albertus was fooling around with 600 years earlier! That's the good news. The bad news is that his images were impermanent because their light sensitivity caused them to darken over time. About twenty years later Frenchman Nicéphore Niépce (1765–1833) came up with a technique for photo-etching images onto metal plates, adding permanence to the process. His photo of the view from his studio window in Saint-Loup-de-Varennes, France from 1826 or 1827 is still with us today.

The downside to Niépce's process is that the exposure times—eight hours to several *days*—made it impractical for most applications. Until his death in 1833, Niépce worked closely with the younger Louis-Jacques-Mandé Daguerre (1787–1851), who continued their quest for faster exposure times. The result was the eponymous daguerreotype, which became the first widely used photographic process in the 1840s. Though delicate and chemically complex, Daguerre's process was faster, though at first it still required portrait subjects to sit in bright sunlight for as long as ten minutes. No wonder they weren't smiling! But within a few years, new chemicals and lenses that allowed more light to enter the camera brought exposure times down to a few seconds.

By the second half of the 19th century, photography was radically changing our world and the way we saw it. As photographic processes evolved so did those of printing, transportation and communication. Now people around the globe could see actual images of people, places and events from all its far flung corners. Exotic colonial destinations naturally attracted many early adopters, and so photography came to Java quite early in its development.

Isidore van Kingsbergen's Early Photography of Java

As Daguerre was dying in 1851, Dutch-Flemish engraver Isodorus "Isidore" van Kinsbergen (1821–1905) was on his way to the Dutch East Indies. Having studied painting and singing in Paris, he joined a French opera group traveling to perform in Batavia. Once there, he began studying the emerging science of photography. Daguerreotypes were falling out of use, with albumin silver prints being the new preferred technique from 1860–90. Van Kinsberen went on to take the earliest archaeological and cultural photographs of Java and Bali, and to open the first photograph print processing shop on the island in Batavia.

Balinese dancer in Singaraja, on the north coast of Bali, the first island east of Java, by Isidore van Kinsbergen, c. 1865.

Isodore van Kinsbergen (1821-1905): photo pioneer and theatre maker in the Dutch East Indies by Theuns-de Boer, Gerda, Saskia Asser, and Steven Wachlin.

The cover features three daughters of the Sultan of Jogyakarta.

Overleaf:

**Dancers of Sultan Hamengkubowono VI in Jogjakarta
by Isidore van Kinsbergen, c. 1863-1868.**

**(Is it my imagination or is one little dancer who got stuck in left field
rather unhappy about that?)**

In 2005, his career was documented by the publication of *Isodore van Kinsbergen (1821-1905): photo pioneer and theatre maker in the Dutch East Indies*, by Theuns-de Boer, Gerda, Saskia Asser, and Steven Wachlin. The description of their book adds perspective to his importance:

> "Isidore van Kingsbergen (1821-1905) is sometimes described as the "sleeping beauty" of nineteenth-century photography, because his remarkable body of work has never been presented in its entirety. Yet he was a flamboyant artist who appeals to the imagination. For the first time, this publication gives a broad overview of the exceptional qualities of this photo pioneer. Van Kinsbergen became famous for the almost four hundred photographs he took of Java's antiquities at the behest of the Dutch colonial government and the Batavian Society. Detailed research has also brought to light a hitherto unknown part of his oeuvre, including the portraits he made at the courts of Yogyakarta, Surakarta, Bandung, Madura and Buleleng (Bali). In his studio, he used his experience as a theatre director to photograph people from various social backgrounds in an expressive manner. Due to his tireless efforts for new cultural projects, he has also been called as the "soul of colonial artistic life in Batavia."[2]

The First Javanese Photographer: Kassian Céphas

Kassian Céphas (1845–1912) was not only the first indigenous Indonesian to train as a professional photographer; he was trained at the personal request of Hamengkubuwana VI (1821–1877), the sixth sultan of Yogyakarta. We know much about his life thanks to the

---

2 Theuns-de Boer, Gerda, Saskia Asser, and Steven Wachlin. 2005. *Isodore van Kinsbergen (1821-1905): fotopionier en theatermaker in Nederlands-IndiëIsodore van Kinsbergen (1821-1905) : photo pioneer and theatre maker in the Dutch East Indies*. Zaltbommel: Aprilis.

Kassian Céphas (1845–1912)

Tari Kraton (palace dance) performers from the court of the Yogyakarta Sultanate posed here as bridegroom and bride by Kassian Céphas.

detailed biography Gerrit Knaap and associates published in 1999: *Cephas, Yogyakarta: photography in the service of the sultan.*[3]

Born in Yogyakarta, Céphas became the pupil of Protestant Christian missionaries and later went with them when they moved to Purworejo in Central Java. When he was baptized there in 1860 he adopted Céphas[4] as his family name. He then returned to Yogyakarta to work as an apprentice to a Dutch photographer working in the royal court of the sultan. There is academic debate as to whether his teacher was Simon Willem Camerik, or Isidore van Kingsbergen, who we just met above.[5] The KITLV digital archive at the University

3 Knaap, Gerrit J., Yudhi Soerjoatmodjo, and Céphas. 1999. *Cephas, Yogyakarta: photography in the service of the sultan.* Leiden: KITLV Press.

4 Aramaic for "rock" (*Kepha*), or The Rock, as St. Simon Peter was known.

5 Morris, Rosalind C. 2009. *Photographies East the camera and its histories in East and Southeast Asia.* Durham [NC]: Duke University Press. Pg. 58.

Garden of the East: photography in Indonesia 1850s–1940s.

of Leiden has 77 photos, mostly royal portraits and palace buildings, credited "presumably" to Camerik c. 1860-1875. In a 2016 paper, Waruno Mahdi[6] states that Camerik mentored Céphas, but does not cite any primary evidence, nor did I find any in my admittedly basic research.

In 1871, supposedly upon Camerik's departure, Céphas became the official court painter and photographer at age 26.

6 Mahdi, Waruno, 2016, "Linguistic variety in later nineteenth-century Dutch-edited Malay publications". In YANTI and Timothy MCKINNON, eds. *Studies in language typology and change.* Nusa 60: 121.

Ad for the photo studio of Kassian Céphas in the Dutch language newspaper *Mataram* in Yogyakarta during the 1870s.

From that point he was responsible for numerous portraits of the royal family, as well as documenting theatrical productions of Javanese Hindu dances and the king's dancers. While his dance images are quite dramatic, French historian Claude Guillot observes that Céphas's creativity was restricted in his royal portraits:

> "Undoubtedly by the will of his illustrious clients who wanted the most 'princely' portraits possible, and because of the technical constraints of the photography of the time, the portraits are rigidly posed. With rare exceptions, all life seems to have disappeared. Nothing indicates a trait of character: there are no close-ups; all the portraits are taken standing, face forward, stiffly posed, under equal light. They are images of dignitaries and not images of individuals."[7]

Two of his royal portraits appear on the following pages for consideration, with additional examples later in this article.

Conversely, his portraits of non-royal subjects were so vibrant as to be chosen to appear on the covers of at least two books: this new edition of *Java Girl*, and the 2014 edition of *Garden of the East: photography in Indonesia 1850s-1940s*,

---

7 Guillot, Claude. 1981. "Un exemple d'assimilation à Java: le photographe Kassian Cephas (1844-1912)". *Archipel*. 22 (1): 55-73.

Unknown princess in the Court of Yogyakarta by Kassian Céphas.

Bendoro Raden Ajoe Danoenegoro seen in court dress. She was a member
of the family of Hamengkubuwono VII, Sultan of Jogjakarta,
who reigned from 1877-1921. By Kassian Céphas.

pictured on the previous page, which features works of all the photographers discussed here.[8]

While the sultan who sponsored his study died in 1877, Céphas became even more prolific under the reign of the successor, Sultan Hamengkubuwana VII. Céphas' position in the court also allowed him to procure the newest technology. In 1886, for example, he acquired a camera that captured photos with an exposure time of 1/400th of a second.

Outside the royal court, Céphas began working on archaeological photography, beginning with the excavation of the hidden base of the Borobudur temple complex in 1885. In the closing years of the century he had many publications, and received numerous awards and honors. Céphas retired at age 60 with his son Sem, who assisted him as court photographer, assuming his duties. In 1911 his Christian Javanese wife, Dina Rakijah, passed away at age 65. Céphas died a little more than one year later in 1912. Though the parents didn't live to see it, the family photography venture ended tragically with Sem's death in 1918 at age 48, due to a horse riding accident.

Despite a lifetime of photography, only a few photos of the photographer himself survived, with the most popular being the one included at the beginning of this profile. I am indebted to Kassian Céphas for many of his images that brought *Java Girl* to life. And particularly to an unexplained series of photos he took of one young lady much more than a century ago...

---

8 Newton, Gael, Matt Cox, Vigen Galstyan, Anneke Groeneveld, Annabelle Lacour, Anne Maxwell, Anne O'Hehir, Susie Protschky, and Alex Supartono. 2014. *Garden of the East: photography in Indonesia 1850s-1940s*. Canberra: National Gallery of Australia. See page 361 for a cover photo.

Unknown subject of Kassian Céphas, photographed at an unknown date.
I chose her for the visual role of Adinda in this illustrated novel.

Who was "Adinda"?

"You cannot call yourself a true geisha until you can stop a man in his tracks with a single look."

Mameha – *Memoirs of a Geisha*
(A book by Arthur Golden and Robin Swicord)

The girl I cast as Adinda in this illustrated version of *Java Girl* was no geisha, but she did stop me in my tracks with a single look. Like traditional archaeologists, my job as a literary archaeologist is to dig. Rather than digging in dirt I dig in archives. Some terrific online resources I use include archive.org, worldcat.org, gallica.fr, archives.gov, loc.gov and, especially for this book, Rijksmuseum.nl.

A far more exciting, albeit rarer, opportunity is digging through physical collections. I've been privileged to work on private archives relating to George Groslier, Jean Despujols, Roland Meyer, Harry Hervey, Makhali-Phal and at François Doré's Librairie du Siam et des Colonies in Bangkok. My Publisher's Notes preceding this article describe how François introduced me to *Java Girl,* but I left out one serendipitous detail: his library is where I saw "Adinda" for the first time.

In perusing piles of his antique French periodicals a few years ago, I found a poorly printed image of a "Danseuse Sundanaise" in an issue of *Extrême Asie: revue illustrée indochinoise.* She instantly enchanted me as her expressive

I first saw Adinda's faded picture on the pages of a now 90 year old magazine...

"Adinda" growing from a girl to a woman more than a century ago.

face conveyed innocence, grace and determination. Luckily, my wife tolerates this sort of admiration for other women, but only for those certified to be at *least* 100 years old.

It was surprising to see her there at all since the magazine promoted French Indochina as the official publication of the Indochina Bureau of Tourism from 1924-1935. The June 1928 issue, however, was a special edition entirely devoted to Java. It featured an article, "Une séjour à Java – Journal d'un touriste indochinois", describing the visit of Mr. M. A. Mignon to the island in August of the previous year. Apparently that editor also found the young lady's photo captivating enough to add to this story.

Years went by and I never saw another image of this girl. But as I began my work on the new edition of *Java Girl* I knew she would grace its cover. The quality was poor so my restoration expert, Artsiom Yatsevich, began working. Then something surprising happened: he found a better quality image. Then I found another image of the same girl. And

Adinda seated in what appears to be formal court dress, by Kassian Céphas.

Adinda in formal dress, by Kassian Céphas.

another. A month after my search began I was still finding images of her for a total of eleven, all included in this book.

The archives don't offer specific dates for any of her photos, only stating "1867–1910," which essentially encompasses the entire career of Kassian Céphas. But in examining the entire collection of her images—seen together here for the first time—we discover that she modeled for him on a number of occasions over a period of many years. She appears youngest in the top left photo of the composite, about ten to twelve years old as confirmed by her outfit described on page 412. Then we see her maturing through adolescence and finally appearing as a woman (see page 327). Fortuitously, her appearance and this progression of time fit in perfectly with the plot of *Java Girl*.

Was she a court dancer? Possibly, but she is not seen in any formal photos of the troupe performing. Was she royal? I think not, as evidenced by her lack of jewelry and accoutrements such as we see in royal portraits (look especially at their rings).

On June 28, 1866 Céphas and his wife had one daughter, Naomi. According to Gerrit's biography, Naomi married a Dutch engineer named Christiaan Beem in 1882 and the couple had thirteen children, eight of whom survived to adulthood. Perhaps "Adinda" was the photographer's daughter, or granddaughter. In any case I am grateful that her images survived, and hope many blessings were bestowed on her during her life, and well beyond.

Studio photo by Woodbury & Page of a woman playing a Javanese xylophone in Batavia. From a photo album, *Gezichten van Java* (*Faces in Java*), c. 1880.

Woodbury & Page Photographers, Batavia

Once again, we have accurate records about this firm thanks to the work of a modern photo-historian, in this case Steve Wachlin who published *Woodbury and Page: Photographers Java* in 1994.[9]

Born in Manchester, England, Walter Bentley Woodbury (1834–1885) trained as a civil engineer but became fascinated with the camera obscura. By 1851, he moved to Australia to continue his engineering work for the Melbourne waterworks, but he had also become a professional

9 Wachlin, Steven. 1994. *Woodbury & Page photographers Java*. Leiden: KITLV Press.

photographer by that time. His employer made use of both talents by also having him do documentary photography on water ducts and local buildings.

In the mid-1850s he met James Page, another expatriate British photographer, and in 1857 the two moved to Batavia to establish the Woodbury & Page studio. The next year, the partners traveled through Central and East Java photographing temples, views and other subjects. In 1959 Woodbury returned to England to buy photographic supplies, but also to begin marketing their photos of Java to publishers, collectors and the media.

On his return in 1860, Woodbury continued his photo tour of the island, now covering Central and West Java, accompanied by his 24 year old brother Henry James Woodbury. In 1861, the firm moved to a new location and changed its name to *Photographisch Atelier van Walter Woodbury*, also known as *Atelier Woodbury*. Apparently Page had moved on, but the studio was now well established in every area of photography: in addition to providing portrait services, views of Java and stereographic images they also sold photo supplies, cameras and lenses. Though Woodbury was forced to return to England in early 1863 for health reasons, the company he founded continued to do business into the 20th century.

He never returned to Java but became a prolific inventor during the last 22 years of his life, securing more than 30 patents for photographic equipment and processes. Meanwhile, his venture made a huge contribution to documenting life in the Dutch East Indies, provided many key illustrations of buildings, hotels, factories, people and views for the book. Today, the KITLV digital archive at the University of Leiden has 2,375 Woodbury photos available.

Studio photo of a seated woman by Woodbury & Page.
From a photo album, *Gezichten van Java* (*Faces in Java*)m c. 1865-1890.

Photographer O. Kurkdjian on the edge of the Sand Sea (Lautan Pasir)
in the Tengger Mountains, c. 1910.

Ohannes Kurkdjian

Ohannes Kurkdjian (1851–1903) was born in Yeravan, Armenia the same year that Isidore van Kingsbergen was sailing to Java for the first time. Like Woodbury, he established a large and popular photography business in Surabaya, East Java.

Kurkdjian's work included dramatic landscapes, some with active volcanos, studio portraits of royalty and individuals, commercial subjects, and rural scenes from around Java. Kurkdjian took on English partner G. P. Lewis in 1897, and upon his death in 1903 Lewis took over the business. The

G. P. Lewis (above, far right) continued operations of the Kurkdjian Studio in Surabaya after the death of its founder, c. 1905-1915.

Lewis (below center) with his staff in 1916.
Thilly Weissenborn is pictured right center.

Thilly Weissenborn retouching a photo at Atelier Kurkdjian, Surabaya, c. 1915.

company continued to grow under his management and in 1913 he hired Thilly Weissenborn (1883–1964), the first important Indonesian-born female photographer. Though Thilly's photographic contributions came later than the other images in this book two of her photos are included later in this article so readers can see her technique.

Today, the KITLV digital archive at the University of Leiden has 753 photos available from the Kurdjian studio.

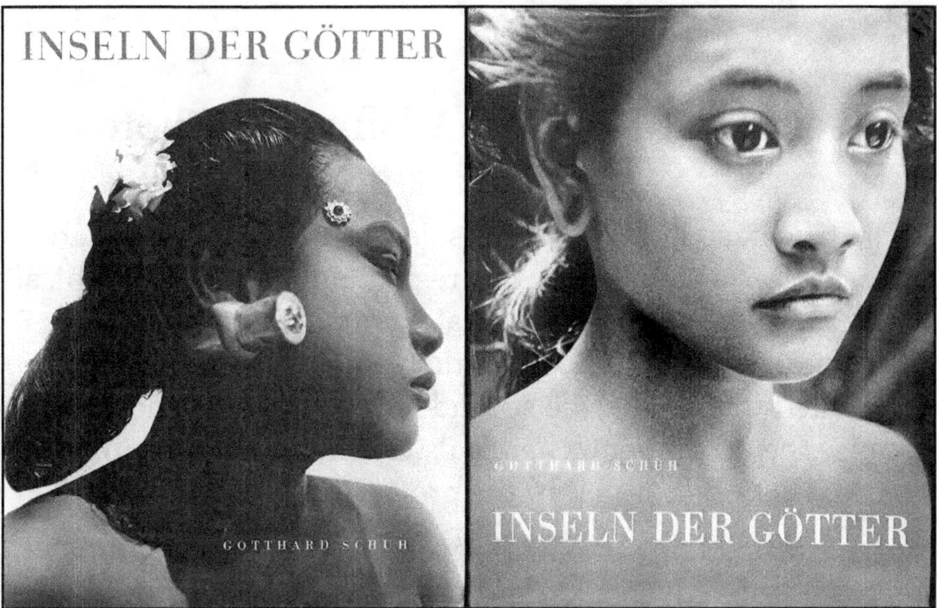

Inseln der Götter by Gotthard Schuh, 1954 and 1960 editions.

Gotthard Schuh

Though he is a "youngster" in this group, I am including mention of Swiss photographer Gotthard Schuh (1897-1969), a pioneer of modern photojournalism. From his 1938-39 Asian photo tour he published one of the most popular photo books about life in pre-WWII Indonesia ever printed:

> The most famous and successful, running to 13 editions, was published in 1941 under the title *Inseln der Götter*. It contained the fruits of an almost 11-month journey to Singapore, Java, Sumatra and Bali, which Schuh had undertaken just before the war. What on the surface could be seen as a mere escape to a paradise populated by beautiful women, turns out on closer scrutiny to also be a successful mixture of reportage and self-observation, a journey inwards.[10]

10 From the exhibition description: "Gotthard Schuh–A Kind of Infatuation" that ran from 30 May to 11 October 2009. [www.fotostiftung.ch/en/exhibitions/past/gotthard-schuh/]

Genres of Javanese Women in Photos

The Java-based photographers described above provided their services as business ventures, though their biographical profiles and their oeuvres indicate that all were personally quite passionate about their work. Commercial photography dominated the field in the second half of the 19th century because the equipment, chemicals and image processing required experts trained in the profession.

They earned their money from studio portraits, selling images in souvenir books, and with an unlimited variety of government and commercial commissions in fields such as archaeology, geography, cultural arts, public works, industry, agriculture, construction, newspapers and advertising. The latter types were invaluable for illustrating scenes and places described in the text of *Java Girl*, just as studio portraits helped to portray characters.

The genres that these photos fall into are determined by their ultimate use and, perhaps most important, by the "eye of the beholder." Here, we will consider the following general categories and topics:

— **Javanese Dancers**

— **Formal Portraits: From Royalty to the Masses**

— **The Age of Image Mass Production**

— **Studio Staging of Woman "at Work"**

— **Postcard Portraits for Collectors**

— **Exoticism**

Studio photo of a Javanese woman in traditional dress by Kassian Céphas.

Studio photo of a Javanese dancer with crown in traditional batik sarong.

Village dancer with orchestra. Date and photographer unknown.

Javanese Dancers

Royal court dancers were frequent photo subjects, whose formal costumes struck me as especially powerful. As it turns out, those female roles are *extremely* powerful in the dance dramas:

When one turns to the archetypal images of womanhood portrayed in the Javanese wayang theatre, however, there is little trace to be found of the simpering Raden Ayu or the passive sex object so beloved of nineteenth-century Dutch writers. Instead, most of the wayang women exude an energy and determination every bit as formidable as that of their menfolk. Dewi Drupadi, the wife of Prabu Yudistira, for example, vowed that she would never again tie her hair

Studio photo of a Javanese dancer with crown and fan, by Kassian Céphas.

into a knot until she had washed it in the blood of Raden
Dursasana, a Kurawa prince who had offended her. This
vow she was later able to make good during the Brathayuda
('Brothers' War') after Dursasana had been slain by Bima,
thus showing that the resolve of women to keep their
promises was even stronger than that of men.[11]

So, despite the demure poses photographers chose for
many female subjects, women historically maintained
powerful roles in Javanese arts, finance, cultural history and
society. Carey's paper goes on to point out

> Indeed, in Surakarta, one of the ladies of the court…bore the
> responsibility for all the contents of the inner court including
> the Sunan's gold and jewelry, as well as the household
> expenses of his establishment. This was regarded as being
> quintessentially 'women's work', just as the oversight of petty
> cash and valuables had, of old, been a female preserve in
> ordinary Javanese families.[12]

Based on that, the popularity of female money changers
as seen on pages 422 and 423 make more sense. Back to
the subject at hand, the photos of Javanese dancers in this
section cover roughly a seventy-year period from the 1860s
through the 1920s.

Overleaf, we have a stunning early image by Kassian
Céphas, circa 1870, showing 8 noble girls carrying the Sultan
of Yogyakarta's crown jewels and sacred accoutrements
under the watchful gaze of their female guards. These girls,
including court dancers, were sequestered in the sultan's
keputren (harem), where they were separated from contact
with males. Apparently the rules were sometimes relaxed for
photographers.

---

11 Carey, Peter and Vincent Houben. "Spirited Srikandhis and Sly Sumbadras–
The social, political and economic role of women at the Central Javanese courts
in the 18th and early 19th centuries." In Locher-Scholten, Elsbeth and Anke
Niehof. 1987. *Indonesian Women in Focus: Past and Present Notions.* Leiden: KITLV
Press. P. 13.

12 Ibid, p. 23.

Princess of the Kraton of Yogyakara by Kassian Céphas. Note her *Paes Ageng*
(*glorious makeup*). **a formal adornment style used by dancers and brides, even today.**

Studio photo of a Javanese dancer in Jogyakarta by Kassian Céphas, c. 1880.

Javanese dancer in festival attire with young assistant, c. 1895-1915.

Javanese dancer in courtyard, by O. Kurkdjian, Co., c. 1912.

Balinese dancer by Thilly Weissenborn, O. Kurkdjian Co., c. 1915–1925.

Formal Portraits: From Royalty to the Masses

Next we'll view examples of studio portrait photography in Java. This quickly became a mainstay of photography businesses beginning with the daguerreotype in the mid-19th century; the first commercial process to speed up exposure times and reduce costs. Before photos, portraits were generally only available to individuals wealthy enough to commission a painting.

While earlier photographic portraits featured royalty and the elite, decreasing prices soon allowed working class families and individuals to create photographic keepsakes of their own. The following pages show royal portraits, followed by studio portraits of individual women, couples and families. While it is possible that the individual Javanese women in this section (or their husbands or parents) commissioned the portraits, it is likely that some were staged by the photographers for resale. We'll explore this concept further in the next section.

Goesti Raden Ajoe Sekar Kedaton seen in court dress. She was a member
of the family of Hamengkubuwono VII, Sultan of Jogjakarta,
who reigned from 1877-1921. By Kassian Céphas.

Raden Ajoe Sriwoelan seen in court dress. Note that the name "Sriwoelan" seems to be of Siamese origin. She was a member of the family of Hamengkubuwono VII, Sultan of Jogjakarta, who reigned from 1877-1921. By Kassian Céphas.

Bendoro Raden Ajoe Danoe Adiningrat seen in court dress. Note that the name "Adiningrat" seems to be of Siamese origin. She was also in the family of Hamengkubuwono VII, Sultan of Jogjakarta. By Kassian Céphas

Wife of Regent of Blora, circa 1860-1890 by Woodbury & Page.

Formal portrait of an unknown woman. Her jewelry, clothing and shoes suggest she is royal or a member of an elite family.

Formal portrait of an unknown woman standing. Note the next two two portraits are taken in the same studio, which one archive linked to Buitzenborg.

Formal portrait of an unknown woman standing with fan.

Another standing portrait with fan, from the same studio.

An undated early portrait of a man with his family, meticulously staged by
Isodore Van Kinsbergen. Note that his foot is *under* the tablecloth.

A village headman from Demang, about 350 miles northwest of Java
on the island of Sumatra, in a studio portrait with his family.
Credited to Woodbury & Page in Buitenzorg, c. 1860-1878.

A couple posing in a studio at the Hotel des Indes in Batavia.

Above: A Javanese mother posing with her Eurasian daughter.

Overleaf: A group portrait of Javanese women in the palace, circa 1901, by Kassian Céphas. In his 2013 book, *Soeka-doeka di Djawa tempo doeloe*, Olivier Johannes Raap suggests that these are not princesses but instead wives of courtiers and lower nobles. He also noted that the woman left rear is pregnant and that "among fifteen girls, a boy becomes a rooster in a chicken coop." Well, certainly in a few years!

Javanese dancers on a postcard.

Batik making on a postcard from Uitgave Boekhandel Visser & Co., Weltevreden.

The Age of Image Mass Production

As the 18th century drew to a close, two things began decreasing demand for professional photography. The first event was when American entrepreneur George Eastman (1854–1932) patented flexible roll film in 1884 (Incidentally, his invention soon led to the invention of motion pictures). In the coming decades, cameras and film evolved quickly, making photography less expensive, more portable and more practical for amateur practitioners. People began to make their own memories so commercial photographers were in less demand. On page 492, you can see his Folding Pocket Kodak introduced in 1900. Finally, not to be a buzzkill, but I was saddened to learn that the great inventor Eastman, who has touched all of our lives, committed suicide due to chronic pain at age 76.

G. Kolff & Co., a postcard publisher in Batavia, 1910.

F. B. Smits, yet another postcard publisher, Batavia, 1902.

The second surprising, but truly world-changing, development was the invention of the picture postcard. In his entertaining, informative and highly readable book, *Paris postcards–The Golden Age*, Leonard Pitt provides a succinct introduction:

> Few people would believe that something as common as the postcard could have such a dramatic history. In the 1870s, before electricity and telephones were part of every household, the introduction of the postcard revolutionized communication and created the first form of social networking equivalent to today's e-mail.
>
> Many deplored the novelty, certain that this new type of message, shorter than the traditional letter, meant that people would forget how to write. Similar objections surfaced when the first photographs began appearing on postcards in the 1890s. It was feared that people, awash in images, would forget how to read. For the educated classes, postcards were considered vulgar. Abbreviations were crude, no better than slang. A missive without proper introductions and salutations was objectionable…

Long after posing in Kassian Céphas's studio, "Adinda" began appearing on postcards, like these two printed by Kunsthandel J. Sigrist in Djocja, Yogyakarta.

In his book, *Soeka-doeka di Djawa tempo doeloe*, Olivier Johannes Raap notes that above she is wearing a *Pinjung Kencong*, a dress traditionally worn by girls older than 10, but before puberty, with a *kemban* (chest cloth) knotted in a triangle, and a batik *wala* belt wrapped at the waist. Her forehead hairline looks like *Paes Ageng* (*glorious makeup*). a formal style used by dancers, or she is dressed for a *Ta Rapan* ceremony (after first menstruation) before changing to adult women's attire.

For this portrait, our cover photo, Raap speculates she could be as old as 25, and observes that her *kemban* (chest cloth) is shiny, so may be made from satin with embroidered motifs. He also notes her cleft chin, speculating that our "Java Girl" may have mixed ancestry of non-Javanese descent!

> By the time the postcard reached its Golden Age, from around
> 1895 to 1915, collecting became a phenomenon and no home
> was complete without a postcard album or two in the parlor,
> second in importance only to the bible... Every city and town
> had legions of postcard sellers, postcard hawkers, postcard
> racks, and whole shops that sold nothing but postcards... By
> 1900, there were international postcard shows, local postcard
> clubs, and magazines devoted to postcards.[13]

As an exotic colonial destination, Java was at the forefront
of the postcard revolution. Photographers sold images to
postcard printers who, through mass production, slowly
diluted the value of and need for custom photos (and that in
addition to the growth of amateur photography). Again we'll
turn to Alloula for his darker vision of colonial postcards:

> The postcard... becomes the poor man's phantasm: for a
> few pennies, display racks full of dreams. The postcard is
> everywhere, covering all the colonial space, immediately
> available to the tourist, the soldier, the colonist. It is at
> once their poetry and their glory captured for the ages; it
> is also their pseudo-knowledge of the colony. It produces
> stereotypes in the manner of great seabirds producing
> guano. It is the fertilizer of the colonial vision.[14]

The images in this section validate his view that staged
photography—and moreover the mass media diffusion of
those images as postcards—created striking, but sometimes
distorted, impressions of colonial life in general, and local
women and cultures in specific. Alloula sets the Golden Age
of colonial postcards between 1900 and 1930, which is why
I've relied heavily on postcards for images in my *other* literary
projects, generally set from 1910 to 1930. But as *Java Girl* was
set in or before 1900, few postcards were relevant. Even better
in this case, I found high quality photos to illustrate the story
thanks to the Rijksmuseum, and similar sources.

---

13 Pitt, Leonard. 2016. *Paris postcards-the golden age.* Amberley Publishing, 2016. P. xi.
14 Malek Allouha, *The Colonial Harem,* p 4.

These photos appeared as postcards advertising the Preanger Hotel (left) and Batavia tourism (right) with the cheery message "Groet uit BATAVIA."

Photos for print advertising were also in demand, like the series from Boehm's Toilet Soaps and Perfumeries, whose owner identified as a photographer himself.

In 1899, Gustav Boehm (1827–1900) set out from Offenbach, Germany on a round-the-world cruise. After passing through the Suez Canal he stopped at more than a dozen ports before reaching Java. At each stop, he added to his gelatin silver photo collection by staging shots with colorful "ethnic types," including women in Java. as seen in the following pages. It seems that he made it through his trip, but perhaps it exhausted him as he died on November 6, 1900.

Whether on postcards, in ads, or on advertising postcards, women have always been popular for adding "sex appeal," regardless of how little their images may have to do with the

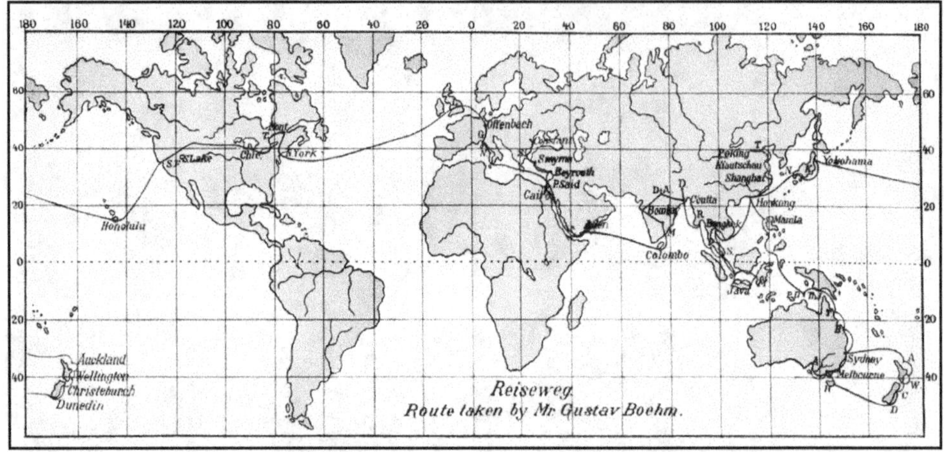

Gustav Boehm's photographic journey around the world in 1899.

products promoted. As the postcard trend swept the world, images of the women themselves often became the product, but some were cast in an educational light by capturing images of daily life in the distant colonies.

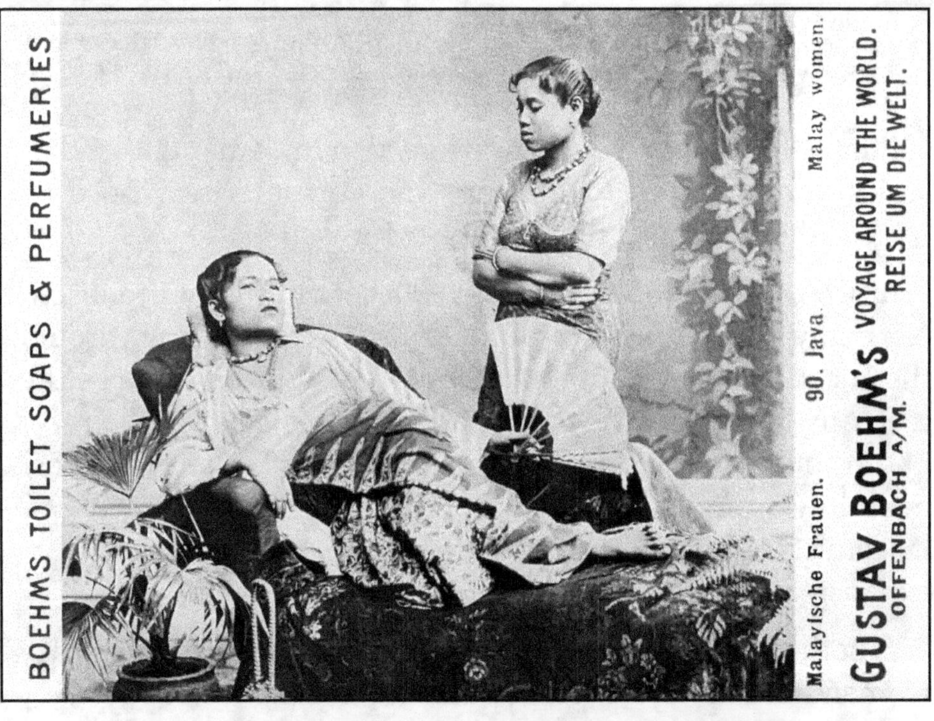

Gustav Boehm's Java series of ads, above and on the three following pages.

BOEHM'S TOILET SOAPS & PERFUMERIES
Javanische Mädchen.   98. Java.   Javanese girls.
GUSTAV BOEHM'S   VOYAGE AROUND THE WORLD.
OFFENBACH A/M.   REISE UM DIE WELT.

BOEHM'S TOILET SOAPS & PERFUMERIES
Malayische Frau.
96. Java.
Malay woman.
GUSTAV BOEHM'S
OFFENBACH A/M.
VOYAGE AROUND THE WORLD.
REISE UM DIE WELT.

BOEHM'S TOILET SOAPS & PERFUMERIES
Malayisches Brautpaar.   97. Java.   Malay bridal pair.
GUSTAV BOEHM'S
OFFENBACH A/M.
VOYAGE AROUND THE WORLD.
REISE UM DIE WELT.

A young couple "cooking" in a studio setting.

Woman at Work and Outdoors

"Photographs are, of course, artifacts…They are clouds of fantasy and pellets of the real."

—Susan Sontag, *On Photography*

Women's vocations were popular topics in the studio and in the field. Later, postcards featured images of women cooking, making batik and lace, giving massage, selling coconuts, playing music, etc.

In the early days of photography, the rarest type of photo was the candid shot due to equipment limitations. By the end of the 19th, and in the early 20th century, photographers portrayed more women in authentic outdoor settings.

Vegetable sellers, c. 1912, by Ohannes Kurkdjian studio.

Money changers were mostly women. The stone set piece identifies this as Kassian Céphas' studio, but archives link the backdrop to Ali S. Cohan. Both this image and the one to the right appeared as postcards by 1908.

The same money changer girl with a different pose..

A trip to the beauty salon…or looking for bugs? In either case, this c. 1890 photo is credited to Ali S. Cohan due to the backdrop. And doesn't that girl look familiar? Let's ask her to turn toward the camera…

Why that's the same girl in the same photo as one of Gustav Boehm's soap ads! Maybe he *didn't* do all his own photography!

Woman with a sheaf of rice in her hands. O. Kurdjian, c. 1912.

Women husking and pounding rice.

Three Balinese women pounding rice, c. 1920.

Girl from Garut selling sarongs by Thilly Weissenborn, c. 1920.

Women shelling cocoa near Buitenzorg, c. 1895-1915.

Women kapok pickers. The photos appear to have been taken at the same place and time, but with different subjects.

Woman sorting tobacco by Ohannes Kurkdjian studio.

Woman with orangutan in Stabat, Sumatra by H. Ernst & Co, c. 1890-1900.

Woman outdoors by Ohannes Kurkdjian studio, c. 1912.

Woman leaning against a stone pole by Ohannes Kurkdjian studio, c. 1912.

Javanese woman in traditional dress by Kassian Céphas.

Postcard Portraits for Collectors

Speaking of staged photos, Jennifer Yee at the University of Oxford makes a number of interesting observations about portrait postcards in her article, "Recycling the 'Colonial Harem'? Women in Postcards from French Indochina." Though her paper is about postcards in French colonies, I find her comments equally valid for the Dutch East Indies.

Yee notes that a number of formal portraits of ostensibly upper class Indochinese women appearing on postcards were formulaic in nature. The same women appeared in multiple poses on a series of postcards, but featuring the same elegant setting with ornate backdrop, draped table, jewelry box, flowers, etc. We see this happening in Java studios as well. Yee's first conclusion is that "In fact this is *not* a portrait of an individual, but an image that stages, or *performs*, Indochinese bourgeois respectability."

Expanding on these images as collectible series of respectable postcards she writes

"These 'portrait' postcards create a tamed version of exoticism, establishing what could in some ways be called an *anti-exotic* aesthetics. These images, read syntagmatically, tell of young women of means, in comfortable cultivated interiors. They can be read within the paradigm of other such photographic images: that is, the portraits of the French middle-class postcard-collecting young lady. This myth asserts the sameness and equivalence of the bourgeois feminine experience as it is lived in France and in France's

Javanese woman in traditional dress by Kassian Céphas.

distant colonies. And yet at the same time the captions affirm that the subject here is not in fact individual but general: they are representations of ethnographic 'types', and also objects to be collected."[15]

Yee found a number of these "anti-exotic" portrait postcards of Indochinese women addressed to women in France. So while we might imagine swarthy French (or Dutch) soldiers sending provocative postcards of "native girls" to buddies back home, her paper suggests that many may have been sent by women, to women. They expressed the "middle-class respectability" that the women shared, "but simultaneously reaffirm exotic difference." Just as men may be curious about women from other cultures, it makes sense that women would want to see their counterparts as well.

While some of the earlier portraits of Javanese women create a faux sense of luxury, the posed studio settings of Javanese women mostly seem to emphasize clothing styles and the beautiful batik fabrics that "René's sisters would have given a pretty penny to own" in the book. Indeed, I see true cultural pride in the images of these Javanese women wearing their handmade fabrics, especially those done by Javanese photographer Kassian Céphas. While Malek Allouha saw only prurient degradation and cultural distortion in images he analyzed in *The Colonial Harem,* I find Yee's balanced view more logical based on this evidence.

Note that most of the images in this book predate the era of mass production, but quite a few eventually appeared on postcards. Still, they were sold as souvenir albums even before that so, with Yee's article in mind, I present this section's portraits as possible examples of "anti-exotic" images that European women may have appreciated as much, or more than, European men.

---

15 Yee, Jennifer. 2004. "Recycling the 'Colonial Harem'? Women in Postcards from French Indochina". *French Cultural Studies.* 15 (1): 5-19. P. 14.

Studio portrait of two Javanese women in traditional attire by Kassian Céphas.

**Studio portrait of two Javanese women in traditional attire
by Woodbury & Page, Batavia, c. 1880.**

Studio portraits of two Javanese girls in Makassar from the photo album entitled *Gezichten van Java* (*Faces of Java*). By Woodbury & Page, c. 1870.

Javanese woman in traditional attire by Kassian Céphas.

Javanese woman in traditional attire by Kassian Céphas.

Javanese woman in Jogyakarta wearing traditional clothing by Kassian Céphas, c. 1870.

Javanese woman in traditional attire by Kassian Céphas.

Organized to commemorate the 400th anniversary of Columbus's landfall in the Americas, the 1893 World Columbian Exposition, also known as the Chicago World's Fair, was a seminal event in American history. Its Midway was inspired by the 1889 Paris Universal Exposition where the French government created living ethnological villages to represent French colonies in Asia and Africa. Chicago also included ethnographic exhibits, but for commercial reasons.

Miss Taojong, above, represented Java at the fair.

Javanese girl wearing *pajoeng* in Jogyakarta by Kassian Céphas, c. 1890.

Javanese woman in traditional attire by Kassian Céphas.

Javanese woman in traditional attire by Kassian Céphas.

This unknown Javanese girl appeared on an early postcard. I'm pretty sure that if you look up "exotic" in your dictionary, you will find her photo there.

Exoticism

"I don't know if all the women in the photographs are
beautiful, but I do know the women are beautiful in
the photographs."

Garry Winogrand
Photographer, (1928-1984)

Having covered "anti-exotic" we'll conclude with images
that seem to capture beautiful women for the sake of their
beauty—with an added dash of exoticism—and, more than
likely, profit motive. Indeed, many "vocation" or "portrait"
images also portray Javanese women as "exotic," thereby
combining genres. Judy Sund offers us an elegant definition:

"The word 'exotic' is rooted in the Greek word *exo* ('outside')
and means, literally, 'from outside'. It was coined during
Europe's Age of Discovery, when 'outside' seemed to grow
larger each day, as Western ships sailed the world and
dropped anchor off other continents.

The first definition of 'exotic' in most modern dictionaries
is 'foreign', but while all things exotic are foreign, not
everything foreign is exotic.

Since there is no outside without an inside, the foreign only
becomes exotic when imported – brought from the outside
in. From the early seventeenth century, 'exotic' has denoted

enticing strangeness – or, as one modern dictionary puts it,
'the charm or fascination of the unfamiliar'."[16]

Few places in the world conjure up dreams of the exotic
as much as the Far East. And here we come full circle, back
to the first page of *Java Girl*, when the young René Van
Landsberg gazed out at the volcanic jungle island from his
ship thinking

**"This was Java—the end of his journey—and he was a little
frightened at all that the suave, exotic name implied."**

Here, in conclusion to my article, are some of the island's
"exotic" inhabitants, as photographers saw them more than a
century ago.

---

16 Sund, Judy. 2019. *Exotic – a Fetish for the Foreign*, London: Phaidon Press.

Unknown Javanese women by unknown photographer, above and overleaf.

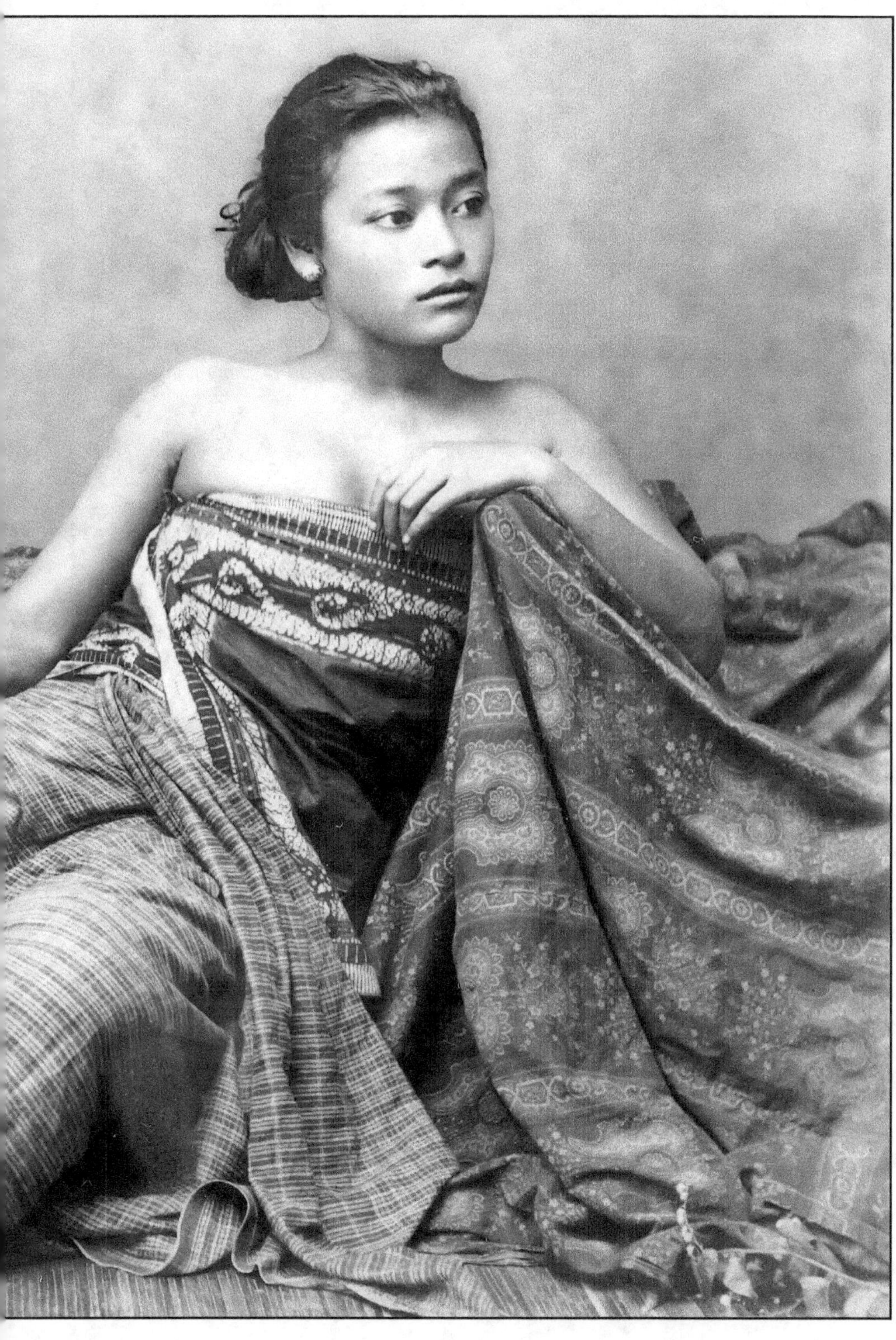

Javanese girl simulating a bath (see water urn and dipper lower left, but floor is not wet), apparently in the studio of Ali S. Cohan, judging from the backdrop. These photos later appeared as popular postcards.

Javanese girl wrapping sarong after her simulated bath. Her Batik fabric pattern is called *Ceplok Grompol* ("gathering together") and is often worn at weddings because it symbolizes a harmonious union. The large decorative motifs are called *Kembang Kopi*, meaning Coffee Flower.

Javanese girl wearing sarong by Kassian Céphas, based on the studio background piece seen in his credited photos overleaf and elsewhere.

Javanese woman wearing sarong by Kassian Céphas.

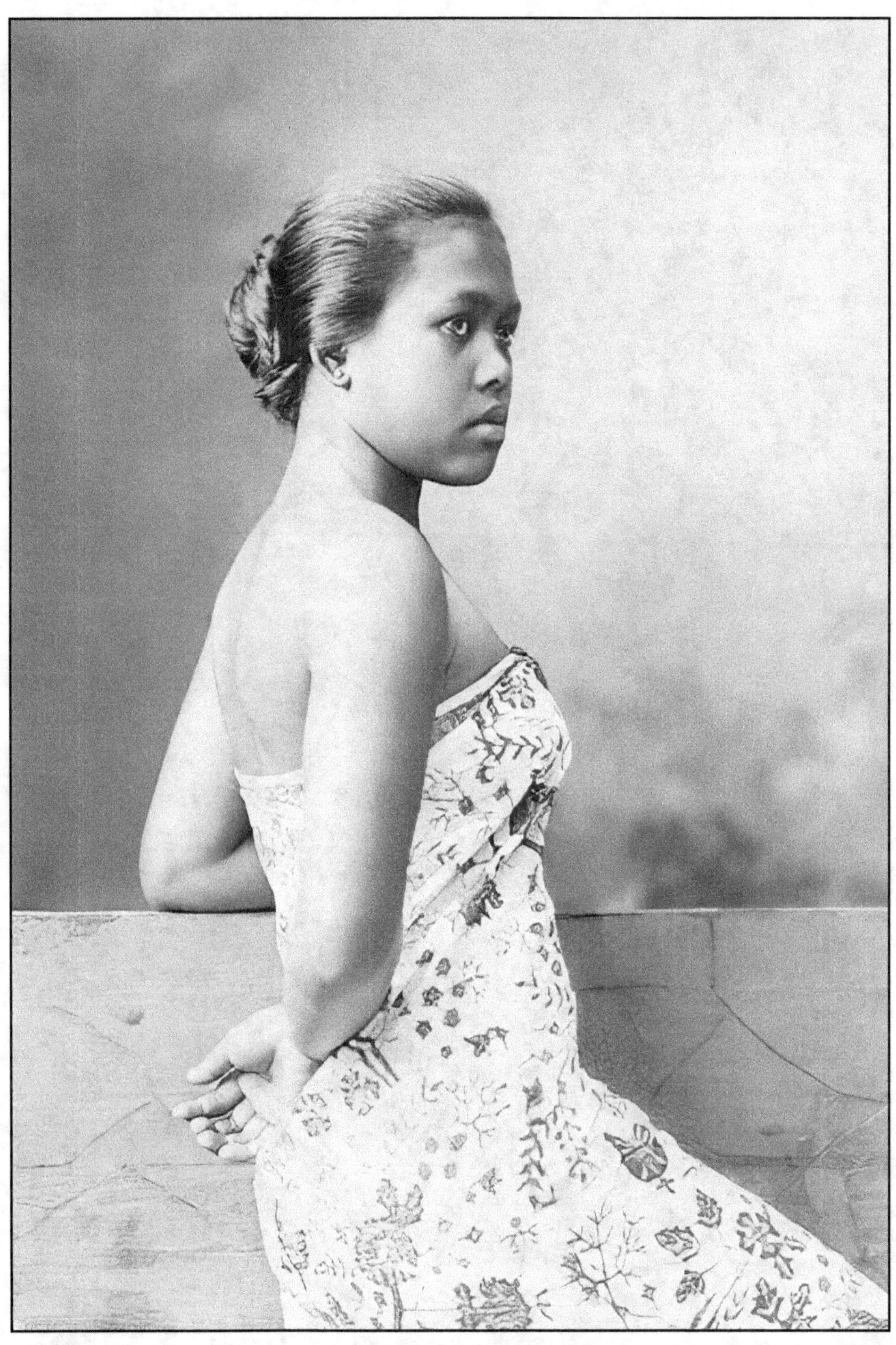

Sumatran girl wearling sarong.

Javanese woman wearing sarong in hut (note dirt floor).

Studio portrait of a Javanese girl balancing basket on her head.

Studio portrait of a young Javanese woman by Woodbury & Page.

The KITLV archive identifies her as originally being from Pontianak, the capital of the Indonesian province of West Kalimantan about 450 miles north of Java. Here she is decribed as being in the service of the Susuhunan of Surakarta, Central Java (Susuhunan is a title used by the hereditary rulers of that region). Given the estimated date of 1870, she was working for Paku Buwono IX who reigned from 1861 until his death in 1893.

The same woman with her hair (and *kemben*?) down.

Above, a woman receiving massage from young boy by Kassian Céphas.
Below, an old woman gives a more credible massage, by an unknown photographer.

Studio portrait by Kassian Céphas.

A Javanese girl photographed by Woodbury & Page, c. 1867.

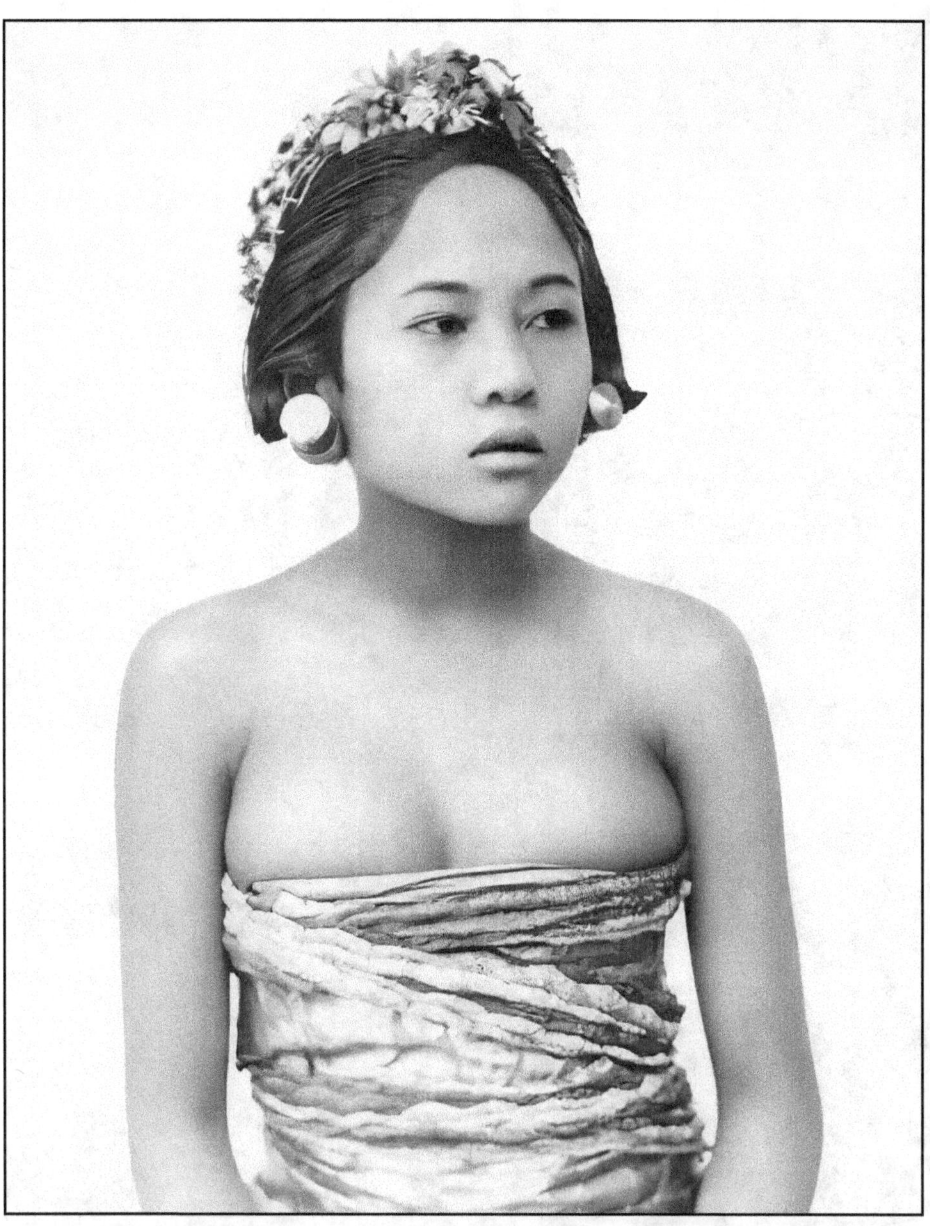

Do you notice *anything* about the Balinese girl above? If so, she listened to her mother.

**"The only things one instructs a young daughter in is [how to be] comely, demure
and of good deportment; to go around with the breasts almost completely
uncovered; not to speak in company, and to adopt a blushing and dissembling
attitude, so that once they are taken into the [royal] seraglio they can make
themselves [...] attractive to the ruler and favoured above all others [...]"**

Peter Carey and Vicent Houben quoting J. W. Winter's 1902 book. See fn. 9.

In the view of Olivier Johannes Raap (*Soeka-doeka di Djawa tempo doeloe*), she may be a *mbok emban* (wet nurse). Her clothing fabric and pattern are worn by the lower middle class, but the baby's sling is expensive batik. Also, upper class Javanese women do not nurse in public. Based on the background we credit Ali S. Cohan.

ISLES OF THE EAST
THE ROYAL PACKET STEAM NAVIGATION Co
TINDALL
AN ILLUSTRATED GUIDE TO Australia, Papua, Java, Sumatra Etc.

Isles of the East – 1912

MODERN EDITOR'S NOTE - The advertisements, text and language lessons in this section are extracted from the first edition of the 360 page "Isles of the East" illustrated guide, edited by W. Lorck and originally published in January 1912.

§

Introduction

Java! There is music in the word when spoken. It sounds like a bar of a soft melody, like the first syllables of a poem appealing to one's sympathy.

And the Island of Java certainly can claim not only one's sympathy, but the greatest interest, may the visitor to its shores be a sight-seer, a man of affairs, a scientist or a *literateur* in search of knowledge.

The field of attraction is so diversified, the horizon of enthralling beauty and scenic magnificence so wide, that it becomes a difficult task indeed to finally settle on a choice of route through the glories of this wonderful Isle of the East—Java.

Round Australia

via JAVA.

"The Garden of the East."

xv.

The following pages have been compiled in the endeavour to place before intending tourists some of the most prominent attractions, in picture and word, touching also to a small extent upon commercial matters of the Dutch Indies.

The Editor.

§

Java Mode of Living

It is advisable to rise at 6 a.m. to enjoy the glorious morning, which will be appreciated as the best part of the day. Take a shower-bath and order your tea or coffee which will be brought by your room "jonges."

If a good pedestrian, a walk is recommended. If driving is preferable, order a carriage from the hotel or engage a public vehicle and obtain a view of your surroundings. Return by 8 o'clock and breakfast.

Further excursions may be made till noon, when all principal stores close, opening again at 4 p.m. Business houses are open all day until the last-named hour.

After tiffin (12.30), rest; rising at 4 o'clock a second bath will be welcome, after which order your afternoon tea or coffee. A visit to the city with a call at the Club will fill in the evening till 7.30 p.m., when it is time to return to your hotel and to dress for dinner (8.30).

To ladies, lightest muslin or silk is recommended. To gentlemen, white clothes and boots for every-day wear are necessary to spend your time in comfort. Very light woolen underwear is recommended. Native laundrymen are quick and cheap.

The stores in all settled towns are up-to-date, and European doctors and chemists are easily available.

Make your complaints, if any, to the hotel manager and not to native attendants.

Important Notice.

Visitors to the ports of Sourabaya and Batavia particularly, have been deceived into the belief that smooth-tongued agents, representing themselves as coming from the Tourist Bureau, are really authorised by the Official Tourist Bureau, which is controlled by the Government. Such is not the case! To avoid misconception, it is well to note, that the Official Tourist Bureau is an institution established for the purpose of affording free of cost or profit every available information in order to assist the visitors to Java. The Official Tourist Bureau does not attend to luggage or baggage; it does not conduct trips through Java, it does not sell hotel coupons in order to make a commission.

The best advice to Tourists requiring accommodation is to wire to one of the leading Hotels (a list is to be found in these pages), and they will attend to luggage, etc., at the recognised rates—without overcharge or commission.

W. Lorck
Sole Editor.

Hotel des Indes

Batavia, Weltevreden,
* JAVA. *

Standing in 15 acres of well laid out grounds, and situated in the heart of the Garden City, is the leading Hotel in the Dutch Indies.

The recognised Home of the Tourist.

Bungalows and apartments replete with every modern convenience.

PERFECT SERVICE.
MAGNIFICENT DINING HALL.
UNSURPASSED CUISINE and CELLAR.

Motor Cars and Carriages at the disposal of guests at shortest notice.

Steamers and Trains met on arrival. Luggage carefully attended to.

All Correspondence promptly attended to.

Telegraphic Address:
" INDES,"
Weltevredren.

THE MANAGING DIRECTOR,

Hotel des Indes,
Weltevredren.

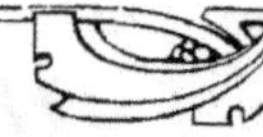

Established 1883.

E. DUNLOP & CO.

General Merchants and Importers

Wine and Spirit Merchants.

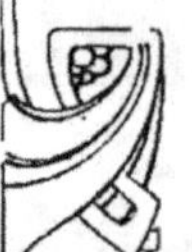

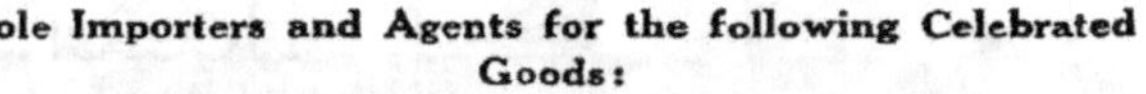

Sole Importers and Agents for the following Celebrated Goods:

Pièrre Chabanneau & Co.'s Brandies and Wines.

The Isle of Skye Whisky.　　Wittkampf Gin.

Usher's Whisky.　　Henkes' Gin.

Amstel Beer.　　Bokma Gin.

Lucas Bols' Gin and Liqueurs.

Gutierrez Hermano's Invalid Port.

Korff's Cocoa and Chocolate Tablets.

Bitters.

Swiss Milk (Bear Brand).

Bordeaux, Greek and Italian Wines.

Champagnes and Brandies.

A. G. Cousins & Co.'s Celebrated Egyptian Cigarette Company, Malta.

Th. Vafiadis & Co., M. Malachrino & Co., and the Anglo-Egyptian Cigarette Company, Cairo.

Also English, Turkish and Russian Cigarettes.

Large stock of Havana, Dutch and Manila Cigars.

Sporting Goods, Bicycles, Japanese Curios, Travellers' Requisites.

Head Office : BATAVIA.

Branches : WELTEVREDEN, BANDOENG, SAMARANG and SOERABAYA.

John Pryce & Co.

Auctioneers & Commission Agents
to the Government of the Dutch Indies.

| Furniture Store: **KALI-BESAR, NOORDWIJK.** |  | **BATAVIA** — **JAVA.** |

DRILLS—Khaki and White. COTTON—Shirtings, Sheeting. PLATE—
—Electro-Plated Goods. KNIVES—"Rodgers'" Pocket, Bowie, etc.
SCISSORS—"Rodgers'" 9in. Cutting-out, etc. RAZORS—"Rodgers'"
Best Ivory Handles.

GUNS—Sporting Double-Barrel, cal. 12, 15, 24, 28, and 12 m.m.

RIFLES - - "Winchester,"
22 AUTOMATIC, 10 SHOT.   22 SINGLE SHOT.

PISTOLS -- "Colts," "Browning" Automatic, cal. 32 and 38.

═══ REVOLVERS ═══
"COLTS" POLICE-POSITIVE. Cal. 32 and 38.
"SMITH & WESSON" D.A., Cal. 38. ———

FILTERS—"Atken's," "Army" en "Navy"
SOAP—"Pears'," "Calvert's," "Cuticle," etc., etc.

Ammunition for foregoing Guns, Pistols, Revolvers, etc.

SPORTING ACCESSORIES—Cartridge Cases, etc., etc.
"TOWER BULLDOG" Pocket Revolvers, 450,etc.

A VARIETY OF ARTICLES FOR TOURISTS, Etc. ..

WINES—Bordeaux, "Chateau Montagne."   BRANDY—Vieux Cognac.
WHISKY—D.C.L , King George IV.

VAN ARCKEN & CO.

BATAVIA and SOURABAYA

JEWELLERS, WATCHMAKERS AND ENGRAVERS

To the Court of the Netherlands since 1854.

Manufacturers
and Repairers
of all kinds of
JEWELLERY

Fancy
Native Handwork
a Speciality.

Workshop for
Electroplating and
Gilding.

Specialists in Repairing
Chronometers
and Fine
Lever Watches.

Grandfather,
Westminster Abbey
Clocks, &c.

SOLE AGENTS for the Netherlands East Indies of the ZENITH WATCH, which represents
the highest grade of perfection in time keeping and excellence in workmanship

Hotel Homann

BANDOENG.

Entirely rebuilt in a complete modern style. Is one of the few Indian Hotels that is specially built for an Hotel, with more than sixty spacious and airy chambers, amongst which Pavilions and rooms with magnificent mountain views. Separate Recreation and Reading Saloons, and a newly rebuilt modern Dining-hall.

Garage for Motor Cars.

The Hotel is throughout fitted with Electric Light.

EXCELLENT ATTENDANCE.

EUROPEAN CUISINE.

Acknowledged to be the most excellent in Java.

Telegraphic Address : " HOMANN, BANDOENG."

Hotel Belle Vue

BUITENZORG,

JAVA,

OFFERS unrivalled accommodation to Tourists and Visitors.

Large, Airy and Comfortable Apartments.

Up-to-date Cuisine and Cellar.

Perfect Attendance.

Moderate Tariff.

A Carriage meets all Trains.

GARREAU FRÈRES,

PROPRIETORS.

Also Managers and Proprietors of the favourite HOTEL DU CHEMIN DE FER, BUITENZORG.

Correspondence receives prompt attention.

MALAY VOCABULARY.

A few every-day single words and sentences, etc., in English and Malay may be useful.

I will go	Saja pigi
Go quickly	Pigi lekas
How much (price) ?	Brapa doewit
How much (quantity)?	Brapa ada
I won't do it	Tida maoe
I won't give it	Tida kassi
I don't allow it	Saja tida kassi
That's enough	Ini sampeh
All right; it is enough	Soedah
Come here	Mari sini
Don't want it	Tida maoe
Go	Pigi
Wait a little	Nanti sedikit
It is no use bothering me any more	Soedah, habis perkara
Hold your tongue	Diam kwe
Be off	Pigi
Here, coolie, take my luggage	Sini, coolie, angkat barang
Two men only	Doewa orang sadja
Five pieces	Lima potong
Are you the *mandoer* from Hotel X?	Kwe mandoer Hotel X ?
Yes, Sir.	Saja Toean
Here is the receipt of my luggage, you take care of it, pay the coolies for me and bring it to the Hotel.	Ini recu deri bagazie, kwe djaga, bajar coolie dan bawa di Hotel.
Here is a quarter (0.25) to pay the coolies.	Ini satoe talen (stali) (f 0.25) boewat bajar coolie.
Where is your bus (waggon)?	Mana omnibus? Kareta?
Everything allright?	Soedah klar?

Go on, then.	Madjoe.
Have you a room?	Ada kamar?
Where is the landlord?	Mana toean roemah makan?
Boy, take my luggage to "No. 50," five pieces.	Jonges, bawa barang di "kamar 50," ada lima potong.
Have you got them?	Soedah ada?
I want some tea or coffee.	Saja minta te (koppie).
Is there no barber?	Tida ada toekang tjoekoer?
Yes, Sir, he will be here after a while.	Ada toean, nanti datang.
Call the washerman for me.	Pangil menatoe.
Here, washerman, are 20 pieces. I want them back in three days; that means on the 29th at 5 o'clock in the afternoon.	Sini, menatoe doewapoeloe potong, minta kombali dalem tiga hari, djadi hari doewapoeloe sembilan, poekoel lima sore.
All right, Sir.	Baai Toean.
Boy, I want some writing paper, some ink and a pen.	Jonges, minta kertas toelis dan penna tinta.
I want some icewater.	Minta ajer ice.
I want a bottle of apollinaris.	Minta ajer blanda.
Where is the lavatory?	Mana kamar ketjil?
Where is the bathroom?	Mana kamar mandi?
Open this bottle.	Boeka ini bottel.
Open this trunk.	Boeka ini kopper.
At what time is dinner, boy?	Poekoel brapa makan, jonges?
Remember, if you don't look after the mosquitos, you don't get your tip.	Ingat, kaloe kwe tida djaga njamok kwe tida dapat presfen.
Wake me up to-morrow at 6 o'clock sharp. I want to leave by the first train to Buitenzorg.	Kassi bangoen bissok pagi poekoel annem betoel. Saja maoe pigi di Buitenzorg (Bogor).

Can I have some breakfast before I leave?	Bisa dapat makan doeloean?
Yes, Sir, breakfast is always ready at 6 o'clock.	Saja Toean. Makanan deri poekoel annem soedah klaar.
I want a carriage and a luggage car.	Saja minta karetta dan karetta bagazie.
I want some half-boiled eggs.	Minta telor stengah mateng.
Let me have a couple of fried eggs or ham and eggs.	Kassi doewa mata sapi atauw mata sapi dan ham.
I want some tea, boy.	Jonges, minta te.
Where is the menu?	Mana soerat makan?
Bring me some soup first.	Bawa sop doeloe.
I don't want any rice.	Tida makan nassi.
Let me have some rice but none of the hot dishes.	Minta nassi, tapi tida maoe sambal.
I want only chicken, eggs and fish.	Minta ajam, telor dan ikan sadja.
Let me have some beef-steak and salad.	Minta biefstuk sama salad.
Boy, I want some bread.	Jonges, minta roti.
Let me have the wine-list.	Bawa soerat anggoer
Bring me a bottle of Claret No. 10.	Kassi satoe bottel anggoer merra No. sapoeloe.
Give me some ice, boy.	Minta ice, jonges.
Give me some fruit, boy.	Minta boea, jonges.
Have you a match for me?	Kwe ada korrek api?

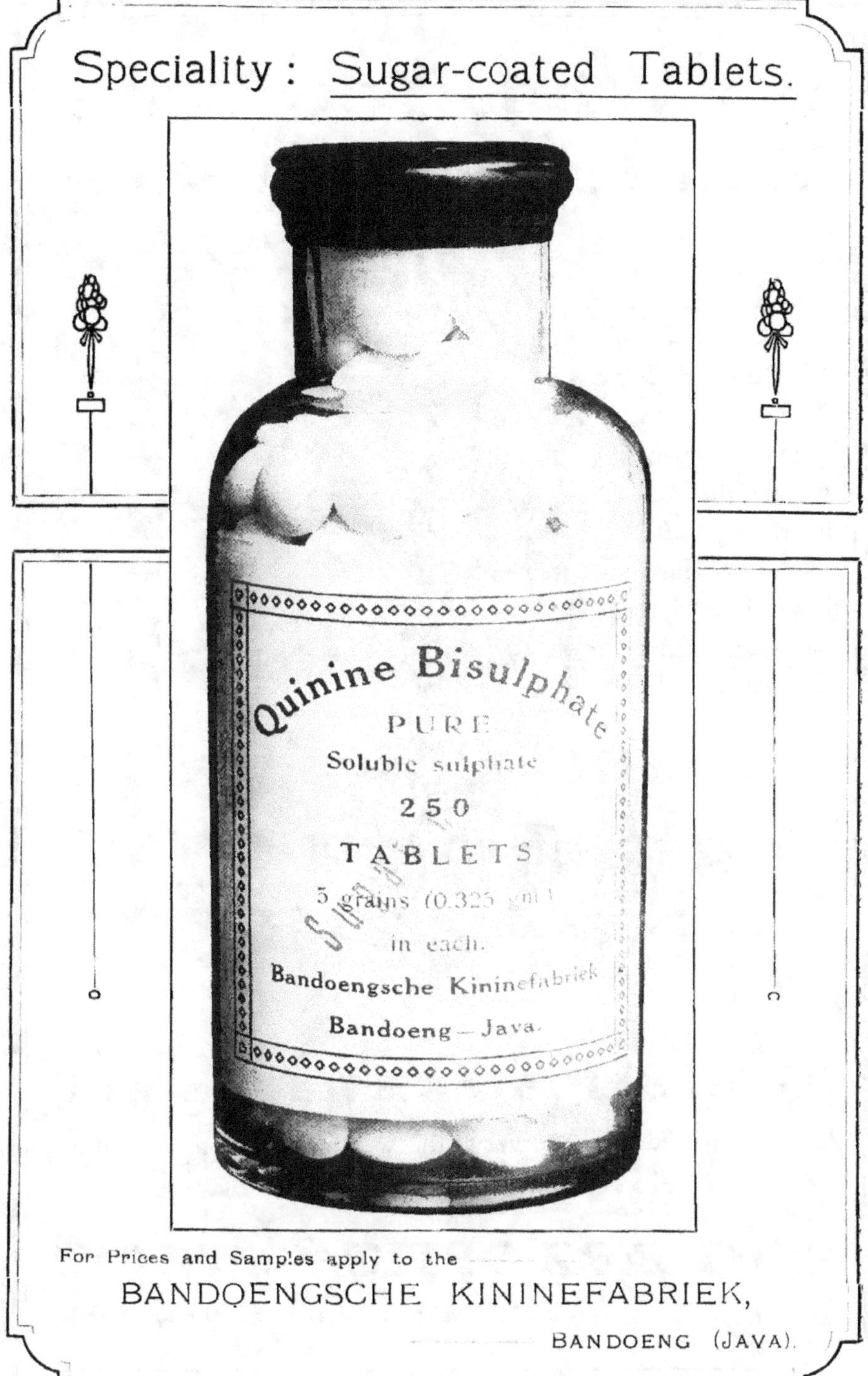
Speciality : Sugar-coated Tablets.
Quinine Bisulphate
PURE
Soluble sulphate
250
TABLETS
5 grains (0.325 gm.)
in each.
Bandoengsche Kininefabriek
Bandoeng – Java.
For Prices and Samples apply to the
BANDOENGSCHE KININEFABRIEK,
BANDOENG (JAVA).

MALAY POISONS
AND
CHARM CURES

by

Dr. John Desmond Gimlette

Malay Poisons and Charm Cures

MODERN EDITOR'S NOTE - This section reproduces the table of contents and first chapter of the 1929 edition, *Malay Poisons and Charm Cures*, by Dr. John Desmond Gimlette, M.R.C.S., L.R.C.P., Residency Surgeon of Kelantan, one of the Protected Malay States.

Originally published in London, 1915, by J. & A. Churchill, 7, Great Marlborough Street, W.

§

Table of Contents

Crystal gazing — Christian Science — Theories as to the origin of disease — Taboo — Origin of cholera — Ideas as to small-pox — Native methods of quarantine.

Chapter III. — Charms and Amulets

Charms against forest demons — Against small-pox — The pĕlĕsit — Snake bite charms — Charms against poisons — The dugong charm — Bezoar stones — Snake stones — The *chĕmara babi* charm — Amulets — Talismans — Love charms.

Chapter IV. — Black Art in Malay Medicine

The spirit-raising *bomor* — Performance of *Main Mok Pek* — *Main Gĕbioh* — *Main Pĕtĕri* — *Berhantu* — *Orang Bunian* — *Main Bĕrbagih* — Waxen images.

Chapter V. — Spells and Soothsaying

A Kelantan manuscript on Magic — Pre-natal language — Divination — Protective formulas — The "waking charm" — Magic squares.

Chapter VI. — Poisons obtained by Malays from Fish

Cat-fish — Carp — Globe-fish — Sting-rays.

Chapter VII. — Other Poisons obtained by Malays from the Animal Kingdom

Tortoises and snakes — Frogs and toads — Moths — Beetles — Land-bugs — Grasshoppers — Millepedes — Slugs and Snails — Worms.

Chapter VIII. — Poisons obtained by Malays from Jungle Plants

Akar Batu Pelir Kambing — *Akar Klapayang* — Bamboo — *Bĕbuta* — *Beredin* — *Chengkian* — *Ibul* — *Jelatang* — *Jitong* — *Kachang Bulu Rimau* — *Keladi* — *Likir* — *Langkap* — *Pĕdĕndang Gagak* — *Rengas* — *Rengut* — *Tangis Sarang Burong* — *Upas* climber — *Upas* tree.

Chapter I

Methods of Poisoning and Malay Charms In General

Murder is commonly accomplished by Malays in a fit of passion or blind jealousy by stabbing with the national weapon, the kris (*kĕris*; a dagger, the creese), with a spear, or by slashing with the narrow-bladed Malay chopper, as well as by the more deliberate use of firearms. Malays are not a timid people, and although in India secret poisoning became one of the most prominent, if not the most prevalent, of Court atrocities under Mussulman rule, the Muhammadan Malay, as a general rule, attempts vengeance by means of poison when he is bearing a grudge and brooding, and when violent or other measures appear to him to be too dangerous or too uncertain. Various poisons obtained from the animal and vegetable kingdoms are used in a variety of ways. Very often when jealousy or malice inspires him, the intention is merely to cause annoyance or injury less serious than death. With this object in view, poison is frequently put into wells and water jars. Malay women are generally held to be the accredited agents, at any rate in many cases of poisoning, because, naturally, the cooking is left almost entirely to them.

Malaya is richly supplied with medicinal plants and herbs; they form the stock-in-trade of the *bomor* or "medicine-man," many of their properties, either deadly (*rachun*) or intoxicant (*mabok*), are known, as well as their medicinal value, to Malays of most classes. This is especially true of the uncultured folk who live in rural districts, but their knowledge is often restricted to the locality, thus explaining the fact of so many various country poisons being used by Malays for felonious purposes. Familiarity with these drugs and with potent imported poisons, such as cyanide of potassium, white arsenic, strong acids and opium, gives considerable scope for the selection of poisons. It is not surprising that the common datura or thorn-apple, with its power of gradually reducing the astutest intellect into a state of drivelling fatuity, and arsenic, which destroys more speedily with symptoms which the most learned native doctors can hardly distinguish from Asiatic cholera, have been used, as in India, as the closing act of a great political contest, as a means of removing a stubborn minister or an intriguing kinsman (Ref. 6).

Some of the poisons used in Kelantan are common to India; for example, Plumbago rosea (*chĕraka merah*), Exccecaria agallocha (*bĕbuta*), Datura fastuosa (*kechubong hitam*), opium (*chandu*), arsenic (*warangan* or *tuba tikus*), the horse-radish tree (*mĕrunggai*), and glass in powder (*sĕrbok kacha*) combined with bamboo and other fine vegetable hairs. Malays do not hesitate to use well-known poisonous drugs as medicines, especially, perhaps, Datura fastuosa, Alocasia denudata (*kĕladi chandek*), Goniothalamus tapis (*kĕnĕrak*), Glycosmis pentaphylla (*nĕrapih*), opium and white arsenic. Indeed, as regards poisons derived from the vegetable kingdom, all those mentioned in subsequent chapters, *except bĕbuta, pokok batu pĕlir kambing, langkup, ibul, pokok ipoh, rĕngas, binjai, rengut and tuba, are used as Malay medicines.*

Malay thieves frequently use poisonous plants to cause no more than stupefaction *(mabok)* of their victims as a preliminary to the main venture. Robbers employ sand, powdered glass, quicklime and other powders to disconcert their pursuers. Rogues claim to be able to cause loss of voice lasting for seven or eight days by the administration of certain poisons by the mouth. Two or three clinical cases have occurred in Kelantan in which it was alleged that witnesses in court could not give evidence for this reason. Aphonia was complete but temporary, but the poison could not be produced. To' Bomor Awang, a Kota Bharu "medicine-man" or *bomor,* said that a powder made with lime used in betel-chewing, and scrapings from the smooth, dry, shiny inner bark of a forest vine *(rotan sĕga;* Calamus, sp. Palmæ), the familiar "cane" of boyhood, was used for this purpose. This was prepared by the "medicine-man" (To' Bomor Awang), and given by arrangement, in a draught of water, to a strong Chinese ward attendant in the State hospital at Kota Bharu, Kelantan, but it had no ill effect on him. The amount of powdered rattan bark was probably too small in quantity, owing to nervousness on the part of the *bomor* who prepared it. He was a vaccinator on the hospital staff.

Suicide by poisoning, or indeed by any other method, is almost unknown among Malays, except, perhaps, when the wild beast part of a distracted man comes uppermost and brooding sullenness changes to frantic frenzy. A Malay may then start to "run amuck" with a stabbing or cutting weapon in his hand, perhaps with the idea of suicide, killing indiscriminately, and expecting to be slain, perchance, at the end of his reckless "running amuck" *(mĕngamok).* Poison mixed with honey is sometimes smeared on the under surface of a knife. The poisoner, sharing a meal with his enemy,

Balinese kris and jewelry by O. Kurkdjian Studio, c. 1912.

divides a water-melon in half with the poisoned blade, but is careful to eat only the upper and harmless portion as his share of the fruit. This method of poisoning is said to be common in Trengganu; cyanide of potassium is employed. In Kelantan a long-bladed kitchen knife, the *pisau ajam,* is used and the ordinary water-melon, *labu China,* chosen.

The Kris. — On the west coast of the Malay Peninsula it has been denied very generally, that the blade of the kris is ever deliberately poisoned, but in Kelantan I have been told by the late Dato' Lela Derja and the Engku Said Husain of Kota Bharu that poison is sometimes smeared on the blades of Malay weapons with criminal intent. Reference to this practice is made in a quaint little book entitled "Six Months Among the Malays" published in London in 1840. The author, Dr. Yvan, who was physician to a scientific mission sent by France to China, writes as follows:

"I changed the subject by inquiring whether it were true that the Malays poisoned their arrows and other weapons. 'As true' he replied, 'as that I am the son of my father.' On my inquiring further into the subject he said he would return on the morrow and show me something relative to it; so on the following day, Abdala arrived carrying a number of small paper parcels which he spread out on the table and allowed me to examine. There were several fragments of a whitish substance which I immediately recognized from its form to be a species of lime; another ingredient reduced to a white powder, some coco-nut oil, a citron and an extract of some kind of a dark colour and virous smell. Abdala took up a long, thin kriss, touched the side of it with the lime, then spread it over with the white powder and squeezed a little of the citron juice upon it; this being done, he exposed it to the heat of the sun and when the blade was quite dry, he took up the black extract and put a small quantity of it upon the part which had previously been covered with lime, touching it lastly with the coco-nut oil. He then proceeded to prepare the other side of the kriss in the same manner, and to convince me that he perfectly understood the whole affair, he wounded a fowl which died a short time afterwards. The white substance was, I found, a mixture of arsenic, and the extracted matter was from the bark of the menispermum coculus; the poisonous properties of the kriss were, probably, owing principally to the latter ingredient" (Ref. 7).

The writer was shrewd in his inference if it is correct. Menispermum cocculus is Anamirta cocculus, Linn., Menispermacere (*Cocculus Indicus* or Levant nut), which used to be used by poachers in "foxing" fish. It contains the poisonous principle picrotoxin, a crystalline substance, easily absorbed through the skin, discovered in the seeds by Boulay in 1812. Two powdered seeds (0.24 G.) or 0.08 G. of picrotoxin are fatal doses in man. Though *Anamirta cocculus* extends southwards from South India to New Guinea, in the Malay Peninsula, Anamirta Louveisi takes its place.

Sometimes the blade of the kris is dipped in human urine with the idea of rendering penetration of the steel more easy when attacking a so-called invulnerable man. Even to-day Malays still think that certain persons can acquire impenetrability of the skin to shot and steel by means of some very powerful charms. About twenty-eight years ago, a notorious Malay rebel — the Orang Kaya Pahlawan of Pahang — was a case in point. This wealthy Malay was endowed with much cunning, great physical strength, courage, and a power of imagination so developed that he could persuade people to believe in the quaint infallibility of his ideas. Except for a silver bullet he was safe. The idea of invulnerability of the flesh was also attached to To' Janggut, a ringleader in the Kelantan rising of 1915, but he was shot dead by the Sikh troops of the Malay States Guides. Charms intended to procure invulnerability nearly always take the form of a belt. A girdle-charm of this kind was found on a Kelantan robber who was speared to death, in 1917, in a seaside village of Northern Kelantan; this particular belt was tied with the knot in front.

Certain Malay weapons are endowed with magic properties, especially the kris and some of the short Malay daggers called *tumbok lada*. In 1917, his Highness the late Sultan allowed a very beautiful and valuable straight, long-bladed kris to be taken from his palace to the hut of an elderly woman living hear the Residency in Kota Bharu. She had been bitten at dusk on the foot by a poisonous snake, and expired at daybreak. Several Malay "medicine-men" were in attendance; she died, however, before the arrival of a very famous *bomor* who had been sent for from afar and into whose hands it was intended to place the Sultan's magical kris. As a charm cure the point of the naked blade is applied by the *bomor* to the punctures of snake bite. No special formula is chanted. Death from snake bite is rare in the Malay Peninsula, although more than thirty poisonous varieties have been described; the royal kris had been borrowed in the hope of restoring the woman to health.

His Highness the present Sultan showed me his father's famous kris in 1921. It is called *kĕris bari*, from the name of the steel, *bĕsi bari*, from which the blade is made; the blade is undamascened and rough like the surface of fine emery paper, it is also black; but this is only due to the fact that, like the blades of all Malay weapons, it has been treated with white arsenic and the juice of the lime fruit to prevent it from rusting. His Highness also showed me another very beautiful gold-mounted kris, which he said

was of even higher quality than the *kĕris bari.* It was a short,
straight kris, also undamascened, called *kĕris melela,* the usual
name for an undamascened blade. The Sultan told me that
in the event of a hair being swallowed and sticking in the
throat, the resulting irritation will quickly disappear when
a little oil in which the point of this kris has been dipped is
administered by the mouth. A Malay dagger *(tumbok lada)*
with a blade forged from *bĕsi bari* is one of the treasured
possessions of the To' Bomor Enche' Harun of Kota Bharu.
This old "medicine-man" told me that in days gone by
his enchanted dagger would float in water, but owing to
repairs to the hilt its magic had been lost. The magic kris is
generally of Javanese manufacture; a rare variety is reputed
to have a blade of steel made by finger pressure alone. One
of these weapons *(kĕris pichit)* is said to be in the possession
of the Raja d'Hilir of Perak. Generally speaking, the value
of the weapon does not depend on its costly ornamentation,
but upon the accuracy of proportion in its blade; while a
kris that has frequently shed blood is greatly increased in
superstitious value. Different forms of damascening produce
different effects — "with one kind the owner of such a kris
cannot be overcome; others are generally auspicious; another
gives luck to its wearer when trading or voyaging" (Ref. 4).
Arrows and darts poisoned by means of the deadly upas sap
are now no longer used for homicide, being confined to the
killing of game by the aborigines living in caves, hills and
plains, *i.e.,* by the Sakai and other jungle folk of the Malay
Peninsula.

Bile. — The bile of reptiles, birds and mammals is a favourite
ingredient of many Malay poisons. Probably its use by
Malays as a practical poison is not very efficacious, and
it may be used only in "make-believe" as an excipient,
or to give a finish to a known deadly combination. Bile is
much prized as a medicine; for instance, that of the bear,

porcupine, snake and crow, especially that of the racquet-tailed drongo or king-crow (Dissemurus platurus), is used by the *bomor* either as a practical or fanciful drug. The dried gall-bladder of the bear is used as a medicine in Borneo; but the Malay *bomor* only administers the bile of the honey-bear (Helarctos malayanus) internally as a "pick-me-up" in cases of accidental falls from a tree or height; it is more commonly applied by him to the navel of children suffering from emaciation caused by intestinal worms. The bile of the large porcupine (Hystrix longicauda) is used in cases of suppressed yaws *(bunga puru ta' jadi)*; that of the king-crow or monkey's slave is used as a fanciful and very disgusting kind of aphrodisiac.

Blood. — Human blood is sometimes used in the making of love charms and gambling charms. The blood must be derived from the corpse of a man who has suffered death from violence, and, for the future success of the charm, it is essential to obtain his forgiveness before his death. This superstition is quite common in Kelantan; Nik Ismail, one of the Kelantan Malays on the hospital staff at Kota Bharu, told me that when cases of murder are in the wards, charm-mongers frequently approach him begging for a little post-mortem blood. The following incident came under my personal observation in 1920. Shortly after the execution of a Malay (Awang Dogol bin Děris) by hanging for murder, a fellow prisoner of the deceased man was caught trying to collect blood (in sufficient quantity to soak a few bits of thread) from the forearm of the dead criminal. The culprit was a Kelantan *bomor* who had been sentenced to two years' rigorous imprisonment for cheating; he said he had obtained the thread from the native gaoler for the purpose of making a charm. His object was the making of a love charm, but the charm could also have been used in playing the Chinese gambling game of Poh *(main po)*. It was to have been prepared by saturating seven pieces of thread in the blood of the dead man and that of a pink water-buffalo, adding the eyes of a tiger and those of a black cat, and burning the whole to ashes. As with other Malay philtres of a harmless, fanciful, or disgusting kind, this one was supposed to have the power of creating love by smearing it either on the skin of the owner, or on the apparel, after mixing the ashes with coco-nut oil.

To appreciate its use as a gambling charm it is necessary to describe shortly the game of Hai Weh, or Poh. This game is played with a die placed in a square brass box fitting it accurately, which in turn slides into a brass cover. The lower end of the box is bevelled, and, the die having been inserted, the box is spun on a board or mat marked with a diagonal cross. The faces of the die are coloured red and white, and the stakes having been placed on the mat, those opposite the red portion of the die when it ceases spinning are the winners (Ref. 2). The blood charm is supposed to enable the owner to see what is inside the brass box by smearing the ashes mixed with coco-nut oil over the eyebrows. Poisonous drugs are not added to, or employed in, the manufacture of Malay love philtres for sinister purposes. Great attention is paid to the proper combination of drugs for curative purposes, and so also with poisonous preparations. Some of the Malay poisons, especially those which act through the skin and mucous membranes, are devised with an almost incredible refinement of cruelty.

"Time-Poisons." — It has often been said, but without authority, that an accomplished Malay criminal can give a single dose of poison and time the death of his victim within three months, six months, or even three years, according to the dose and the particular combination he uses. The possibility of the existence of such a poison which will kill at any distance of time according to the dose is supported by the tale of La Spara, who was hanged in Rome in 1648 with thirteen of her companions, while a number of her clients were whipped, half naked, through the streets. Hieronyma Spara, the reputed witch, supplied young matrons who wished to resent the infidelities of their husbands with an elixir which was a slow poison, clear, tasteless and limpid, and of strength sufficient to destroy life in the course of a day, week, month or number of months, as the purchaser preferred. A similar organisation was led by Tofania, an old woman of Naples, who was tried and strangled in 1730, after she had caused, directly or indirectly, the deaths of more than 600 persons with her Aqua Tofa'na, or the Manna of St. Nichola of Bari (Ref. 1). The same tradition exists in Persia to this day. I tried to verify the Malay story in an up-country district of Southern Kelantan known as the Ulu Kesial district. This part of the State had long enjoyed an evil reputation for efficiency in poisoning until the District Officer, Mr. A. J. Sturrock, treated it with a considerable amount of judicial attention in the year 1912. Many of my notes have come from Ulu Kesial; but of late years it has become increasingly difficult to chat about poisons in this part of Kelantan. Native experts there say that the idea of a

time-poison is unfounded *(bohong)*, but that the effect of a
certain deadly poison, presently to be described, is greatly
accelerated or delayed if certain fruit and vegetables, such as
papaw, water-melon, pumpkin and cucumber, happen to be
eaten soon after the ingestion of the poison, or not until some
days after its administration. This Ulu Kesial poison serves
as an example of the great attention to detail which must be
paid in the preparation of old-fashioned Malay poisons. It is
said to cause the spitting of blood with fever.

The fruit of a poisonous palm *(ibul)* and of a poisonous
jungle climber *(rengut)* are taken as well as a pill-millepede
and the gall-bladder of the honey bear, that of a common
toad and that of a horned toad-frog; each is carefully and
separately dried and then toasted over a fire. They are then
pulverised, and kept in separate packets until the time
arrives to use them. If it is desired to administer this poison
in water, an equal quantity of the six powders is taken,
mixed together, and put into the water jar. If it is to be mixed
with food, the galls of the frog and the toad must be fresh,
and, when fresh, mixed with the four dry powders, and
the resulting mass then heated over a fire until it becomes
black and sticky like opium prepared for the pipe. It is
now ready to be put into a curry or any kind of rice-broth.
In three or four days the victim is said to cough blood. A
fine black powder, prepared by an Ulu Kesial villager and
said to contain all the ingredients, was sent to me in 1920
to experiment with. It was given to a dog, but the result of
the experiment was not known owing to the pariah slipping
its chain and escaping shortly after it had swallowed the
poison. This particular combination is said to be so deadly
that it must not be prepared inside a house or in a market
town, but in the solitude of thick jungle. An evil-doer (Mat
Hasan), I am told, neglected this precaution when making
it, only a few months ago, and so caused his own death. He

was getting it ready in his house, had reduced the millepede
to fine powder and the galls of the bear and the toad, when
a puff of wind blew the dry powders into his mouth and
nostrils and he died in three days. The villagers said he had
died of fever, but those who "knew" declared Mat Hasan
had accidentally poisoned himself.

Some apparently quite harmless things are avoided (*pantang*)
when combined, because they are said to be poisonous
(*mabok*) in combination: for example, mangosteen fruit with
sugar, for fear the sap of the rind will mix with the sugar;
water-melon with honey, for the same reason; the heart
(*umbut*) of the coco-nut tree with shell-fish; the heart of the
nibong palm with oysters. Fish and other food must be fried
only with vegetable oil, *i.e.*, coco-nut oil; a stew made of
the flesh of the mouse-deer and pineapple is said to cause
death. It is said that the durian fruit must not be eaten with
brandy, so also even in England that eating a banana with
a glass of Curaçoa at dessert is "very unwise." On the other
hand, tradition says it is unwise to eat the pear without wine
("Pear, Wine and Parson" — Cotgrave's Dictionary, 1650): —

> Apres la poire,
> Le vin ou le pretre (priest).

And again in the "Art of Preserving Health" by doctors of
famous schools of Salerno (Italy) early twelfth century (Ref.
3) : —

> La poire crue est un poison . . .
> Elle charge trop l'estomac. Etant cuite,
> Elle y porte la guerison . . .
> Quand on a mange de la poire,
> Que le premier soin soit de boire.

> (Translation of Brunzen de la Martiniere, 1749.)

In Kelantan no spells are muttered during the process of

mixing drugs with criminal intent: no special "precious rod"
of gold or silver is used as in ancient Egypt, but no doubt
magic enters during the preparation of the compositions.

Serious cases of poisoning are recognised as being beyond
the power of the *bomor*, but he has antidotes for every
poison, many of them being made up of products from the
animal and vegetable kingdoms. Emetics do not seem to be
specially employed as in Western practice. Fresh coco-nut
water is promptly used as a household remedy in nearly all
cases of Malay poisoning. It is slightly acid, diuretic, and
contains much sugar with a small proportion of fat, and may
be of practical value. Should the supernatural aid of magic
be sought, the prospect of cure by charms rests entirely on
the power of the formulas chanted by the *bomor* and on the
significance of his blowing *(tiup;* Kelantan *siup)* upon the
face or body of the patient during the process of the cure.
This practice is called *jampi, jampi;* the cure depends, in fact,
on the patient himself, on his faith in the talismans and
amulets that he happens to be wearing for good luck; on his
conservative belief in old traditions and on his faith in the
bomor who is called in to cure him.

It is said, in Kelantan, that a criminal with poison concealed
about his person can be recognised by the absence of the
top part of his shadow—i.e., the shadow of his head and
neck is not projected. Many think that poisoned food can
be recognised by the shadow of the right hand and fingers
not being cast when eating rice. Some say that a stirring rod
of ivory will become dusky if poison should have been put
into food, such as curries and other stir-abouts. In Perak a
spoon made of the beak of a hornbill is said to turn black if it
touches poison.

The *bomor*, like Mithridates the Great, king of Pontus and
Bithynia, can make an antidote for any kind of poison;
his compounds differ from the royal prescription, which

consisted of "two dry walnuts, and as many good figs, and twenty leaves of rue, bruised and beaten together, with two or three corns of salt, and twenty juniper berries, which taken every morning fasting, preserveth from danger of poison and infection that day it is taken" (Ref. 5). For instance, one is prepared from the wing-bone of a goose, the horn of the wild goat, the spine of the sea porcupine, the tusk of a toothed whale, and various yet unidentified jungle roots and barks. These are to be rubbed down in hot water on a stone, and after careful straining the water is to be given by the mouth. A formula must be recited and a powerful rendering given at the same time by the *bomor* who owns the charm. This prescription was used by the late To' Bomor Enche' Abdullah, a "medicine-man" to H.H. the late Sultan of Kelantan; the charm that he used is given on p. 46.

Burnt tiger's whiskers in coco-nut oil as an internal remedy for chronic rheumatism; the ashes of a cat's whiskers in liquid opium as an antidote to poison; hairs from an elephant's tail as toothpicks in the toothache of children, and medicines derived from the sperm whale, and such a rare local animal as the Malayan wild goat, strongly suggest the idea of "make believe" or sympathetic magic on the part of the *bomor*, much in the same way as the digging foot of a mole serves to cure cramp in Devonshire.

REFERENCES.

(1) CHAMBERS, W. & R. (1901.) "Chambers's Encyclopædia." "Poison." London.

(2) DENNYS, N. B. (1894.) "A Descriptive Dictionary of British Malaya." "Gambling." London.

(3) LEROY, A. (1879.) "Dictionnaire de Pomologie," Vol. I., p. 65. Paris.

(4) McNair, F. (1878.) " Perak and the Malays." London.

(5) Parkins, Dr. (1814.) "The English Physician," p. 330. London.

(6) Simpson, A. P. (1871.) "Native Poisons of India." *The Pharmaceutical Journal and Transactions, 3rd series, II., p. 602.* London.

(7) Yvan, Dr. (1840.) "Six Months Among the Malays and a Year in China," p. 145. London.

Illustration Credits

The editor expresses his gratitude to the original models, artists, photographers, and to the archives that have made it possible to create this illustrated modern edition of *Java Girl*. Images are identified by subject; source credit; and page number in the book. Credit abbreviations shown in [brackets].

Artists and Photographers

Ali. S. Cohan [AC]

Andries Augustus Boom [AB]

Anonymous [A]

C.H. Graves & Universal Photo Art Co [CG]

Dianelos Georgoudis [DG]

Eugene Delacroix [ED]

Franz Wilhelm Junghuhn [FJ]

Gemma Frisius [GF]

Gotthard Schuh [GS]

H. Ernst & Co. [HE]

Howard Pyle [HP]

Isidore van Kingsbergen [IK]

J. Vanderheyden [JV]

J.J.R. van de Wilde [JW]

Joh. Braakensiek [JOB]

Jan Brandes [JB]

Johannes F. E. ten Klooster [JK]

John Lewis Marshall [JLM]

Kassian Céphas [KC]

Kent Davis [KD]

O. Hisgen & Co. [OH]

Onnes Kurkdjian [OK]

Thilly Weissenborn [TW]

Woodbury and Page [WP]

Sources

DatAsia Press [DP]

Koninklijk Instituut voor Taal-, Land- en Volkenkunde [KIT]

Nationaal Museum van Wereldculturen/Tropenmuseum [NMW]

Periodical/Postcard [PP]

Rijksmuseum.nl [RM]

Royal Netherlands Institute of Southeast Asian and Caribbean Studies, and Leiden University Library/Wikimedia Commons [RLW]

Wikimedia, Wikipedia, Wikimedia Commons [W]

#	Subject	Artist	Source	Page
ii	Javanese dancer woodcut print	JK	RM	ii
vii	Peacock cul de lampe	APP	RM	vii
01a	Javanese dancers	KC	RM	2
01b	Passing small fishing craft	A	PP	4
01c	Cheribon Bay	A	RM	4
01d	Volcano view	OK	RM	6
01e	Men at the club	A	RM	8
01f	Horse and carriage	A	RM	10
02a	Batik workers	OK	RM	12
02b	Batik workers	OK	RM	12
02c	Cheribon road with trees	A	RM	13
02d	Busy village market	OK	RM	14
02e	Native soup seller	A	RM	15
02f	Women carrying baskets	A	PP	16
02g	Javanese countryside painting	FJ	RM	18
02h	Rice field and mountain view	WP	RM	19
03a	View of sugar factory	KC	RM	24
03b	Busy *kampong* (village) street	A	RM	25
03c	Alfred's house	WP	RM	26
03d	Alfred's *njai*, Missah	A	RM	28
04a	Rear of Alfred's house	WP	RM	31
04b	*tokke* lizard	JB	RM	33
05a	Cart with sugar cane	A	PP	37
05b	Postcard with Javanese mailman	A	PP	38
05c	René's girl Betty	A	RM	42
06a	Alfred and René's garden	WP	RM	48
07a	Men drinking at the club	A	RM	51
07b	Landscape panorama	WP	RM	52
07c	Adinda standing	KC	RM	55
08a	Sandlewood horse and carriage	A	NMW	60
08b	Natives walking on road	A	PP	61
08c	*Kampong* Koevang Tengah	WP	RM	62
08d	Chinese *warong* (store)	A	PP	63
08e	Tropical fruit	A	NMW	64
08f	Workers harvesting sugarcane	OK	RM	65
08g	Laying sugarcane train tracks	OK	RM	66
08h	Irrigation ditches	KC	RM	67
08i	Sugar factory with Mt. Tjirmai	KC	RM	68
09a	Clouds forming over mountains	A	RM	72
09b	Deserted streets in the *kampong*	WP	RM	74
09c	Cutting and pressing sugarcane	A	NMW	75
10a	Dinner with the van Heecks	A	RM	79
10b	The van Heecks home	WP	RM	80
10c	European-Javan family	WP	RM	83
10d	Mountain resort	A	PP	85
11a	Flying fox	A	PP	88
11b	Native festival	CG	RM	89
11c	Javanese dancer with band	AC	RM	90
11d	Mata Hari	A	W	92
11e	Javanese male dancers	KC	RM	94
12a	Sugarcane factory	OK	RM	98
12b	Sugarcane factory	OK	RM	99
12c	Sugarcane factory	OK	RM	99
12d	At the club	A	RM	101
12e	A free-lancer from *Ivanhoe*	A	W	103
13a	Alfred on the ship	A	PP	110
13b	Grand Hotel barber	A	PP	111
13c	Hotel des Indes dining	A	NMW	111
13d	Ship to Batavia	A	RM	112
14a	Native servants	A	RM	116
16a	Lace making	A	PP	126
16b	Lace making	A	PP	126
16c	Concordia Club	WP	KI	130
17a	Rice farming	A	NMW	133

17b	Men on mountain trail	A	RM	135
18a	The de Kock's house	WP	RM	141
18b	The de Kocks	A	RM	141
20a	Horse and carriage	JV	PP	154
21a	The club in Cheribon	OH	RM	157
21b	Dinner at the Club	A	NMW	157
21c	Sugar factory, New Tersana	OK	RM	160
21d	Sugar factory, New Tersana	OK	RM	160
21e	Bandoeng train station	A	PP	162
21f	Hotel Preanger, Bandoeng	A	PP	163
22a	Winkelstraat, Bandoeng	A	PP	165
22b	Concordia Society, Bandoeng	A	PP	165
23a	Hotel der Nederlanden	A	PP	170
23b	Hotel der Nederlanden	WP	RM	171
23c	The de Jong family	A	RM	172
23d	Tennis in Java	A	RM	173
23e	Daisy Vermeer	A	RM	174
24a	Chatting on the hotel veranda	A	RM	181
25a	Adinda's gold bracelet	JW	RM	186
26a	The Inger house	KC	RM	191
27a	The ship to Cheribon	A	PP	198
27b	The house at Tjidani	WP	RM	199
27c	The view of the valley	WP	RM	199
27d	Tea picking by Mt. Salak	A	PP	200
27e	René on his white horse	AB	RM	201
27f	The household servants	A	RM	202
27g	The active volcano Gedeh	A	RM	205
27h	Illustration from *Faust*	ED	RM	206
28a	René on his white horse	AB	RM	211
28b	Women picking tea	A	KI	211
28c	Inger's photography hobby	A	RM	212
28d	Visit to the Homan's house	A	RM	213
28e	Oerip and her baby	OK	RM	215
30a	Waterfall	A	NMW	224
30b	Jungle village	HE	RM	225
30c	Bellevue Hotel, Buitenzorg	A	PP	227
30d	Hotel river view	WP	RM	227
30e	Bathers in the river	A	NMW	228
30f	Formal dinner	A	RM	229
30g	Circus poster	A	NMW	230
31a	River view	WP	RM	234
31b	Botanical gardens palm	WP	RM	235
31c	The Homan house	WP	RM	236
31d	Palace of the governor	WP	RM	237
31e	Stable boy	JV	PP	238
32a	Women picking tea	A	KI	242
32b	The dead tiger	A	RM	243
33a	Saina and René's *mandoer*	A	NMW	247
35a	Inger's mansion gates	WP	RM	258
35b	Inger's manion	WP	RM	259
35c	Inger with a drink	A	RM	260
35d	René in the Inger carriage	KC	RM	262
35e	Colonel and Mrs. Vermeer	A	RM	263
36a	Captain Cramers	A	RM	266
37a	Inger's *ngai*	A	RM	272
37b	The Vermeers' house	WP	RM	273
37c	Mrs. Vermeer	A	RM	274
37d	The Lorelei	HP	W	277
38a	Botanical Garden gates	A	RM	280
38b	Cathedral footpath	A	RM	281
38c	René riding home	A	RM	286
39a	Tea factory	WP	KIT	290
39b	She was all Javanese...	KC	RM	295
41a	Mountain stream	A	RM	307
41b	Dr. Jansen	A	KIT	308

42a	René and Adinda's home	WP	RM	314
42b	Adinda decided	KC	RM	317
42c	Javanese herbal remedies	KC	RM	319
42d	Dutch apothecary	WP	RM	319
43a	Adinda came in	KC	RM	327
	Appendices			
	"Nederland's kostbaarst sieraad"	JOB	W	330
	Librairie du Siam	KD	DP	334
	François Doré	KD	DP	334
	The Rijksmuseum	JLM	RM	336
	Java Girl binding	KD	DP	339
	Schwartz phone number	A	PP	340
	Java Girl binding	KD	DP	342
	Java Girl cover	KD	DP	343
	Kent and Sophaphan Davis	KD	DP	345
	Garuda Mahambira	A	PP	345
	Adinda in frame	KC	RM	347
	Adinda dance pose	KC	RM	348
	Barong	A	PP	349
	Camera obscura	GF	W	351
	Shroud of Turin	DG	W	351
	Balinese dancer	IK	KIT	354
	Isodore van Kinsbergen cover	IK	PP	355
	Dancers	IK	KIT	356
	Kassian Céphas	KC	RM	359
	Dancers	KC	RM	360
	Garden of the East cover	KC	PP	361
	Céphas studio ad	KC	PP	362
	Unknown princess	KC	RM	363
	B. R. A. Danoenegoro	KC	RM	364
	Adinda standing formal	KC	RM	366
	Adinda in EXTRÊME-ASIE	KC	PP	368
	Adinda composite	KC	DP	369
	Adinda seated	KC	RM	370
	Adinda standing formal	KC	RM	371
	Woman playing xylophone	WP	RM	373
	Seated woman	WP	RM	375
	O. Kurkdjian at Sand Sea	OK	KIT	376
	G. P. Lewis in studio	OK	RM	377
	Lewis with staff	OK	KIT	377
	Weissenborn retouching	OK	KIT	378
	Inseln der Götter covers	GS	PP	379
	Javanese woman sitting	KC	RLW	381
	Javanese dancer	A	RM	382
	Village dancer	A	NMW	383
	Javanese dancer	KC	RM	384
	8 noble girls	KC	KIT	386
	Princess of the Kraton	KC	RLW	388
	Javanese dancer	KC	RLW	389
	Javanese dancer	A	RM	390
	Dancer in courtyard	OK	RM	391
	Balinese dancer	TW	NMW	392
	G. R. A. Sekar Kedaton	KC	KIT	394
	R. Ajoe Sriwoelan	KC	KIT	395
	B. R. A. D. Adiningrat	KC	KIT	396
	Wife of Regent of Blora	WP	RM	397
	Sitting portrait	A	RM	398
	Standing portrait	A	NMW	399
	Standing portrait with fan	A	KIT	400
	Standing portrait with fan	A	KIT	401
	Amputee with family	IK	NMW	402
	Village headman family	WP	RM	403
	Couple posing	A	NMW	404
	Mother and Eurasian daughter	A	RM	405
	Palace women	KC	RM	406

	Javanese dancer postcard	A	PP	408
	Batik making postcard	A	PP	409
	Kolff postcard	A	PP	410
	Smits postcard	A	PP	411
	Adinda postcard	KC	PP	412
	Adinda postcard	KC	PP	413
	Preanger and Batavia postcards	A	PP	415
	Gustav Boehm map	A	PP	416
	Gustav Boehm ad	A	PP	416
	Gustav Boehm ad	AC	PP	417
	Gustav Boehm ad	A	PP	418
	Gustav Boehm ad	A	PP	419
	Couple cooking	A	NMW	420
	Vegetable stand	OK	NMW	421
	Money changer	KC	PP	422
	Money changer	KC	NMW	423
	Hair styling women	AC	KIT	424
	Hair styling women	AC	KIT	425
	Shelling cocoa	OK	RM	430
	Kapok pickers	OK	RM	431
	Woman sorting tobacco	OK	RM	432
	Woman with orangutan	HE	RM	433
	Woman outdoors	OK	RM	434
	Woman leaning on stone pole	OK	RM	435
	Javanese woman seated	KC	RLW	436
	Javanese woman standing	KC	RM	438
	Two Javanese women	KC	RM	440
	Two Javanese women	WP	KIT	441
	Two Javanese girls	WP	RM	442
	Two Javanese girls	WP	KIT	443
	Seated woman	KC	RLW	444
	Standing woman	KC	RM	445
	Seated woman	KC	RLW	446
	Seated woman	KC	RM	447
	Taojong, World's Fair	A	PP	448
	Standing woman	KC	RLW	449
	Seated woman	KC	RM	450
	Seated woman	KC	RM	451
	Standing woman postcard	A	PP	452
	Standing woman	A	RM	455
	Woman reclining	A	RM	456
	Simulated bathing	AC	RM	458
	Simulated bathing	AC	KIT	459
	Simulated bathing	AC	RM	460
	Standing woman	KC	NMW	461
	Balcony woman	KC	NMW	462
	Sumatran girl	A	NMW	463
	Standing woman	A	RM	464
	Woman with basket	A	RM	465
	Seated woman	WP	KIT	466
	Seated woman	WP	RM	467
	Massage woman with child	KC	RM	468
	Massage woman	A	NMW	468
	Standing woman outdoors	CG	RM	469
	Javanese standing	WP	KIT	470
	Balinese girl	A	PP	471
	Woman with child	AC	RM	472
	Javanese bottle	A	RM	493
	Javanese bottle	A	RM	498
	Kriss and jewelry	OK	KIT	500
	Malay dagger	A	W	503
	Javanese bottle	A	RM	505
	Javanese bottle	A	RM	506
	Map - Greater Indonesia	A	KIT	514
	Map - Netherlands East Indies	A	KIT	516

Serimpi Ritualized Dance
Johannes Frederik Engelbert ten Klooster, 1919. Rijksmuseum.nl

Glossary of Malay Terms in the Text

aya-aya	we are here, we are here
baboe	nursemaid
bawa kabaya	bring my negligee
baleh-baleh	low bed of split bamboo
di dapoer	in the kitchen
djoeroek	lemon
goedang	warehouse; pantry
kampong	native village
klamboe	mosquito netting
knapa?	why?
kalong	large bat; flying fox
klewang	dagger
mandoer.	native overseer
njai	native housekeeper
nona	Miss
sarong	batik skirt
sakit	sick
saja	yes; (also) I
sama djoega	it is all the same
tuan	Mr. or master
totok	newcomer
toekang ayat	water carrier
tokke	large lizard
titjak	small lizard
tida apa apa	nothing
tida taoe	don't know
tabe	good morning, (also) goodbye
topie	pith helmet, (also) hat
toetoel	member of the cat family smaller than a tiger
tida	no

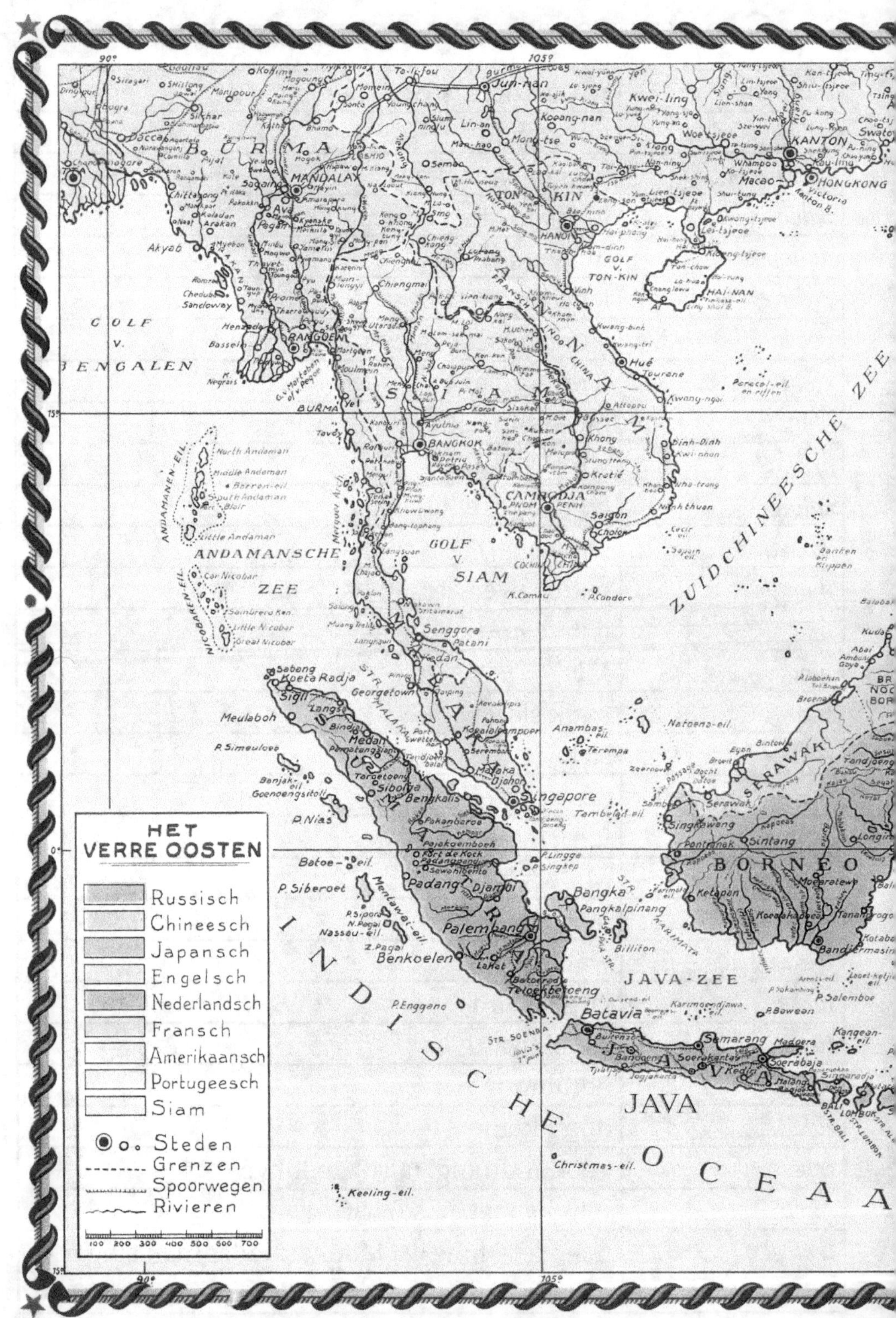
HET VERRE OOSTEN
Russisch
Chineesch
Japansch
Engelsch
Nederlandsch
Fransch
Amerikaansch
Portugeesch
Siam
Steden
Grenzen
Spoorwegen
Rivieren
100 200 300 400 500 600 700
BURMA
MANDALAY
Ava
Pagan
Akyab
Bassein
RANGOEM
GOLF v. BENGALEN
ANDAMANSCHE ZEE
North Andaman
Middle Andaman
South Andaman
Little Andaman
Car Nicobar
Little Nicobar
Great Nicobar
SIAM
BANGKOK
TON-KIN
HANOI
GOLF v. TON-KIN
HAI-NAN
Hué
Tourane
Kwang-ngoi
CAMBODJA
PNOM PENH
Saigon
Cholon
GOLF v. SIAM
COCHIN-CHINA
P. Condore
KANTON
HONGKONG
Macao
Whampoa
Swato
ZUIDCHINEESCHE ZEE
Sabeng
Koeta Radja
Sigli
Meulaboh
Medan
Siboga
Benkalis
Padang
Palembang
Benkoelen
Telok betoeng
P. Nias
P. Siberoet
P. Enggano
Georgetown
Singapore
Malaka
Bangka
Billiton
SERAWAK
Serawak
Singkawang
Pontianak
Sintang
BORNEO
JAVA-ZEE
Batavia
Buitenzorg
Bandoeng
Semarang
Soerabaja
Soerakarta
Jogjakarta
JAVA
BALI
LOMBOK
INDISCHE OCEAAN
Christmas-eil.
Keeling-eil.

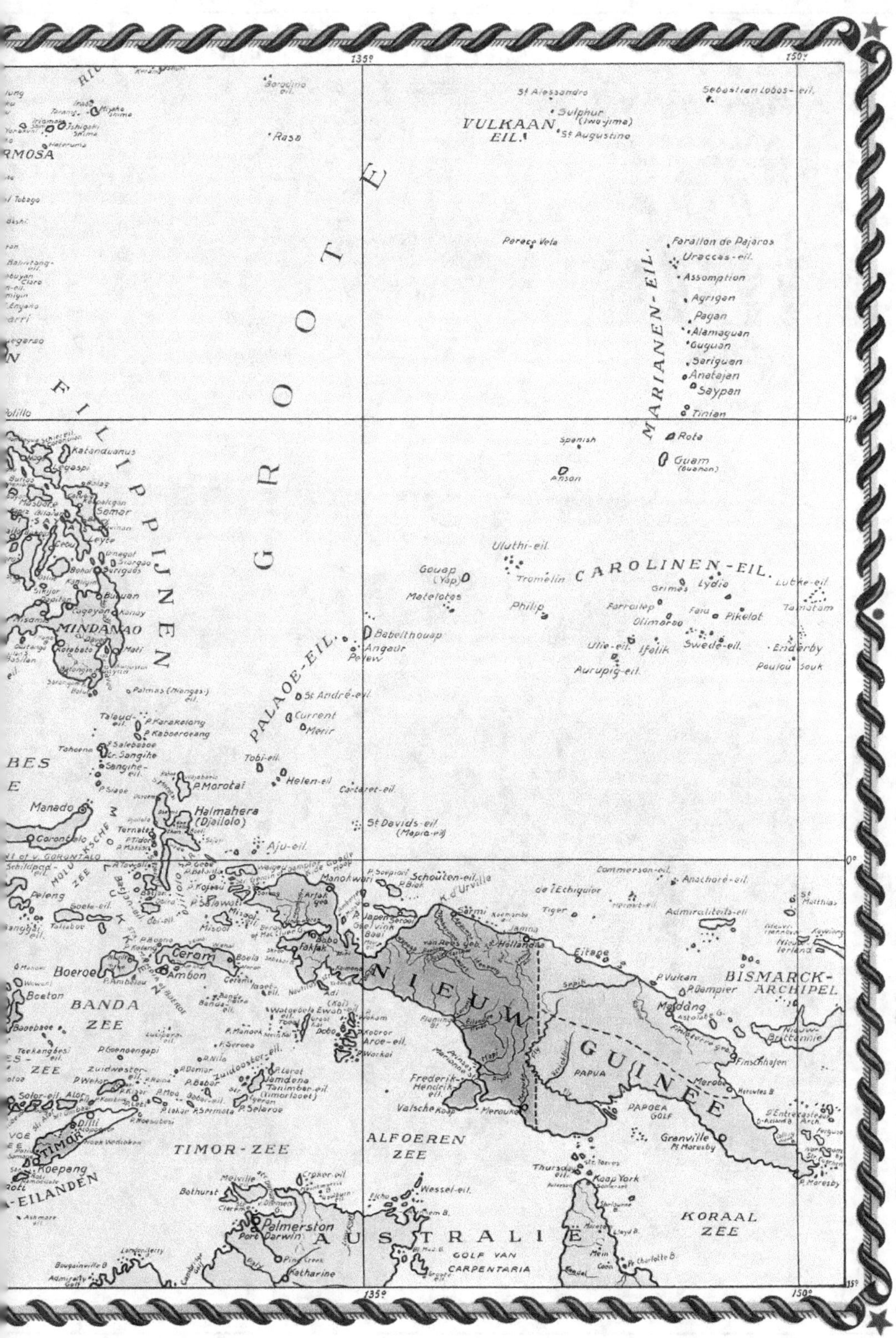
VULKAAN EIL.
St Alessandro
Sebastian Lobos-eil.
Sulphur (Iwo-jima)
St Augustino
Parece Vela
Farallon de Pajaros
Uraccas-eil.
Assomption
Agrigan
Pagan
Alamaguan
Guguan
Sariguan
Anatajan
Saypan
Tinian
Rota
Spanish
Guam (Guahan)
Anson
MARIANEN-EIL.
Saradino eil.
Rasa
FORMOSA
FILIPPIJNEN
GROOTE
Katanduanus
Legaspi
Samar
Leyte
Bohol
Dinagat
Siargao
Surigao
Buluan
Cagayan Sulu
Mindanao
Cotabato
Mati
Palmas (Nanggas) eil.
Talaud eil.
Karakelang
Kaboeroeang
Salebaboe
Gr. Sangihe
Sangihe eil.
P. Siaoe
P. Morotai
Tahoena
Manado
Caroneelo
Halmahera (Djailolo)
Ternate
Aju-eil.
Uluthi-eil.
Gouap (Yap)
Matelotas
Tromelin
Philip
CAROLINEN-EIL.
Grimes
Lydia
Farroilep
Faru
Pikelot
Olimarao
Ulie-eil.
Ifelik
Swede-eil.
Enderby
Aurupig-eil.
Poulou Souk
Lutke-eil.
Tamatam
Babelthouap
Angaur
Pelew
PALAOE-EIL.
St André-eil.
Current
Merir
Tobi-eil.
Helen-eil.
Cartaret-eil.
St Davids-eil. (Mapia-eil.)
CELEBES
Manado
Peleng
Manokwari
Schouten-eil.
Commerson-eil.
Anachoré-eil.
de l'Echiquier
Admiraliteits-eil.
St Matthias
Sarmi
Tiger
Arfak
P. Japen
Geelvink Boei
Jamna
Hollandia
Eitape
P. Vulcan
Dampier
BISMARCK-ARCHIPEL.
Nieuw Brittannie
Madang
Finschhafen
NIEUW
GUINEE
Salawati
Misool
Fakfak
Ceram
Ambon
Boela
PAPUA
PAPOEA GOLF
Marobe
Hercules B.
Boeroe
BANDA ZEE
Dobo
Aroe-eil.
Workai
Frederik-Hendrik-eil.
Valsche Kaap
Merauke
Granville
Pt Moresby
Zuidwester-eil.
Tanimbar-eil. (Timorlaoet)
P. Selaroe
Wetar
TIMOR
Dilli
Koepang
TIMOR-ZEE
ALFOEREN ZEE
Thursday eil.
St Torres
Kaap York
KORAAL ZEE
Melville-eil.
Croker-eil.
Wessel-eil.
Bathurst
Port Darwin
Palmerston
AUSTRALIE
GOLF VAN CARPENTARIA
Bougainville B.
Katharine

EN Nederlandsch
OOST-
INDIË

ENKELE GEGEVENS
LANDOPPERVLAK:
60 x Nederland
of ⅕ van Europa

SUMATRA — 13 x Nederland
BORNEO — 22 x Nederland
CELEBES — 5 x Nederland
JAVA en MADOERA — 4 x Ned.

AANTAL B
70.00

AAND
WERELDP

Kinabast 90%
Peper 85%
Coca 81%
Kapok 64%
Palmolie 46%
Copra 41%
Rubber 33%

Nederlandsch Oost-Indië

Java

Verklaring der teekens:
Kinabast
Peper
Coca (Cocaïne)
Kapok
Palmolie
Cocospalmen (Copra)
Rubber
Rietsuiker
Sisal
Mangaanijzererts
G Goud en Zilver
Aardolie producten
Tin
Tabak
Bauxiet
Thee
Rijst
Kruidnagelen
Muskaatnoot
Foelie
Koffie
Cacao
Steenkool
N.
W.
O.
Z.
BOEKHANDEL
N. VOORHOEVE
EINDHOVEN

Exotic Visions of French Indochina

A romance of colonial Cambodia.
ISBN: 978-1-934431-16-0

A romance of colonial Cambodia
ISBN: 978-1-934431-94-8

First Study of Cambodian Dance.
ISBN 978-1-934431-12-2

Masterwork on Cambodian Dance.
ISBN: 978-1-934431-29-0

Exotic Visions of French Indochina

An American in 1920s Indochina.
ISBN: 978-1-934431-82-5

A sensual novel of East and West
ISBN: 978-1-934431-88-7

Fantastic folktales from ages past.
ISBN 978-1-934431-21-4

1912 Exploration in Cambodia.
ISBN: 978-1-934431-90-0

A Travel Journal of the Cambodian Mekong — 1929
Edited by Groslier biographer Kent Davis, foreword by Henri Copin, and literary translation by Pedro Rodríguez. This full color edition features 70 hand-tinted vintage illustrations, including Groslier's original photos; appendix articles by Paul Boudet, Dr. Paul Cravath and Solang Uk; and the complete original French text.
ISBN 978-1-934431-87-0